Time Undone

Book Four of the Talus 3 Series

Peter Sandor

Time Undone, 1st Edition.

Rev. 13, 06-07-25

ISBN 978-1-7383943-3-3

Copyright 2024 by Peter Sandor

Read other books by Peter Sandor

The Wyld Wynd Trilogy

Book 1 – Wyld Wynd The Rising

Book 2 – Wyld Wynd The Unrest

Book 3 – Wyld Wynd Unleashed

The Wall Plug Boys – a hilarious, adult comedy.

The Talus 3 Trilogy

Book 1 – Arctic EMP

Book 2 – Galactic Illusions

Book 3 – Forsaken Drifter

Paperbacks, hardcovers and ebooks are available from Amazon.

Contents

Prologue

September 25th in the year 2084.

Zurich, New European Union

I opened my mouth unnaturally wide as I slid a spoonful of cereal past my lips. At the same time, my eyebrows lowered as I stared at Jena, my seven-year-old girl. My wife, Mariam, was not so amused, her stern gaze reminding me my comical face was not appropriate at the breakfast table. However, it did not stop Jena, or her ten-year-old sister, Arina, from breaking out into boisterous laughter.

"I must have missed something important."

My head turned to see our house guest, Romy, in the wide doorway to the kitchen. Motioning my hand towards the empty chair, I offered, "Please, come and sit."

Just before he sat down, Mariam slid a large bowl in front of him, while her other hand pointed, first to the cereal box, then the plate of assorted fruits. Through a wide smile she said, "Get started, Romy, and don't let the kids distract you." She lowered an eyebrow while turning her gaze to the children sitting across from Romy. They had been staring at the strange visitor prior to her gaze, but now turned their eyes to each other, both failing in their attempt to stifle their childish giggles.

"So, what are you two up to today?" my wife inquired.

Romy peered up from his bowl of cereal, but I interrupted before he could reply. "You know our rule, my dear, no *shop talk* outside of working hours."

"That might have worked at the dinner table last night, Yevgeni, but it won't work this morning. I would like to know a little more about the man who is eating all our food. Besides," her gaze shifted to the electronic numerals on the wall mounted clock. "It's 9:05 in the morning, well into normal working hours."

With Romy's spoon frozen a few centimetres from his open mouth, I softly slapped the back of his shoulder. "No worries, just keep eating." My eyes lifted to my wife who was now in front of the kitchen sink. "Romy is an author. He is writing a book about modern space exploration. For some reason he thinks I have something to offer."

She turned, leaning the arch of her back against the edge of the countertop. "All I can say, Mr. Gunn, is that I hope you learn more about his work today than I typically do here at home."

"In a few minutes, we will retire to my study for the discussion you say will likely never happen, my dear." My wife recognized my sarcastic tone and opened her mouth. Before she could reply, I interrupted, pointing at the coffeemaker beside her, "It's all primed to go—if you could just flick that switch."

The corner of her lip turned up as her face exuded just enough reciprocated sarcasm for me to notice. She flicked the switch on. "My apologies, Romy, but your discussion might not offer the most entertainment for the children since I am sure they would be listening with their ears to the study door." Her gaze shifted to me. "After breakfast, I'll be taking the kids to my mother's house for the day."

Nodding, I rose, retrieved two cups and poured coffee into both. I preferred mine black, but in spending the past two days with Romy, I knew he preferred cream and sugar in his. I placed his cup down in front of him, so he could use the condiments on the table as he saw fit.

Leading Romy to my study, we moved up the half flight of stairs, down the hallway and through the door at the far end. Our house was, in fact, a large, three-story townhouse within a group of five, facing the Limmat river in Old Zurich. It had been completely renovated two years ago, bringing it up from its original construction in 2025. Each townhouse in the row was half offset, allowing for large picture windows on both sides of the southwest corner of the study. It gave an excellent view of the grove of elm trees bordering the river, the grove still filled with the fog the morning heat had not yet burned off.

The room had old maple floors covered by a colourful, red and grey Moroccan carpet. On one side, in front of a wall-to-wall bookcase, was my antique desk. Across from it were two smaller chairs, and behind them was a short, thickly-padded, black sofa and a just-as-comfortable looking, matching chair.

Romy did not sit; rather, he moved to the window, his fingers clasped together behind his back. "I have been in Zurich for a week now, and I think this is the first time I have seen a hint of full sunlight."

I stood just behind him, bent from the waist and gazed up. In fact, he was right. You could see the partially obscured ball of yellow. Now, in the year, 2084, climate change and pollution had left a thin haze covering most of the planet. Today, when you could see the sun through it, was rare, occurring only perhaps five or six times a year.

I took a drink from my coffee cup, considering the difference between Earth and the world Romy had described to me. Two days ago, he had kidnapped me and brought me to a yacht where I woke, well off shore on Lake Zurich. Some might find it odd I accepted his means to an end after he explained his reasoning. Romy had a story to tell, one originating from a pact between my grandfather and his great grandfather, many years ago.

On the yacht, over the past two days, he had told me the entire story, beginning with the fact his great grandfather was from an alien Korian race, when he met my grandfather who was part of the Russian secret service. Together, they thwarted an effort by a third alien race, the Sholites, to destroy Earth and the Korian populated asteroid they called home—the massive, hollowed out asteroid known as Talus 3.

After being saved from the disaster, Talus 3 continued on through space, its Korian inhabitants searching for their own planet to call home. My grandfather and Romy's great grandfather, bonded as friends, had made a pact where, if and when the Korians found a new home world, somehow, a message would be sent back to my grandfather. If by then he had passed, then the story would be brought back to his descendant—and that was me. That is why Romy was in Zurich, and his goal was to finish the telling of the story, now in its third day.

It was a story no one in their right mind, including me, would believe. But, on the first day, when he pricked his finger, I saw his blood was blue, not red. My grandfather had foretold to me this unique nature of Korian blood many times in my youth. This irrefutable evidence was the game changer. Who was I not to believe when I saw the blue drops of blood make a small pool on the glass table, before turning clear as it oxidized? Even in our modern age, seeing is believing.

Romy placed his tablet on the table in front of the couch he lowered into. He crossed one foot over his other knee and said, "So, I am an author writing a book on modern space exploration?"

I sat on the plump cushion of the chair to his left. As I sunk in, I replied, "I don't like lying to my wife, so when I told her this, there is truth in it. You do have a story, and I suspect all of it is not yet written."

Creases formed on Romy's forehead in front of his flowing, brown hair, long enough to cover his ears. It was the odd look I had seen on his face several times in the past two days, a hint I knew something I should not.

I was right as he brought up the most recent such instance. "I made a point of not telling you who I was, yet you figured it out. How did you manage that?"

After another drink of my coffee, I answered. "It was not difficult. In the story, you told me of life with the Korians after leaving Earth, you described a Romy Gunn, you described pureblood humans who have psychic powers, and finally, that Romy found himself to be one of them. Not only that, but Romy was a very unique pureblood, one with the ability not only to hop between planes of reality populated by pureblood humans, but to also travel in time. As you told me, such a time travelling pureblood, one other purebloods called a *time drifter*, occurred only once every few millennia."

I paused, taking another drink of coffee.

As one eyebrow raised, the look on Romy's face was more quizzical. "That in itself would not identify me."

My eyes rolled. "I have already said, I am the descendant of my *grandfather*, known as Nick Anderson. You are the *great grandson* of Rowan Gunn." When I saw he was still confused, I elaborated, "Nick Anderson and Rowan Gun would have been around the same age when they met, yet you are here even though, as descendants, there is a one generation gap between us. Further, our ages are not too far apart. The only way you could be here, is if you time travelled."

Romy grinned. "You are clever. I can see why you are respected as an experienced spaceman, scientist and medical doctor."

I motioned my chin towards the tablet. "You have said there is more to the story."

"It will take some time, likely all day. You might want to freshen your coffee."

Leaning forward, I placed my cup on the table. My eyes widened. "We can do that later. I was dying all last night through dinner, then I barely slept having been so anxious to hear the rest of the story now that Romy and his father, Ryder Gunn, were reunited."

His finger pressed on the tablet, bringing it to life. Once he found the correct file, he glanced up. "Best you relax and sit back."

I did sit back as he began to read, but my level of anticipation did not subside as he continued to recount the story of the Korian and Sholite peoples, now residing in Alpha Centauri.

Chapter 1: The Beacon

The 18th day of the 2nd month, Alpha Centauri year 0024.

Deep Space

"Distance?"

"Maintaining one kilometre, Sir."

"Excellent, Mr. Fasedy. Keep it tight," Captain Snyder replied to his navigation officer.

The command center of the *Predator,* the latest jaguar class destroyer out of Metro, housed the captain and five officers. Fasedy had been the navigation officer since the vessel was commissioned, three months ago. The other four officers were, respectively, in charge of propulsion, environmental systems, scanning and weapons. They were all focused on their scanners, the quiet in the room an indication of their underlying, collective nervousness. The *Nova* was a scant one kilometre away, and one kilometre between ships wasn't close—except if both vessels were moving at 25 per cent the speed of light (SOL).

The *Nova* was an explorer class vessel tracking an asteroid they captured on their long-range scanners the day before. The powerful telescope in their hold was deployed, and the asteroid inspected. It was a bent oblong, roughly 250 metres across, and it was moving at 43 thousand kilometres per hour. Between the scanners and the telescope, there was a strong suggestion of a high metal content mixed in with the rock.

Captain Rock Snyder was only 40 years old, considered young for his commission as the lead on the *Predator.* The other officers on the command deck all had seniority above his own. However, he was the up-and-coming officer, shooting through the ranks, now with responsibility for probably the most modern warship in the fleet and in all of Alpha Centauri. His officers trusted him as did the other 90 crew members looking after the day-to-day activities aboard the vessel.

"Hail the *Nova*, Ensign Chara."

Immediately, Ensign Chara pressed a series of coloured buttons on his console and said, "*Nova*…Captain Snyder for Captain Mason."

"One minute," came the reply.

The feminine voice of Captain Nico Mason came across the speakers. "Good afternoon, Captain Snyder. How can I assist you?"

Captain Snyder snickered. "Our ship has been out here in the dark of space for six weeks now, so long that I've personally lost track of day and night. But if it helps, well, good afternoon to you too."

"Grumpy," came the reply.

Snyder ignored that and asked, "How long before we break our warp bubble?"

A distant discussion could be heard from the speakers before Captain Mason answered, "Just over 22 minutes. Our comm is open. Have your navigation officer latch onto it and sync your controls."

Snapping his fingers, Snyder was about to relay the command when he was cut off.

"Already on it, Captain," Ensign Fasedy growled.

The process of slowing down was easy. Of course, it was much more difficult to slow down from 25 per cent SOL without ripping the ship apart. And since their velocity amounted to 250 million kilometres per hour, even a difference of a second in timing could find the two ships easily a million kilometres apart. So, the next 20 minutes were travelled in quiet, both ships on a shallow arc, coming around to parallel the path of the oncoming asteroid.

A minute later, Ensign Edy, the propulsion officer, said, "Countdown is set for 60 seconds on my mark." A few more seconds went by. "Mark."

The large digital clock above the multiple screens spread across the front of the command deck began the countdown.

"Belt yourselves in, Ladies and Gentlemen," Snyder ordered as he clicked in his own shoulder belts over and down his chest to the central latch. It was protocol, but Snyder thought it silly. If there was any type of issue breaking out of SOL, the ship and all the occupants would be splattered across the cold vacuum of space, irrespective of the restraints.

Snyder pressed a button on the armrest. "Crew, this is Captain Snyder. Lock yourself in for warp break in—" he glanced at the timer "—47 seconds."

There was only a slight buffeting for 30 seconds as the ship decelerated. When it stopped, Fasedy reported the *Nova* was three kilometres ahead of them.

"Catch us up, Mister Edy. Put us 500 metres behind them."

Once in position, both vessels had their external cameras locked on a point in space where they knew the asteroid would appear. Sure enough, a few minutes later, on the view screens in both ships, they could see the big rock slowly tumbling towards them. When it was close, both ships matched the path and speed of the asteroid. A series of 20 marker missiles were launched from the explorer ship. They were timed such that the markers would impact into the asteroid at evenly spaced locations around its surface area during its roll.

Now, as the sensors from the markers spiked deep into the rock and metal surface, a light at the top of each marker began to strobe. Only one, damaged from its impact, remained dark. There was silence for the next ten minutes as the crew of both ships watched and waited for the analysis to be complete.

Ensign Chara glanced at Captain Snyder. "Captain Mason is hailing us."

"Captain Snyder here."

In the background, from the explorer ship, there was boisterous cheering. Above it, Captain Mason yelled, "Platinum, Captain! There is a large mass of platinum in that big, beautiful rock!"

"Congratulations, Nico. You're going to follow it into Metro space?"

"Yes, Captain," Nico Mason replied. "At this speed, it will take about 35 days to get to the mining trawlers, but we will make sure it gets there safe and sound."

Captain Snyder decided, "We're going to escort you for two days, until you're clear of any possible Haven ships. You'll be on your own after that."

Forty hours later, three low beeps from Captain Snyder's bedside panel caused him to shift in his slumber. A few seconds later, the beeps emitted again. The captain's eyelids lifted to see the low, muted light level within his cabin. As he rolled over, he grumbled, "Lights, 50 per cent." The cabin lights brightened, and he pressed the communications button on the console. "What is it, Mr. Ronlan?"

Jake Ronlan was the engineering officer assigned to the *Predator* and also his second in command. As his voice came through the speaker, Snyder, in his mind's eye, could picture his relatively squat body, his round face covered with a thick, black beard and the beads of sweat that seemed perpetually on his forehead. "Sorry to wake you Cap, but there is an odd disturbance in sector 48."

Rolling his legs off the short cot-like bed, the corners of Snyder's mouth turned down in a frown. For the most part, space was a big empty vacuum of nothing. However, there were asteroids and comets, gas clouds and dust clouds that could be of interest, but sector 48 was known to be an area of nothing. He growled, "Sector 48—there's nothing of interest there, and certainly, nothing of enough interest to wake me!" Snyder's fingers came up and scratched the side of his head. "Damn! Our sensors don't even reach sector 48."

After an electronic click and a pause, Ronlan added, "That's exactly what I told Captain Mason on the *Nova*, but she reminded me the sensors aboard their explorer class vessel can see much further than we can, and they have a higher sensitivity."

Rising to his feet, Captain Snyder said, "And you can't handle it?"

"Captain Mason didn't say that exactly, but that's the vibe I got. She insisted it was important enough to wake you."

"I'm on my way."

Snyder left his cabin, turning left down the grey, metal-plated hallway, wide enough for two people to easily pass by each other. Several crew members passed him on their way to the aft portion of the ship. Each nodded to their captain and Snyder nodded back. The nod was the customary acknowledgment of respect used in the Metro navy for one of superior rank.

Each of the crew members had the required uniform: dark claret almost black pants and a matching long sleeved shirt. On the left side of the chest was a six-centimetre circle of white, and printed on it was a large letter *M*. Snyder's uniform was exactly the same except his shirt had a light-blue patch atop each shoulder, a visual indication of his captain's rank. If he was a squadron captain in charge of a group of ships, the patch would be yellow, and if he ever made admiral in charge of an entire fleet, red patches would sit atop his shoulders.

He pulled up the zipper on the front of his claret-coloured jacket also having the light-blue patches, while he waited for the elevator door to open. Three flights up the door opened, and after a thirty metre walk down the main corridor, he entered the command deck.

He saw a few nods and heard a few say, "Afternoon, Captain," as he walked to a point beside his command chair.

Ronlan popped up, wiping his brow before giving a curt nod. "The command is yours, Cap."

Captain Snyder slapped the top of Ronlan's shoulder. "Relax, my friend. It was almost time for my shift in any case." He looked over Ronlan's shoulder and said, "Ensign Yosaka, please hail Captain Mason aboard the *Nova*. Let's see what all this excitement is about."

There were three full teams aboard the *Predator*, each a complete five-man deck crew, that rotated through the command deck every five hours. Yosaka was presently the communications officer on shift. She hailed the *Nova*, and a few seconds later, a response was received.

"Good morning, Rock. I hope you slept well," Captain Mason chided.

"Yeah, yeah, Nico. What's got your panties in a knot," Snyder grumbled.

"Careful now, Rock. I don't want to have to report you. It would be such a waste of time to have you go through harassment training again. I mean, how many times so far—three?"

Lowering back into his command chair, Snyder grinned. "Four if you include the initial training, but who's counting?" Before Captain Mason could give another smart-assed comment, Snyder added, "Get to the point, Nico. What're you seeing?"

"Being an explorer ship, our long-range sensors are always scanning. Ahead of us, on the starboard side, we picked up a massive electromagnetic disturbance. And before you ask, no it wasn't some type of stellar collision. There is no debris. But the signature was massive. It lasted ten seconds, then it was gone."

Rubbing the stubble on his chin, Snyder mumbled, "And you say there was nothing left behind?"

Mason corrected him, "I didn't say there was nothing left behind. I *said* there was no debris."

Stopping the chin rub mid-stroke, Mason's eyes narrowed. "And?"

"We popped out the big scope and had a look. No debris, as I said, but there is a metallic sphere. It looks perfectly round. It's a long way from our position, but we estimate the diameter at 15 metres. There is also an energy signal."

"Is this something the Haven navy is doing?" Captain Snyder asked.

"Unlikely. I haven't seen the technology to create this size of disturbance in their arsenal, and we don't have that capability either. I'm suggesting, as the explorer ship, we go to the sphere and investigate. You can continue on with the asteroid towards the mining trawlers."

Almost jumping out of his chair, Snyder blurted, "Not on your life,

Mason! Seeing as it's an unknow risk, and we don't know for a certainty it's not some type of Haven weapon, I'm declaring it a security risk. That makes it a military matter."

A chuckle came through the speaker. It wasn't only Mason's, but the *Predator's* command crew could also hear Mason's crew snickering in the background. Snyder's one eyebrow lowered, and he could feel the flush on his face. Apparently, the explorer captain had been pulling his leg.

Her voice came over the speaker. "Keep your shorts on, Rock. It's all yours, but—" her tone became slower and more serious "—keep safe out there. I'll have a drink waiting for you back on Metro."

"You too, Nico," Captain Snyder replied before nodding towards Yosaka. "Disconnect, Ensign." He then glared at Ronlan. "What are you still doing here? I need you in Propulsion to fire up the engines! I want to be at that sphere in 12 hours."

Ronlan gave a curt nod and all but ran out of the command deck.

The long-range coordinates of the unknown sphere were received from the *Nova*. The formidable mass of the jaguar class destroyer slowly veered away from the asteroid and the explorer ship that continued on with its babysitting duties. Soon, visually, where the *Nova* should see the *Predator*, they would see nothing but black space and a patch of space missing the background stars. The *Predator* was covered with one-metre, metal plates, each set slightly off angle from its adjoining panels, and each was coated with a nano tech paint that trapped light in the coating. Of course, the light, being trapped energy, would heat up the panels, the heat subsequently recovered and repurposed by the ship's advanced energy control systems.

The three-hundred-metre-long vessel pointed its rounded nose towards the coordinates of the beacon. It did indeed look like a devil, the round, blood-red laser gun ports on either side of the nose looking like eyes and the command deck, protruding up from the fuselage, much like a forehead. At various locations down the length of the fighting ship were appendages, bristling with laser cannons and torpedo ports. The naval ship accelerated, and a blue, opaque aura formed, first around the rear propulsion ports, then expanding forward until the ship was engulfed. It took time to reach the desired speed, in this case, 35 per cent SOL.

Captain Snyder was just completing a report in his cabin when three beeps sounded. It was only ten hours since they had left the asteroid. He was writing a report giving details of the *Nova's* findings regarding the location and unusual nature of the disturbance in space and the sphere left behind. He finished typing the final few words, hit the sequence to encrypt the message, then *enter* to send it. It would arrive at Metro Naval Headquarters in an estimated 14 hours.

The beeps sounded again.

"What is it, Mr. Ronlan?"

"Three Haven naval ships on our radar. A frigate and two cruisers, Sir. Distance—20 million kilometres and closing."

Captain Snyder instantly shot to his feet. "Bring all stations to battle alert, Mr. Ronlan." He ran at a full tilt as the strobing red lights and the associated whoop of the siren, filled the hallways. Two minutes later, he landed in the command chair beside a fidgeting Mr. Ronlan. Snyder didn't need to dismiss his second in command, since he was already on his way to Propulsion.

"Ensign Fasedy, set camera shift to every ten seconds," Snyder ordered.

There were many cameras mounted to ports around the *Predator*. All could be accessed and their views shown, however, there were four main cameras most often utilized. One, on the right front of the ship, monitored their zero to three o'clock position. The second, mounted near the rear of the ship, monitored the three o'clock to six o'clock position. Two more cameras monitored the mirrored quadrants on the other side of the vessel. By directing the camera shift to ten seconds, that meant each camera would pan their 90-degree quadrant in ten seconds. The sweeping pattern would repeat with the four images being shown on the four large monitors along the front of the command deck.

"Mister Mallin, weapons status?"

Mallin, the weapons officer of the deck, looked down at his monitor. "Primary laser supply is at 100 per cent. Backup power banks, one, two, three and four are all at 100 per cent."

"Excellent. And torpedoes?" Snyder asked.

"All 30 tubes are primed and have a green light."

A large sigh escaped Snyder's lips. "Load tubes one, two, nine and ten. Be ready to arm them immediately on my command, Mister Mallin." In a quiet, but firm voice, Snyder added, "This is not the time to daydream. Be alert. That goes for all of you."

"Mister Fasedy, what are the positions of the Haven ships?"

"Eighteen million kilometres and still closing."

"Ensign Chara, hail the Haven ships, all standard bands," Captain Snyder ordered.

Chara made attempt after attempt, but there was no response. Captain Snyder hated playing these games. The Haven navy knew the much newer Metro ships, especially a destroyer, were more formidable than all three of the pursuing Haven vessels combined. The eagle class cruisers and the wolf class frigate, would be blown out of space with barely any effort if they approached much closer. And they knew it.

Snyder could hear the static on the last channel tried. Chara nodded. They both knew the Haven captains were listening.

Captain Snyder announced, "This is Captain Rock Snyder in command of the Metro naval destroyer, *Predator*. We are not on a military mission. But if you come closer, we will consider it a hostile act, and you will be fired upon. This is your only warning."

There was no response. Snyder waited ten minutes before asking Ensign Fasedy, "What is their position?"

"They are no longer closing. They are maintaining a course mirroring ours at a distance of 18 million kilometres."

"Excellent. If that should change, let me know immediately, Ensign Chara."

Ninety minutes later, Fasedy announced, "Sir, we are four million kilometres from the sphere's coordinates. Should we begin deceleration?"

"Of course, Mister Fasedy." He looked at Shara Mal, the propulsion officer on deck. "Between you two, slow us down at your discretion, but keep it smooth. I better not slide out of this chair."

"Aye, aye, Sir," Ensign Mal replied.

The *Predator* came to a stop 100 kilometres from the sphere. Upon maximum magnification, via the front cameras, the command deck crew could see it was not just a sphere, but it could be better described as a beacon. It was indeed spherical with a wire mesh frame surrounding a smooth outer shell, each square of the frame approximately one metre square. There were only two irregularities in the pattern. The first most obvious one was a ring a quarter of the way down from the top of the wire mesh frame. It went right around the entire grid, and on a regular cycle, a bright, white, pulsing light was emitted. After a few minutes, it was easy to determine the pulses came 125 seconds apart.

The other protrusion from the smooth surface was not as obvious. On the left side, what looked like a handle attached to a small door, could be seen. Snyder pressed the button on his armrest. "Ronlan, are you seeing this in Propulsion?" Both the propulsion and science teams were under Ronlan's command. That's why the question was directed to him.

"Yes, Sir. I have my science and engineering leads here." There was some muttering in the background, then Ronlan suggested, "Captain, in our opinion, this did not originate from Haven. We have been reviewing the file the science team aboard the *Nova* sent us, the one analyzing the original disturbance. That information, along with the visual of this beacon, are not consistent with Haven technology."

Leaning forward, Snyder squinted. "What is it made of? It looks like gold."

On some worlds, gold is a rarity, so quite valuable. But in the totality of space, gold is a common element, easily found in many asteroids. As such, it was not a surprise when Ronlan replied, "It sure looks like it, but we won't know until we get closer and do a scan."

It was at that moment Snyder had second thoughts. *Maybe we should have let the Nova handle this. Something doesn't smell right.*

"Ronlan, take two members of your team, and get a shuttle ready. I'll bring the *Predator* closer, but keep us a respectable distance back. You'll take the shuttle in and do a closer inspection."

The *Predator* was brought in to a position five kilometres from the beacon. The strobing, white light continued to pulse every 125 seconds. Snyder was just finishing an updated report on the beacon. He described the strobing white light, their initial observation distance and, now, their new position. He felt it prudent to send the encrypted message before the closer examination, as protocol required.

"Ronlan, you're clear to launch," Snyder said into his microphone.

There was a barely perceptible shiver through the *Predator* as the docking clamps released the six-man-shuttle. A few moments later, the shuttle could be seen on the front right monitor within the command deck. It was slowly closing towards the beacon that continued to pulse, a pulse that all on the command deck were finding more than a little irritating.

"Chara, keep comms open to the shuttle," Captain Snyder commanded.

Chara nodded, while pressing a sequence of buttons on her console.

Snapping his fingers, Snyder looked at Fasedy. "I almost forgot. How are our Haven friends doing?"

"They are parked 18 million kilometres off our port side. I think they have settled in to watch the show."

"Awesome," Snyder mumbled. His train of thought was interrupted by Ronlan's voice over the speaker.

"We're going to make a few circles around the beacon and do a good visual."

The command deck crew watched the action as the shuttle made seven loops around the beacon, the gold glistening in the high-power light from the shuttle.

"There's nothing odd here, Captain." Ronlan gave his opinion. "Other than the handle and what looks like a hatch, the outer shell of the sphere is as smooth as a baby's bottom."

"Let's try a standard energy scan, Mister Ronlan," Snyder suggested.

The shuttle made another slow round of the beacon, and when it returned to its original position, Ronlan reported, "Nothing, Captain. Just that infernal light is driving us crazy."

After a few seconds, Captain Snyder suggested, "Let's try an x-ray scan and see what's inside that thing."

Without hesitation, Ronlan replied, "Aye, Captain. Countdown from five."

Whoever was in the shuttle with Ronlan began the count. "Five...four...three...two...one...mark."

There was only silence amid the tension on the command deck, but nothing else. It was Ensign Chara who noticed it first. "The strobing has stopped."

She was right. It must have been at least 40 seconds since the strobe should have gone off. "Ronlan, stop the scan!" Snyder shouted.

There was no response, and then Shara Mal said in a staccato voice showing her nervousness. "Energy buildup detected from the beacon, Sir. It's increasing quickly!"

"Ronlan, get out of there, maximum speed!" He said the same to Fasedy and Mal. "Get us the fuck out of here, now!"

On the front right screen, the shuttle was seen speeding away from the sphere. At the same time, the *Predator* jolted, veering right as it accelerated quickly away from the beacon. One of the aft camera's was still locked on the beacon, maintaining the image on the front, left screen.

"Energy levels from the beacon are off the scale, Captain!" Mal shouted, her voice at a higher pitch, the staccato still evident, but now, from fear and not just nervousness.

Captain Snyder slouched back in his chair. There was nothing else to be done. They were accelerating at their maximum. The distance from the beacon was increasing exponentially. He thought, *we just might make it.*

Those hopes were shattered when the left screen was engulfed by an instantaneous flash of white light. *Damn*, Snyder thought. A moment later, on the right screen, they saw the shock wave hit the shuttle, disintegrating it on contact.

He knew the *Predator* had perhaps five seconds. Captain Rock Snyder did not have a wife or children. He was a career military man—the up-and-coming officer who was going to set the Metro navy alight. And now, the only thing that was going to be set alight was his ass. His very last thought before the shock wave hit was, *I guess those Haven ships are going to get quite a show, after all.*

Snyder was wrong. It was six seconds, not five when the shock wave hit. Being further away than the shuttle, the ship did not disintegrate, but there wasn't a piece of the *Predator* left that was bigger than one of those one metre by one metre black, outer panels; the panels that a few minutes before, were part of the hull of the most modern warship in the Alpha Centauri system.

Chapter 2: A New Beginning

The 13ᵗʰ day of the 4ᵗʰ month, Alpha Centauri year 0024.

Haven, far orbit.

Ryder Gunn stood across from his son, Romy. They hadn't seen each other, nor had they had any contact with each other, for the past eighteen years. Yet, to Ryder, these last few metres between them seemed insurmountable. For all those years of absence, guilt wracked him. There were good reasons why he'd been away. He would explain them to his son, and he could only hope Romy would accept them. Yet, his feet were frozen to the ground, his fear holding him in place.

However, when Ryder's eyes caught his son's, his knees almost buckled. Romy's eyes were moist, the sudden shock of his father's appearance making him instantly vulnerable. Now, at 30 years old, his son had grown into a handsome, strong man, but at this moment, his face appeared pale and haggard. Ryder wondered if it was due to his son's recent incarceration at a Korian minimum security penal facility, or the close encounter he had with his delivery to a maximum security, Korian penal ship, the one Ryder and his fellow crew members had just rescued him from. Or possibly, the look of despair, perhaps even defeat, might be due to his father's sudden appearance.

That look of despair on his son's face, along with his hand on the desk supporting him, gave Ryder the strength to move his feet. It surprised Ryder how quickly he wrapped his son in his arms. There was an instant of anticipation that seemed to last forever, until Ryder felt his son's arms return the embrace. Then, both men were sobbing.

Romy had not had a father for the last 18 years. During that time, he sometimes wondered if his father was dead. The population of Haven certainly thought he was. After all, 18 years ago, he and many of his compatriots from the Korian Explorer Corp. turned the noses of their ships to the cold, dark unknown of deep space. To most, survival would be a miracle.

Yet, it seemed a miracle had indeed occurred. Romy squeezed his father tighter. In his youth, Romy and his father always had a close bond. It was eerie whereby the elder Gunn and his son had an almost psychic bond. It was as if they could see inside the other, sensing moods, feelings and often words even before they came out. That ended when Romy was 12 years old, when his father left, but even after that, he felt a supernatural bond to his father. It was one that belayed the death mongering thoughts of Haven's population. It was not that he knew his father was alive, more so, he would have felt it if his father had died.

The two men finally pulled apart. Ryder, for a moment, could not suppress a wide smile before he wiped the moistness from his eyes. He then slapped his son on the shoulder and whispered, "Finally—after all these years."

Romy had recovered from his temporary vulnerability. He pulled himself up to his full height, at least three centimetres above his father. His face firmed up, and his eyes brightened. He had been freed from his life sentence at the penal facility, and now, his father was here. *His father!*

Romy had to do a quick calculation in his head to come to the realization his father was 64 years old. Although Romy had recovered, he thought, right now, his father looked at least every day of those years. Romy did not know where his father had been or what adventures he had survived, but they had aged him. There were wrinkles under his eyes, and the creases on his forehead were deeper than he remembered, especially now as they were strained. Under his beard, at the corners of his mouth, the skin drooped as did that at the front of his neck. However, his body looked lean and strong. The slap on Romy's shoulder had been impressively powerful. To Romy, it all added up to the fact, where ever his father had been, it had been a hard life.

"Where are we?"

His son's words brought Ryder out of his daze. Ryder wrapped his arm around his son's shoulder and coaxed him across the room to two chairs. Once they were sitting, Ryder explained their situation.

"We're aboard the Metro naval ship, *Shade*," Ryder explained. "It's a barracuda class cruiser. We're cloaked and hiding in a high orbit, 50 kilometres above Haven—hiding in plain sight, so to speak."

Romy paused, holding back the urge to ask questions about the words just mentioned. He had never heard of *Metro*, whatever it was, and within the classification of space vessels, naval or otherwise, he had never heard of a barracuda class. Within the Haven navy, cruisers were an eagle classification. However, he was not interested in these details. Looking at his father with an expectant gaze, he waited for him to continue, hopefully with the answers he was looking for.

Ryder looked down for a moment, pushing his fingers back through his hair, a habit that had been passed down to his son. When he looked back up, after a deep breath, he said, "Yes, it's been a long time." In his lap, Ryder's hands were clasped together, his fingers rolling over each other. "Eighteen years, in fact. I'm sure they've been long years for you, just as they were for me." Ryder awkwardly gulped a breath of air. "Just before I left, we had a long talk. I explained to you why I had to leave. Do you remember?"

"Of course. How could I not? But please, tell me again," Romy replied, his voice barely above a whisper. "Maybe it will help me understand things."

Involuntarily, Ryder drew back into the chair. *Understanding?* He gathered himself, knowing his words in the next few minutes could make or break their foregoing relationship. "You'll remember, I was not a popular person on Haven. Your mother and I…"

"My step mother," Romy interrupted.

"What?"

"I'lish Mann, by blood is my aunt, so not my mother. Then, as part of this subterfuge fooling all the Korian and Sholite people, she adopted me. That would make her my aunt and my stepmother."

Clearing his throat, Ryder continued, "We both know the story, Son. You also know if we didn't go through with the farce of a marriage, the Sholite and Korian fleets would likely have destroyed each other well before they reached Haven. The false marriage, that between a primor of a powerful Korian family and the acting president of the Sholite people, showed the population we could all get along."

Romy flicked a piece of lint off his pant leg. "My stepmother has red blood, the red blood passed down to her from her Earthen great grandmother. Yet, she was born on Talus 3 as a Korian."

Smiling, Ryder made an effort not to be patronizing. "Your stepmother was raised as a Sholite and has always considered herself a Sholite."

In his own right, Romy made an effort for his twisted smile not to appear overly sarcastic. "How would you know? You have been away."

With a slight tilt of his head, Ryder gave a reply, the nonchalant nature of which he instantly regretted. "Oh, your stepmother and I have been in contact over the years."

Shooting to his feet, the words burst from Romy's lips. "Mother knew! All this time, and she knew!"

Ryder's hand came up in front of his chest before he slowly pressed it down, as if to push the tension in the air away. "Relax, Son. Sit and I'll explain."

Lowering his gaze, it was now Romy's turn to press his fingers back through his hair. He mumbled, "It seems I have been the only person who did not know you were alive. Is that it? It's like I've been living in a bubble." He snapped his face up, his eyes narrow slits. "Do you know what it has been like being the son of Ryder Gunn? Common knowledge has you as the highest-ranking traitor of Kor."

This is the last thing Ryder wanted, but it was expected. He'd left his son 18 years ago. For many, they would use the word—*abandoned*. There had been many assassination attempts on his life, sourced from some on the ruling council, but when those threats expanded to his son, Ryder knew he had to leave. At least, that's the story Ryder kept telling himself every day since he left his son. He left to ensure his son's safety. That was it. If he was gone and thought dead, there would be no point in attacking his son. It all made sense, yet in Ryder's mind and heart, it had never settled well.

"Father, I understand why you left. I think any strong man would do such in that situation. But there is a question."

"Yes, what?"

Romy's voice lowered to barely a whisper, and the words came slowly. "Why didn't you ever come back for me?"

The tension in the room was interrupted by a beep from the direction of the desk.

Raising a finger in the air, Ryder said, "We'll finish this conversation later." He rose and walked to the desk before pressing a button on the comms device. "Yes, Captain Brand."

"Admiral Gunn, we are ten minutes from making our departure. Would you like to join us on the command deck?"

"Be right there, Captain."

Turning back to his son, he was relieved the call interrupted their conversation. They needed a few moments to take a few breaths. "Join me. This should be interesting." Ryder snapped his fingers. "I almost forgot. Let's get you out of those orange penal coveralls." He pointed to a locker. "There are civilian clothes in there. Get changed, but be quick."

Romy changed, glad to be free of the orange suit. His father frowned as he took note of several wounds on his son's body. Ryder knew his son had been drawn into the rebellion and then the Korian civil war. Even though he could not return to Haven, Ryder always had people close by his son. Barrett Fexman was one of his close associates, and Fexman kept a close eye on Romy. Then, there was Rico, another close friend of Ryder's. He was saddened when he heard of Rico's death.

Thankfully, the pants and jacket Romy pulled on were claret red, the same colour as his father's. The outfit was similar, except his father's had a white circle over his chest, and in the middle was a red letter *M*. He assumed the *M* represented the *Metro* his father had mentioned earlier, even though he did not know what it meant. His civilian version of the shirt did not have the crest on it.

As they walked out the cabin door, Romy said, "Admiral?"

Ryder led the way, and his words came back to Romy. "I'm not in the military. I'm an admiral of the Explorer Corp., and I'm an advisor to the prime minister."

In a way, it surprised Romy that his father was not the person in charge. Many thought Ryder was a born leader. He and his stepmother took control when the joint fleet of Korians and Sholites travelled to Haven, and then again when his father left Haven, many explorer ships and even a few naval vessels went with him. They all followed Ryder, so to Romy, it was odd that his father was on his way to the command deck where another person was captaining the ship.

They walked down the same hallway Romy had already travelled after his rescue, then up the same elevator, but they walked in the opposite direction to his original passage through it. Ryder led him towards the front of the vessel and explained, "Metro is the name of our home. Leave it at that for now, and I'll explain more later. We've been making our own ships for some eight years now. With the help of the Mabuza and their advanced technology, these vessels are much more formidable than what the Haven navy has."

Romy's jaw dropped. "You know about the Mabuza?"

His father raised a finger. He said, "Later, Son," as the door to the command deck opened.

A middle-aged man, perhaps 45, turned and smiled at the two newcomers to the deck. His head was shaved, his eyes close set. Romy thought, *much more predator than prey.*

Ryder introduced his son to Captain Xavier Brand who then introduced Romy to the other four officers on his command deck. There were many nods before the captain invited Admiral Gunn and his son to sit in two of the chairs bolted to the back wall of the circular room.

Once in the chair, Ryder whispered to his son. "We're about to come out of our cloaking cover. Keep in mind, our escape isn't risk free."

Romy leaned over, whispering back. "I don't understand. Cloaking systems only work in an atmosphere, not in the vacuum of space."

"We've made some advances. You're correct in that a cloaking system needs molecules to realign, and they're not available in space. However, we've come up with a system whereby a thin layer of helium is released around the ship. These molecules then, in turn, are realigned by the cloaking system."

"Impressive, but aren't the sensors still a problem?"

"Quite right, Romy. The sensors and even the cameras cannot penetrate the cloaking shield. There is an additional problem in that the engines cannot be used when we're cloaked. The shield won't hide the signature," Ryder elaborated.

Leaning forward, Romy turned and looked at his father. "You mean we are just floating out here, blind? There's probably Haven ships all around us."

Ryder replied through his chuckle. "Yes, isn't it exciting."

"Ensign Fortay," Captain Brand stated, "Enter coordinates 002, 200, 450."

A few seconds later, "Done, Captain," came as confirmation.

"Jorge, on my mark drop the cloak and give me five seconds at 20 per cent standard drive."

The captain then turned to his communication officer. "Rolston, do a scan sweep while the cloak is down."

Jorge, the propulsion officer, pressed buttons on his console, then nodded without taking his eyes off the screen.

"Mister Jorge, mark!"

The four screens across the front of the command deck came to life as Ryder and Romy were pushed back in their chairs from the g force. After five seconds, the load on their chests stopped, and the screens blanked out once again.

"Jorge, status?" the captain asked.

The propulsion officer put his face closer to the screen, reviewing the recording of the five second burst. "When we went dark our velocity was 940 kilometres per hour with an acceleration of 50 kilometres per hour squared."

"Fortay, put the sensor map on screen 2."

The navigation officer pressed a button on his console, and a map appeared. It showed the planet Haven at the centre of the screen. The *Shade* was a large red dot. The three orbiting control stations, Haven Control one, two and three, were shown in blue. There were six other smaller, red dots close to Haven and four more distant. Each had a letter overtop the dot indicating the calibre of the Haven naval warship. Of the six in closer proximity, there was one battleship, two destroyers and three cruisers. The four vessels further out were all frigates.

Captain Xavier Brand mumbled, "I hope your son is worth this effort. They won't make this easy."

Brand turned and winked at Ryder with a huge smile on his face. Romy saw this as well, realizing the captain was enjoying the challenge.

Ryder leaned towards Romy and whispered, "At least four of the Haven ships will move towards the vicinity of our energy burst from the engines. Because it was so short, they won't know a direction, but they'll know we're somewhere in this vicinity."

"That doesn't sound good," Romy muttered.

"No, not at all. They'll likely fire out a scatter of space charges—what some might call a plethora," Ryder added.

Romy was usually cool and collected, but he could see his father was much more in control than he was. A space charge was a large explosive device sent out into space, set with a timer. If a broad pattern was required, 15 or 20 could be fired out simultaneously, set for different times to cover a large area of space. Fortunately, in space, unless the explosion is a direct hit, it is not dangerous. Without a medium such as an atmosphere to carry the shock wave, even a short distance away from the blast centre is safe. Additionally, since sound does not carry in the vacuum of space, there was absolutely no way of knowing what was happening outside the Metro ship.

A clock countdown had begun when the cloaking device had been turned back on. It was now at five minutes. Romy thought it odd the captain was so fixated on exact timing in this situation. Two more minutes went by when Captain Brand bellowed out a new set of coordinates.

"Rolston, once again, full scan and have a peek at the Junkyard as well," the captain ordered.

Romy's eyebrows lowered as he thought, *the Junkyard. What on Haven does he want with that?* The Junkyard was a zone of over 400 derelict Korian and

Sholite ships left over from the armada that originally came to Haven 24 years ago.

"Prepare for another five second burst at 20 per cent, Mr. Jorge," the captain calmly stated.

At eight minutes and thirty seconds, Captain Brand said, "Steady, Mister Jorge—on my mark."

At exactly nine minutes, Captain Brand yelled, "Mark!"

Once again, Romy saw the screens come to life. This time the ship's occupants were pushed to the right as the *Shade* made a hard starboard turn. The most immediate concern on the forward-looking screen was a large amount of space debris. Further in the distance, two Haven destroyers could be seen in a crossing pattern.

Ryder whispered as he saw the debris was from space charges, "They weren't that far off."

After five seconds, the screen shut off and the increased acceleration stopped. They were now coasting in the general direction of the two destroyers. With any luck they would not hit any space charges, and they would manage to travel undetected between the two Haven naval vessels.

"This is crazy," Romy whispered.

Captain Brand turned, winking at Romy this time. "Rolston, play the recording of the Junkyard."

One screen lit up, showing the vast fleet of bent and damaged metal ships. After two seconds, quite incredulously, one of the ships lifted up and out of the centre of the Junkyard, just before an explosion was set off below it. The day prior to the rescue of Romy, the crew of the *Shade* had set up the explosives and the diversion in the Junkyard.

Rolston said, "Just before we recloaked, one of the destroyers broke off and headed for the ship we just sent off as a diversion."

Clapping his hands together, Captain Brand exclaimed, "Well, that means we only have one destroyer to worry about!"

Except for Captain Brand, who seemed to be enjoying the adventure, the rest of the crew were tense for the next hour. For the next hour after that, it slowly eased. Since they were accelerating the entire duration, Brand was sure they were well out of the range of the Haven military. They had slipped away.

The captain ordered the cloaking system shut down, and after a quick scan of the sector showing no contacts, he ordered, "Ladies and Gentleman, set trajectory for Midpoint, 35 per cent SOL."

"Midpoint?" Romy whispered towards his father.

Ryder rose to his feet and stretched his arms above his head. "Let's go for a walk, Son." He gazed towards the captain. "Captain Brand, request permission to use your nav room."

"No problem, Admiral. If you can, join me for dinner in my quarters in— let's say—three hours," Brand offered.

"Of course, Captain," Ryder replied before he led Romy off the command deck.

Once in the hallway, Ryder opened the first door on his right, leading his son in. There were four chairs on swivels in the centre of the room. Ryder sat in one, offering another to Romy.

Ryder said, "Lights off," and then, "Map, origin, 0,0,0."

The lights did indeed turn off, and a holographic image of the planet, Haven, floated in front of them. They both sat transfixed by the image for a long moment, each man thinking of the memories gained on it. They both also wondered if they would ever set foot on the planet again.

Ryder mumbled, "It looks the same as the day, 24 years ago, when, on the bridge of the *Pathfinder,* I first saw the planet."

Romy felt his father's memories were deeper than his own, so he did not interrupt.

"If you recall," Ryder began, "Haven was actually first found by a Sholite explorer ship. It orbited in the habitable zone of what we called the star, Alpha Centauri B. It's an orange star, so middle aged as far as stars go." Ryder had donned a pair of gloves while he spoke. Now, holding the index finger on each hand back against each respective palm, each glove was energized. He stretched out his hands, then quickly brought them in twice. In response, the holographic image zoomed out, now showing Alpha Centauri A and Alpha Centauri B. They were slowly rotating around a central point between them. "Alpha Centauri A is a younger, yellow star, and in years past, myself and other explorer ships visited and analyzed the three planets rotating around it. None of them were in the habitable zone, so they were of no interest as far as supporting life. However, there were many mineral deposits found. In fact, one of the planets was loaded with vast amounts of gold."

"I am surprised we still call the system Alpha Centauri," Romy interjected.

Ryder smiled at a fleeting memory from his distant past. "We knew nothing of this star system until we passed Earth. Through their long-range telescopes, they did, and they'd called the system Alpha Centauri. Your great grandmother, Natalie Gunn, continued to call the system by this name as we travelled towards it." Ryder turned his smile towards his son. "I guess the name just stuck. It's part of her legacy."

Spreading his hands once again and drawing them in emphatically, four times, the holographic view zoomed out extensively. Now, in a greater view of the system, a third star, far out from Alpha Centauri A and B, could be seen. Ryder pressed his hand forward, then slowly drew it back. The third star became larger and larger as he did so, until it filled the space in front of them.

"This is Proxima," Ryder said. "It's a smaller, red star, much older than the other two. The *Pathfinder* had been to this system several times prior to my permanent departure from Haven. In fact, a month prior to that date, we performed a detailed review of a planet orbiting Proxima."

Lifting his hand and slowly pushing it forward, the view backed out, Proxima became smaller, and three planets appeared orbiting the star. Ryder pointed to one of the planets, the one closest to the sun and explained, "This is the planet of interest."

Shrugging, Romy blurted, "How can that be of interest. It is so close to the sun."

Ryder nodded in understanding. "That was our first thought as well, but the luminosity of a red sun is much less than the yellow or orange suns of central Alpha Centauri. In fact, the luminosity of Proxima is one twentieth that of Alpha Centauri B, and that puts this planet, even as close as it is to Proxima, right in the middle of the sun's habitable zone."

"So, that's where you've been all these years."

"Yes. We named the planet Metro. That name should bring back a memory."

"Indeed, it does, Dad, but I can't put my finger on it."

"Think back to your ancient history lessons," Ryder recounted. "Many thousands of years ago, when the inhabitants of Kor and Shol were in the middle of their ongoing war, a younger group—what many called a cult, created a settlement on a moon of a third, nearby planet. The group was about three thousand people, a combination of Korians and Sholites."

"Now, I do recall. The settlers wanted to show the politicians and generals the two races could coexist. Unfortunately, instead, they viewed the cohabitation as blasphemy. The entire moon, called Metro by the inhabitants, was destroyed by a joint task force."

Ryder let out a sarcastic laugh. "Odd, I think that was the only time the two warring forces pulled together in a joint endeavour. How ironic." His voice trailed off for a moment before he turned his gaze to his son. "We called our planet Metro after them, a second attempt to show Korians and Sholites can coexist—and we have."

"So, your home is on Metro?"

Ryder opened his gloved hands wide, then slapped them together. The holographic view backed out to a view of the entire Alpha Centauri system. Then, he waved his hand across it as he said, "That is my home. It's wherever a ship will take me, to new surprises and adventure."

Romy had turned his gaze to his father's light-blue eyes. Earlier, in his cabin, Romy thought they were sad and tired. Now, as he talked about space exploration, they came to life, the colour seemingly transformed to a steely-blue. It reminded him his father, who many thought a born leader, never wanted any part of it. Circumstances, at the time, thrust him into leadership, but the first chance he could, he left it behind. He left it to explore space, the vocation he truly loved.

"Are we going to Metro?" Romy asked as he put his hand on his father's shoulder.

"Not yet." Ryder dragged his hands inwards and centered the view on a point between Haven and Metro. There was a small, metallic object there. "We're going there. It looks small, but it's actually a massive space station, maintaining a position halfway between Metro and Haven. It's appropriately named, Midpoint. A little over 20 thousand Metronians live there.

Romy was about to blurt out a response, but he paused. It was obvious he would not be able to return to Haven. He was an outlaw, just as his father was. He would have to start a new life, and if he had a choice, he would rather do so on a planet as opposed to a piece of space metal.

"I would prefer to go to Metro."

"No, you wouldn't."

"Why?"

"Because Efi will be waiting for you at Midpoint."

Chapter 3: Midpoint

The 13th day of the 4th month, Alpha Centauri year 0024.

Somewhere between Haven and Midpoint station.

It was surprising to Romy Gunn how, in a short span of twelve hours, his life had so completely changed. That was putting it lightly. Twelve hours ago, he was on his way to a high-security penal station orbiting Haven. He had been despondent and convinced he would spend the rest of his life there. His sarcastic frame of mind, at that time, looked at the positive aspects of the dilemma. He was the son of the outlaw Ryder Gunn, and to some criminals, they might find a bond there. But more—likely many more—would see him as a criminal in disguise, a political criminal with no right to be incarcerated within the dishonourable brotherhood of real criminals. It was probable they would kill him, something Romy thought would have been merciful.

Romy was looking out the round porthole within the cabin assigned to him. It was smaller than his father's, but large enough for a single military bed, a small writing desk and a double locker. As he looked out at the blackness of space, it did not surprise him to see the short, curved lines of light from distant stars. If the *Shade* was motionless or even travelling at a lower sub-light speed, the lines would have been bright dots. However, since the *Shade* was travelling at 35 per cent SOL, it was fast enough for the light to appear curved.

As his gaze took in the sight, he realized this is the furthest he had been from Haven since he was a young boy travelling within the flotilla of ships after the destruction of Talus 3. Earlier in the evening, when he and his father had dinner with Captain Brand, he asked the question of their position. After a quick call to the command deck, he told Romy they were still 600 billion kilometres from Midpoint, a distance they would cover in a little over two days.

When his father had told Romy he knew Efi Kuma, it came as a shock. Once the information settled in, Romy had many more questions. It seemed his father knew all about Efi, the Mabuza tribe and their pureblood clan, the Bantu. He knew they were more advanced than the Korians, Sholites or the Metronians.

Upon further questioning, Romy discovered his father knew about the seven races of pureblood humans and their psychic powers. What Ryder Gunn did not know was that the Mabuza leaders were also see'ers of the future, and they had long ago prophesized Romy Gunn to be one of the most important people in this era and a powerful pureblood in his own right.

Romy's daydream was interrupted by a knock at his door. He opened it to see his father looking more refreshed than he did the day prior.

"Did you get some sleep, Son," Ryder asked.

Ryder stepped aside to allow his father to enter. "Only a little. There's a lot on my mind these days."

"Like that Mabuza woman, Efi. I hear she is beautiful, and smart."

Ryder rolled his eyes. "Yes, she certainly is. But there is…"

"Do you love her?" Ryder interrupted.

Romy was sure the flush colouring his face told his father the answer. Romy knew he loved Efi deeply, just as he knew Efi loved him. But Efi chose to keep her distance, so her affection would not influence his training and position as a *drifter*-what the Mabuza people referred to in their language as the *msafiri*—or time traveller. Outside of the five see'ers and a few other high ranking Mabuza officials, no one else knew this, not even his father.

Frowning, Romy waved a hand over his head. "No…no. I don't want to talk about Efi. I want to finish the unfinished business between you and I."

"Which is?"

Romy sighed. "The whole business about why you never came back for me. I love you, and will always love you, but I need to understand."

There was a twitch at the edge of Ryder's eye. "Okay, son. I'll try again to explain. But let's at least walk the ship. There are other things you can learn as we talk." He put his hand on his son's back, coaxing him out the door. Ryder's voice faded as he tried to explain his departure while interrupting often, pointing down a corridor or into a door opening, to better explain the configuration of the warship.

It was Romy's conscious thoughts that bothered him, but it was his subconscious that held the answer he needed. Romy didn't need to understand, he didn't need circumstances explained again. He needed something his father had not yet offered. He wanted an apology. He just hadn't realized it yet.

Forty-five minutes later, Romy had all but given up on his needs as his father smothered the conversation with his description of the ship, often interrupted with a tale of his space exploits. Each time this happened, he saw how his father's face would brighten. It was difficult for his father to disguise where his passion was. As such, Romy was beginning to get an inclination of the answer to his sensitive questions even before his father answered them—which he still did not in any case.

With one hand on the door handle, Ryder passed the interlink imbedded into his other wrist in front of the sensor beside the door. There was an audible *click*, and Ryder pulled the door open. Once inside the propulsion centre, Ryder continued to teach, describing almost every console and switch.

When they moved to the centre of the room, Ryder pointed to a six-metre-high glass dome. "This is the heart of this ship—the engine, so to speak."

In the middle of the glass dome was a series of three stainless steel boxes, and on top of the middle one was a smaller glass dome. This one was narrower and tall. There were tubes, hoses and wires connected at many locations, the bigger ones passing through the floor board, while smaller ones connected to a series of four control panels beside the larger dome.

"We discovered *bluranium*," Ryder said as he pointed again, this time to the bottom of the central dome where two cubes of blue metal were suspended. Two narrow laser beams, one bombarding each cube, scattered upon impact.

"Bluranium?"

Ryder nodded. "Yes, in our explorations we found a new element within a few asteroids we corralled. The easiest way to explain this element is it's similar to uranium, just with less volatility. Yet surprisingly, it has a much higher energy value. As such, the radiation levels are significantly lower."

"But a couple of asteroids wouldn't provide enough supply?"

"Correct, but it gave us the incentive to search harder." Ryder turned from the bluranium reactor towards his son. "Remember, yesterday, when I showed you the Proxima system. There were three planets orbiting the red star."

Romy, still transfixed by the bluranium cubes, just nodded.

"Well, the third planet out, what we thought was a cold piece of useless rock and iron ore, actually has huge deposits of this new element."

"The ruling council of the Korians and Sholites must be envious," Romy estimated.

As Ryder led Romy out of the propulsion center, Ryder replied. "Only the higher levels of Haven society, the ruling councils, and the military know about us, and even a smaller circle know how advanced and formidable we've become."

"Do they know about the bluranium?"

"Just as we have spies, they have spies, so, yes, they know," Ryder said with a shrug. "There's a rumour we're still verifying that the Haven government is revealing this information to the general public. We suspect this decision was caused by your sudden abduction. I mean, what would they tell their people? Revealing the fact Metro is out there will divert the people's thoughts from the embarrassingly easy manner in which we were able to retrieve you," Ryder added in a matter-of-fact tone.

"They will want some of that bluranium," Romy suspected.

"Surely, since they found a small quantity themselves, but that's only wet their appetite. The second rumour, knowing we've found a vast amount, is they're sending a negotiating committee to discuss trade, peace borders, etcetera."

There was a pause. It seemed Ryder knew what would come next and conveniently looked at his wrist interlink. He slapped Romy on the shoulder and smiled. "I'm late for a meeting. Keep out of trouble as best you can."

Romy was left behind with his jaw open.

This was the pattern for the next two days. Ryder Gunn appeared a busy man, spending some time with his son, trying to eat most meals with him, but whenever Romy tried to once again broach the topic of Ryder's absence from his life, there always seemed to be a meeting or a conveniently timed call to the command deck.

Two days later, Romy was in his cabin, reading from a tablet. Having the time, he decided to read as much as was available about the history of Metro. A beep from the intercom interrupted his thoughts.

"Romy Gunn, please come to the command deck."

He was surprised. There were several times now whereby Romy had attended the command deck, but always as a guest of his father. This was the first time his presence was requested directly. He pressed his feet into his boots and hurried up one level to the command center.

Captain Brand gave him a tight smile when he entered. "Hello, Romy. We have already decelerated to 10 per cent SOL on our approach to

Midpoint. We are about to go sub-light, so strap yourself in beside the admiral."

Romy followed the command and sat beside his father. The command deck was busy with activity, commands and responses going back and forth as sub-light was achieved.

"Ensign Fortay," Captain Brand requested, "Put Midpoint on screen two. Magnify to give us a good image."

Romy leaned forward in anticipation. The image came into view, and it was difficult to make out clear details. It just looked like a long cylinder on one side, with an even larger rectangle of steel hanging off the opposite side. He couldn't determine the size without some frame of reference. His jaw dropped when he finally found one.

He nudged his father with his elbow and whispered. "Is that what it looks like?"

Ryder chuckled quietly. "That cylinder on the left is the former Sholite space station, *Ryfoss*. It's been significantly modified and lengthened over the past 12 years. In fact, its length is double what it originally was."

Romy pointed. "And the huge rectangle?"

"More of our modifications. In all, Midpoint is five times the size of what *Ryfoss* was. That's not including the five substations just outside this field of view. One of those substations is purely military, while the other is for the Explorer's Corp."

Romy's eyes opened wide with another realization. "The station is not rotating! There is no simulated gravity!"

Captain Brand, without turning, snapped. "Quiet on the deck."

Leaning into his father, Romy continued in a subdued voice, "The Sholite stations would rotate, and through that, the centripetal, outward force would simulate gravity."

Ryder whispered back. "The lack of rotation is thanks to the Mabuza. They share their advanced technology, except where it could be directly incorporated into military weapons. In this case, they introduced us to another liquid material, when mixed with a second carrying material, be it cement or an iron-based metal, will simulate a much higher density. If enough is used in our flooring material, it'll simulate low level gravity."

Romy's eyebrows were lowered in a confused gaze.

"Think of it this way." Ryder simplified the explanation. "Historically, we used magnetic boots, and we made this process extremely efficient. This new concept uses an increased gravitational force rather than an electromagnetic force. It's just the next level up."

As the *Shade* rounded the massive space station, Romy did a double take of the screen. The back of the station was like a massive, three-dimensional spiderweb, except there were long ends hanging off the sides. At various locations, space ships of every size were docked at interspaced points, making them look much like insects caught in the web.

Romy caught the last message over the intercom.

"*Shade*, you are clear to dock at port 45."

"Understood, Midpoint tower," came the reply.

"Keep an eye on your port side. There will be a hydrogen trawler going out. They've been delayed for a while."

Captain Brand thought, *yup, we better. Trawler captains were known to take too many risks at the best of times.* "Keep us well clear, Ensign Fortay."

Thirty minutes later, after a slight bump with the boarding hatch, Ryder and Romy Gunn thanked the captain for the ride. They departed the vessel and strode down the long cylindrical walkway, opening into a much larger corridor, easily nine metres high and 20 metres across.

Romy was glancing upwards and around in awe, when he heard his name.

"Romy!"

The second shout brought his gaze down. Ten metres away stood Valre and Efi. He smiled at Valre, but his attention quickly came to Efi. She looked different out of the wilderness attire Romy had become accustomed to when they were together in the Wildes. Now, in a purple pant suit with a white blouse and a matching purple jacket, she looked like a banker or a barrister. When he lifted his gaze, however, this was the Efi he knew. Her eyes were bright, a contrast to her light-brown skin. Her hair had grown out a bit but was still comprised of many tightly curled, brown spirals of hair, the end of each being tipped with a streak of golden colour. Her lips were full, and when she smiled at Romy, he began to stride towards her.

Halfway there, she ran the last two steps and wrapped her arms around him. He reciprocated the warm embrace, kissing the side of her head.

She mumbled under her breath, "You idiot," before she slid her face towards him, giving him a passionate kiss on his lips.

Romy had missed her. They were in love, but could not allow it to overcome them and the other efforts still needed. There had been several such kisses, and just like those, Efi eventually pulled away. Her eyes were moist.

"Thank goodness, you're here," she said through a widening smile.

He chuckled. "You're a Bantu, so clairvoyant. You knew I would be here."

"True enough," Efi replied. She took a step back, half bowed with a wave of her hand in front of her. "After all, you don't think I *just* bought this outfit, do you?"

Romy's response was cut off.

"Hey, we're here in the room," Valre said as she waved from a position beside Ryder.

Blushing, Romy strode over to Valre and gave her a massive hug. "It seems like forever since I gave you one of those," he said after he released her.

Valre, who had been Romy's butler as he grew up, was one of the most important people in his life, along with his father and his stepmother, I'lish Mann. *Butler* wasn't a fair term as Valre had been pivotal in Romy's upbringing while taking care of his affairs. In this sense, she was more of a combination, loving aunt, lawyer and accountant.

There were many other travellers in the massive corridor: some military, some workers and some just travelling the system. The people and the station left Romy in awe of how far the Metronians had come in what really was just a few short years. When his father first told him of Metro, then Midpoint station, he thought it would still be a life of hardship, but he realized now it would likely be anything but.

By the time he was advised of his accommodations, Romy was exhausted, but more than that, he was hungry. Before Ryder went to his own quarters on the opposite side of the station, they agreed to continue to the Black Star restaurant, centrally located along the curved section of the old *Ryfoss* station.

The food was rich and plentiful, as was the drink. Since all four of them were there, Romy could not further discuss the most pressing issue in his mind, and that was the still unanswered question of his abandonment on Haven when he was 12 years old. However, he realized during the last two days, and especially since they arrived at Midpoint, his need, what initially seemed insatiable, had reduced, and he would wait for the right moment to ask that question again.

Instead, Ryder and Valre were curious about their adventures on Haven, Romy and Efi's trek through the Wildes to their time in Hagaza, the Mabuza capital, as well as their brief time in Bellantor where Romy was finally captured. All this was explained with Ryder often interrupting with questions, hungry for more details. As Romy answered, he thought, *my father, forever the explorer.*

After dinner, Ryder, even more exhausted than Romy, was the first to insist it was time for all of them to retire for the night. Romy was quick to second the motion, his own eyes feeling heavy, but he was anxious to be alone with Efi. The kiss between them at the arrival dock was passionate, but too quick for his liking. He wanted more.

Outside the restaurant, Ryder gave Romy and each of the women a hug before looking to his left. The corridor curved underfoot as it followed the shape of the station. "We'll catch up tomorrow," he said, before making his way up the corridor. Then, he was gone.

Romy, Efi and Valre walked in the opposite direction, towards the central core of the station to a main, traffic corridor. There, they caught a train towards the rear of the station where their quarters were located.

By now, Romy had seen the Metronians, formerly Korians and Sholites who were still easy to distinguish by their dress, and some Mabuza, lived intermixed in this society. In the area where their quarters were, there were a higher percentage of dark-skinned Mabuza, and Romy thought that might not be by accident. The see'ers considered him one of the most important purebloods, one who they had plans for, and one they would protect. It was likely some of the Mabuza, casually about in the common areas, were actually covert security personnel.

Valre said her goodbyes before turning down a side corridor to her room. Efi and Romy's rooms were side by side. Efi arrived at hers first and invited Romy in.

"Are you sure?" Romy questioned with a raised eyebrow. "It's late."

"It's also been a while since we've seen each other." She pressed open the door and stood to the side, the opening a clear answer to his question. He entered and looked about the room while he heard the door close behind him. When he turned, her hands were already moving, stretching around his neck, her face turned sideways. He leaned down and kissed her. It was more passionate than before—much more passionate. It lasted for a long time, their lips sliding, their breaths mingling.

Eventually, Efi pulled away as she kicked off her shoes. Romy took the hint and did the same. She took his hand, leading him to the soft, cushioned couch in the center of her room. She plopped herself down, pulling him with her. Her eyes, golden in colour, smiled at him. She truly looked happy and relieved to see him.

Their fingers were still intertwined while the fingers of Romy's other hand played at her shoulder. "What are we doing here, Efi?"

Her fingers tightened on his, giving him instant reassurance even before her words came out. "I don't know, exactly. Perhaps we're just taking it one day at a time. And on this day, I think we both need to be close."

"Maybe we should be close all the time." Romy leaned in. "You know how I feel about you. I…"

Efi's finger flashed up, pressing against his lips, staying the words—the exact words she knew would have followed. "I know exactly how you feel, and yes, I feel the same. However, there is more to this than just you and I. We can be together, but we need to go slowly. We cannot let our love consume us. It would be too distracting."

Romy felt his heart skip a beat when she used the word, *love*. He would have liked to press his own love more, but her words were enough for now. It was especially so when she leaned forward, placing a hand behind his neck, drawing him into another kiss. The kiss spread to her ear and neck as both of their hands wandered, exploring, but when it seemed too much, Efi placed a hand on his chest, pushing him back.

Her face was flushed, her breaths heavy as she managed, "We have an early morning. Tomorrow, we begin your testing. You will need your rest."

An involuntary noise came from Romy's lips. It originated deep within his core, somewhere between a grumble and a growl.

Efi blinked while tilting her head sideways. Through a smirk she said, "Oh, really."

Romy grinned. "As you wish, I will not push my advances because, if I did, you would find a new found meaning for words like passion—" Romy's voice lowered, barely above a whisper "—and even lust. Such would be your utter and complete surrender to 'what if.'"

With his last words, Romy's lips had come very close to hers. Suddenly, he jumped to his feet, smiling wide. "Goodnight!"

As he headed to the door, Efi heard him chuckling. She shot to a sitting position, her face still flushed, her hair disheveled, buttons on her clothes still undone revealing her smooth skin. She threw a pillow after him as he left the room, his chuckle by now growing to all out laughter.

Chapter 4: The Test

The 18th day of the 4th month, Alpha Centauri year 0024.

Midpoint station.

Romy sat on a plastic-covered, soft cushion in a narrow booth situated in the corner of a dining room. The booth was one of four booths strung across the back wall of the restaurant. To some, the beige floor tiles and contrasting blue plastic seat covers would be aesthetically appealing, but to Romy things did not match; the entire restaurant just did not seem right.

The three booths next to his were filled with people, mainly older seniors with only a few younger folk mixed in. Quiet conversation buzzed through the room until it was interrupted by the entry of two men and a young woman. One man and the attractive woman had lighter skin, while the second man had tinted skin, not unlike the light-brown coloured citizens within the Mabuza population. In all, the three of them looked quite ordinary until the woman turned her head, revealing her short, red hair highlighted by a pink streak angled across her front bangs.

An ache passed through Romy's head, and his vision blurred for a few seconds. Then, his vision came back into focus. The newcomers caused a commotion. Several people rose to meet them, and, based on the hugs between the redhead woman and one older man in particular, what Romy was witnessing was a warm reunion.

Another ache, and his vision blurred again. When his senses cleared, the people in the room were flat down on the floor, hands covering their ears. Through a wide, plate-glass window at the front of the restaurant, Romy could see a large vehicle. From behind it, two men with weapons were firing into the restaurant and towards a second pair of men out in front of the building.

Romy saw an old woman, who was prone on the floor, rise up and draw a concealed weapon from her purse. She was bringing it to a firing position when Romy, instinctively, shot up and ran over to her. He lunged forward in what he thought would be just in time. His hand came down on her arm, his eyes opening wide as his fingers passed right through her forearm. The old woman did not react at all. It was as if he was not really there.

The gun fired, and a middle-aged man was shot before collapsing to the ground. The redhead woman, in turn, shot the older woman, then knelt beside the shot man. Beside her, also kneeling, was the young man who entered the restaurant with her.

Romy, his voice shaking, said, "How can I help?"

There was no response. He seemed invisible to them. He leaned closer to the man and shouted, "What's happening!"

Still, no response.

As Romy shifted his gaze towards the redhead, her face tilted up, her smoldering gaze boring into him. She growled, "You don't belong here." At the same moment, her fingers flashed up, clenching on Romy's throat.

Romy took in a deep, gasping breath as he shot to a sitting position in his bed. The breath turned into a sequence of sputters and gasps as he brought his hand up to his throat. After a second massive gasp, he realized he was in his bedroom. With no portholes, he was in complete darkness.

It was another dream, one of those dreams he had more often than he liked. Of course, he had dreams as normal people do, where a few seconds after waking you forget all about them. However, there were other dreams, like the one he just had, where it was more than vivid. It was as if it really happened. Even now, he could still feel the woman's fingers clamped on his throat.

He cleared his throat before muttering a curse under his breath. He followed this with, "Lights—30 per cent."

The lighting in the room came on to the desired level. The bedroom was four metres by four metres. It was attached to a larger common area: one section filled with wide, thick cushioned seating, another with a small dining table and, finally, a small pantry style kitchen, one well suited for making snacks but totally unacceptable for cooking full meals.

Throwing his feet off the side of the bed, they hit the carpeted floor. He rose and strode into the attached bathroom, completing all his morning affairs, finishing with a hot shower. Efi had given him a hint of what would come this day, so he scanned through the closet for clothing that would suit a day of activity. He pulled out dark-brown, loose-fitting cotton pants, a jacket made of the same material, just light-brown in colour. That was pulled over a white, short-sleeved shirt.

As he entered his common living area, it was to hear a knock at his main door. He opened it to find Efi, a wide smile on her face. Her outfit indicated she also appeared ready for a day of activity.

"Hi, Handsome," she offered. "You look ready to go." She raised her wrist, glancing at the time on the interlink. "That's good because your father and Valre will be waiting."

He recalled the four of them had made arrangements to meet for breakfast at what had been described to him as a small, quaint café. It took the two of them only five minutes to walk to it, where they saw Ryder and Valre waiting. Romy again noticed there was a high population of Mabuza in this section of Midpoint station, and he saw when food was brought for them, it was Mabuza fare, something he had come to enjoy during his previous time spent with Efi.

With everyone refreshed, their discussion during breakfast was livelier than the night before. Romy was enjoying the time spent with his father and the two women, but at the front of his mind, he still needed to spend more time alone with his father.

Turning to Efi, Romy asked, "How long will we be busy today?"

Efi had just taken a large bite of a wonderfully crusted biscuit. She held her finger up as her chewing quickened, Finally, after clearing her throat, she replied, "We will be gone all day, but back for dinner at the 18th hour." She obviously thought that was sufficient as, after her last word, her teeth chomped down on another bite from the warm biscuit.

"Great," Romy replied. He shifted his gaze to the two women. "My apologies, but I would like to have dinner tonight with just my father and I. We have 18 years of catching up to do." He smiled affectionately at the two, trying to enhance the sincerity of his apologetic words.

He turned to his father. "You okay with that, Dad?"

Ryder shrugged and smiled at the same time. "Sure, Son. Sounds like a plan."

They finished their breakfast with Romy and Efi leaving the restaurant in the opposite direction travelled by Ryder and Valre. Moments later, they were in the main corridor waiting for a downstream train. In this environment, devoid of compass directions, downstream was towards the docking stations, considered the back of Midpoint.

The train whooshed into the station. They boarded and sat. By now, Romy suspected where they were going. "Are we going off station?" he asked.

She patted his thigh, stating, "If I answer that now, then you'll have many more questions. If I answer those, you will have even more after that. Just wait a few minutes, and one picture will be worth all those words."

Although he did appreciate the touch of her fingers, he could do no better than a grunt in response. There were always unanswered questions, and he could not help his mind going to a place of insecurity. The Mabuza see'ers had a plan for him. They told him he would play an important role in the Athar. In fact, *critical* was the word they used. At first, it boosted his ego, but eventually, there was a sense he was not in control of his own destiny. He was a pawn in a big game. At least, that was the thought difficult to set aside.

When they departed the train, it was only a short walk down two corridors to a waiting space shuttle. He took a moment aside to look out a large porthole, examining the vessel. It was indeed a small, bright-silver shuttle, unlike anything he had seen before. It was not extraordinary in any way, just—then he came up with the right word—*Alien*. That is what his eyes told him.

The small shuttle had three prongs on the front. The two side prongs had glass, bubbled fronts, allowing the passengers to see out in a forward direction. The longer, middle prong housed the pilot. They were seated and belted into the port pod where they could see out the glass dome. There was a slight jostle as the docking clamps let loose. The ship lurched forward, then made a wide, sweeping turn.

Once the shuttle's path straightened, Efi pointed ahead. "That is where we're going."

In front of them, still far in the distance, was a massive, silver shape. As they came closer, Romy estimated the vessel was 300 metres long while the cylindrical shape was 70 metres in diameter.

"That is the *Aramis*, a Mabuza starship. Actually, it's the flagship of our small fleet," Efi explained.

Romy's jaw was slack, the shock quite apparent on his drawn face. The starship was sleek in its design. Some would say it was aerodynamic, except with no atmosphere, *aero* was not relevant. Still, the nose was nicely curved to a point as were the leading edges of the twin outriggers, jutting out from the fuselage. Romy knew the curves could easily deflect space dust, and even smaller asteroids. The lack of sharp corners and the presence of continuous curved surfaces, would make the ship exceptionally strong in the case of impact from a larger asteroid, or even a missile in the case of war.

The shuttle was now underneath the massive vessel, elevating into an open dock. Once they were in proximity, docking clamps clutched onto the shuttle, shifting it towards the docking gate. The whole process was smooth, right to the minor bump when they made contact with the air-tight gate.

As they deboarded, Romy questioned, "How many of these do you have?"

"There are two more, a bit smaller than the *Aramis*. Then, we have smaller vessels, making our navy not much different from that of Haven or Metro." One eye narrowed as she glanced at Romy. It was a coy look. "We have less vessels, but as you will see by this one, ours are more advanced, in both technology and armament."

They had been walking down a long corridor for some time when Romy noticed two security personnel, a man and a woman, had fallen in a few paces behind them. Romy pointed over his shoulder and was about to ask when he was interrupted.

"It's protocol when a foreigner is aboard." Efi commented.

Chuckling, Romy chimed, "But I am—*the drifter*—one of the most important purebloods of all time." Romy lifted his chin while sweeping his hand forward, panning it slowly in an arc in front of him.

Both of Efi's eyes narrowed. "Yes, and at least right now, a clumsy Korian, one too curious for his own good who might lose a hand or even worse, if put in the wrong place."

"Really…"

Shrugging, Efi clarified, "Hey, they're following you, not me."

That doused the conversation into silence as Efi led him down several corridors until they arrived at a massive, locked door. Efi placed her wrist against the sensor, and the door unlocked, the light above it flashing green.

As they passed through, Efi nodded to the guards who took up a soldierly stance against the wall opposite the door. Once the door was closed, Efi said to Romy, "The only people to pass this door are you and I. This, in fact, will be our home during your training period."

"But I have dinner with my father this evening."

"That won't be a problem. Today is only testing. Tomorrow, we begin your training. Once started, neither you or I will be permitted out until I deem it safe."

Romy turned and saw they were in a wide hallway. It was white and sterile, making it hard to distinguish where the floor ended and the walls began. It was about 40 metres long. On the left were two doors, and on the right, only one.

Efi led him through the first doorway on the left, revealing an austere room: a narrow bed, a clothes locker, desk and a bookcase filled with books.

"Wow!" Romy exclaimed. "Who reads books anymore?"

As Efi led him in through the second door, she agreed, "True enough. But from tomorrow, your time here must be focused and uninterrupted by the outside world; no video screens, no communication devices. Nothing except the books to relax your mind from time to time."

As they walked through the door on the other side of the hallway, leading into a massive, white room, Romy added, "I still have my wrist interlink." He lifted his wrist to remind her.

In a hushed voice, Efi explained, "This room is like an elaborate faraday cage. No communications or energy of any type can get through the walls. She knocked on the white surface beside the door. These are a metre of thick concrete, heavily reinforced with metal. A steel-tungsten mix to be specific."

As Romy inspected the room, he asked, "Why?"

Efi turned, facing Romy. "This room was made for you. It has been waiting for some time. Once your training starts, we will touch internal energy you do not know you have. Like riding a wild beast, there could be unexpected and powerful results. This reinforced bunker will contain you."

"We know I have the power to teleport, and, even in a crude mode, the ability to time travel. Aren't you afraid I could accidentally be lost?"

"No. Our engineers are excellent. The walls are spiked with compounds that restricts transposition or teleportation of purebloods," Efi elaborated.

"Seems you have thought of everything," Romy mumbled as he walked past her. He examined the room, again all white and mostly empty. The roof and walls were curved, again, much like a long cylinder with a flat floor. There was a table and chairs at the far end. Around them were several eight-foot-high cabinets. There was a preponderance of cables going in many directions, from cabinet to cabinet, some through the floor and a couple to an extra chair off to the side of the seating configuration.

"When do we begin?" Romy asked.

"In 30 minutes." She grasped his wrist, removing the battery from the interlink. She tilted her chin upwards. "There are clocks in all the rooms."

Romy walked back to his room, inspecting the contents of the clothes locker. There were at least 30 sets of coveralls, again following the all-white theme. He was thirsty, so after a large drink of water, he lay down on the bed until the clock indicated it was time to start.

He quickly donned the white coveralls, and when he entered the long testing room, he found Efi similarly dressed.

Once they walked to the table, Efi snapped her fingers and pointed to a chair. "Sit there."

Through a grin, Romy mumbled, "So, that's the way it's going to be."

She sat across from him, giving him that wide smile that always lit up her face. "Yes and no. The bond we have will help you, but it must be clear, I am the teacher, and you are the student."

Romy paused, wrinkles appearing on his brow. He knew he had powers, but all this talk of psychic abilities and time travel was surreal. He wasn't sure about anything except he knew he could not return to Haven. He was at a Metronian enclave with very few options, so he calmly replied, "Understood."

From a drawer under the tabletop, she retrieved a tablet and put it between them. "We must first investigate your psychic powers before we delve into transposition, teleportation or time travel. But, even before that, let's refresh your memory about pureblood humans."

Intertwining his fingers on the table in front of him, Romy chirped. "Yes, let's do that first."

Rolling her eyes, then tilting her face down towards the table, she grumbled, "And so it begins."

Thirty minutes later, Efi had summarized the details of the seven pureblood races of humans. These were the races who had the capability to utilize the significant portions of the human mind that, to doctors and scientists, had remained unknown for many years. These areas the purebloods had control of, allowed them to transposition to an infinite number of planes of reality. It changed the perception whereby sight determines our reality, to one where our brain tells our eyes what it is seeing. Romy always had trouble with this concept of cosmic consciousness, so Efi gave an example.

There was a cart beside her, holding ten small rubber balls, each a different colour. She picked one up and asked, "What colour is this?"

"Red."

"And how do you know it is red?" Efi added.

He laughed. "Because it is red."

Efi held the ball up, waiting for a better answer.

"Okay, I will play along." He took a minute to think. "Long ago, when I was a child, my father would have taught me colours. He would have told me that colour was red," he said as he pointed to the coloured ball.

"Of course, but he would know that because that was what he was taught. That pattern would go back forever," Efi said. "But what if what you saw as red, your father really saw as blue. There is no way to know, and as long as this concept was consistent no one would ever know."

"So, that's because that's what my mind tells me."

"Exactly. The different planes of reality are an expansion of that concept where the mind controls what our senses see, feel and hear."

Romy took a deep breath. "I'm not sure I will ever be able to wrap my head around that idea."

"We have testing to do for each of the seven psychic powers. It won't take that long, but it will tell us, at the least, if you have potential. Some of the tests are quick and do not utilize aids, while for other tests, we need to measure your electrical impulses." Efi's chin lifted towards an electrode covered helmet hanging on a hook.

Romy turned his head towards the cabinet supporting the hook. "You expect me to wear that?"

It stung. The ball left Efi's fingers with a great velocity, hitting the side of Romy's chest. He yelled out, spinning his face towards the Mabuza woman. He was about to yell again, when he saw the second ball leaving her fingers, faster than the first. Flinching, Romy saw the green electrostatic field form around him. It was purely involuntary, and when the ball hit, it deflected off to the side. Romy did not feel a thing. The green shield only formed for an instant, but it was enough.

Efi calmly picked up the tablet and spoke as she typed into it. "The power of the shield, an ability rooted in the Celtae, pureblood race. Test one complete. Check!"

Romy rubbed his chest where the first ball hit. "*Check?* Did you say *check?*"

"From our time together in the Wildes, I already had a good idea you had this ability. I just needed to catch you off guard, so your subconscious mind would bring it forth."

"I hope the other tests aren't as painful," Romy grumbled.

In fact, they weren't. The next test was for the ability to move objects, an ability natural to the Ionian race. In this test, a glass was put in the middle of the table. The helmet was put on his head, and Efi turned on a switch mounted to the cabinet. The electrodes on the helmet lit, and for the next hour, Romy attempted to move the glass with the power of his mind. It didn't budge, nor did the needle on the gauge Efi was monitoring, move. There was no electrical stimulation observed.

The next test was for clairvoyance, or the ability to see into the future. For this, Efi once again utilized the balls. She pushed him the tablet and asked him to write down which ball she would pick up. He did so, and Efi picked up a ball. It was yellow. Romy turned the tablet and showed her what he had written. It read, *green*. The process was repeated for the next 30 minutes. Out of 150 selections, Romy correctly identified only 21.

"That's no better than random luck," Efi concluded. "You are one for three in abilities, so far."

The next test was for the power of illusion, a trait common to the Kush people. Efi asked him to concentrate on the red ball, and make it appear in the middle of the table. He focused. Sweat even broke out on his brow. Efi watched the gauge closely. The needle vibrated but did not move from its home position.

"Almost, Romy. It might come to you in time as your powers develop and become stronger."

Romy took off the helmet and pointed to his stomach. "I'm hungry."

Glancing at the clock high on the wall, Efi agreed. They left the main training room to the initial door to the training complex. Efi opened it, retrieving the two covered plates of food from the cart outside. She smiled at the same two guards who were sitting in chairs on the opposite side of the hallway. Returning to the main training room, they ate their fill of fruit, cheese and smoked meats.

"Three more tests to go," Romy said as he sat down in the now familiar chair.

"Only two," Efi corrected. Teleportation is the transference of oneself from one location to another in the same plane of reality. It is the ability of the Anasazi people. It's a power I suspect you have, but it is raw and likely uncontrollable." She giggled. "If you tried to move yourself, you might wind up bouncing off the walls. We'll revisit that test after you have other powers well under control."

"What's next, then?" Romy asked.

"I'm going to test you for energy bursts." She handed Romy the helmet. However, this time, she connected two pincer type electrodes joined to the end of long cables, one to the index finger of each hand. "The Toltec have the power to reformulate their bodies energy into balls of energy on their hands. They can then throw them as highly effective, deadly weapons."

"We will start now," Efi said. "Focus on your hands. Send your energy towards them."

Romy did not even begin to know what that meant, but he focused on his hands. In his mind, he envisioned his thought consciousness flowing from his mind, down his neck, then towards his hands. He was surprised when he felt the pins and needles in both hands. It tingled, almost painful. He looked up at the gauge. The needle on the gauge was bouncing wildly. He turned his gaze back to his hands. They looked orange.

"Stop!" Efi yelled. "Stop, now!"

Romy bolted upright in the chair, shaking his head. He pulled the electrodes off his fingers and shook his hands, trying to avail them of the stinging feeling that was now slowly receding.

"That's a very definite, yes," Efi concluded. She was impressed. The reaction was more powerful than she expected.

Efi asked Romy to remove the helmet as she took the seat across the table from him. "This is an easier test: no electrodes, no thrown balls, no pain. The Shang pureblood race had the power to read minds. We'll see how you do."

Romy straightened himself, interlacing his fingers on the table.

Typing into the tablet, Efi said, "I am thinking of a number between one and ten. Focus, and tell me what it is?"

He narrowed his eyes for five seconds, then said, "6.9."

Efi threw back her head. When she brought it forward, she chided, "No. A whole number. I want a whole number between one and ten!"

"If you wanted a whole number, you should have asked for a whole number."

Her face was flushed. Through clenched teeth, she growled. "Tell me the number I am thinking of."

He lifted a finger.

"What?"

"Is it the number you are thinking of now, or the number you were thinking of before you got angry?"

"Now, you idiot. Tell me the number."

"Seven," he blurted.

Efi slammed a small fist on the table. "You are right! I was freaking thinking of seven!"

"Awesome. I can read minds," Romy concluded in a patronizing tone.

Efi leaned forward. Her face was a darker brown. Her lips were full, but the tips were curled, like a predator's snarl. The words came slowly. "What am I thinking right freaking now?"

Grinning, Romy waved his hands in front of himself. "No, I am wrong. I cannot read your mind, for if I could, what I am sensing could not possibly come from such a sweet, beautiful woman."

She looked away, closing her eyes tight, hoping it would clear her mind for even a few seconds. When she finally returned his gaze, he winked at her, and she could not help but let out her laughter.

They repeated the same, *guess the whole number game,* for the next hour. Romy did poorly, only guessing the number correctly nine more times. Clearly, the first correct guess was just a fluke.

The day had moved quickly. Looking at the clock, Efi said, "It's 17:00 hours, and we are done for the day. We will have to hurry back to Midpoint station for you to make your dinner date with your father."

They quickly retraced their steps from the morning, boarded the shuttle, and then they were on their way back to the massive space station. Once they docked, Romy was about to head to the upstream train. Efi clutched his arm, turning him. She leaned up and their lips met. It was as passionate a kiss as they would allow with so many bystanders in the unloading station.

She slid her lips over to his ear and whispered, "After dinner, come find me."

Suddenly, dinner with his father did not seem so important. The thought came that an apology from his father tonight could wait.

Efi, who was clairvoyant, blushed before she slapped him on the chest. She pushed him away. "Best you go now." She turned and strode away to her own preplanned dinner with Valre.

Twenty minutes later, Romy sat down in the restaurant opposite from his father. This was a high-end establishment with a large bubbled-glass port hole along one wall. The table where they sat was right in the middle of the window, a good indication of the respect and influence Ryder Gunn had in this community.

They both ordered fish, something that might sound odd since they were billions of kilometres from a lake, sea or river. Romy said as much, to which Ryder pointed to a ship 30 kilometres removed from the station.

"That's an aquarium ship," Ryder explained. "Massive water tanks fill it—water and lots of fish."

As they ate, Ryder asked many questions about the day's testing. Romy told him all, thinking he would leave his own sensitive questions until dessert. That was the plan—until it fell apart.

An officer in the claret uniform of the Explorer Corp. marched to the table. "My apologies to both of you, but this is important." He handed Ryder a piece of paper, then turned and left.

Ryder unfolded the paper and read the message. His face snapped up, his eyes bright. "I have to go, right away." He stood to his feet.

"Go where?" Romy mumbled, his eyes wide in surprise.

"I have to leave the station immediately."

"What can possibly be so important?" Romy asked. "We haven't even had dessert!"

Looking down at his son, there was a moment of sadness, then Ryder pursed his lips into a tight line. "Son, I'm a space explorer. Another alien beacon has been found, and that means this is my time." Ryder's eyes lit up with life as the words continued. "This is when people expect me to lead. It's not optional." Without another word, he turned and left, his stride firm, his chin held high.

Chapter 5: The Third Beacon

The 22nd day of the 4th month, Alpha Centauri year 0024.

Deep Space.

"Admiral, 150 kilometres distance."

Ryder Gunn, although an admiral of the explorer fleet, was also captain of the *Wayfinder*, a second-generation explorer class vessel. It wasn't the 'latest and greatest' but it was significantly more advanced than the *Pathfinder*, a predecessor he captained when leaving Haven, 18 years ago.

From the elevated captain's chair, he ordered, "Ensign Sny, take us down to ten per cent sub-light." He rose and stood on the platform in front of his chair. "To all of you. No scans or sensors. I want only one camera on. Put the front screens in multi screen mode. I want to see the sphere in full when we get close enough."

The front screens, which had been showing the scans of the four quadrants around the *Wayfinder*, changed. Now, the screens were synchronized, showing the blackness of space, and in the distance was a small dot of light.

"The beacon," Ryder mumbled under his breath.

Ryder was being extremely careful. The first beacon had been discovered by Captain Snyder of the *Predator*, who had been an excellent, young officer. Through his training, he was known to make excellent decisions. The safety of his ship and the men under him would have been of paramount concern. Still, he was young, and young officers, especially men, are eager. Space is generally empty where, normally, you have to make an extreme effort to run into anything dangerous. Then again, sometimes danger has a way of finding you.

That's exactly what happened to Captain Snyder a little over two months ago. The last message from the *Predator* was that a shuttle had been sent out and was about to do an x-ray scan of the beacon. As was protocol, they reported their last known position as 100 kilometres from the mysterious device. It wasn't far enough.

Two Metro frigates were sent to investigate after the *Predator* had not reported in for 24 hours. No one within the Metro forces thought Haven had a military vessel capable of taking out one of their latest jaguar class destroyers. Ryder thought it must have had something to do with the sphere.

The frigates had arrived, hoping to find the destroyer in distress, or at least some wreckage. However, all they found, and it was with significant effort, were small pieces of jagged debris. All this added to the mystery of the beacons.

"Take us in slow, Mister Sny. One per cent sub-light and no more." Ryder said.

The beacon became larger on the screen. It showed the same characteristics as the first beacon. Its surface was smooth, the golden sphere covered in a symmetrical wire mesh. And as had been reported before, the white ring of light across the top of the beacon strobed every 125 seconds.

"Sny, circle the beacon at a distance of 500 metres." Ryder's words were quiet, his mind focused on the view of the alien device.

Ryder's fingers were clenched tight on the arm of his chair. He half expected the sphere to explode due to their proximity. But it didn't. The beacon just kept strobing.

Locating a button on his armrest, he depressed it and commanded, "Lieutenant Jenholin to the captain's room. Find Valre on your way, and bring her along." He shifted his gaze to the navigation console. "Ensign Sny, you will also join us."

His eyes moved to look at his propulsion officer, Ensign Krlson. "You have command, Josh. Maintain this distance from the beacon and…"

There was a pause where Ryder lowered an eyebrow, followed by Krlson raising his own.

"And?" Ensign Krlson whispered.

"And, don't break my ship," Ryder chirped before he strode towards the aft door followed by Ensign Sny.

Metro ships had many different sizes and configurations. For military vessels, a larger size usually meant more weapons, shuttles and personnel, but a slower speed. However, aerodynamics, by default, did not matter, and to a large degree, neither did weight. Most often, and this was especially the case for explorer ships that did not carry more than a couple of weapons, a crucial factor in deciding a configuration was how efficiently the vessel could be built.

The *Wayfinder* was a second-generation ship, and subsequent builds were improved with two more revisions after it. Relatively short with an 80-metre length, there were five outriggers that ballooned out from the curved nose. Ballooned described it well, as the outriggers joined together half way to the primary central cylinder, giving it the illusion of a flower in bloom. The central core of the ship, where visible, was painted black while the outriggers were red, a colour that for many thousands of years had been used to identify explorer vessels. The thirty-metre-high outriggers allowed for multiple level decks inside the ship. Consequently, Admiral Ryder's captain's room was just aft of the command deck, one flight up.

Ryder Gunn and Sny were the first ones to reach it. There was a desk on one side, and a comfortable seating area filled the room in front of it. Ryder snapped his fingers and pointed to an armchair opposite a long, low table, while he lowered into a wider, softer armchair facing Sny. This black, leather chair was known to all as off limits to anyone except the admiral.

Moments later, Valre strode into the room, followed by Lieutenant Marcy Jenholin. Marcy was tall and lean, and her long face and high cheek bones made her attractive. Her short-cropped, blonde hair, cut three centimetres high in a military style, gave her a no nonsense look some saw as a conundrum to her beauty.

"Evening, Admiral," Jenholin curtly said as she stood at attention.

Marcy Jenholin was Ryder's second in command, and when he was on the ship, his engineering officer responsible for engineering, science and propulsion. Ryder knew her as one of the smartest Sholites he had ever met.

Pointing to the couch beside him, the two women sat down and shifted so they could see the screen on the wall opposite the desk.

Ryder, after collecting the remote, brought the screen to life with the same view of the beacon as seen on the command deck. His fingers came up to scratch the side of his head. "So, what do we do now?"

Silence followed except for the sound of Edy's pant legs rubbing on the leather cushion as he shifted himself, showing his nervousness.

"Come on, folks! I have you all here on my ship because you're the best of the explorer class. Tell me something."

Lieutenant Jenholin crossed one leg over the other. "It might be a good idea to go over the facts we know," she offered. Her dark eyes shifted back and forth, and seeing no objections, she continued. "This is the third beacon of the exact same size, shape and colour."

"And each of them had the strobing white light with the exact same 125 second cycle," Edy added.

Ryder interrupted, "The beacons seem to have some type of self destruct mechanism. The first one exploded when the *Predator's* shuttle applied an x-ray scan. The second one, since we knew not to scan it, was investigated with a robotic drone. It circled and took pictures, focusing on the hatchway evident on one side. Eventually, it made sense to try and gain access, but as soon as the drone's arm touched the handle, the self-destruct mechanism was armed."

Fortunately, Jenholin broke in, "the *Morenta* was keeping a cautious 200-kilometre distance from the beacon. The explosion was massive, but only caused a buffeting of the explorer ship."

Ryder glanced down at the remote and loaded the video from the *Morenta*. They watched the 30-minute clip through to the explosion.

"Thoughts?" Ryder queried.

"It could be a navigation marker," Ensign Edy offered.

Lieutenant Jenholin chuckled. "We're in space, in the middle of nowhere. A flashing light is not going to help anyone."

"Keep it civil, Lieutenant." Ryder admonished her through a frown. "Everyone, throw out your ideas, no matter how dumb they might sound." He grinned and winked at a red-faced Ensign Edy.

Valre leaned forward. Ryder was surprised since she was not scientifically inclined. She came along on the trip to keep him company more than anything else. She said, "Agreed that a space marker does not make sense. Let's look at basic facts." The others looked on with interest, so she continued. "The device is not from Metro and not from Haven. That would make it an alien device."

"Agreed," Ryder whispered.

"If an alien was going to come to a new region of space, what would be the first thing they would do?"

Ensign Edy smirked and said, "Say *hello?*"

All four of them laughed in response until Valre raised her finger. "That's funny, but I think you are right. If the people who made the beacons are civilized, and it seems from this technology they are, then they would likely only want to say *hello* if we're also civilized."

Ryder's lips widened in an admiring smile. "I think you're on the right track. These beacons, and now this one specifically, are some type of puzzle for us to figure out. If we do, they would deem us worthy, so to speak."

Jenholin frostily added, "And, if we don't, they blow us up."

"Then, what is the white light?" Edy asked.

"Part of the puzzle," Ryder quipped. "We agree it's not really a beacon light." He rubbed his chin. "Maybe it's as simple as sending back a reciprocal white strobe. Maybe that'll satisfy the beacon."

Shaking her head vehemently, Jenholin said, gruffly, "Wouldn't do that. We've no idea what reaction we would get. It might really piss them off."

"Does anyone have a better idea?" Ryder took a second, eyes searching each of his advisors.

"Anyone?" he repeated.

Jenholin shifted nervously but kept her lips tight.

"Very well." Ryder clapped his hands, then looked at his wrist interlink. "In two hours, we'll send out a drone." He pointed at his lieutenant. "Affix a light bar on it. Make sure it's back lit so it can be seen across the vacuum. Make sure the intensity, duration and spacing match that of the beacon, exactly. Any questions?"

There were none, so he dismissed the three advisors. Lieutenant Jenholin was going to be the last one to leave. He called her back.

"You have concerns, Marcy?"

She shrugged. "Of course, but it wouldn't be the first time, would it?" She grinned knowingly, a look he was not seeing for the first time.

"We have to do something," Ryder said, his voice low, showing he had some doubts himself. "We can't just sit here and watch it blink every 125 seconds."

"To that, I agree. Besides, if this one blows up, I'm sure there will be another."

"How do you know?"

"There have already been three. Whoever is sending them is persistent." She tipped her head and said, "With your permission, Sir, I need to get that drone ready."

Once the lieutenant left, Ryder inhaled deeply. He scrunched his nose and looked from side to side. Once he realized the faint acrid smell was body odour, and since he was the only one left in the room, he looked at his interlink. He had more than enough time for a quick shower.

His berth was two floors down, half way back along the main fuselage of the space ship. There, he washed and trimmed his beard. He let out a guffaw as he looked at himself in the mirror. *At least if he was going to die today, he would look good doing it.*

He dressed in a fresh Explorer Corp. uniform, one of many hanging in his closet. There was a knock at the door, whereby he replied, "Enter!"

Valre entered. "Do you have a few minutes?"

He took a quick glance at his interlink. "Sure. Have a seat."

He sat down opposite from her. "What's up?"

Valre was ten years younger than Ryder. Her white, shoulder-length hair framed a pretty, still wrinkle-free face, with cat-like, wide eyes. "I am worried about you."

Frowning, Ryder replied, "How so?"

"It's more that I am worried about your relationship with Romy."

Ryder's frown grew longer. "Things aren't the best, but we've been apart for 18 years. It'll take time for things to heal."

"It won't heal easily with you here and Romy on Midpoint."

Ryder's hand wiped down his face, ending with his eyes gazing into Valre's. "My place is here…"

"No, it's not. Right now, you should be with Romy."

He pointed through the wall. "You see what is here. This beacon is from an alien race, possibly with gifts of advanced technology."

Leaning back, Valre calmly replied, "I know. I know. And they could be on their way here right now to destroy us all. Anything is possible."

"So, you do understand!"

"Not at all, Ryder. Your second in command is more than competent. She could have handled this."

Ryder rolled his eyes. "She is the smartest person I know, but not always the most decisive. You saw. I had to tell her to send out the drone."

Valre shrugged. "She would have come to it eventually, even though it might not be the right decision."

Creases of frustration crossed Ryder's forehead. "We can't sit here and do nothing. This beacon is important. I can feel it in my gut!"

She rose to her feet, flashing out a finger at Ryder's nose. "You haven't changed! I bring up a discussion about your son, and we wind up talking about how important your exploits are." Valre took a deep breath and added, "You were without your son for 18 years, but what you don't realize is your son was without a father for that same time period. Are you so fixated on this emptiness of space that, with your son now so close, you are going to push him even further away?"

She did not wait for an answer. Rather, she turned and briskly walked out of his cabin.

For the next 30 minutes, alone in his cabin, Ryder's mind was troubled. Thankfully, the call from Lieutenant Jenholin came over the intercom. The drone was ready. He made his way to the command deck, putting the thoughts of his son aside. He had to focus on this mission. After all, the lives of his 35 crew members depended on him.

He saw Jenholin seated facing an auxiliary console on the left side of the deck. Once the admiral took his seat she said, "The drone is ready to launch, Sir."

He faced Ensign Edy who was back at his navigation console. "Launch the drone, and park it 30 metres from the beacon. Once it's there, get us to a distance of 250 kilometres."

Once the *Wayfinder* was in position, with a good magnified view of the drone and the beacon on the front screen, Admiral Gunn said, "Okay, let's get this started."

Jenholin nodded towards him, indicating all systems on the drone were ready.

"Lieutenant, start the strobing sequence exactly 30 seconds after the beacon strobes."

"Aye, aye, Admiral."

The command deck was filled with nothing but silence. The beacon strobed. Everyone was frozen, their eyes transfixed on the screens. In their minds, they were all counting. After 30 seconds, the light bar on the front of the drone flashed a bright, white pulse.

"Now, we'll see," Ryder mumbled under his breath.

After 125 seconds, the drone flashed its strobe again.

"Sir," Lieutenant Jenholin said. "The beacon missed a strobe. It's gone dead."

A red light flashed on her screen. "No—correction! There is a significant energy build up!"

"Ensign Edy, full reverse. Get us as far away as you can."

Ryder, along with the other crew members, were pressed forward as the

Wayfinder's sub-light engines came to life. Ten seconds later, the camera, still on high magnification, sent the image of white light that filled the front screens. The explosion instantly vaporized the drone and was now continuing towards the *Wayfinder.*

"Cameras, standard mode!" Ryder yelled.

It didn't make sense, but, to Ryder, it was something. The shock wave would not be visible in space. He hoped just giving a command of some type sent the message to his deck crew that they were still in charge of the situation.

"Five seconds," Jenholin said.

The crew members all pushed back in their chairs and tightened their security belts. For most, they tightened their fingers on the armrests and waited.

Two...one...

The ship buffeted, the nose pressed down, and they rolled to their left.

"Stabilize, Mister Edy! Keep us true!" Ryder bellowed.

The *Wayfinder* responded as vibrations continued through the ship for a few more seconds. Then, there was only the silence of space. The view on the screens was clear, blackness with a few stars in the far background.

Faintly, Ryder admitted, "Maybe that wasn't the best idea, after all."

Four hours later, Ryder was in his cabin, more tossing and turning than actually sleeping. Still, the beep from the console beside his bed was annoying. The second beep, even more so. He pressed his finger onto the intercom button and cursed, "What the hell is it?"

It was Lieutenant Jenholin. "Come to the map room immediately." There was a pause before she added, "Sir!"

There was an obvious, audible *click* indicating the connection had been terminated at her end. Good thing, as he was about to give her a mouthful of expletives describing her lower rank. However, he knew she was thorough to a fault. If she was short with him, she had good reason. Consequently, he pulled on his pants and shirt, foregoing the jacket, socks and shoes.

The map room was one floor up. He passed two crew members along the way, who nodded but looked at him strangely considering his disheveled hair and bare feet. He entered the map room to find Jenholin in the centre of it, impatiently tapping her foot.

"There you are!"

Ryder yawned. "Don't you ever sleep?"

She ignored the question. "Sir, something has been bothering me ever since Ensign Edy joked that the purpose of the beacon was to say hello."

"This floor is cold," Ryder grumbled, looking at his feet.

She ignored his random words. "One thought was, who are they saying hello to? I think I have found the answer to that question."

"That's interesting. Who?"

Waving her hand in front of her, she said, "I'll get to that, but first, let's talk about the fourth beacon."

"There is no fourth beacon."

"Not yet. But let me show you something." Her hands, donned with the electro gloves, flashed in the air. She pointed, and a hologram of a gold beacon appeared. "This is the position of the third beacon." Before he could respond, a second gold beacon appeared. "This is the position of the second beacon." Her fingers pointed again, and another beacon appeared.

"And the first beacon, I presume, Lieutenant," Ryder said.

"Yes. Tell me what you see?" Jenholin asked, her words fast paced with excitement.

Ryder lifted a hand, his curled finger pushed under his chin. One eyebrow raised. "The three beacons are in a line."

"Actually, an exact line," Jenholin clarified. "What else?"

Ryder rubbed the finger against his beard. "They seem equally spaced."

"Exactly equally spaced," she repeated in her excitement. "The distance between the three beacons is exactly, evenly spaced, and they are in a straight line. With that, we can predict where the next beacon will be by extrapolating the pattern."

As his eyes lit up, dismissing any weariness that had been left in them, he blurted, "Excellent work!"

"There is more."

Ryder gazed up at the pattern of three beacons, the line that had been added and the projected location of the fourth beacon. "More?"

"The time between the first and second beacon was exactly 50 Alpha Centauri days or one Alpha Centauri month. So was the timing between the second and third beacon."

"So, we know when the fourth beacon will appear," Ryder mused.

"Exactly!" The lieutenant tempered her excitement. Her admiral had not yet seen the real importance of the discovery. "Sir, the Alpha Centauri month is unique to the people living here, those on Haven and us Metronians. So is the 125 second interval. This is a standard unit of time in our quinary numerical system."

"The beacons are not random."

Jenholin whispered, "They are sent with the intention for us to find them."

"'Us,' would be those on Haven or us from Metro, I assume." Ryder thought to clarify what he was hearing.

"There's more." Jenholin's hands clapped together and the holographic view shrunk. "We know if we extend the line between the three beacons, we will come to the predicted location of the fourth beacon. But, being forever curious—" she grinned "—I thought, what is in the other direction?" Her finger traced out in front of her. Since the view was significantly shrunken, the line extended many billions of kilometres into space outside the Alpha Centauri system. Once satisfied, she snapped her fingers, and a red X appeared in the view. Above it, were the three-dimensional coordinates of the location.

"Do those coordinates look familiar, Sir?"

Squinting, he looked at them. She zoomed in so he could see them better. "There is something about them that's familiar, but I can't put my finger on it. Help me out."

Her voice became sombre. Even though her ancestry was Sholite, she spoke softly out of respect for Ryder Gunn. "That is the exact position where the asteroid ship Talus 3 exploded on the way to Alpha Centauri."

Ryder's jaw dropped. "What?" was the only response he could come up with.

"Whoever is sending the beacons knows about Talus 3. That means they have been watching us for a long time. These coordinates, along with the time intervals unique to this system, tells us these beacons are meant for the Korians."

Ryder's shoulders sagged as he felt the enormity of the revelation. He mumbled, "What are we getting into?"

"I don't know, Admiral. But we need to be very careful."

Chapter 6: P Central

The 40th day of the 4th month, Alpha Centauri year 0024.

Hagaza, the Mabuza capital city on Haven.

Mist was a beautiful woman. Her black face was highlighted by features perfectly proportioned. Long, straight, black hair flowed down her back to her waist, a stunning contrast to the long, yellow dress she wore; it served well in accentuating her lean, tall figure.

My, my, Elki thought as she watched Mist walk towards her. *What I'd give to be young again.*

As Mist moved closer to the bench Elki sat on, even though her footfalls were light, the contact of each sandaled foot against the polished stone floor of the departure hanger echoed around the vast room. The walls had a similar polished-stone façade, except they were light-blue, a contrast to the dark-blue floor. It was no accident these colours were used since they were the colours of the Mabuza flag, and this was the departure area for dignitaries of the Mabuza, used exclusively for officially approved transpositions.

Mist gracefully lowered onto the bench beside Elki, kissed her on the cheek, then offered, "We still have 20 minutes to our departure. I thought I was early, but you always seem to be ahead of me."

"You're taller than I, younger and more beautiful. So, keeping a step ahead of you, in this aspect, is the least I can do for my ego," Elki replied with a wink.

Mist crossed one leg over the other while turning towards the older woman. "You forgot I am also smarter than you, even though you are the senior see'er among us." She poked Elki in the shoulder, her eyes twinkling as she enjoyed this type of banter.

Slapping her hand away, Elki did her best to frown while glancing up at Mist. "Now that I see you up close, you do look tired. Did your visit to your sister not go well?"

"Actually, it went very well, but it's a long trip to Relion 2, plane 6334."

The purebloods inhabited the Athar, an infinite number of planes of reality, accessible to the more powerful and tuned pureblood minds. And the number of new-found planes continued to grow as pureblood explorers discovered new civilizations.

"How is Tashia? I hope you told her I miss her," Elki offered, her words spoken in a softer tone.

Mist noticed. "It has been over 20 years since Tashia left the see'ers. She is at peace with her decision, and she is happy."

A wide smile monopolized Elki's face. "That makes me happy, then. It was an awkward time for her, you and I, when she made her decision."

Shrugging, Mist replied, "She met a man she deeply loved. To some, it was unfortunate he was an Anasazi. Mixed pureblood could not be allowed within the see'er's circle."

Elki's white afro vibrated as she shook her head. "But it sounds so racist when you say it in such a simple and matter-of-fact tone!"

"I suppose it is. However, as see'ers, we have a purpose to foresee the future and look into the past, ultimately to make corrections as required for the betterment of the Athar. Our psychic powers as Bantu purebloods needs to be pure, or we will fail in our calling."

Elki let out a sigh. "Of course, you're right. Your family blood line was 99 per cent pure Bantu. It made your older sister's psychic powers formidable; that's why she was groomed towards the see'er's council. When she decided to forego her calling, that left you as her obvious successor." The smile returned to the older woman's face. "And we're not disappointed."

Mist heard the words, but her mind was elsewhere. She was still thinking about the racist qualities of pureblood societies. The seven pureblood races: Bantu, Anasazi, Celtae, Kush, Shang, Ionian and the Toltec, each having unique psychic powers, defined by small differences in their DNA. Inevitably, there were cross relationships, resulting in mixed blood offspring. After a few generations, it was realized that as bloods became more mixed the psychic powers weakened, until eventually, only almost indiscernible, latent powers would remain. It was discovered that the DNA code had a survival mechanism, and when mixed would fight competing alien DNA.

Sculls were the result. These were psychically impotent descendants of purebloods. The sculls and purebloods lived side by side. For the most part, purebloods tolerated sculls. In fact, they got on with them well, but what purebloods could not tolerate, were purebloods from other races who would potentially water down their own pureblood caste. Consequently, it was natural for purebloods to be at war with each other for longer than anyone could remember. But then, the Ionians took charge.

Mist lifted her mind out of her daydream, gazing across the room at the four Ionian guards. She shivered; their appearance resembled blue ice on a windswept tundra of blowing snow. Their skin was pale, their long hair white, and their eyes were pink. Their light-blue and white attire added to their frigid appearance. The light colouring was the side effect of all seven psychic powers residing in their bodies. Impossible as it once seemed, the Ionian scientists had discovered a formula to allow the different DNAs to coexist without the psychic powers being significantly degraded.

The Ionians, now more powerful than any other race, took charge and brought peace, or at least a semblance of it, to the Athar. Many purebloods embraced the ability to have all psychic powers, and they converted. Many more, as is the nature of people, were resistant to change and preferred to continue on with their race as is. But there were a few, a few who thought the mixed blood as blasphemy. They would not have their pure blood tarnished by others they thought lower than they were. These were the true racists, people having no need to keep their blood pure other than for a fear of something that is different from what they are.

Mist tried hard to remind herself the purity of their Bantu blood had a purpose, a necessary one for the betterment of all purebloods and sculls residing in the Athar.

Grodin, who had been standing with the Ionians, strode over towards the two women. The tall man had broad shoulders befitting someone who took the security of others in his charge seriously. He had been one of many security personnel ensuring the security of the citizens of Hagaza until the day Efi and Romy, haggard and dirty, transpositioned to a little used transposition terminal. Recognizing Efi, he brought them safely to the see'er council, and was charged with their safety while in the Mabuza city. Having performed well, he was promoted, now a senior officer on the see'er's personal security team.

Grodin was in serious mode, his lips in a straight line, devoid of any semblance of a smile. His lips cracked open. "Ladies, it's time to depart. The four Ionians at the front. I will follow their wake. The two of you on my shoulders."

The Athar, to purebloods, was seen by their mind's eye as a vastness of yellow, red and light-blue markers. Instinctively, a mature pureblood can home in on any given marker, and, as such, each of the travellers could have transpositioned to their destination independently. However, when travelling in groups, it was more efficient for one traveller to lead, and the remaining travellers to follow in that person's psychic wake.

That would be the case now as the four Ionian guards took up a position in the centre of the large room. They formed a tight square after which Grodin took a position behind them, his hand gripped down on one of their shoulders. Immediately after, Elki and Mist, one on each side and just behind Grodin, each put a hand on his shoulder. They were all linked.

One of the front guards, tilted his head back, and in a loud voice said. "Just checking. None of you have any energy sources on you?"

As all purebloods learned in their childhood, purebloods could not transposition with any type of energy source. In doing so, the energy signature would combine with the pureblood's molecules, so that when they recombined, they would be reordered, resulting usually in a grotesque mound of disjointed flesh and bone. This explained why the Ionian guards, the most modern soldiers in the Athar, were only armed with a sword strapped over their back and a dagger hanging off their belt.

Elki's eyebrows lowered. "Of course, we don't! I'm sure I've been transpositioning since long before you were suckling on your mother's teat!"

Elki saw the two forward guard's heads tilt towards each other. They were likely snickering. The corner of her lip curled up in a snarl, she whispered lightly, but loud enough to know the guards would hear, "No-good, baby-faced albino's…"

The words were cut off as the guard announced, "Focus. We are going now."

At that moment, as the lead guard focused on the destination marker, his mind's eye view was transferred into the mind of each of the other travellers, causing the destination marker to light up like a beacon. They all focused, and as a group, a larger shimmering sphere formed around them. First, it was clear, then opaque. The figures within distorted and faded. When the circle cleared, all seven travellers were gone.

It was something Mist never became accustomed to. She focused on the bright marker transferred to her mind's eye. She felt the same queasy feeling in her stomach every time she travelled. It lasted only a few seconds. Then, as it always did, there was the feeling of falling forward. She was young and strong and knew not to put her foot out. Her arrival would be elegant.

And it was. When the opaque circle around them cleared, they were assaulted by humid, midday heat. Glancing up through squinting eyes, she saw the bright sun was directly overhead. They had arrived on P Central on plane 4000. P Central was a large planet, a full half larger than Haven. As such, the Bantu visitors, in addition to being assaulted by the heat, were also burdened by the increased gravity. Mist felt it when she tried to turn and look about their surroundings, groaning as she tried to move her legs.

From beside Mist, Elki chirped. "I'm already sweating. This just won't do."

The lead guard turned to the side, his hand flowing across his body. "This way, please."

They were in a large courtyard, surrounded on all four sides by three-story-high, red brick walls. On each level, a wide walkway ran just inside the brick, visible through the many arched openings, capped in larger, grey concrete blocks. Elki and Mist had been here many times before, so they knew this was one of four courtyards in the massive Bantu pavilion.

As the guard moved to the side, ahead of them in the shade of a cantilevered awning, a man waited. As the group walked towards him, the lead guard and Grodin exchanged words, after which the Ionians veered towards a doorway on their left. With their mission complete, they were no longer needed and began their walk back to the Ionian pavilion.

The man under the awning waved as the three Bantu travellers joined him. "Welcome, once again, to P Central."

Rodri was a senior Bantu ambassador to the Pureblood Court. He was the third highest ranked Bantu on P Central.

Nevertheless, Elki quipped, "Hello, Rodri. Where's Eversha?"

Rodri shuffled back a step, his hands gyrating apologetically. "The High Ambassador sends her apologies. She is in meetings day and night. But I assure you, I will see to all your needs."

Elki did not push her disappointment, since in reality, she wasn't disappointed at all. Eversha was extremely intelligent, while Rodri was competent at best. Since the Mabuza are a tribe of the Bantu, they are required to report significant events to the Bantu leadership. They knew about the Mabuza infatuation with time travellers, something not all Bantu found as relevant. The report they came here to give was a formality. It was business Elki preferred to keep under her control, so she preferred to deal with someone as mundane as Rodri.

"What time is it?" Elki asked.

Rodri carried a small tablet. He swiped his finger across it. "It's an hour after midday."

As they walked into the coolness of the building, Elki clapped her hands together, a wide smile on her face. "Excellent. Our timing is perfect. There's a wonderful restaurant just down the block. I've been thinking about it all morning. We must go there for lunch."

"But…but your report?" Rodri replied.

"I will have none of that. I'm hungry," Elki said. "We'll eat, then rest. Look at Mist." She pointed to her companion. "She travelled yesterday and again today. We'll rest overnight, then provide you with our report in the morning at the same time we give it to the Ionian representative."

"Of course, Elki," Rodri acquiesced.

One block away was actually three blocks away. On Haven, they would have walked, but here, in the heat and higher gravity, it was not recommended for off-worlders. Instead, Rodri led them down two levels to an underground rail station. It was one of 14 such stations adjacent to a circular rail line in the shape of a three-kilometre circle. There were seven pavilions above the underground railway, equally spaced on the circle, two stations per pureblood pavilion.

It did not take long for them to hear the electric hum of an incoming train. It was a short trip as they deboarded at the next station under the Celtae pavilion. Once at street level, Elki saw the restaurant, one of her favourites, and gave out a whoop.

Surprisingly, even with the heavier gravity, Elki was out front. She turned to Grodin, Mist and Rodri. "Stop dallying!" she urged.

They entered the coolness of the restaurant, finding a more than adequately cushioned booth with a wooden, semi-circular shaped table. They slid in after which a waiter promptly appeared. He put a menu on the table for them to share, as was the custom.

Elki pushed it towards Mist. "I know exactly what I want. The vegetable stew here is excellent, probably better than any I have tasted in my travels. I highly recommend it."

Elki and Grodin took her advice and ordered the stew along with a cool drink. Rodri declined the food, ordering an alcoholic beverage in its place.

Once the waiter left, Rodri leaned forward, his elbows on the table. "So, how is your—what do you call him—your msafiri doing?"

"His name is Romy Gunn," Elki replied. "I told you, we'll give you our report in the morning." She leaned towards the senior ambassador. "Rather, tell me about the goings on in the court. What priorities threaten the Athar?"

Rodri could not tell if Elki was being serious or sarcastic, but clearly, discussion of Romy Gunn would not happen until the morning. So, he set about explaining the present issues in front of the court. For the most part, peace had settled over the Athar, with only an occasional flare up of tensions between races.

The food and drinks arrived. Elki stirred the thick stew with her spoon, then tested the first small mouthful. She drew in a breath trying to cool the morsel of root vegetable before rolling it in her mouth. Two bites and she swallowed. A satisfied smile crossed her face as she asked, "How are the Bantu warriors faring?"

Forty kilometres away was a massive complex of military barracks. When the Ionians pressed for peace across the Athar almost a century ago, led by the Earthman, Nolan Harrison, it was decided a muti-race, military force needed to be established. Although there are bases throughout the known Athar, the one on P Central was the primary and largest base. Occupying it were 200 thousand Ionian soldiers and 50 thousand from each of the other six races. Of the Bantu, three thousand were from the Mabuza tribe.

"Our Bantu warriors commend themselves exceptionally," Rodri answered. "Of course, the Celtae with the power of the shield, the Toltec with the ability to throw energy blasts from their fingers and the Anasazi with the ability to teleport about, are more formidable when it comes to war. Our ability to foresee what is to come is more useful in missions requiring stealth, and they do very well in that regard."

After a mouthful of food almost too large for her mouth, Elki needed a moment before her next question. "I assume the Ionians are the best of the best?"

Chuckling, Rodri had a twinkle in his eye. "They like to think so, but they are not as strong as they would think."

"How so?" Mist interjected.

"As you know, the Ionians took it upon themselves to discover the secret of having mixed pureblood without reducing the psychic powers that go with it," Rodri elaborated. "But when the facts became available, it was clear, there was some degradation. Ionians have all seven psychic powers, but their strength is about 65 to 70 per cent that of a pureblood who is not mixed or tainted."

Grodin looked up from his stew. "That still makes them more powerful than any of the other races."

Rodri nodded. "In some situations, yes, but in others no. You see, considering other races, and take ours for example, if we exclude those who have significantly mixed bloods, 80 per cent have strength at 80 per cent or more. Ten per cent of the Bantu have psychic strength over 90 per cent."

He shifted his gaze to the see'ers. "And some, such as the two of you, have psychic strength over 98 per cent."

Grodin pulled Rodri's gaze back to him. "So, in certain situations, a strong Bantu, or Toltec, could have an advantage, at least in using their specific psychic power."

A coy sideways grin came across Rodri's face. His voice was lower, his eyes shifting back and forth. "If used in stealth with sufficient planning, while catching an Ionian unawares, most assuredly."

Having finished her stew, Elki slapped her spoon against the table. "That's enough! People would think we're a group of insurrectionists here." She laughed, letting anyone listening know their comments were not serious.

For another half hour they talked about nothing important, just idle banter. Once Elki thought enough time she considered polite had passed, she announced it was time to seek their lodgings in the Bantu pavilion.

Early the next morning, Elki and Mist woke refreshed. They met in the wide hallway leading to a large common room where Rodri awaited. The floor was a lacquered wood with a purple tinge to it. This wood, only found on a far continent on P Central, was rare in the Council City. The same wood covered half way up the walls with small intricately-carved mythical figures perched every two metres.

Grodin joined them a moment later, and they enjoyed a light breakfast while continuing the idle gossip from the afternoon before.

"Who will we be meeting at the Pureblood Parliament?" Mist asked.

"Minister Chouvrin is the one assigned to our region of the Athar," Rodri replied. "She's the same Ionian we met the last time—what was it—eight months ago?"

Taking a final drink from her cup of tea, Elki said, matter-of-factly, "We best be going, then." She rose to her feet, indicating it wasn't open for debate.

They made their way outside, just in front of the Bantu pavilion. This was the first time Mist took the opportunity to appreciate the beauty her eyes beheld. The seven pavilions, one more breathtaking than the other, were in a ring above the lower rail line. But, here, at ground level, there was a wide ring road made of golden-coloured blocks. On the other side of the ring road was an equally wide swath of grass, although on P Central the grass was a dark-blue colour. Finally, inside the grass ring was the Pureblood

Parliament, a massive white block building, adorned with spires and arches throughout its façade.

The whine of an electrical vehicle pulling up in front of the group brought Mist out of her daydream. Rodri urged them aboard, and the black vehicle began its trek around the ring road. As they came to a point on the opposite side from the Bantu pavilion, there was a bisecting road, just as wide as the ring road and also made of the same golden-coloured brick. The end leading away from the ring, allowed egress from the political centre to a residential zone, and even further, to the military complex. The other end of the bisecting road, led towards a circular driveway in front of the parliament building's entryway.

Once the group left the black vehicle, they took a moment to look around their surroundings. Here, there was a buzz as many people were in front of the grand, glass entryway. Mist saw a group of three men, easily recognizable as Toltec by their shorter stature and dark features. At the top of a long set of stairs as wide as the entire entryway, stood a man and woman arguing. The man, dressed in light-brown leather, had a long, braided, black ponytail. Every few seconds he would throw up a hand as he tried to convince the white-haired Ionian woman in front of him of his argument.

The three Mabuza travellers and Rodri snaked their way through the people on the stairs and into the building. Elki shook out her arms in the cooler inside air. "Thanks for that," she mumbled. "I have to wear these clothes all day." The clothes she, Mist and Grodin wore were the same as that from the day prior, just they had been laundered overnight.

The vestibule they were in was as grand as the façade. The alternating rows of black and white blocks went up the walls for four stories. Mist saw the sign two metres up. Two metres wide by one metre high, it read,

The Harrison Parliament Building.

Mist thought it ironic, here they were in an area dedicated to Nolan Harrison, a man from Earth who unbeknownst to him had latent pureblood powers. In fact, once his powers developed, he became the most powerful pureblood ever known. He began as a figurehead for the Ionian cause to end the ongoing pureblood wars, but quickly, he became their leader.

However, what the Ionians, nor Nolan Harrison, knew was, Romy Gunn, the man they were here to discuss, was related in the family lineage to Nolan Harrison. Whereas Nolan developed mighty pureblood powers, Romy was developing into a pureblood having some psychic powers, but more importantly to the Bantu, the ability to travel in time. He was a *drifter*.

Elki, as wise as she was, thought it best to keep the family link a secret from the Ionians. They didn't need to show unsolicited interest towards the young man.

A hallway off the vestibule led them to an elevator. They exited on the third floor where Rodri led them into a large meeting room. There were comfortable lounge chairs for at least ten people, and near the far wall was a long conference table with the same number of chairs. Elki set the tone by lowering into one of the lounge chairs. Mist did the same. Grodin, always at the ready, preferred to stand.

Rodri was about to sit when an Ionian scurried into the room. He nodded a greeting to the guests, then whispered a message to Rodri before leaving as quickly as he came.

Rodri relayed the message. "Minister Chouvrin will be 30 minutes late. There are drinks available if you wish." He pointed to a cabinet against the far wall.

Giving a loud sigh, Elki wanted to ensure Rodri saw her frustration, but in reality, she wasn't disappointed. The fact the minister would be late showed her level of disinterest, the same disinterest Chouvrin showed at their last meeting. This meeting would be no more than a formality.

None of them took up the offer of a drink. Rather, they waited, mostly in silence, until 40 minutes later when Minister Chouvrin rushed into the room. She wasn't fat, but she looked soft, which was odd for an Ionian. She wore a simple white shirt under a short, black jacket and matching black pants. She had the albino look all Ionians had, but her hair was cut short, making the short bristles barely visible against her scalp.

"My apologies, Elki," Minister Chouvrin announced. "So much to do and so little time."

Elki rose and gave a slight bow which the minister returned. She said, "You remember Mist, I'm sure, and this is Grodin, our security lead."

The minister nodded to each of them as well as Rodri, before they all sat. She brought her tablet in front of her, swiping a finger across it. "Remind me again," she mumbled. A few seconds went by before her eyes lit up. "Oh, yes! You have a skull named Romy Gunn that is of interest."

"You might recall, at our last meeting, we told you we assumed he had psychic powers. Today, we can verify that he does," Elki replied.

Eyes down, Minister Chouvrin mumbled, "What race?"

Without hesitation, Elki said, "He's a Celtae and has the power of the shield."

Mist waited for more, but Elki finished the lie with finality. She had difficulty keeping a straight face knowing Romy had multiple powers, raw as they were. Elki was playing a dangerous game.

Minister Chouvrin's pink eyes glanced up. "During the last report, you indicated Mister Gunn might have the ability to time travel." The minister couldn't hold back a slightly twisted smile. "Is that still your assertion?"

"That hasn't changed," Elki replied. "We visited him yesterday, and he's still being tested."

Mist's knuckles were white as she gripped the thick arm of the chair. Elki just lied again–twice! She knows this Ionian has the ability to read her mind if she saw the need. The lie could be easily discovered. Mist tapped a finger on the chair, drawing Elki's attention. Her eyes widened slightly, giving the senior see'er a *what are you doing* look.

Elki, seeing the minister preoccupied with typing, winked at Mist. Elki knew the young minister thought the whole subject of their time traveller as inconsequential, beneath her and a waste of her valuable Ionian time. Of course, the minister could scan her, but purebloods could sense when this was done. It was considered an assault, unless the person doing the scan had a good reason. Elki knew the minister was much too preoccupied to think such an action was required.

Chouvrin glanced at the digital clock mounted on the wall, and let out an, "oh my!" Her foot started to tap on the floor. "When will you more exactly determine these time travel abilities?"

Shrugging, Elki replied, "Eighteen months, perhaps even longer if…"

"One year from today," Minister Chouvrin announced. "That's when you will provide the next update."

"Of course. Might we be honoured with your visit to Hagaza for the next update? By then, meeting him might be suitable," Elki proposed.

A patronizing smirk came across the minister's face. "P Central is the centre of the Athar, politically and geographically. The meeting will be here. Bring him if you think it will be helpful."

Mist knew she and Elki were thinking the same thing. On this plane, just like every plane, the universe was infinite. And, as far as the purebloods knew, the number of planes were also infinite. So, since an infinite space has no defined borders, how possibly could anyone know where the centre was? *Stupid woman!*

Glancing at the clock again, the minister cursed under her breath, then rose to her feet. "If there is nothing else critical, I am late for my next appointment." Not expecting a response, she turned and walked towards the door. One hand caught the door jamb. She turned her face back. "One last question. Can you control this man?"

Elki had already risen to her feet. This was the first question that caught her off guard. It caused her to pause a moment before answering, "Yes. He has committed to a path supporting the Mabuza people. He will do as we ask of him."

The minister noticed the slight hesitation. It caused her also to pause a moment, and she almost turned back to investigate further. However, another glance at the clock, and she verified her priorities. She gave a curt nod and left the room.

By now Mist was on her feet. She knew Elki was confident in her last answer. But Mist, without being overconfident, knew her powers to foresee the future were more powerful and more accurate than her older mentor. Both women knew Romy Gunn had a rebellious side to him. That's one of the reason's Efi was arranged to be with him. She would have influence. If Romy's allegiance needed some coaxing, surely, Efi was totally committed to guiding him.

While Elki thought her plan to be without a weakness, Mist was worried. What she saw in her dreams of the future proved Romy to be helpful, but also to be a man following his own path. What was not as clear was where Efi really stood. She was committed to the Mabuza people, but she was falling in love with the Korian man. That could change things, no matter what Elki or any of the see'ers wished.

Chapter 7: Psychic Training

The 41ˢᵗ day of the 4ᵗʰ month, Alpha Centauri year 0024.

The Aramis, Mabuza starship, just off Midpoint.

Romy took a deep breath, his eyes narrow, predatory slits. His elbows were bent, his fingers clenched into tight, white-knuckled fists. His knees were bent, one foot slightly in front of the other.

The light on the distant wall turned green. He pounced to his left and snapped the spear off the rack. Sliding to his left he tilted back, his kinetic energy coiling. Knee bent, one leg came forward, slamming into the floor. The two-metre-long spear sprung from his hand. His momentum carried his arm around his far shoulder, but his eyes stayed in line, following the flight of the steel-tipped spear. The ironwood shaft vibrated, letting off a noticeable *hum*. It lasted only a second, replaced by the *thud* as the tip sunk into the centre of the cork target beside the green light.

He was already moving. Five metres to his left, he grasped the bow from the second rack. His feet took a sideways stance. Pulling an arrow from the quiver on his back, he cocked it. Pulling the twine taut, he took a second to take one deep, relaxing breath. His finger twitched, and the arrow released, hitting the same target, ten centimetres from the spear.

Two more arrows were released, each as he moved to a new position, incrementally, five metres to his right. He growled, seeing these two arrows both hit the target 30 centimetres below centre.

Speed and accuracy were both important on this test. He covered the short distance to the curved sabre on the wooden table. He gripped the handle even before the bow he had just thrust from his hand, clattered against the floor. He hefted the gleaning blade, and in a fluid motion, sliced the razor-sharp edge towards the centre of the thick, two-metre-long bone hanging from a sturdy chain. A loud *crack* echoed across the training room as the bone fractured, the split half falling to the floor. One stride to his right and a backhand, turning stroke hit the second bone. The result was the same as that on the first hit.

The third long bone was thicker. Two running steps and a lunge later, he grunted as the blade flew towards the bone. There was a resonating *clunk*, then a *twang* as the blade sent vibrations up his arms, rattling his elbows. The swaying bone bent but didn't separate. Romy swore under his breath, coiling and sending a second thunderous strike into the weak point. The lower half of the bone easily fell away.

He threw the sabre to his right. It clanged against the wall. By the time he heard it, he was already at the next table. He grasped the assault rifle from it without stopping. Once beside the edge of the table, he dropped to one knee, facing the wall to the left of the cork target. Here, three targets were moving side to side, one slowly, the next quicker and the last faster yet. Romy knew he was behind. He didn't take the relaxation breath he should have. The first bullet trailed the first target, missing. After a slight shake of his head, he took the breath, then nudged the trigger. The second target exploded into a hundred fragments. His hand supporting the barrel lifted. His shoulders rolled to the left, then another nudge on the trigger. The third target was destroyed.

To his left, he heard Efi's voice yell out, "Twenty-three seconds!"

Rising to his feet, Romy replaced the rifle on the table and stretched his arms over his head before moving to Efi's side. "Way too slow," he muttered.

Efi's smile lit up her face. "There's always room for improvement, but that was your best time yet!"

Training with conventional weapons was only half of Romy's requirement, but it was a critical half. Purebloods, when they transposition, could not take energy sources with them. That included any type of projectile or energy weapons. Often, if a raiding party travelled to another plane, they would take such weapons with them, minus the battery packs or ammunition. Then, their first course of action would be to find these power sources at the new location. However, this was risky, and it was advisable for the soldiers to have conventional warfare weapons with them and to have the ability to use them effectively.

Romy lifted the back of his hand, wiping the beads of sweat from his brow. "This is the 25th day of training. I should have cracked the 20 second mark by now."

"You've made great progress since you've been here."

Romy offered, "You do know, I have been trained on everything here before. Being in the Patriotic forces required these skills—everything except the bow. That is new to me."

Efi slapped his shoulder with the back of her hand. "Come, let's set up the course again. We can do two more rounds before our visitors arrive."

Already shifting towards the course, Romy froze and glanced back. His appearance did not require words. She knew exactly what he was thinking. *What visitors?*

The opaque circle of rippling waves cleared. Mist, her fingers gripping Elki's shoulder, took a deep breath. For Mist, this was the third transposition in consecutive days. Each time a pureblood completed a planer hop, it used up some of their psychic energy. However, Mist was a strong Bantu pureblood, probably stronger than Elki ever imagined or knew.

Mist wrinkled her nose. Even though the humid air of P Central was somewhat oppressive, at least it was not clinical, ventilated air such as that irritating her senses right now.

Two Mabuza soldiers, dressed in the customary black and blue uniforms, approached Grodin and the two women at the centre of the arrival room within the *Aramis*. The lead soldier, stiff lipped, gave a nod to the two see'ers. His lips cracked open. "Welcome aboard."

After Elki and Mist nodded in return, the guard's lips spread wider into a smile. "Good to see you again, Grodin."

Returning the smile, Grodin replied. "I didn't know you were stationed here, Marcus. Well met." Grodin tilted his head, peering around Marcus to gaze upon the second guard. "If my memory does not deceive me, you are Rowland. Good to see you again, also."

Rowland's eyes widened, surprised Grodin would remember him. Having met him only briefly, once or twice, he was thrilled the senior officer would have any recollection. But Grodin was earning a reputation as an officer serving the soldier rank. Roland was seeing first hand where that came from.

"Sir...Sir," Rowland stuttered. "Welcome aboard!" Lost in the moment, the young soldier forgot about the see'ers. Finally, realizing his error, his feet shuffled as he faced the women. The stuttering continued. "My apologies. I...I...well, welcome!"

With many experienced years behind her, Elki knew how to handle almost any situation. Her voice changed; her calm words sang off her tongue. "Why thank you, Rowland. Can you please lead us to the training room."

Rowland had large teeth, and hadn't yet lost a single one. It allowed for a great smile. "Of course!" He turned sharply, leading them towards the exit door.

The transposition room was near the back of the starship, on the second level. Since it was centrally located, it took only a few minutes to arrive at their destination. There, since the see'ers were high level dignitaries, the Captain of the *Aramis* and his first officer awaited them.

After cordial greetings, Elki stated, "I don't want to interrupt your activities. I'm sure you're both very busy with much better things to do." The captain opened his mouth to reply, but Elki's word's cut him off. "I'm sure Marcus and Rowland can take care of any needs we have." Her downturned hand waved the two officers away, a clear indication any argument would be futile.

Marcus moved to a position beside the training room door, Rowland placing himself on the other side. Rowland, standing at attention—in fact, more perfectly at attention than he ever had, announced, "Of course! There won't be any problems."

The captain could do nothing but shrug. He said his goodbye before retreating to the command deck along with his first officer.

The main entry to the training complex was one floor below them. This secondary entrance led to a second level observation room. Once inside the room, Elki relaxed, kicking off her shoes, flexing her toes. "Can you please get us some fruit juice, Mist? And for you, Grodin?"

Grodin, having taken up a position beside the inside of the door, fingers clasped behind his back, replied, "No, thank you, Ma'am."

Mist didn't mind such requests, knowing how much Elki had helped her over the years. She walked towards a counter along the back wall of the room and retrieved a drink for each of them. She also poured a glass of juice for Grodin. Handing him the drink, she said, "Relax a bit, and sit down."

Begrudgingly, Grodin accepted the glass, but his feet remained fixed in place.

Lowering an eyebrow, Mist insisted, "Sit. Consider it an order if you have to."

The room was painted in a calming beige, with the back wall a slightly darker shade. It was large enough for a couch and two smaller lounge chairs in the centre of the room, situated around a large, round table. Grodin lowered himself into one of the arm chairs. Behind the seating area, on the wall opposite the bar, was a wide, short window, wide enough for both of the women to sit on the stools in front of the window and peer out at the training room below.

Romy grunted as his feet slid back on the floor. There was barely time to recover. The next energy blast from the machine was already on its way. The green energy shield, in a mesh pattern around his figure, glowed. The energy ball slammed into his shield. Sparks, green and purple, splattered in front of him.

He heard Efi's voice. "Break!"

Romy relaxed, the psychic energy shield surrounding him dissipated. He had taken four blasts, each pressing him backwards. "What energy level did we get too?"

Shrugging, Efi replied, "The last two blasts were at 20 per cent machine capacity."

"Only 20 per cent! You have to be kidding me!"

Efi didn't look up from the tablet. Her only response was another shrug.

Striding towards her, Romy's face was red, his eyebrows tilted inwards. "And what's with the shrugging? What's that supposed to mean?"

Efi took up a stance facing him, her fists planted against her hips. "What do you want me to say?"

"Maybe something encouraging!"

"Encouraging?" Efi growled in response. "There's nothing encouraging about your progress. We've been in this complex for 25 days. You should be further ahead. It's frustrating."

Choking on the words, he barely managed a reply. "Frustrated? You're frustrated? Really!" His chest was heaving as he took deep breaths. His gaze changed. It was an evaluating look. Even though Efi was in the same white coveralls he wore, it hugged her curves in a way that enhanced her figure. It brought back memories, constant memories of the game they were playing. They both loved each other. They knew that, but the love was held at arms length, sometimes allowing a cuddle or a passionate kiss. But it went no further. Efi prioritized the training, and Romy was a gentleman. He would not press himself on her. Yes, he was frustrated, but not for the reasons Efi assumed.

Efi's eyes softened. She lifted her hand, her fingers grazing across Romy's cheek. For a moment, she pressed herself against him, the momentary glow in her eyes telling Romy how she felt. But when she left the moment there, backing away, Romy sighed, realizing Efi and he weren't on the same emotional level, at least, that is what he chose to assume.

An awkward silence ensued. Romy broke it, as he glanced up at the mirrored window. "They're watching, aren't they?" Earlier, in the late morning, she had told him Elki and Mist would be visiting.

Now, in the mid afternoon, Efi gave an affirmative nod. "Let's do the next exercise."

"Wow! Did you see that!" Elki exclaimed.

Mist certainly did. They had been observing Romy for two hours now. For the last 40 minutes, he had been practicing releasing energy balls from his fingertips, a psychic power attributed to Toltec pureblood DNA. There had been several attempts whereby Romy could only muster a few sparks of orange energy. A few attempts later, he managed a slightly larger fireball. He released it, but it fizzled out halfway to the fire-resistant target placed by the far wall.

"I am seeing the same thing you are. Efi has been vague about his progress in her reports, but certainly, the reports were not glowing." She sighed. "I can see why."

"Efi needs to get with it," Elki nattered.

"As far as we know, there have only ever been five drifters. With so little history, we can't predict how long Romy will take to hone his powers," Mist responded. "He might never be ready to do what we ask of him."

It wasn't very often Elki scowled at Mist, but now was one of those moments. Her head snapped towards the younger see'er, her complexion darkened, her eyes as if aglow. "Don't even go there. We have a cause and Romy's a part of it. We dream on events in the Athar. Sometimes it takes us to events in the past, sometimes into the future. From that, we determine if corrections have to be made. He's a critical part of that process."

Mist did not respond, yet a sigh escaped her as her face softened.

Waving her hand in front of her, Elki blurted, "Don't get all sentimental on me. I like Romy as much as you do, but he's a tool for the corrections I speak of. He'll serve that purpose." Her gaze shifted back to the window, indicating the finality of her answer.

However, Mist had known her mentor for many years, too many for her to be summarily dismissed. "What if he chooses not to serve us and the cause?" she whispered.

Noticeably, Elki's breathing paused for a few seconds. She did not turn her gaze from the window, lest Mist perhaps catch sight of her own insecurity revealed in her eyes. "He'll help us. He has to. Many billions of lives depend on the work we do."

Mist saw Romy differently from Elki's perspective. He was not a person easy to tame or fall in line without questions. In fact, she thought he had a rebellious element to him, teetering on reckless. "When Romy begins to travel in time, he could be faced with the time shift paradox. It could have disastrous results," Mist offered.

"We don't know much about the paradox.," Elki replied. "Between the five previous drifters we know of, the paradox only came into effect a few times. They were able to deal with the situations that arose. Romy, if nothing else, is quick on his feet. He will deal with it as the need arises."

Grodin rose from the couch and approached the two women. "Excuse me. I have been assigned to the see'ers for some time now. Before that, for a short time, I was assigned to Romy and Efi. From that, I know Romy is a time drifter, and I know you have plans for him." Grodin had an odd, adolescent look on his usually stoic face, one showing his embarrassment. Through it, he said, "I'm all in, so could you please explain what this time shift paradox is?"

Elki took a moment to consider Grodin's request before she responded. "I know no one more loyal to us than you, Grodin. Still, I will clarify first, there are very few who know about Romy's potential as a time drifter. The fewer people that know, the better."

"Of course, Ma'am. That is a given!" His voice was louder, showing it was difficult for him not to be offended by the inference of mistrust.

Elki's eyes brightened, and she gave Grodin a smile. She was good with people. She could read them, and in instances like this, she knew exactly what they needed. "When a drifter travels back in time, there might be certain situations that arise which defy logic, and by that, I mean the logic of the Athar." Confusion was evident on Grodin's face as Elki continued. "The Athar is the collective consciousness of all beings: animals, sculls and purebloods. It defines everything we see and do. Some call it our reality. Some might say it is just our perception. In any case, even for a time drifter, there are logical rules."

"I understand your words, but I'm not sure exactly what they mean," Grodin muttered.

"The past drifters were vague about the definition of the paradox. The best they came up with was calling it a 'logical impossibility.'" Seeing the confusion hadn't left Grodin's face, Elki added, "Let me give you the best example. Let's say Romy goes back in time and kills his grandmother. That means his father would not have been born, and, in turn, he would not have been born. If he was never born, how could he go back to commit the murder?"

The blank look in Grodin's eyes had left him. "Yes, I see the logical impossibility."

Clapping her hands together as she laughed, Elki said, "Well, you understand it now as well as I do! We don't really know what happens from there, other than the Athar, being a supreme power, has a way of interfering. It does not appreciate the lack of logic."

Mist had zoned out the conversation. She was still focused on Romy, pondering his future with the see'ers. She would not go as far as to voice her own reservations about Romy's expected fealty. But her dreams had Romy in a different future from that Elki anticipated. Her thought process was shattered by a flash of bright orange from the other side of the observation window.

Elki tilted back, almost falling off her stool. Immediately, Grodin strode to the window, gun drawn.

"What was that?" Mist asked.

"The boy is out of control," Elki snapped. "He just attempted another fireball. It was small, as his previous ones were, when, suddenly, it grew to a massive size. Not knowing what to do with it, he threw it towards the target, but it veered off to the right and exploded. See there," she added, pointing to the spot.

Mist and Grodin saw what Elki did. In the right corner of the room was a wooden table, the flames encircling it being extinguished by the room's fire-retardant system. The once-pristine white walls were scorched, and black smoke was collecting along the roof line.

Elki pushed herself off the stool. "We better get down there before someone gets killed."

A few minutes later, Elki, Mist and Grodin arrived in the massive training room. Their noses were assaulted by the acrid scent of the *almost* catastrophe. Elki led them towards Efi and Romy under the guise of normalcy, ignoring the carnage before them. "It's wonderful to see you again—both of you." Elki focused on Romy. "I see you're working hard to tune your powers."

Romy could do no better than to spit out a bitter response as he glanced at the charred table. "Tuning—is that what you call that?"

Laughing, Elki offered, "No worries. We have many tables." Elki was an expert at conceiving positive motivation, when need be, and if there was ever a time it needed to be, it was now. She touched Romy's shoulder and confided her thoughts. "You're frustrated because you aren't progressing as fast as you think you should. I think you need to take a day off, relax, then continue with a fresh state of mind." Her fingers tapped Romy's shoulder several times. "You can do this," she added.

Romy liked Elki—a lot, but not so much at this moment. It didn't matter exactly the framing of her words. In fact, it probably didn't even matter who said the words to him, it would still have that patronizing edge he read into them. He didn't know what to answer while remaining polite. When the words finally came out, he felt foolish. "I will try my best."

Elki slid her arm through the crook at Romy's elbow, turning him towards the exit. "Excellent! Let's talk a little more, just you and I." She turned to Mist and winked. "Spend a few minutes with Efi. Get her thoughts."

Mist knew the wink. She had seen it before in negotiations. *Divide and conquer.*

Once Grodin, Elki and Romy left the room, Mist turned to Efi. She got right to the point, one she saw, but she suspected even Elki had not. "Do you agree?"

Efi was a centimetre shorter than Mist. She tilted her golden gaze up. "Agree with what?"

"Do you think the lack of adequate results is causing his frustration?"

"Well, that is obvious."

"Maybe not. I would offer another possibility," Mist replied. "Could it be, that the cause and effect are in reverse?"

Efi scratched her chin. "I have no idea what you mean."

"Perhaps the frustration comes first, and is causing the lack of results."

Efi's scratching fingers moved up to her temple. "What do…"

Mist walked towards the door and turned just before she exited. She grinned at Efi, a grin that was more sinister, a message visible in that itself. Her voice was a purr. "Think on it. You'll figure it out."

Mist left, leaving Efi dumbfounded. A few moments later, after considering the tone of Mist's voice and her odd gaze, she suddenly realized the inference. Her eyebrows shot up. The words came involuntarily. "Oh my." Her eyes opened even wider. "Oh, my!"

Chapter 8: The Fourth Beacon

The 17th day of the 5th month, Alpha Centauri year 0024.

Deep Space.

The Haven ice mining trawler, *Recovery Two*, was travelling through space at 20 per cent SOL. I'lish Mann, sister to Ryder Gunn, received a message from her brother ten days ago. It was short, but by no means simple. It stated,

> *Sister:*
>
> *Meet me at coordinates 3312, 248, 1475 on exactly the 17th day of the 5th month. Don't be late. I mean, you can't be late! Don't tell anyone except your immediate crew requiring this knowledge. And don't tell them until you're well on your way.*
>
> *I need you to bring me something—only one thing. Find me an expert in light waves and computers. I need a geek, but someone I can tolerate. The person you bring needs to be the most technically smart person you know.*
>
> *See you there.*

The *Recovery Two* was one of 24 space ships I'lish had in her fleet. At 66 years old, she was semi-retired and no longer active in the day-to-day operation of her company. She left that to others, only becoming involved at quarterly board meetings and annual reviews. However, she still carried more than significant clout. Decisions critical to the company's direction and future were not approved without her. She had veto power over everything and anything.

It really wasn't a bad fate. She thought, *it could have been a whole lot worse.* Quite a few years ago, more years than she cared to count, she was the president of the Sholite people. She held the position during the critical time when the Sholite fleet, having travelled across space for thousands of years, along with the remnants of the Korian fleet, finally arrived at Haven. It was a successful arrival, and one that would not have been so peaceful if not for the efforts of I'lish and her brother, Ryder, no matter that the efforts were dubious and deceitful. She chuckled as she recalled the consequences as, *taking one for the team.*

Once discovered, their political futures were annihilated. They were fortunate not to be in jail. In fact, perhaps it was a fortunate turn of events. She didn't have to deal with politicians. She could focus on her business and her family. Although she was shunned by many Korians on Haven, amongst the Sholites, she was well respected and considered a leader in their community.

Sitting in a comfortable armchair within one of two lounges aboard the mining trawler, she was gazing out the two-metre-wide, port-facing observation window. The scene in front of her made it easy to daydream. There were two nebulae in the far distance: the one slightly left was a swirl of yellow, while the one on the right was larger, most of it pink with a fiery red tail curling from the mass of space dust, helium and hydrogen. All this was backed by a plethora of stars, some barely visible, others so bright as to excite I'lish's mind with wonder of the unfathomable forms of exotic life they might support.

Her thoughts were interrupted by the clank of footsteps. Captain Josh Roskov was heavy set, but surprisingly light on his feet. With one hand sliding down each handrail, he skipped down the metal treads, his feet hitting only two of them. I'lish turned her head and smiled at the young captain as he took a seat beside her.

"Two hours to our destination," Captain Roskov reported.

As all the crew were, the captain was dressed casually, only dark blue coveralls giving him the distinction of his officer rank. Only he, his second in command and his engineering boss wore blue. The rest wore red, or white. It kept things simple. White coveralls were for labourers, cooks, clerical types and the such; there were very few of them on the vessel. Red was for maintenance and engineering personnel. These were the men and women who could make a difference in an emergency. Everyone knew, if the situation was critical, look for red coveralls to help you.

"Thanks, Josh," I'lish replied. She liked the man. She was the primary force behind him obtaining his own ship, even though he was only 24 years old. She saw him as decisive. He didn't panic in tough situations, and he cared for the people under him. A wry smile crossed I'lish's face. "You were one of the first babies born on Haven when we arrived, were you not?"

I'lish knew the answer, but Josh knew she liked to pester him about the fact. Josh sighed, then stated, "You know I was. When will you finally let that go?"

Her shoulder's rose in a shrug. "I was born over 1.5 light years from this location on Talus 3. I lived all my younger life in space, and at that time, I thought that's where I would die. There are days when I still feel odd when my body is held by the natural gravity of Haven, or when I breathe fresh, unprocessed air." She pointed out the window. "So, whenever I come back to space, there is a warm, comforting feeling, like that felt by a baby held by the arms of her mother. Out here—this will always be home."

Josh Roskov contemplated the awkward moment. He could remain silent, leaving I'lish to her thoughts, as many younger people do to elders. But that wasn't in his nature. "Many think of space as being empty. I was one of them." He grinned. "Do you remember my first space trip? I stowed away on one of your ore miners, almost freezing to death before the crew found me. At that point, there was no turning back, and the mining code does not allow free rides. So, even though I was only 16, the crew put me to work, and from that point, there was no turning back." He whispered the last few words. "I fell in love with space."

A wide, proud smile crossed I'lish's face. She knew the captaincy was only a start for Josh. He was a born leader. She knew, one day, he would rise to heights he would not expect. The thought pleased her. She tapped his thigh. "I know you're busy, but sit with me for just a few minutes. It's nice to share that space out there—my space—with you."

"Of course, Ma'am."

Josh stayed for 20 minutes before he made his apologies and left for the command deck. A little over an hour later, I'lish heard Josh's voice on the ship's intercom. "Prepare yourselves for deceleration as we break our warp bubble—in 30 seconds."

She felt the familiar bump at that time. Even though, as an experienced space flyer with space legs, she waited the recommended ten minutes before she rose from the chair. She headed to her cabin where she washed and prepared herself to meet her brother, Ryder, in less than an hour.

Her heart rate was increasing as the meeting came closer. She hoped Romy would be there. She hadn't seen him for five months, and even that was during a short furlough he had from the PAT forces during the Korian civil war. There was so much that had happened since then. She had been afraid for Romy when he was captured, and relief swept through her when she received a message from Ryder saying they had rescued their son. At times, it still felt odd when she thought of him as *her son*. As Ryder's sister, she was Romy's aunt. However, she adopted Romy when he was six, raising him in her own house. With Ryder being away exploring space for a large part of the time, she was the adult in Romy's life. She earned the right to the title, *Mom*, every time Romy called her by it.

It was time. I'lish made her way down to the lower level. She backed down the ladder into the shuttle where Captain Roskov was already waiting.

After lowering into one of the hard, molded seats, identical to the one the captain sat on, she asked, "Where's Marty?"

"Coming."

A few moments later, another set of feet became visible through the access hatch. Marty sat beside I'lish and, with a nod to her and the captain, said, "Howdy."

The ladder was lifted through the hatch that was then clanged shut. Once Roskov heard the familiar sound of the hatch locks being engaged, he lifted his wrist up towards his lips. He ordered. "All set. Let's go."

Immediately, the shuttle locks disengaged. The pilot, just in front of the three passengers, fired a vertical thruster, and the shuttle moved away from its mother vessel. Once clear, the main engines were fired, and the shuttle was on the way to its target. Through the curved front glass, three kilometres distant, I'lish saw the looming shape of the *Wayfinder*, Ryder's explorer spaceship. Beside it were two smaller vessels; Metro navy spider class gunships. When she saw them, it surprised her. She still had no idea what Ryder was up to. *Why did he need the protection of the gunships?*

It only took a few minutes before they docked under the *Wayfinder*. The hatch was cracked and another ladder lowered. Once the three visitors climbed out of the shuttle, Ryder was waiting for them along with his second in command. Throwing any and all formalities aside, Ryder sprang forward, enveloping his sister in a great hug while lifting her up on her tip toes. I'lish set her initial feelings of foolishness aside, returning the embrace.

Once they separated, Ryder, with a cheeky grin monopolizing his face, introduced his second, Lieutenant Jenholin. I'lish reciprocated, introducing Captain Roskov. She was about to introduce Marty, when Ryder interrupted, pointing, "Who's that?"

"That's Marty Mortenson, the scientist you asked me to bring along," I'lish replied.

For a moment, Ryder's eyes widened. But the look changed as they narrowed under lowered eyebrows. "He's just a kid!"

"*She,*" Marty corrected.

Ryder was a little above average height for a Korian. Marty was a head shorter and thin. Her hair, shaved short on the sides, was dyed an unnatural red colour. Many short bundles of hair, twisted in different directions, covered the top of her head—as if the locks had never seen a brush. That, along with the black pants and loose jacket, made it difficult to determine her gender.

Ryder set his feet in a wide stance, his fists bundled into his waist. He glared towards I'lish for a moment before turning his gaze down onto Marty. "Okay, *she's* just a kid! You don't look older than 14!"

Marty let out a snicker. "That's what Max Knudson said when he first met me, but at least he was astute enough to know I was a girl. By the way, I'm 22."

Mouth open, Ryder paused. Max Knudson was the most renowned Sholite astrophysicist on Haven. He was beyond famous. Finally, his jaw muscles worked. "You know Knudson?" Ryder scoffed.

Marty leaned on one leg, slouching to the side, giving the impression of boredom. "Yup. I worked under him for two years." Sarcastically, she snapped her fingers, then pointed at Ryder while her tongue pressed against the roof of her mouth, giving off a sharp *click*.

Ryder crossed his arms. "He must've got sick of you holding him back."

"Actually, he asked me to leave because he said he was holding *me* back." Before Ryder could reply, she added, "Do you have any snack bars on this tub? I'm hungry."

I'lish saw Ryder's knuckles turning white as he gripped the sleeves of his jacket. Before her brother said something he would really be sorry for, she blurted, "Ryder, before you get too wound up, why are we here?"

Realizing it was best for Ryder not to add anything, for the moment at least, Lieutenant Jenholin added, "We have a brief presentation explaining why. This way."

The lieutenant led them from the arrival area, down the hallway to Ryder's captain's room. Along the way, I'lish asked about Romy. He answered that Romy was safe, but not here. Her jaw fell, but only for a moment before Ryder told her they would see Romy in a few days.

Once they arrived at the ready room, Lieutenant Jenholin presented a series of slides showing the three previous beacons that had arrived in Alpha Centauri space. She explained the details regarding the timing and location of the beacons, and the Korian link. She finished her presentation by saying, "That means the next beacon will arrive..."

"Tomorrow." Marty had been quiet through the entire presentation, but now, after doing the mental math, finished Jenholin's sentence.

"That's right," Ryder added. "The strobing light seems to be the key to the beacon's purpose." During the presentation, Ryder considered Marty's self-described resume and thought, *perhaps he should not judge her so quickly*. "You must be smart," he told the young woman. "That's why you're here."

Placing her ankle on the other knee in a masculine pose, she pointed at I'lish and made the clicking noise with her mouth, again. "She's the smart one."

"How so?" Ryder asked.

"Well, she brought me, didn't she?" Marty replied.

All five of them burst out laughing. It was a good moment. Ryder raised his hand. "Okay. I get it." He looked at the young scientist. "I'm sorry for misjudging you. We're glad to have you here."

Lieutenant Jenholin rose to her feet. "Marty, you should come with me, and we can further review the details about the past beacons. We also have a lab set up for you."

Marty rose, but an odd look came across her face. It looked—hopeful.

Jenholin's eyebrows lowered, then they rose in realization. "Yes, we'll get a few snack bars along the way!"

The next day, in the first hour, I'lish and Marty arrived on the command deck. Ryder and Lieutenant Jenholin were already there. The beacon was expected somewhere in the zone pictured on the four screens at the front of the command deck, sometime today, but there wasn't an exact time. So, they waited.

And they waited longer. Four hours later, after Marty had made her way through three snack bars, Jenholin noticed it first. Wisely, their sensors were off. They were 250 kilometres from the target coordinates. On the front screens, where there had been just a pattern of distant stars, in the centre, the stars were out of focus. Soon, the stars were gone, replaced by a patch of black. A minute later, an electric-blue rim of light appeared around the blackness. The light pulsed around the blackness as it got larger. Finally, a gold sphere flowed out of the blackness, into the target area. The electric-blue light pulsed a last time, then faded as it shrunk away. The stars were once again within view, but now, a golden sphere was in front of the panorama. A few seconds later, it strobed the expected white light.

I'lish was the first to speak. "Wow!"

"Damn right, wow," Marty added. "That was some type of time-space shift. You're right. It's alien and much more advanced than we are."

"We think the key to discovering why the beacon is here, lies in that strobing, white light," Ryder offered as he peered at Marty. "What do you think?"

Marty shrugged. "Give me a little time and more of these snack bars, and I'll figure it out."

"That's great, *Kid*." Ryder replied with a wink.

I'lish wrung her hands together. "This is going to be more than interesting!"

"Well, not for us—at least not yet," Ryder said. "You and I need to leave for a bit. Marty will stay here, working on the beacon with Jenholin to help her," Ryder stated. "If they come up with anything, we'll be back quickly."

"But…but what could possibly be more important?" I'lish sputtered.

Ryder put his arm around his sister's shoulder and whispered in her ear, "Come with me." He led her off the command deck into his captain's room. After he closed the door, he continued. "Romy is at Midpoint. I received a message that he'll be travelling to Metro shortly. He might even be there already."

"So, we're going to Metro?"

Nodding, Ryder clarified, "If it's okay with you, The *Wayfinder* and one of the spiders will stay here. We can take your trawler to Metro with the other gunship."

"Sure." I'lish's face was aglow. She would see her son! But then, creases formed across her brow. "He's going to Metro." She added, barely above a whisper, "Does he know?"

There was a barely perceptible shake of his head. "Nope."

I'lish fell back into a chair, her legs stretched out. "Oh, shit."

Chapter 9: Metro

The 19th day of the 5th month, Alpha Centauri year 0024.

Midpoint station.

Forty-eight days. That's how long Romy had been isolated within the training area on the *Aramis*. Sitting on the edge of his bed, his feet felt the cold of the floor. It really wasn't cold, but in the morning, everything felt cold against them, especially after having been under the warm blankets all night. The tablet he had retrieved from the end table was on his lap. As he changed the duration in his log from 48 to 49 days, he questioned how long he would be locked up.

He liked the idea of having Efi all to himself, even though they held back the onslaught of emotions and remained at arms length. Although, Romy had noticed, since Elki and Mist's visit 27 days ago, Efi was more intimate with him. The moments of close contact between them, that had been infrequent, were now more often. Without that, by now he likely would have quit. Still, in those intimate, loving moments, when their passions were about to succumb to all out carnal need, she would become lukewarm to downright cold. She always put a stop to it before things went too far—at least what she considered too far.

A beep emitted from the communication device on the end table. It was the signal from Efi that breakfast had arrived. Rising, he pressed his feet into the leather slippers. He let out a frustrating grunt. The slippers were white, matching the pajama's he wore. They were white as well, as were the walls and the floor, the toilet in the bathroom, the towels and the toilet paper. Then, he remembered, and a sly grim crossed his face.

A few minutes later, Romy arrived in Efi's next door apartment. He smiled as he caught sight of her light-brown face, easily found in the sea of white. She was sitting at the table, serving the food onto his and her plates. Yes—white plates. She smiled at the sight of him, but even more so at the object he carried under his arm. Once he was near, he sat on the chair opposite her, placing the object in the middle of the table.

Efi's smile widened. It was the unique smile Romy loved. The center of her upper lip was always raised, like she was pouting, but the corners of her lips curled up into deep dimples. Romy, in his mind, tried to describe it. The best he came up with was, it was innocent, but so sexy at the same time, at least, if such a thing was possible.

"Where did you find that?" she asked through the smile.

The vase was bright red. Circling it were thin, light green rings, five of them in all. The width of Romy's smile now matched Efi's. "A few days ago, I couldn't sleep, so I searched through some of the cupboards in my room. Stuffed in the back of one, I spied this thing."

Efi leaned her elbow on the table, her chin supported by her palm. "It's ugly."

Romy had a forkful of food half way to his mouth when he paused, his blue eyes playful. "It's not ugly. It's really, really ugly. But at least it's not white!"

Efi starting eating. Between forkfuls of fruit, she pointed the business end of the fork at the vase. "There was a day when someone picked that colour combination. That's sad."

"Maybe it was an accident. A mislabelled can of pigment, or maybe the artist, if we can refer to her as an artist, forgot her eyeglasses that day and picked up the wrong can."

"He, not she."

"What are you talking about?" Romy replied, a quizzical look on his face.

After swallowing a mouthful of smoked meat, she twirled her fork towards Romy. "A woman wouldn't have selected those colours, but if she did, she would have destroyed the evidence. That vase—" she made a short jabbing motion towards Romy "—is a guy thing."

Momentarily, Romy froze, but then his head angled back, and he laughed uproariously. When his eyes came back even with Efi's, they were moist. He wiped away the tears about to form and muttered, "You're so precious." The words came through the last couple of snickers.

Leaning back, Efi crossed her arms, her one leg crossed over the other had her foot bobbing nervously up and down. "What did you say?"

Romy had recovered. He tilted forward on his chair. "I said, I think you are the most precious thing in this whole Athar. That's why I love you so much."

She melted. She rose to her feet, barely holding back her tears. Once near him, she backed down onto his lap, her arms thrown around his neck. She whispered, "And I love you," just before she tilted her face, pressing her lips to his in a lingering kiss.

Finally, Romy pulled away. His eyes that were dark and passionate, brightened as they widened. "Star fruit."

"What?"

Speculatively, he slid the tip of his tongue against his teeth. Pointing to the fruit plate, then her mouth, he said, "Seems you passed me a bit of your star fruit."

As he micro-chewed, she gave him a playful slap on his cheek. He had been learning the Mabuza language and was becoming quite proficient, but the string of fast paced words she spilt out were unfamiliar. Since he wisely thought it was best not to ask, he just assumed these were Bantu curses she was now sharing for the first time.

As she walked towards the bedroom, she tilted her head back and offered, "I had some things brought for you. They are in your room." Without waiting for the barrage of expected questions, she continued into her bedroom, closing the door behind her.

Tilting his head to the side, in a mocking, high-pitched tone, he muttered to the closed door, "Well, thanks for that, Sweetheart." In a subdued whisper, he added, "Thanks for waiting."

Once he entered his own apartment, he saw nothing of interest to break the sea of white. He moved into his bedroom. On the bed was a suit of clothing: black pants, a dark-blue shirt and a black jacket. On the floor were a pair of shoes—and they weren't training shoes. These were higher cut with a thick tread on the bottom. *They were hiking boots!* Then, his eyes returned to the blue shirt. He couldn't help himself as he blurted out, "The shirt has a collar! The shirt has a collar!" He strode to the wall, the one that separated his bedroom from Efi's. He pounded on it.

In response, barely audible, he heard her reply, "What is it?"

He yelled, and for some reason spoke slowly, like it would help Efi hear him through the wall. "Where—are—we—going?"

His eyes were wide, appearing perplexed when he heard her snicker. They became narrow slits when he realized what he heard as a snicker on his side of the wall, was surely a boisterous laugh on her side. When this subsided, he heard her reply, mocking as it was. "We—are—going—to—Metro."

He took a few steps back. "We are leaving?" he mumbled. He let out a howl and jumped, throwing a fist in the air. "We are leaving!"

An hour later, they were entering the departure hanger aboard the *Aramis*. The clothes Efi wore were similar to his in their cut, but her pants and jacket were dark blue, her shirt, light-blue. They were elegantly matched.

Efi placed her arm around him, her hand settling on his far shoulder. "You've only hopped a couple of times, so focus. It shouldn't be a problem. You've been training and improving your psychic powers. That will have strengthened your psychic connection to the Athar."

"Like before, just follow in your wake," he replied, his voice calm, a contrast to the basket of nerves he felt inside. He was hopeful the nerves were because of his excitement of their impending arrival on Metro, and not the fear of the transposition. Whichever it was, in a few moments they would find out.

As Efi moved into the centre of the room, he placed his hand on her shoulder. She whispered, "Here we go. Follow the marker." Right after her last word, the mind's eye view of the Athar exploded in his mind, brighter than he had ever seen it in the past. One light, a yellow one, was much brighter than the rest. He took slow, deep breaths, relaxing as he focused on that one point. He felt the queasiness in his gut, then the sense of falling forward. He resisted the urge to take a step forward for balance. He forced his eyes to stay open. He was moving through the beacons as they sped past him, accelerating until they were only seen as blurred lines. After a few seconds, the entire panorama blurred, the lights replaced by a hazy grey. When the haziness cleared, he almost fell forward. His fingers gripped Efi's shoulder for balance. He sighed in relief knowing she was still there.

"This is Shalkar, a Bantu world on plane 4456. It's a stopping off point for travellers, one of many such stopping off points for purebloods," Efi explained.

Efi had not divulged their connecting location prior to leaving. After all, it wasn't relevant to him. His feet shifted as he made a small circle. On one side of the platform was a large, steel and concrete building painted green. Without counting, it had to be at least 30 stories high. On the other side of the platform from the building was a narrow road. It was straight for about a kilometre in the distance, before it curled to the right. Finally, it was lost to sight as it entered a pass between two high mountains. Somewhat in awe, not so much at the beauty of the mountains; rather, he was in awe of the beautiful mountains on a different planet on a different plane of reality.

Efi poked her arm under his, pulling him towards the road. He now saw the complex of buildings on the other side of it. It was a small city, comprised of many different buildings having different sizes and heights. By the time they crossed over, Romy was panting.

"You did well, considering this is your third hop ever. But it's not a surprise you're tired. As you do more of these, it will be easier."

Efi led him to a building in the distance on their left. The lobby receptionist, a wide smile on his chubby face, offered a greeting. "Welcome back. So good to see you again, Miss Efi." Once the receptionist gave her a key, and before they left the counter, she ordered food to be brought to their room.

They took an elevator to the third floor, then, as they walked towards their room, Efi explained, "Normally, it would take about three hours for a pureblood to recoup enough of their body's energy before their next hop. You might need a bit longer."

By now, Romy was almost dead on his feet. He could do no better than to mutter, "Agreed."

Once in the room, he threw himself on the bed. He was asleep even before his head hit the pillow. Five hours later, he woke, feeling the massive hole in his stomach. Efi waved, urging him to the table where two plates of native food awaited them. He had no idea what it was, but it tasted fantastic. There were spices he had never experienced, and it reminded him there was so much that would be new to him.

The food helped, but he still felt weary. This time, Romy changed into pajamas he retrieved from the closet. Efi did the same, and they curled together in the bed. Romy quickly fell asleep, but Efi was troubled. It didn't help when Romy, in his slumber, pushed his hand up inside the back of her shirt. That in itself was not the problem. What was, was she liked the feel of his hand there. She loved Romy and wanted more of him, but she had always resisted the temptation.

Maybe Mist was right. Efi always wanted Romy's primary focus to be on his training and his purpose as the *drifter*. But, even though his progress with conventional training was exceptional, his psychic training was lacklustre at best. She always assumed his lack of progress was a vicious circle, beginning with his frustration, which in turn was caused by his lack of progress.

Mist had suggested an alternate theory. Romy and Efi loved each other intensely. That was obvious to them and anyone else who observed them together. But that also caused frustration. They had not had that most intimate moment people who loved each other as they did, had. Mist suggested that perhaps that was the source of Romy's frustration. Efi just didn't know it.

She felt Romy's hand shift under her shirt, his fingers dragging across her back. An involuntary growl slid past her lips. She rolled over and poked him in the shoulder. He stirred but did not wake. She poked him harder. "Wake up!" she hissed.

Romy's eyes shot open. "What?" His vision cleared, and he saw Efi undoing the buttons on her shirt, then she slid it off her back. She curled closer and pressed her lips to his—hard. Her hips twisted and turned as she wriggled out of the pajama bottoms. Now fully awake, Romy helped her free him from his own pajamas. Her fingers attacked the buttons on the shirt, while he all but ripped off the pants.

Their naked bodies slid against each other, their hands exploring areas they had never tested before. They left not a centimetre of flesh unexplored. It did not take long before Efi coaxed him to his back. Straddling him, she slid down with a sultry groan. As she moved on him, their eyes remained locked. It felt so good, Romy did not want it to end, but like a man on a mission, he lifted his shoulders as he wrapped an arm behind the small of her back. He lifted further, twisting as he pulled her under him. Her legs wrapped around his waist as he now led. He kissed her, then lifted his head. He wanted to watch her, and he wanted her to watch him.

It didn't take long. Her body began to shake. For him, that was it. He could take no more. His body jolted, then again for a second time. He leaned down. She thought he wanted to kiss her, but he bit softly on her lower lip. He held on until her body stopped shaking. Then, he kissed her—then, she cried, softly.

Once he rolled off her, she reached over, intertwining her fingers in his. There was no reason for words. The soft touch said everything. To her right, out the large picture window, she saw the sun just cracking the horizon. They could sleep for two more hours. She whispered an alarm command to the communication device on the small table beside the bed. Then, her eyes closed. Letting out a deep sigh, she felt content and happier than she ever had in her life. Sleep came easily.

By late morning they had washed, dressed and eaten again. Right after they left the apartment, Efi stopped and fumbled with the four thin bracelets on her right wrist. Two of them were black and two were silver, and each of the four had an intricately etched design. Removing one of the silver ones, Efi handed it to Romy. "You recall there is a clock on the end table beside the bed?"

"Why—yes," Romy stammered, confusion clouding his eyes.

"Put the bracelet on top of the clock. Leave it there."

"I don't get it?"

"You don't need to *get it* right now," Efi explained. "I gave your father an estimated arrival time. Hurry now, or we're going to be late."

Romy started to turn, but hesitated.

"Go, go," Efi urged, her downturned hand shooing him towards the door.

Shaking his head, Romy complied. Once in the room, he took a good last look around, then placed the bracelet on top of the clock.

When he returned to the hallway, Efi asked, "What time was it on the clock?"

Shrugging, Romy replied, "The numbers read 10:44—whatever that means in their time system here."

"You sure?"

"I'm not an idiot. Of course, I'm sure."

"You're sure it wasn't 10:43?"

Leaning down slightly, Romy put one hand on each of Efi's shoulders. He was frowning, and his eyes were dark. To keep himself from yelling, he forced himself to a low tone. "Efi, I don't know what you're playing at. The time wasn't 10:43. It wasn't 10:45. It was 10:44—exactly."

"Okay, just checking. We don't want to be late." She ducked down, freeing herself from his hands before striding down the hallway.

Romy was still shaking his head as they walked to the transposition platform. Efi asked, "So, are you ready for this—going to Metro?"

"Oh yeah," Romy replied.

Recognizing a new found tone, bordering on cocky, Efi raised an eyebrow and warned, "Now, don't get all weird and different on me. You still have a lot of training to do. It's going to continue on Metro with even more intensity."

"Yes, Ma'am. I'm in your wonderful hands," he snickered.

There were two groups ahead of them at the departure platform. As they waited, Efi mentioned, "I expect your father will be waiting for you."

He sighed. "I would like to think so, although he seemed to be fixated on those beacons."

"I sent him a message three days ago, indicating we would be going to Metro: date and time."

It was now their turn, so they loaded onto the platform. They repeated the same process as the day before. Romy put his hand on Efi's shoulder, but now, things felt different—she felt different under his touch, and he liked it.

His thought process was interrupted by the Athar appearing in his mind's eye. A red marker in the centre of the panorama glowed bright. He relaxed and let his psychic energy flow to it. When the haziness cleared, he felt strong, the feeling of vertigo only lasting a second. As such, he had his first look at Metro, the planet his father had led the explorers to, the world his father had led them to build.

The first thing noticeable was the dim level of light. He tilted his gaze up, and no matter how much someone would have described the scene, it would not have prepared him for what he saw. The sun was not just large. It was massive, covering most of the visible sky. For a moment, it shocked him that he could even look at it with the visible eye, but he could. This sun was a red star, with probably only a couple of billion years left in its life. The luminosity was 20 thousand times less than that of Alpha Centauri B, but then, they were much closer, only eight million kilometres away and well within the star's habitable zone.

His stupor was interrupted by a shout from his left. He turned to see a man walking briskly towards them. Just behind, matching the pace, was a woman. Once the man was in front of him, he saw he was no man; rather, he was a teenager, appearing about 16 years old. He had jet-black hair, flowing back and down to his shoulders. He was tall for his age, almost matching Romy's height. Distinct sharp features highlighted his face, and when the woman arrived to stand behind him, it was easy to see the woman was his mother. Yet, there was something familiar about him.

The boy's eyes were bright, even though they were dark-brown in colour. He was excited, exhibited by the words leaving his lips in a fast staccato. "You must be Romy Gun, correct?" Before Romy could answer, he shifted his gaze. "And Efi Kuma?"

"Correct on both counts. Where is Ryder Gunn?" Romy asked.

The boy smiled and the familiarity Romy saw grew. "Father sends his apologies. But he assured me he'll be here in two days."

His eyes wide, Romy's cheekbones sank, and his skin turned pale as if a great sickness just overtook him. "What do you mean, 'Father?'"

A silly grin came across the boy's face. "I wasn't sure he told you." He mumbled, "I guess I know now."

"Told me what?"

The boy lifted himself, shoulders square. "My name is Shayne. I'm your brother."

Chapter 10: Cliffside

The 20th day of the 5th month, Alpha Centauri year 0024.

Cliffside, Planet Metro, orbiting Proxima Centauri.

"You're my brother!" Romy yelled. He crossed his arms. "How did that happen?"

Shayne's lips widened as his nose wrinkled into the smirk to come. "I'm only 16, but I understand it's a process."

"Oh, you're a funny guy," Romy growled.

"I'm Naala." She stepped beside her son with a well-timed interruption.

"Naala Gunn, I take it you're my father's wife?" Romy challenged.

Naala was pretty and about ten years younger than Ryder Gunn. She smiled a really nice smile, and it softened Romy's mood. Her voice flowed, almost musical. "Yes, your father and I married 17 years ago."

Seeing Shayne open his mouth, Ryder snapped his fingers in front of his brother's face. "Don't bother. I know how that process works as well."

Naala, seeing Efi fidgeting nervously, stepped forward and gave her a great hug. Once she pulled back, she said, "You must be Efi. We heard you were coming with Romy. Welcome to Cliffside."

Efi thanked her, then let her gaze fall on Shayne. She gave Romy a nudge with her elbow. "He might be better looking than you are."

Letting out a guffaw, Shayne chirped, "What'd ya mean, 'might be?'"

Rolling his eyes, Romy muttered, "This is *fucked* up."

Naala, chattering with Efi, froze mid sentence, tilting her gaze to Romy. She waggled a finger. "I know what that word means. Ryder learned it from his grandmother from Earth." She cracked a smile. "But you're right. This is *fucked* up."

Efi and Shayne had blank, oblivious stares on their faces.

Turning to Efi, he whispered, "I'll explain it later." He shifted his gaze to his younger brother and, in a deeper voice, said, "I'll explain it to you in two years."

Shayne and the two women had a good chuckle and began a conversation Romy zoned out. He took in his surroundings. They were standing on a balcony, but because of its size, he considered it more of a small plateau. It was obviously man made since the plateau was a cutout in what he now saw was a rock cliff. As he tilted his gaze upwards, he saw there were many more cutout plateaus above him—at least 20, and each plateau was set back a short distance from the one below it.

The numerous plateaus were built into a tall, angled cliff, and as he scanned to the left and right, he saw the cutouts continued as far as the eye could see, some smaller, some vastly larger. He returned his inspecting gaze to the cliff wall on their balcony of rock. There were doors at ground level, the one in the middle being a wide façade of glass. Above this level were three more levels of windows and smaller balconies. The plateau he was on was 200 metres wide, and as he looked to his feet, he saw the rock they were on was the same as that constituting the back wall. The rock was black, with sparkles of silver in it. He saw the sparkling black rock as far as he could see in any direction.

Curious as to what was below their plateau, he strode to the edge of it, followed by Shayne, who left the two women to their chatting. There was a one-metre-thick, one-metre-high railing, made of blocks of the same black material, what Romy now assumed was a form of granite. Beyond the railing was a scene that took Romy's breath away. In contrast to the pink sky, monopolized by the massive sun, the panorama well below them was a sea of dark-green. It was thicker close to their location, thinning as his gaze moved further out. In the far distance, there was more grey than green, until he narrowed his eyes, bringing the mountain chain there into focus.

The far mountains were monumental, but the chain only ran for what he estimated to be 40 kilometres, and the peaks in the middle were higher, then, they progressively became lower near the two ends of the chain.

Shayne saw his brother's focus there, so he interrupted his stupor. "Those are the Meteor Mountains."

"Meteor?" Romy questioned.

"Over the past 20 years, our scientists have researched the formation of this planet. It seems during the planet's early, formative years, when it was just a cooling mass of rock, metal and dust, another cosmic entity crashed into it. The meteor was massive, leaving a great depression on the other side of the mountains, lifting the still pliable surface upwards on this side of it. As you might've guessed, on the other side is a depression, 250 kilometres in diameter. Now, filled with water, it is the Great Meteor Sea."

Romy was at a loss for words. He inspected what was in front of him.

Now, in the pockets of green and grey, he saw other pockets of water: small lakes and even some rivers running between them. As his gaze turned lower, he realized how high they were from the foothills below. There were at least another 40 levels of cutout plateaus below them, and running at the base of the cliff, again, to points as far as he could see in each direction, was a wide snaking river.

His lips parted, his jaw slack, Romy was hypnotized by what lay in front of him.

Shayne provided some added details. "There are about 20 thousand Metronians who live on this planet; 15 thousand live in this city, Cliffside, while five thousand live in a smaller settlement on the other side of the Meteor Mountains. It's called Meteor City."

The words were masked by an electrical whir from above them. Romy looked up and saw a shuttle flying overhead. It was white with a blue stripe along its length on each side. The women also noticed it, reminding Naala it was time to depart.

She yelled to her son, who turned towards her, his hand grasping Romy's elbow as he had to drag him away from the view of the foothills below.

They walked through the glass doors, into what Romy didn't expect. He expected the interior of Cliffside to be no more than a series of roughed out caves. Instead, the atrium was as elegant as any he had ever seen. There were small amounts of rock visible, but more was covered with coloured stucco and wood.

They continued down a wide hallway, leading further into the black granite of the cliff. After a few minutes, Naala stopped them at a series of three doors on their left. As they had walked further into the complex, other Metronians appeared. They passed several cross hallways, where even more people were visible. To Romy they looked no different than what he would have seen on Haven, although he could see a more even mix of Korians and Sholites. There were also many Mabuza, but here, they lost their rustic façade found on Haven, now wearing elegant clothes in bright colours.

Shayne pressed a button, and a minute later, the double doors opened. Two people were already aboard the elevator. The group entered, along with two Mabuza who had been waiting beside them.

Once the electric whine of the motors put the elevator in motion, Romy whispered to Shayne, "Where are we going?"

"Father has a large home 20 pods north of us. He rented an apartment close by for you and Efi."

"But we're going up," Romy replied, his brow furrowed with confusion.

Chuckling, Shayne said, "It'd be a long walk, so we need to catch the bus." He saw his brother's brow furrow even more, so he elaborated, "The blue and white shuttle is used if you want to go between even numbered plateaus. There are red and white ones for odd numbered plateaus. That keeps down congestion. At level 50 and at ground level, there are a series of air buses going south to north. At level 20 and 60, the same air buses travel north to south. It's how we get around Cliffside."

The elevator's climb was angled, matching the angle of the black, granite cliff. Once they arrived at level 50, they walked down a similar hallway towards the plateau. Back out under the pink sky of Metro, Romy saw a small group of people around each of two small structures in the middle of the platform. People were boarding a red and white shuttle at one building, while those at the other platform, instinctively looked to the south. A few minutes after they joined the other passengers, a blue and white shuttle landed in front of the small building.

There were five people already aboard the shuttle. Naala, Efi and the two men boarded, along with five others. Once seated, Romy saw Naala key the number 82 into a keypad by her seat. He assumed correctly that this was the pod number. So, their destination was level 50, plateau 82. The number lit up on a LED sign above the pilot, along with two other numbers.

Four stops later, they arrived at platform 82. Another elevator took them down to level 10. This is where Ryder and Naala had their home. Naala led them towards a cross hallway, but Romy saw the light from the plateau entrance ahead. He took Shayne's arm, leading him towards it. "We'll catch up with you in a few minutes."

Not waiting for a reply, Romy pulled Shayne out onto the platform, and sat on the edge of the black granite block wall. He looked upwards. "It's darker."

"I can explain that. Remember Great Meteor Lake. Well, that was made by a great big *fucking* meteor."

Smirking, with an eyebrow raised, Romy thought, *so he does know what the word means.*

"Our scientists say the massive amount of kinetic energy almost split the planet in two. But it didn't. What it did, though, is it created a massive crack down the entire centre of the planet. The two cooling halves shifted, but didn't come apart. That shift caused a cliff that goes around the entire planet. On one half, the cliff faces east. On the other side, it faces west."

"How does that make it darker?" Romy asked.

"The planet's rotation has a 20-degree tilt. So, for the first half of our daylight period, this area of the cliff faces towards the sun. In the latter half, we are in the shade. But soon it'll be night."

"You talk like a scientist yourself, Brother."

"I'm learning. I'd like to understand the stars better," Shayne admitted.

His eyes darkening, Romy scoffed, "You sound like Dad. You don't want to go there."

The distaste in Romy's tone was obvious. Shayne knew some of it since his father spent much of his time in space. There were times when it was hurtful to him, but he still saw Ryder Gunn often, something that had been stripped away from his brother. "You have unsettled business with our father," Shane concluded.

Romy slid off the wall, turned and slapped the top block. "Ya think? I haven't seen him in 18 years. We finally meet, and right away he is off exploring. Even though I am here, he still doesn't have time for me."

"He talks of you often. It's not been easy for him, either."

Slowly turning, it was as if his stare was burning a hole into Shayne. "You have no idea. He was here. He told you about me." His voice raised to a yell. "I didn't know about you," he continued, pointing a finger at his brother. "I didn't even know he was alive!"

"I'm sorry," Shayne whispered.

Romy's voice was nothing more than a whisper. "You're not the one who has to say he's sorry."

Romy felt his brother's hand on his shoulder. "You're right. I was lucky I knew about you. That way, I could look forward to this day when we'd meet." His own voice broke as he continued. "The day, I could tell you I love you, Brother."

Turning to face his younger brother, words escaped him. His eyes were moist, and before the tears flowed, he pulled Shane into a massive bear hug. Shane returned the embrace. Both of them silently cried. It was a beginning for the two of them.

Chapter 11: Bad Dreams

The 21st day of the 5th month, Alpha Centauri year 0024.

Deep Space.

Ryder's eyes opened easily. It was the ease resulting from not having been in a deep sleep. At first, he wasn't sure where he was, but the familiar hum of an electromagnetic drive told him he was in space. Yet, the hum was not as smooth as that of his own ship, the *Wayfinder*. It only took a second for his mind to clear. He was aboard the mining trawler, *Recovery Two*.

"Sentinel, time." He grumbled. The small cabin that had been so dark he could not see the end of his nose, brightened with the glow of green numerals on the ceiling. The voice matched the numerals. "It's 2:10."

"Sentinel, 30 per cent light." The ship's communication system reacted immediately with a low light level illuminating the guest quarters. Ryder rolled on his back while his hand wiped down his face. For a moment, he thought he should continue the effort to sleep, but that's what he had tried for the last four hours. For most of that time, he rolled from side to side, with an occasional, short slumber, but whenever he checked the time, it was to discover his eyes had only been closed for a few minutes, at best. Although the bed wasn't as comfortable as the one on his own ship, or at his home on Metro, that wasn't the issue.

The restlessness attacked him at least once a week, sometimes up to four times a week, notwithstanding which bed he was in. It was a pattern having haunted him over the past 18 years. Even thinking about it as he was now, just made it worse. He muttered a Korian curse before slinging his legs off the edge of the bunk. He pulled on his pants and the jacket, minus a shirt, then shoved his feet into his ankle-high boots.

It was the sleep cycle aboard the *Recovery Two*, so he tried to be silent. He gingerly opened the cabin door, moving out into the hallway. Here also, the ceiling lights were set to 30 per cent, as they were in the main lounge he arrived in after quietly stepping down the four steps from the hallway. He glanced around the lounge, seeing it empty, as he expected at this late hour. He strode to the counter to his right, again gingerly opening one cabinet door, then the next. The third open door revealed what he was looking for—the blue bottle of alcoholic fruit wine. There was also a small fridge from which he retrieved a cold glass, then ice from the freezer above it.

He made quick work of the first glass of wine, downing it in one gulp. He was refilling the glass when a familiar voice surprised him.

"It's a little early for that, isn't it?" I'lish asked.

Ryder paused, but only for a second, before refilling the glass. His eyes shifted to the observation window across the room. Just in front, her face peaking around the headrest of a high-backed chair, was his sister. "Not when I can't sleep," he grumbled in a hoarse reply.

As her brother shuffled towards her, she asked, "Does that happen often? I don't mean the drinking; rather, the lack of sleep."

Falling into the chair beside I'lish, Ryder stared off into space through the wide window. "It's nothing for you to worry about," he replied in the most reassuring tone he could muster.

"That's not convincing. Maybe all this time in space, all the responsibility, and now the beacons, are a bit much. Your second in command seems more than competent. Leave it to her for a time."

"She is, and the *Kid* seems really smart. But it's not the beacons," Ryder admitted, before taking a deep drink from the glass.

Ryder appeared visibly different than I'lish had ever seen him before. She couldn't put her finger on it. He was a confident man, and he didn't ever appear weak. Then it came to her. He appeared vulnerable. She reached over and put her hand on his. "What's going on, Ryder?"

For a moment, Ryder was silent as he rotated the glass, the fruit wine and ice swirling within it. He hadn't seen his sister in many months. Maybe it was time for him to confide in her, so he did. "I'm not as strong as you might believe."

I'lish's brows lowered. "How so?"

He swirled the wine again, then threw back his head, letting the contents of the glass empty into his mouth. The thought was that the wine would lubricate his mind, making the words easier, but they weren't. They still stung when he said them. "I'm a coward."

Bolting upright, I'lish would hear none of it. "No, you're not. You're one of the bravest people I know. You've done more for the Korians, Sholites, and now the Metronians, than anyone."

"Except my son," he replied, his voice cracking.

"This is about Romy?"

A heavy sigh escaped Ryder's lips. "Yup. The lack of sleep, my misgivings and my hesitations are because of what I've done to Romy."

"I was with him. He was…"

"Yes, you were, and I wasn't!" The crisp words cut through the air.

A realization came over I'lish. "Surely, you talked to him about this when you travelled from Haven to Midpoint."

"He tried several times. I kept pushing him away."

"Ryder!"

Even through the dim light, Ryder could see the anger in his sister's eyes before it turned to disappointment. He could not look at her, so he looked at his glass, wishing there was still some alcohol in it. But it was empty, so he shifted his eyes, gazing off into space. He shrugged. "I told you, I'm a coward."

Chapter 12: Finally

The 21ˢᵗ day of the 5ᵗʰ month, Alpha Centauri year 0024.

Cliffside, Planet Metro, orbiting Proxima Centauri.

The dimness of the sun at this mid morning hour closely matched the forever twilight she was most accustomed to on Haven. Or so Efi thought, as she walked a few paces behind Romy and Shayne, giving them the space she assumed they needed. After breakfast, Romy had requested a visit to the surface of Metro, so that's where they now were.

The boardwalk they were walking on was comprised of long, flat boards of exotic wood, each three metres long, secured along their long edges. The wood was charcoal coloured, making the grain almost invisible, but from above, it was easy to see the boardwalk with the thick border of yellow, long grass on either side of it. Since the boardwalk mirrored the winding river at the base of the cliff, their path curved until, just ahead, they saw a vast amount of water gushing out from the cliff's base. The torrent of water angled upwards as it left the confines of the black marble, then fell into a large pond, which in turn, flowed into the winding river.

Efi hurried up alongside Shayne. "Where does the water come from?"

"From up there," Shayne replied, pointing to the top of the cliff, some 900 metres above them.

Both Efi and Romy looked skyward, seeing only the black edge of the cliff against the pink morning sky.

Shayne added, "On the vast plateau above us, the black rock is prominent for 200 metres back from the edge. Beyond that is fertile soil and the plants, animals and water sources that tend to go with it. When the explorer settlers first came here, at many points overtop of where the city is now built, waterfalls cascaded down the black cliffside. Of course, the engineers within the group set to building sluice channels at various points. The water that likely, for many thousands of years, flowed over the cliff, now flows down the channels and into reservoirs like this one here."

"You take advantage of the flow converting it from potential to kinetic energy?" Efi asked.

Shrugging, Shayne replied, "We do, because it's there, but in reality, we have all the energy we need, ever since bluranium was discovered."

Romy scratched his head. "Why did you build the city here? If the cliff goes right round the planet, why not pick a location where the water above is not such an issue?"

"Two reasons," Shayne explained. "We do need water, but the main reason is the *Armatods*."

In unison, both Romy and Efi said, "Armatods?"

A laugh burst from Shayne's lips. "Wow! It's like you were singing." Not hearing Efi or Romy join his laughter, he cleared his voice and answered their continued curious stare. "Right—Armatods—it's easier to show you." On the last word, he turned and led them away from the rush of water. Half way around the pond was a beautiful round patio, surrounded by stone benches. Behind the benches were tall grasses, but not the same as the yellow variety bordering the boardwalk. These were as pink as the sky, and the thick stalks were adorned with massive green and purple flowers. The flowers had multiple petals with each being at least 30 centimetres long and again half as wide.

Efi grasped Shayne's elbow, bringing him to a stop. "The flowers are huge."

"All the vegetation on Metro is oversized. The luminosity of the sun is low, and the plant life needs as much sunlight as they can get. This is what flowers on this planet have evolved into."

A snicker escaped Romy's lips as he poked his younger brother. "'Luminosity'—that's a big word for a 16-year-old."

Ignoring the moment of sarcasm, Shayne turned and strode off, down the pathway leading towards the river. The path ended at a stone bridge, and when they were half way across it, Romy stopped and peered over the side.

"Fishing is good here. But be careful. There are larger carnivorous fish," Shayne warned. "We keep them out of this part of the city with metal screening at the city's two ends."

Shayne slapped Romy on the shoulder, urging him on, the look in his eyes showing he was becoming impatient with his older brother.

As soon as they crossed over the river, Shayne led them into the tree line. The grass was knee high at first, but as they delved deeper into the forest, at least half the sunlight was blocked by the massive leaves on the trees. As a result, the grass was shorter and only appeared in swaths surrounded by areas of bare soil. These trees appeared to all be of the same variety, relatively short, but the huge dark-green leaves spread at least 15 metres from the black, gnarled trunks.

Once they were 50 metres into the forest, Shayne turned, leading them on a heading parallel with the river. Shayne lifted his finger to his lips, indicating Efi and Romy needed to be silent. They became more aware of forest signs. Now that they were further away from the cliff, a slight breeze rustled the large leaves, and the massive connecting stalks groaned with the movement. Yet still, they could hear the signaling of several varieties of what they assumed must be birds.

The setting was serene, but it changed instantly when Shayne led them into a small clearing. Within it, there were mounds of raised soil in three rows, with five mounds per row. At the head of each mound, flowers had been planted.

Efi was confused, not sure what to make of them. Still, she asked, "Flower beds?"

Shayne snapped back, "Close. They're graves." He knew a sarcastic comment was being formulated, but he didn't wait for it as he strode towards the closest row of graves. Once they were at the edge of the row, under the shade of one of the massive leaves, he warned, "Make sure you stay at the edge of the cemetery. They don't like it if we walk through."

"*Who* doesn't like it?" Efi asked.

"The Armatods." Shayne squatted as he pointed to the other side of the graves. "See the footprints in the soil there."

Romy squatted as well, and he saw them, large footprints, double the size of his own, but the more interesting feature was whatever foot made them, sunk four centimetres into the soil. "They're big," he stated.

Rising back to his full height, Shayne explained. "Armatods are an indigenous species we found on the planet. I'm careful with the term species since they're at the point in their evolution where they are turning from a species to a people. And they aren't so much big as they're heavy. They have blue blood, and we suspect they began their life cycle as a crustacean species. They grew in size, became upright, and over the millions of years of evolution, they've lost half of their protective shell. Critical areas are still covered: their skull, shoulders, back, knees and elbows, but the remainder has become soft tissue, allowing them greater flexibility and movement."

Romy noticed three of the graves had long spears on top of them. "They have weapons?"

Nodding, Shayne replied, "Crude spears, shields and knives. They haven't discovered the bow yet, but that'll happen soon."

Efi interjected, "Do they attack you?"

"There are two subspecies of Armatods: Reds and Whites, each named for the colour of their skin. The Reds are more intelligent and quite docile, except when they come across Whites. They don't like each other. When we arrived, the Reds looked upon us as higher order gods. That's why they bury their dead close to us."

"Where are the Whites?" Romy asked.

"There are many more Whites than Reds. The Whites live on the other side of the planet. They're not as smart, but they're more aggressive. That's why we chose this location for our city."

Romy, in particular, didn't want to leave, hoping to catch a glimpse of a Red, but Shayne insisted they had been there long enough. As they retraced their steps back to the bridge, Shayne showed Efi and Romy pictures of Reds and Whites on a small tablet.

"There's an intelligence in their eyes. Can they talk?" Romy questioned.

As they recrossed the bridge, Shayne said, "It's not talking, but they have 20 distinct sounds they can make. They've started to sequence the sounds, so we've distinguished 32 distinct communications."

Efi added, "So, they can communicate in a crude manner?"

"Yes, Shayne offered. "At this point in their evolution, their language is forming."

They were now on the boardwalk when Romy opened his mouth to ask another question.

Interrupting, Shayne offered, "Let's do something else."

"Like what?" Romy asked.

"Anything that isn't me explaining and teaching you stuff."

"Smartass!" Romy quipped.

Shayne winked at Romy. "I'm only 16. You should feel bad since I have to explain so much of this to you, newcomer or not."

The three of them laughed together at Shayne's wit. But Shayne was serious. He had enough teaching for the day. Shayne reminded them Ryder would be back the following afternoon, so not to be scarce. His mother, Naala, was excited for an actual family gathering, for which she was having a festive meal prepared. Shayne gave Romy and Efi a hug, then left them at the hallway to the apartment that had been arranged for them.

As Romy walked into the apartment, facing away from Efi, he muttered under his breath, "Father and the word 'scarce' in the same breath. That's cute." He could only roll his eyes at the thought.

Ironically, late morning the following day, Shayne was about to knock on Romy's apartment door, when he heard *squishy* noises coming from the far end of the hallway. He saw two silhouettes framed against the light from the glass doors at the end of the hallway. Once they came closer, he saw they were Romy and Efi, both dripping wet.

A silly grin crossed Shayne's face, but before he could send out a smart comment, his older brother flashed a finger under his nose. "Don't say a word," he warned.

As Shayne followed them into the apartment, Romy headed straight for the bathroom, pulling off soaked pieces of clothing as he went. Before Efi followed him, she whispered to Shayne, "Don't go away. You have to hear this."

Shayne walked to the wall-to-wall windows looking out over the foothills below. They were on the second floor on pod 82 on the tenth level. The apartment was beside his father's, although his was bigger with two luxurious floors. Turning, he surveyed the main room. It was open concept with a sitting area, dining table and a food preparation area. He thought it resembled his own apartment, one floor down, just his was not as neat and tidy.

A few minutes later, Efi appeared from the bedroom, a towel being stroked back and forth across her hair. She threw herself down on the cushion beside the one Shayne was sitting on. Her hand came up to cover her lips, trying to muffle the giggle that wanted to burst free. After she regained her composure, she set about explaining their water adventure.

"After you left us yesterday, I decided we should take some time with some pureblood training. Your brother has only hopped twice, so it was a good time to get a few more under his belt."

Shayne knew about his brother's pureblood powers, and that the Bantu people considered him special, hence all the added attention he was getting.

Efi continued, "We decided to leave from the patio by the pond we saw yesterday. I led the way to Rejilon, a beautiful planet with millions of islands in a vast planet-wide ocean. He followed in my wake," Efi added with a questioning gaze.

Waving his hand, Shayne interjected. "I know what the wake is."

"Well, we arrived—no problem. We stayed five hours, then hopped to another plane, a desert world." She leaned closer to Shayne. "Your brother is strong. He has great potential."

There was a twinkle in Shayne's eyes. "Not much water on a desert planet."

Tilting her head, Efi agreed, "Point taken. Now, in these hops I have always led. I told your brother it was time for him to lead. He was skeptical, but I insisted he lead us back to the patio beside the pond."

Chuckling, Shayne said, "I can see what's coming."

"The good news is, he led us back to this plane. It was his first such successful endeavour. Now, the bad news was his aim was a bit off. He must have been distracted by the thought of the pond rather than the patio."

"Oh, no!" Shayne cried out.

"Oh, yes!" Efi replied. "When we materialized back on Metro, it was to find our toes tickling the surface of the pond. From there, basic physics dropped us into the cool water."

Shayne was already laughing, uproariously, when Efi joined him. This was the scene Romy saw and heard when he came into the living area. He dropped himself into a chair opposite to them. For a moment, they paused, but when their gaze fell on Romy, his hair still dishevelled from his shower, they burst out in laughter once again.

Romy lifted his foot on top of the table in front of him, then lifting the other to cross his ankles. "Enjoy it while you can," he grumbled.

Eventually, the laughter did subside. Shayne said, "I didn't come here just for the fun, but, honestly, it made the visit much more worthwhile."

"Then, why did you come, Brother?" Romy replied, dryly.

"My mother told me, 'The two of you need to be at father's apartment for 17:00 hours.' He will be back, and mother says he has a surprise for you."

Romy scoffed, "What, like he might spend some time with me?"

Confusion clouded Shayne's eyes, "What?"

Waving his hand, while shaking his head, Ryder said, "Never mind. I don't think you'd understand."

Shayne's eyes softened. He just got the realization the relationship between their father and Romy was more fragile than it should be. "I'm told he'll be staying for a bit."

There was no point in Romy venting at his brother, so he stopped the line of discussion. He was genuinely thrilled at discovering he had a brother. He was impressed with his intelligence and, at the same time, he seemed practical. He gave Shayne a wide smile. "I'll see you there. I'm looking forward to it."

Once Shayne left, Romy realized they had a few hours free. He looked across at Efi, and his heart stirred. *He loved this woman,* he thought. She returned his gaze, one she had come to know well. Even before he tapped his thigh, she was on her feet, moving to him. In a fluid motion she straddled him, leaning in with a passionate kiss. Pressing down, she moaned, causing him to stir. He tangled his fingers in the hair at the back of her neck, tugging her lips away.

He whispered, "You know we'll have to have another shower."

Her eyes were half closed, her voice a sultry purr. "Uh, huh." Then she leaned into another kiss before they lost themselves in each other's loving embrace.

Just before 17:00 hours, Romy knocked on the door to the Gunn household. Naala answered a moment later, smiling wide at her step son, then embracing him in a hug. She was about to do the same to Efi, when she glanced at her face. She grasped her shoulders and said, "Efi, are you okay? You look flushed."

Efi let out an awkward chuckle. "Everything is great. I just got out of a hot shower."

Naala ushered them in. There was one other couple Romy didn't know. They were in a discussion with Shayne. To the right, in front of an expansive window, he saw his father, speaking to a woman facing away from Romy. It took Romy only a moment to recognize the long, black hair. He rushed over, yelling, "Mother!" Before she fully turned, Romy had his arms around her, lifting her up on her tip toes. "You're the last person I expected to see here!"

I'lish had tears in her eyes as she settled down to her feet. She clasped her son's face, giving him a kiss, first on one cheek, then the other. "It's been about eight months since I saw you last."

Wrapping his arm around his mother's waist, Romy turned towards his father, looking sharp in a dark blue suit. "Hello, Dad."

Not to be out done, Ryder took a step closer and hugged his son—and even gave him a kiss on the cheek. It was at that point when Ryder noticed the difference. "You shaved."

"Even though my beard was brown, I didn't want people mixing me up for you," Romy said.

"Not a chance of that," I'lish interjected. "All this space travel is putting years on your father."

"Maybe he should spend less time in space, then," Romy added. "What do you think, Dad?" The words were playful, but Romy's gaze, not so much.

"What do I think? I think you need a drink." Before Romy could reply, his father was off towards the bar.

"You see that, Mom. I have barely seen him since he rescued me, but each time I allude to the fact we need to have a serious discussion, he deflects the way he did just now," Romy explained.

I'lish turned, looking into her son's eyes. Softly, she said, "I don't have a position on this. It's something the two of you need to resolve."

Efi, who had been with Shayne, walked over, and leaned in the last metre. "I'm not interrupting anything, am I?"

"Have you met Efi before?" Romy asked his mother.

"Once, briefly, when she came to visit Valre."

Stepping beside Efi, Romy wrapped his arm around her waist, then faced I'lish. "I love Efi, and I'm going to spend the rest of my life with her."

"Really…"

"I thought I should get that out there," Romy added.

Ryder came back carrying four drinks on a tray. "I heard that," he said. "Congratulations." Then, he handed a drink to each of them. "I'll drink to that."

Romy and Efi met the other couple. He was Naala's brother, and the woman was his wife, both younger than Naala. Things were going very well, allowing Romy and Efi to relax. There was no training, no hopping, just banter between family and two new-found friends.

After an hour, Naala clapped her hands together. "Dinner is being served. Please follow me."

Naala had hired caterers who had been busy. From the living area, they were led to the dining room, where they saw the caterer's work. The large square table was covered with white silk, gold plates and cutlery. It seemed Shayne knew his place, moving behind a chair backing onto the window. Ryder moved to the center chair on that side. Efi and Romy moved to the adjacent side and were about to sit, when Ryder said, "Romy, I've waited for this moment to have both my sons beside me. Please," he offered as he held his palm open to the chair on his right side.

Walking around behind Efi, Romy answered, "Of course." He continued in a whisper, "I mean, it's only been 18 years."

I'lish and Efi, sitting closest to the three Gunn men, heard the comment. They also saw Ryder whisper in Romy's ear, while his hand gripped his son's shoulder, urging him to sit.

The first soup course came, and the banter was light, mainly with Shayne and Naala's brother, Mason, updating Ryder on the comings and goings on Metro. The second course was a meat course. The discussion changed as, by now, whenever someone began a discussion about Metro, or for that matter, anything, somehow it was twisted into a discussion about Ryder's space exploration—and the mysterious beacons.

Romy shoveled the forkfuls of meat and vegetables into his mouth. He wasn't even aware what the meat was, or was that last bite a vegetable? Such was his distraction with his father's obsession.

Efi noticed, placing a hand on Romy's, but he pulled his hand away, his gaze like dark darts of warning. She thought, *this isn't going to end well.*

A fruit pudding was brought for dessert. It was so elegant, they felt it would be a crime to disturb it with a spoon, but they all did. And it tasted even better than it looked. However, Romy didn't notice, as his father continued to describe his exploits. There came a point where Ryder realized he was carrying too much of the conversation. He looked at Romy, then Shayne, and through a smile said, "This is the first time I've had both my sons by my side. This is absolutely great!"

"No, it's not," Romy muttered.

"What?" Ryder asked, turning back to his older son, furrows forming on his forehead.

"I said, 'No it's not.'" Romy rose to his feet, the chair skidding backwards. "It's not fucking great!" He yelled, the last word drowned out by the sound of his fist slamming into the table.

As Romy's pudding bowl and spoon, slid off the table, clattering onto the floor, Ryder's eyes were unnaturally wide. "Son, what's come over you?"

Romy's face was a deep red, his eyes were boring down into his father's.

He spat out the words. "You left me behind for 18 years, now you want to act as if it never happened. It's time I told you, it did!" His fingers were curled into white knuckled fists. Efi leaned away, thinking Romy might actually strike his father.

Ryder's jaw was slack, his lips open. He looked at Efi, a pleading look. There was no support there, so he looked to Naala, but when their eyes met, his wife turned her gaze downwards. Finally, he looked at his sister. "I'lish, talk to your son."

I'lish rose to her feet, throwing her napkin on the table. "No, *you* need to talk to your son."

Each word stung Ryder as he shrunk back in his seat. It didn't matter that it was awkward. Naala knew as well that this confrontation would come one day. She rose, also placing her napkin on the table, more elegantly than I'lish had. She clapped her hands and a servant appeared. "Prepare after dinner drinks." She glanced around the table and clapped again. "Everyone up—into the living room."

Ryder shifted his chair back, but Naala gave him a, "no, not you. You and Romy need to talk." With that, Naala and the guests left the room. She gave a look back at her husband, giving him a reassuring smile. Then she closed the door.

Romy sat down and for a good five minutes, neither of them said anything. Finally, Ryder offered, "Damn, Son this is a bit extreme, don't you think?"

Sighing, Romy replied in a low voice, "Not really. Leaving me behind for 18 years, letting me think you were dead—I would call that extreme."

"I always had people watching over you."

"They weren't my father. You're my father."

"It was all to keep you safe. Out here, in space, there were…"

Romy's words had an edge to them as he interrupted, "It wasn't about my safety." He glared at his father as his voice rose. "You were more interested in exploring space!"

Ryder shot to his feet, the chair falling back on itself. "You have no idea how hard it is to be Ryder Gunn!" His hands began to gyrate in the air as he paced behind the table. "On Haven, I was the hero turned to a zero, considered the biggest traitor the Korians had ever seen. Then, out here in space, I'm supposed to be the explorer's saviour. They came out here following me. Do you really think I wanted any of it!"

Romy jabbed a finger towards his father. "Don't tell me how hard it was for you. Do you know what is harder than being a traitor or a saviour?"

"What!"

Shooting to his feet, Romy yelled, "Being the fucking son of a traitor or saviour!" He jabbed Ryder in the chest. There was venom in his voice. "Being the son of Ryder Gunn."

The words cut Ryder as surely as if a sword just ran him through. He leaned forward, his fingers clenching the edge of the table. He turned his face away from his son, and his body began to quiver. An uncontrollable sob escaped his lips. He didn't dare look at his son, but he needed to say his piece. The time had come. Through the sobs that now racked him, he said, "I'm not a zero, Son—certainly not a hero and not a saviour. I'm somewhere in between, just a man with faults." He brought his sleeve up, wiping it across his nose. He cleared his voice, then continued, gaining some strength in his voice along with a momentary spurt of conviction. "I'm a coward, Son. And I've been selfish. I've lost a lot of sleep over it, but you're right. It's not about me." His voice cracked. "I can't take it back." His voice grew louder. "All I can do is try and make up for it now." His face turned towards his son. His cheeks were wet with tears. "I love you, Son. I'm so sorry." Another sob caught in his throat. "Please forgive me, and let's start again—please," Ryder begged.

It was like a mighty weight lifted off Romy's shoulders, one that had been there for 18 years. Tears were streaming down his own face. He lunged forward, wrapping his arms around his father. They embraced for a long time, until the wracking of their sobs subsided.

Romy realized he really didn't say very much. It was his turn. "It's all good, Dad. I can get over the past. I do forgive you for that."

In the living room, Efi, I'lish and Naala remained after Naala's brother and his wife made a hasty departure. It had been a good half hour since the yelling stopped. The three women argued about who should check on them. The two older women convinced Efi she had the least to lose, so she crept to the door, quietly cracking it open. She let out a sigh of relief as she waved the other two women over. The door was cracked wider, and the three women saw Ryder and Romy facing each other, beside two bottles of wine, one empty, the other almost there. It appeared the two men were telling stories, making up for the last 18 years. It was good to see them smiling and to hear the laughter a father and son should share.

Chapter 13: The Harshlands

The 26th day of the 5th month, Alpha Centauri year 0024.

Cliffside, Planet Metro, orbiting Proxima Centauri.

The Gunn family had just finished a plentiful dinner of smoked meat and barbequed root vegetables with two round loaves of freshly-baked bread. Ryder, Romy and Shayne sat along one side of the table situated in the middle of the large patio adjacent to Ryder and Naala's home. On the other side of the table sat the Gunn women, Naala, I'lish and Efi: present, past and soon to be.

The temperature was markedly warmer than Romy had felt since he arrived on Metro. His father explained Metro's orbit around Proxima Centauri was only 11 days, and with the tilt of the planet at 20 degrees, up to a five-degree temperature shift is felt at opposite sides of the orbit. When Romy arrived, Cliffside was five days out of its coldest zone. Now, five days later, this location, which was well into the southern hemisphere, was at it's warmest time.

For Romy and Ryder, the past four days had been wonderful. Having left the women behind, Ryder focused exclusively on Romy, showing him everything worth seeing at Cliffside. This included, the five shopping complexes, the farmlands just off the northern tip of Cliffside, the spaceport at the southern tip, and of course, the Science and Technology Centre.

At the same time, I'lish and Efi got to know Naala. They found her sharp as a whip with an exceptionally outgoing personality. They could see why Ryder married her. Naala also showed them the sights, although most of their time was spent in the shopping complexes.

Slouched back in his chair, Ryder rolled his hand over his stomach. "That meal was awesome. I couldn't eat another bite."

"But there is dessert to come," Naala suggested.

Romy waved his hand. "I agree with Father. I'm stuffed. Maybe we can save the dessert for later?"

"Of course, Romy," Naala replied. "It's sweet nut…"

"Sweet nut pie," Shayne interrupted. He pushed his chair back, rising to his feet. "I'm a growing boy, so, I'm going to the kitchen to get a piece now." Then, he added, "And another later with the rest of you." Before his last word left his lips, he turned towards the aroma of the baked goods.

I'lish's eyes followed Shayne, then turned to Romy. "He reminds me so much of you when you were that age."

Romy smirked. "What—he is as smart as I am?"

I'lish cocked her head, grinning. "No, I was thinking you ate a lot in your youth."

They all broke out in laughter. They were all happier than they could remember, and I'lish would have liked to stay longer. When the laughter subsided, she stated, "I have to leave tomorrow."

"Why?" Romy asked, suddenly alert. He wanted to spend more time with his mother.

"I won't be far." She paused for a moment, thinking how best to share the news. "In two days, there is a meeting between Haven officials and several members of the Metro council, including the prime minister. Although, officially, we are not at war, our relationship is fragile at best. So, this is a meeting to develop a lasting peace."

"And to get at our bluranium," Naala added.

Before taking a drink from the glass of water I'lish just picked up, she agreed, "That too."

Ryder's brow furrowed. He was confused. He knew both he and I'lish were forbidden from any involvement in political affairs. He took the opportunity to remind his sister of it.

"You should know politicians are fickle. They make, keep and rescind agreements and proclamations as long as it suits them," I'lish explained. "The Haven government has asked me to lead the negotiations."

"But why you?" Romy asked.

"It should be obvious. They think I have leverage with your father, and from that, leverage with the prime minister."

Ryder responded, "But I have very little influence in political circles."

I'lish opened her eyes wide while tilting her head; it was a comical look. "That's what I told them, but they didn't believe me. Nevertheless, that means I'm taking the *Recovery Two* to the meeting coordinates, tomorrow."

"But that's my ride back to my ship!" Ryder exclaimed.

"Hopefully, you have more influence with your Explorer Corp. than you have with the politicians," I'lish said with a smirk. "You can try and hitch a ride with them."

Efi had been silent through the conversation, since she had her own announcement. It appeared this was as good a time as any for it. "Romy and I are leaving tomorrow, as well."

From behind Efi, he heard Shayne's muffled words. "Leaving to where?" he said, plate in hand, another forkful of pie on its way to his mouth.

Romy turned his face to Efi, one eyebrow lifted. They had talked of this, but he was unaware this would happen so soon.

Efi continued, "You all know about Romy's unique powers. We have been training, but now, we come to a crucial stage. There are too many distractions here. We need a few weeks away for him to continue his progress."

Swallowing the last chunk of pie, Shayne repeated, "I ask again, where to?"

"It's not too far from here, relatively speaking," Efi said, her voice a tone lower. "We're going into the *Harshlands*."

Just before leaving Cliffside, Romy and Efi had a debate as to who would drive the land crawler. Romy convinced her the four-wheeled vehicle was similar to some of the all-terrain vehicles he had driven when he was in the PAT military forces. As such, Romy was behind the steering wheel as they drove on the main highway between Cliffside and Meteor City. The scenery was stunning, their view on both sides filled with the fat, gnarled *Marcatta* trees they had seen monopolizing the shores of the winding river at Cliffside. But after ten kilometres, that changed. Some Marcatta trees were still there, but there were just as many trees of a different variety, these having brown trunks with large orange leaves. Then, there were vast areas where there were no trees at all, only thick groves of tall bushes.

When Efi had explained to Shayne what type of area they were looking for, Shayne programmed a location into the nav system. Now, she was concentrating on the screen in the centre of the console of the vehicle, and the flashing red arrow on the map.

"Slow down," Efi directed. "There should be a roadway coming up, on your left."

"Shayne said there would be a massive tree. He said, we couldn't miss it," Romy added.

Shayne was right. Just before the cutoff, there was a tree taller than any they had seen on their travels on Metro. The thick trunk curled up from a mass of exposed roots, the bark black, covered at many points with grey moss. There appeared a central joint, high up, where all the thick branches joined. The massive gnarled knot there looked like a face, giving the tree an eerie ambience. As they turned off the highway, Efi felt as if the old tree was watching them, smirking at their foolishness.

"That's one ugly tree," Romy muttered.

"It's called a *postree*," Efi clarified. "A Sholite explorer came across the species shortly after her arrival on Metro. Her name was Kira Post, so, as it often is with such discoveries, the species was named after her."

Romy was only half listening. The road was now little more than a pathway, mostly covered with gravel, but occasionally, there were larger rocks to avoid as well as the frequent instances of puddles at the lower points of the road's undulations. Some of the puddles were shallow, but when travelling through some, the water was half way up the door of the land crawler.

They were now travelling through a jungle environment—what the Metronians had come to call the *Wilderlands*. There were more postrees here, but not as many as the other wide-leafed species that flourished.

They drove for another hour, rounding a bend, when Romy slammed his foot against the brake pedal. The land crawler screeched to a halt, throwing Efi, who had been intently watching the map on the navigation system, against the front console. When she lifted her gaze, her eyes were as wide as Romy's.

There, on the road ahead of them, were two lines of natives, at least 20 of them. This was their first encounter with the Armatods, and they didn't know what to do. Thankfully, the Armatods did. The two lines parted, moving onto the grass shoulders. One of them, appearing to be a male, waved his arm forward while grunting a noise. It was clear, they wanted the vehicle to pass.

At a speed just above a crawl, Romy moved the vehicle forward. Once they were almost within the natives, they saw the Armatods each raise a hand, palm up, while they also bowed their heads. As they passed through the two lines, the Armatods began to chant—or was it a hum? It was an unnatural sequence of repetitive sounds; sounds a Korian or Mabuza could not imitate. Ironically, the odd noise was melodic and peaceful, leaving Efi and Romy feeling safe within the group.

As they passed through, it was easy to see why they were called Reds.

Even though their leathery skin was grey, the shells covering their more critical joints and the crown of their head had a red edge, fading to grey. The males and females could be differentiated, and there were children. Two of the females had bundles slung over their backs, dark eyes in tiny grey faces poking out from the cloth wraps.

They had rudimentary clothes: cloth pants, foot coverings, and many had straw hats. Then, there were the spears and knives they carried. Romy thought they must be adept in their use, the evidence being the carcass of a large animal slung between two of the males. There was enough meat there to feed all of them.

Once they passed the group, Romy drove faster, but still, progress was limited because of the tree limbs, rocks and gulleys constantly attempting to reclaim the gravel roadway back into the jungle.

By now, the roadway was no more than two gravel paths, forging through the tall grass. This lasted for another hour, when Efi let out a loud gasp. The Harshlands surrounded them before they even realized it. The trees were left behind, as was the grass; even the soil was scarce, visible in small pockets between what they saw as an endless panorama of rocks.

Now that they had a moment to think, they thought 'rocks' was not the right term. Rather, in front of them were massive, flat stones, sedimentary in nature with distinct layers. They were random sizes, strewn aimlessly on top of each other, resulting in elevation changes up to ten metres high. However, as they continued along the road, now utilizing the flat, stone base, they saw the stone configurations were less, with more of the Harshlands being just large areas of flat rock in a wide, dry plain.

The roadway was harder to determine. Thankfully, there were red flags on the ends of metal poles marking the road. They must have been there for a long time since many of them were nothing more than tatters of cloth.

Another hour went by before Romy asked, "How much further is it?"

"We should see it any time now. Shayne said the place is called, *Lucky Postree Ridge*."

They started to notice a change in the landscape. In the soil deposits, in between the stone formations, there was colour. Green and purple could be seen, and as they drove further, they saw a small stream, complete with waterfalls, winding through the rocks. Now, the ground cover was predominant, and Romy and Efi could see the colours were actually a short, green ground cover with purple flowers.

Two stone formations appeared just ahead, and when they drove through, the land crawler skidded to a halt for the second time within a few hours. Ahead of them was a wide stone ridge. On the right side of it was a massive postree, the largest one they had yet seen.

Slouching back in his seat, Romy offered, through a chuckle, "I can see why that postree is considered lucky. It's the only tree we have seen since we left the Wilderlands, two hours ago."

"Shayne said there would be water here," Efi said as she shooed him forward with a flick of her hand.

Once they exited the vehicle close to the base of the ridge, they saw a narrow stream of water, coming from a thin waterfall, flowing over the far edge of the ridge, then meandering off through the landscape of green and purple before disappearing into the distance.

Fortunately, there were stairs cut into the stones, allowing them easy access to the top of the ridge. On the other side was a large pond fed from a waterfall coming from within the rock itself.

"Shayne told me there aren't many natural springs in the Harshlands, but there are a few. This is one of them," Efi explained.

It didn't take them long to assemble their tent underneath the shade of the postree leaves. Just in front, they set up a table and two small camp chairs. They had packed clothes, bedding and enough food for at least a week, so they were set and could finally relax.

The sun was setting, and on Metro that meant the bulk of the red dwarf sun was being lost due to the rotation of the planet. Soon, it would be dark. They heated up two of the packed meals they brought with them. Romy had placed several blankets against a smooth stone face near the fire they had made. He leaned back against them, while urging Efi to a position within his arms.

It was the kind of place where they could forget about troubles and responsibilities. It was indeed a harsh land, but in its own way, it was exotic and beautiful.

Yet, one can only evade their responsibilities for so long, before they creep towards the forefront of thought, unwanted as they might be. That's where Romy's mind was right now. "Can I confide something to you?"

Efi, her eyes half closed, purred a "mm hmm" in response.

"Remember when we were training on the *Aramis,* and Elki and Mist came to visit?"

Efi purred the same response again.

"Do you also remember, Elki took me aside, leaving you and Mist on your own for a while?"

By now Efi could sense a bit of tension in Romy's voice. She opened her eyes wider and cleared her throat. "What of it?"

"Well, Elki and I had a boisterous debate."

"You mean an argument."

Romy let out a nervous chuckle. "Yes, you could say we locked horns."

Sitting up straight, Efi turned to look at Romy. "What was this about?"

"It was about Talus 3. I have asked several times as to their visions about the catastrophe that killed millions of my people almost 25 years ago. Again, she deflected my question, indicating there were more important things for me to do."

"And that got you angry," Efi surmised.

"Of course it did. Millions of Korians killed, and she is belittling the event. I told her I needed her and the other see'ers to dream hard on it, and find a positive sign. Otherwise, I would go back in time and find out for myself."

Knowing this was a good time to stay silent, Efi did so.

Romy continued, "Then, she got angry—real angry. I think if she had the ability to throw a fireball at me, she would have. Instead, she scolded me, reminding me my time travel training hadn't even begun."

"True enough," Efi agreed.

"Then something happened that I cannot get out of my memory. Elki began to cry, and it wasn't from anger. She was sad, and I could tell she was sad for me and for what my life would hold as a servant of the see'ers, working for the Athar."

"She said that?"

"Oh, no. But I could see it in her eyes," Romy clarified. "In the end, she did not close the door on Talus 3, but she urged—almost begged—patience."

"Did you accept her answer?"

Romy sighed. "I guess I did. She had me swear that Romy Gunn would not go to Talus 3 until we discussed it again after my training was complete."

"So, that is the end of it for now?"

"Absolutely not," Romy replied a little too quickly, his face set in a stern frown. "I told her that because I had enough of her words. She, along with the other see'ers, think of me as a doll on a string, ready to do as they desire, whether it be from whim or fact."

"But there is a great cause whereby you can make a real difference in the Athar."

"I know that," he chirped. "And I will help, but I will also have my own life with my own priorities, not just theirs." His voice lowered, audible just above the cracking embers. "There will either be a fair balance, or there will be no balance at all. I will just walk away from it, if need be."

Efi tilted her head to the side, pressing her ear against Romy's chest, his heart beating strong into her being. Yet, she closed her eyes and stayed silent, knowing the question that was coming next.

"Where do you stand on this, Efi?"

"I also have to find a balance," she whispered. "But if it comes to a decision…" Her fingers tightened in Romy's shirt. "Since I was young, I have been told of your coming—the drifter. And in that time, I was prepared and trained so you could serve the see'ers."

Romy felt a hesitation in her words. "So, you serve the see'ers and are loyal to them."

"Loyal above all else, or at least that's the way it was before I met you. I learned, yes, you are the drifter, but more so, you are Romy Gunn." Her voice cracked, yet became stronger. "The man I love like no other."

For a time, Romy remained silent. Then he said, "It is likely, one day, I will have to go back to Talus 3."

Her face slid against Romy's chest as she nodded. Then, it surprised her how easily the conclusion came to her. "And if the time comes when I need to make a choice between the see'ers and you, my love, I choose you. You are everything to me."

Chapter 14: The Science Kid

The 29th day of the 5th month, Alpha Centauri year 0024.

Deep Space.

Even though he held an elevated rank and reputation in the Explorer Corp, Ryder Gunn, like any other guest, wasn't allowed on the command deck of a spider class gunship of the Metro navy. It was simply that the command deck was too small for more than three people to occupy it, and it took three to operate the vessel's controls.

It wasn't that the *Dauntless* was small, but it was tight; more a mass of deadly weapons attached to a state-of-the-art power unit, with cramped living accommodations for the seven crew members as an afterthought. Captain Dumont Lessier was the only one afforded a cabin, small as it was. The rest of the crew and any guests had to make do in the constricted barracks in the aft part of the gunship.

That's where Ryder was now, lying on a narrow, lower berth, listening to the snoring of the crew member above him. That slumbering person was one of three people who made up the second command team, now on their rest period, while the captain and the two crew members assigned to him were piloting the *Dauntless*.

Notwithstanding the snoring, Ryder had just finished a restful sleep, for the most part because his relationship with his son was vastly improved, and he was back in space. Sliding to a sitting position, he took a deep breath of the conditioned air, enjoying the familiar metallic tinge, much as an addict feels the euphoria when he injects drugs into his veins.

Rising, he shimmied between the two rows of bunks, then out the opening into the small mess area. He saw two of the crew members there, giving them a nod. They knew who he was, but still they gave him no more than a cold nod in return. The soldiers who made it onto a gunship were the toughest of the tough. The man looked the part, solid with the side of his head just a wrinkled burn scar where his ear should have been. The woman beside him had a nice smile, but her eyes were cold, her fingers tensing then relaxing, like she was a killer ready to spring. She looked like she could take the man, if it came to it.

Ryder poured himself a mug of tea, then returned to his bunk. With only three more hours to their rendezvous with his ship, the *Wayfinder,* he was anxious. Two days ago, he had received a message from his second in command, Lieutenant Jenholin.

It read, *Come now. The Kid has found something.*

He knew Jenholin to be a good judge of a situation and not prone to panic. The message was short and direct, leaving no doubt as to her evaluation of its importance. As such, he immediately contacted the Explorer Corp., but a ship would not be ready to go until the following day. He contacted the navy office, and fortunately, a ship was going out on patrol, leaving in two hours. They could drop Ryder off at the *Wayfinder* since it would not take them far from their assigned patrol area.

With not much else to do, he lay down on the narrow mattress. He must have nodded off again, until a slight jostle woke him. It was the familiar motion when a vessel breaks its warp bubble. They were slowing down.

Thirty minutes later, an announcement came over the ship's speaker system. "Admiral Gunn, a shuttle is about to dock. Make your way to the airlock."

Retrieving his small duffle bag, Ryder moved down the narrow hallway towards the rear of the *Dauntless.* On his left, he saw the seventh crew member of the ship waiting for him in a small side room. This woman was not one of the command crew; rather, she was a junior officer, someone who took care of business the other regulars felt was beneath them. Or she would fill in, in the event one of them was injured or killed.

The ship jostled again, and a light on a control console beside the junior officer began to flash yellow. From below them, on the other side of the sealed hatch, Ryder heard a *woosh* of compressed air. A few moments later, the flashing light changed to a solid green. The hatch was opened, and the officer shuffled back from the ladder below. "Pleasure having you on board, Sir," she stated.

Ryder had done this trip before. Once his feet were over the opening, he knew the simulated gravity of the floor would be lost. With a push on the railing, he floated down the hatch until his feet hit the floor of the shuttle.

Lieutenant Jenholin pushed off and floated to him, grasping his shoulder. "Good to see you again, Admiral." Once she heard the hatch above them click shut, and she saw Ryder was belted in, she did the same. She tilted her face to the pilot. "Let's go," she commanded.

Through the front window of the shuttle, Ryder saw his ship, and beyond it, he saw a flash of white light. "Is there anything new with the beacon?"

"With its behaviour, no," She replied. "But as my message indicated, the Kid has come up with something interesting."

"What?"

"Honestly, it's hard to explain. She will have to show you."

Fifteen minutes later, even though Ryder had the urge to go directly to the command deck and take control of his ship, he asked Jenholin to lead him straight to the lab set up for the Kid. It was near Engineering, so a short walk and an elevator ride later, they entered the lab.

It looked much different than when he had left Marty to it. A quick circumspection of the room told him she had relocated some of the equipment and modified other units. She had set up a large table in the middle with a garbage container at each end, filled with empty snack wrappers.

Marty was sitting on a stool, facing away from the doorway, intently viewing a monitor in front of her. Her boots were on the floor beside her, and Ryder lowered an eyebrow towards his lieutenant when he saw the Kid was wearing shorts.

With no excuses, the lieutenant just shrugged.

Ryder cleared his throat as he walked towards her workstation.

Finally hearing him, she turned her face towards Ryder. Grinning, with a hand pushing off the table, she spun herself on the stool to face him. "Well—the man—the legend—has returned."

Ryder glanced around the lab. "It looks like you've been busy."

"Now that you mention it, I have." She spun the stool back round, her fingers clicking on the keyboard in front of her. "C'mon over here. You're going to want to see this."

She was pulling up several files on her computer, the results showing on the large screen mounted to the far wall. She was flipping from window to window, loading files so quickly Ryder was feeling dizzy. "I've been focusing on the white light," she began. "I mean, it's just a white light—right?" She turned her questioning gaze to Ryder. Before he could reply, she interjected, "Nope, not at all."

She hit the *enter* key on her keyboard and a tall, horizontal white line appeared across the screen.

"I took the white strobed light from the beacon and ran it through every filter I could come up with: ultraviolet, red scale, infrared, x-ray and different gamma rays. The scans came up empty."

She hit a key, and at first, Ryder thought there was no change to the white line, until the Kid pointed out something. "It was luck, really, that got me on the right path. You see, my computer froze, and in that instant, this is what the white light looked like."

"It's still white," Ryder concluded, dryly, wondering where this was going.

An odd chuckle came from Marty. She didn't even try to hide her demeaning tone. Pointing to the screen, she said, "Look there—and there. Those two areas are more grey than white." Before Ryder could interrupt, Marty continued. "White light is really a combination of all other colours, the primary ones being red, yellow and blue. And each has a different wave length. Of course, all other colours can be made by a specific combination of those primary colours."

"Of course," Ryder repeated, in a mocking tone.

"So, I videotaped the strobe light, and as the word would indicate, the light strobes at a very high frequency. From the grey areas I happened upon, it is clear, something is happening within the white light. So, I started to slow down the framerate and this is the result."

As the framerate slowed, more areas of the white light band, turned grey. Soon, it was all grey. Then, as the framerate slowed even more, there were hazy areas of colour, first red, then blue, then green and yellow. The blurred colours cleared, and soon the band of white was no more. In its place, were narrow bands of colours, each distinct in what appeared to be a random order.

In a glib tone, showing the pride at her finding, Marty said, "If white light is a combination of all colours, then, it shouldn't be a surprise you can separate it into colours." She added in a more solemn tone. "The bands are not as random as they first appear. They are sequenced."

"It's a message within the light?" Ryder asked.

The kid hopped off the stool, then walked around to the screen. She pointed to the red bands spaced at different intervals across the bands of colour. "The red bands appear to be end markers. They don't really combine with the other coloured bands, or let's call them mini sequences." Seeing the confused look on Ryder's face, she added, "It's either the end of a letter in an alphabet, or more likely, the end of a word."

Lieutenant Jenholin asked, "Why would anyone send us this type of code? Is it a test of our intelligence?"

"Not likely," the Kid replied. "What would be the point? I suspect whoever or whatever is sending the beacon is far advanced to us, and I also suspect light is their medium of communication." Before Ryder could deny this, she continued, "Our eyes can only see light within a very narrow wavelength. I suspect these creatures, whoever they are, have advanced optics where they can see a far wider wavelength band, and at a much higher frequency. They see words in light bursts, the same as we see them written on a page."

"The obvious question is, 'What's the message?'" Ryder asked.

Marty threw her hands in the air. "I don't know!" Once her hands came back down by her side, she added, "Each message is short, but they're all different."

"What about the first message?"

"The *Predator* exploded before the video of the light strobe could be sent out. Unfortunately, I suspect the first beacon would have supplied the key to the cipher, or the alphabet, if that's what we prefer to call it."

Ryder sat on the stool Marty had vacated. "Maybe we should just send back a message in their alphabet, just with a different mix. It'd show them we understand their language."

"But we *don't* understand their message," Marty emphasized. "Sending such a response would just be foolish, indicating we don't know how to spell."

Ryder jumped to his feet, clapping his hands together. "You've made great progress, Kid. Keep it up." He looked around the room, then said to Jenholin, "Move some of that stuff aside, and bring a cot in here for Marty."

Ryder grinned at the Kid, even though her eyes had narrowed and her gaze was boring into him. "Whatever you need, just let us know. We'd stay around and help, but it would just dumb down the room."

Following his lieutenant, he was leaving when his hand caught the door jamb. His face turned back, and Ryder said, with his best effort at motivation, "Hey, Kid, if it was easy, anyone could do it! We're counting on you!"

Chapter 15: A Close Call

The 30ᵗʰ day of the 5ᵗʰ month, Alpha Centauri year 0024.

Lucky Postree Ridge, The Harshlands.

Staggering backwards, Romy took a deep breath. He brought his wrist up, wiping the sweat from his brow. He had always been fit, but since the day he began his training with Efi, what little fat content he had, burnt away. Without a shirt, under the red sun, his skin glistened with a sheen of perspiration, highlighting the ridges defining his taut build.

Efi stood across from him, feet spread, knees bent as she was about to continue her onslaught. With one short spear in each hand, she shimmied sideways before thrusting one spear tip forwards. Romy easily parried it with the long dagger he held. They had sparred many times now, and he was familiar with her patterns. He knew the thrust was nothing but a feint, and the spear in her other hand would be the challenge. When it unleashed, speeding towards his chest, he slapped it aside with the sword carried in his other hand. Taking a stride forward, inside her guard, he lifted the dagger, the tip stopping just before it entered the soft skin under her chin.

The motion was lightning quick, giving Efi no time to react. Feeling the sharp tip pressing her flesh, the fingers of both her hands opened. The spears fell to the ground. She saw Romy's eyes dark and calculating, his long breaths predatory. She opened her eyes wide, providing as innocent a look as she could manage. Through her pouting lips, she whispered, "Love you."

Pulling the blade away, Romy grinned while giving her a wink. "Good thing. This would be bad if it was only me loving you this much."

Moving to her tip toes, she put a soft kiss on his lips. Her fingers came up, settling on his cheek. "Let's go for a swim."

Romy knew what that really meant. He walked past her, grasping her hand to pull her along the path leading around Lucky Postree Ridge to the spring water pool on the other side. After pulling off their clothes, they dove into the clear, brisk water. The short swim to the other side of the pond was enough to wash the sweat from them before they popped up on the other side. There, amongst a bed of yellow and purple ground cover, was a large blanket, one they had used every day for their lovemaking.

Today would be no different. He slid on top of her for their joining, their groans and growls raw with passion, as if it was their first time once again. When they finished, Romy rolled off her and pulled her close such that her face was nestled against his chest. The large, red sun was only half visible as it was retreating into night, bringing the chill that came with it. With their limbs intertwined, he pulled the blanket overtop their bodies, the chill pushed away by their combined warmth.

It didn't surprise Romy to hear Efi's breaths change to that of slumber. For the past four days, since their arrival at Lucky Postree Ridge, they had continued to train in the use of every form of weapon: spears, swords, bow and arrow, pistol and rifle. Romy, with his past training in the Haven military, was already quite proficient in the use of most of these, but with Efi's training, he surpassed her in almost every aspect of skill. He was now an expert, a formidable adversary for any in the Athar who might challenge him.

A growl brought Efi out of her slumber, causing her head to turn from one side to the other. "What was that?" She managed through a jaw vibrating yawn.

"That—was my stomach," he replied, pointing to his belly.

Efi shook out the blanket before they dove back into the large pool. The sky was dark and would have been pitch-black except for the incandescent rock that lay sporadically across the base of the pool. Romy intended to ask his brother about it when they met. All he knew was there were spring water pools sparsely throughout the Harshlands, and many of them had veins of this strange geological marvel. Somehow, the rock, and only when submerged, collected energy from the sun just as a solar battery would. Then, at night, the energy would be released as light, spraying tendrils of brightness across the night sky.

Once back at their campsite, Romy stoked the fire, adding several logs of dry wood from the back of the land crawler. Two blue packets of food were heated and devoured in no time. The contents were plain, but with the constant training and effort each day, the meals tasted glorious.

In the morning, after their breakfast consisting of the contents of two yellow breakfast packets, Romy was preparing for another day of physical training. Placing a hand on his arm, Efi stopped him.

"You don't need more practice with physical weapons. It's time to work on your psychic powers," Efi decided.

That was the plan for the next four days. Romy didn't need much practice with his energy shield, the power of the Celtae race. By the end of the second day, Efi fired a volley of energy blasts from a laser rifle. *All were deflected quite easily,* Efi thought, and with Romy suffering only one step backwards from the barrage.

Mastering the power of the fireball, a psychic skill from the Toltec race, was a challenge. Intermixing training in this skill with practicing his energy shield, built his confidence. With little to worry his mind, he progressed rapidly.

On the morning of the fourth day, they heard the electrical whine of an electromagnetic drive. A minute later, they saw the silver and red shuttle come over the ridge to the wide, flat plateau they were using for their training. The shuttle landed, and Shayne hopped out.

"Don't stop on my account," Shayne said. "I saw some of the fireworks from the distance. It's awesome."

"Again," Efi said after turning away from the newly arrived visitor.

After a quick wave to his brother, Romy turned to face the grouping of massive, flat rocks. There were three of them on the far side of the plateau, 30 metres away. The two on the bottom, oddly, supported a larger flat rock, wider than the two underneath it put together. There were black scorch marks covering the upper rock, evidence of Romy's efforts for the day. Romy tilted his neck in a stretch before returning his focus to the rocks. A glistening of orange energy began to form on Romy's right hand. The tendrils of energy, like lightning, moved faster as the glow turned into a round, orange ball, 30 centimetres in diameter.

Sliding into a sideways stance, he pulled back his arm, then flung it forward. His body bent over, but his face remained high, his gaze intent on the far rocks. A moment later, the energy ball struck the top rock, sparks showering in every direction. When they cleared, there was an additional scorch mark added to the pattern.

"Wow!" Shayne exclaimed as he ran towards his brother. Once beside him, he slapped Romy on the back. "You'll have to teach me that, one day."

"When you're old enough, I guess we'll find out," he replied just before giving Shayne a great hug.

Efi was soon beside them and asked Shayne about the supplies. He pointed to the shuttle, indicating the food supplies, fuel and wood were in the shuttle storage compartment.

"There's enough for five days," Shayne clarified.

After unloading and storing the supplies at the campsite, Efi asked Shayne to stay and have dinner with them.

"Sorry, I have to get back—big date tonight." Shayne answered, smugly.

"You're only 16," Romy scoffed. "I didn't go on dates at that age," he added, almost grumbling.

Shayne's lips tilted into a sideways smirk. "Women have been asking about you. There's lots of interest since you showed up at Cliffside. You know—son of Ryder Gunn—woohoo."

Her hands pressed into her hips, Efi interjected, "Really! I hope you told them he was taken."

Shayne's silly grin turned to Efi. "Of course. I told them an exotic Mabuza woman had her claws sunk into him—and deep."

Expecting a reprimand, Shayne was surprised when Efi's response was, "Excellent!"

Romy was sad to see his brother go. Not only did he love him, but he had become quite fond of his happy-go-lucky personality.

The next week was spent continuing to work on Romy's ability with the fireball, but now, intermixed with these tasks, they began to work on teleportation. Whereas transposition was the ability to hop from one plane to another, teleportation was the ability to move from one location to another in the same plane. This was a psychic power in the Anasazi race's DNA.

All in all, it did not go badly. He only had two bruises, matching the two drag marks in the scorched pattern on the rocks where the solid surface had interrupted his intended path. Efi couldn't help but laugh the first time he reappeared with his feet a metre off the ground, his cheek pressed flat against the rock face.

But if you don't try, you don't succeed. After the fifth day, he was able to teleport three times from the campsite to the other side of the grouping of three rocks. He had mastered these short hops, but Efi knew a longer teleportation would be a much more significant challenge.

In the late hours of the fifth day, Shayne returned with more supplies. This time, he accepted Efi's invitation to stay the night and leave in the morning after a hearty *yellow packet* breakfast.

It was in that morning when trouble found them. Romy was poking the fire, focused on bringing it to life. Shayne was behind his back, not doing much of anything as 16-year-olds are prone to do, when a glint of metal caught Shayne's eye. The grouping of three scorched rocks was visible in the distance, 30 metres away. And there, again, he saw the flash of metal at the edge of the rock pattern.

Inside the tent, Efi was tidying up the blankets used the night before when she froze, but only for an instant. Her Mabuza ability to foresee the future had kicked in. In her mind, she saw Romy and the ominous presence of death.

She strode for the canvas flap, but stumbled with only her head managing to press through the opening. Before she could yell a warning, she heard the firing of a projectile weapon.

A second later, she saw Shayne snap his hand across his body. Fortunately, Efi said a silent prayer for the shooter's inaccuracy that seemed to be fulfilled.

The *crack* of the gun and the splinters of stone shrapnel around them brought Romy's attention back from the flickers of flame. He spun instantly and saw the man with the gun duck behind the protection of the three rocks. Without thinking, Romy pulled back his hand, then snapped it forward. The energy ball was on its way, but in fact, it was no energy ball. As soon as it left his fingers, it stretched out into a line, much like a laser burst. Shayne's mouth gapped. He had never seen energy move so fast.

Less than a second later, it smashed into the bottom of the top rock, at the joint between the lower two. This time, there were no scorch marks as the rocks were shattered, fragments being thrown tens of metres into the air. When the dust cleared enough, Romy saw the assassin running away from the scene. A second snap of Romy's hand had a second bolt of energy speeding towards him. It hit him square in the back, throwing him to a prone position 40 metres away. The only movement was from the column of smoke spiraling up from the smoldering hole in his back.

Efi joined Romy and Shayne as they ran, covering the ground to the body at a fast pace. Romy turned him over. It was obvious he was a Mabuza—a dead one. Efi leaned down, checking his pockets for identification. There was none to be found. She lifted one arm, then the other, pausing as she saw a tattoo on his right wrist: a pattern of five small, interlinked circles.

"Who is he?" Romy questioned, his face a grim pose.

Rising to her feet, Efi replied, "I'm not sure, but the tattoo says he had Mabuza military training. It makes sense this is an assassin sent by the leaders of the Mabuza resistance on Haven."

"I thought Ruut Nkosi was in jail," Romy quipped.

"He is, but where one leader falls, another takes their place," she answered.

Romy turned and was striding back to the campsite. "I'll get a shovel."

Efi watched the two Gunns'. Shayne was bouncing up and down as he walked beside his brother, his words filled with excitement. "What kind of freaking fireball was that!"

His answer, if there was one, was lost in the distance to Efi. His unique energy blast was indeed impressive. She assumed, in the emergency, his true potential came forward. But that was not bothering her. There was something else.

She had not lied to the men in that the assassin had military training. What she did not divulge was each circle told of his proficiency in marksmanship. One circle was little better than a beginner, while five was the highest level a sniper could receive. A Mabuza with such training would not have missed from 30 metres.

Her eyes narrowed as she watched Shayne in the distance. She remembered the wave of his hand as the shot was fired. In her mind, there was no doubt. Shayne had the power of telekinesis. He had deflected the bullet.

Chapter 16: A Message Received

The 35th day of the 5th month, Alpha Centauri year 0024.

Deep Space.

It couldn't be helped. Ryder was worried about the Kid's progress. She kept to herself as she tried to figure out the code to solve the messages sent by the alien beacons. The lack of communication had Ryder going crazy. The only thing keeping him from pulling his hair out, was it was during a similar lack of communication period when Marty solved the initial mystery of the white light. So, he bit his lip and left the young woman to her work.

It was now six days—six long days—since she had solved the first part of the beacon's puzzle. She didn't explain why, the day after her revelation, she had asked for a message to be sent back to one of her friends back on Haven. Because of the distance, it had taken two days for the message to arrive there, and a return response had taken an additional two days. That meant it had taken Marty's associate two days to investigate and compile the reply.

Ryder held the hard drive containing the return message in his hand as he strode towards her lab. He found her in her typical position, her face close to the computer screen, her fingers rattling the keyboard.

"Hey, Kid, the reply finally came in," he offered as he moved to a position beside her.

As he lifted his hand, she snatched the hard drive from it. "About time," she muttered.

She fumbled with a cable, but finally connected the drive to her computer. She noticed Ryder was still fixed in position beside her. She tilted her head up, her eyes narrowing below her mop of red hair. "Thanks, but you need to leave now."

Leaning a hand on the table top, he shook his head. "Not a chance. I've been waiting six days to see what's in that message."

Marty spun on the stool before crossing her arms in front of her. "Much as I appreciate the father figure persona, you're more of that *creepy* father figure when you hover over me."

The low growl that emitted from his clenched teeth, fortunately, held back the harsh words he could not have taken back. After a moment, he composed himself and said, "This is the 35th day of the month, Kid. A new beacon comes on the 18th of next month, and we've managed to explode each beacon before the next one arrived. I'm not sure what'll happen if this beacon is still here on the 18th of next month. You understand what I'm saying?"

Marty's demeanor changed. Her face softened, and her eyes widened. The sarcastic appearance she often had was lost. "Admiral Gunn, I know how important this is. We're talking about contact with some alien species, unknown except for the fact we know they're far more advanced than we are." It surprised Ryder when she placed her hand on top of his on the table. "I'm thankful to be here and to be part of this. So, I'm putting everything I have and know into solving this. With a little luck, we'll have this figured out in a couple of days."

For a few moments, Ryder was speechless. In those few moments, the Kid changed in his eyes. All he heard was the truth, not only in her words, but in the sincerity they were spoken with.

Marty ended the awkward pause by adding, "If you leave, I can put all my attention to this." As Ryder turned to walk out, she said, "I'll give you an update every 12 hours."

Thirty minutes later, Ryder was at his favorite location on the *Wayfinder.* At the tip of one of the five outriggers, joined to the main fuselage, was an observation room. It was roughly four metres by four metres, enclosed in a glass bubble, in turn, covered by a retractable metal canopy. He moved to the control console and pressed a sequence of buttons, resulting in the retraction of the canopy.

He sat in one of the swivel bucket seats and, using his feet, slowly rotated himself through the entire panoramic view. When he saw the beacon, he stopped. The *Wayfinder* was orbiting the gold sphere at a distance of ten kilometres, making it only a small dot. Then there was a flash as the white light strobed. Instinctively, he gazed at his interlink and silently counted with the visible numerals. At 125, he lifted his gaze and, as expected, the white light burst from the beacon once again.

As if on cue, Lieutenant Jenholin walked into the observation room with the flash of light. She was carrying two cups of tea, handing one to the admiral. "You look like you could use one of these."

"Sure," he grumbled. "Anything to distract me from this waiting." Leaning forward, he took the cup as Jenholin sat in the chair opposite to him. "We explorers aren't built for inactivity."

"So true," Jenholin agreed. "And you won't mind some added distractions, then?"

"Like what?"

"News from Haven."

Rubbing his chin, Ryder said, "We haven't heard anything for a few months. I bet things began to unwind when we plucked Romy from their filthy Korian claws."

Laughing, Jenholin replied, "You're right. Between the mysterious raids Metro had been enacting on their Junkyard and the sightings of mystery ships in space, it was inevitable they would discover we were well established in Alpha Centauri. Our prime minister sent a message to the council and the new senate, along with the Sholites, detailing our successful existence on Metro."

"I suspect they weren't overly surprised."

She nodded as she continued. "It was more of a verification, but now if they didn't reveal this news to the public, it would certainly leak out. That would be worse."

"So, they announced it?"

"As delicately as they could. They kept your name out of it, but the people of Haven know you are a critical part of Metro."

Ryder took a drink of his tea. "And as I like it, an ever-reducing influence on the political and military affairs of state." He lifted his cup in a mock salute.

"In what, surprisingly, was less of an uproar and more of a socially confused state, the Mabuza thought it was a good time to add to it."

Ryder's eyes brightened. "They didn't!"

"Oh yes, they did. They invited the lead politicians and military officials from both the Korian and Sholite camps to Hagaza, their capital. They let them in their restricted areas, including their underground military base. The Mabuza showed the visitors they were not quite the inept, quiet, rustic race the Korians and Sholites perceived them to be."

Leaning forward, his interest piqued, Ryder quipped, "That must've been a shock!"

"Not as much of a shock as when they revealed they were one of seven pureblood races, each with unique psychic powers."

Ryder had just taken another drink of tea, and when he heard the lieutenant's words, he almost spat it back up.

"Apparently, since their own powers of premonition are less visible, the Mabuza had a couple of Ionian friends there to demonstrate all the psychic powers," Jenholin stated.

After a long sigh, Ryder said, "The universe is changing for us all. I imagine the Korians and Sholites feel much less important than they did a few short months ago."

"I think it has put some fear into them. The civil war just ended, but there is a great call for unity among the former PAT and MAT forces and the Sholites. They all feel threatened."

Ryder mumbled, "Maybe they should be." He saw the confused look in Jenholin's eyes. "As we speak, my sister, I'lish, is representing Haven in peace talks with the Metro prime minister."

"That clarifies that, but, speaking of your family, isn't your son a pureblood, and wouldn't that make you a pureblood?"

Waving away the comment, Ryder explained, "The psychic powers run in my family, but only seems to show up every few generations. The Mabuza have discovered my son does have some powers. That's why they're training him."

Ryder didn't want to divulge too much information about Romy, so he pointed at the beacon that just flashed again. The conversation focused there for the next 20 minutes before Ryder took his leave.

The report from the Kid, after 12 hours, was simple and underwhelming. She was making progress, but she had nothing firm, yet.

At the next 12-hour interval, Marty's voice was a higher pitch as she told Ryder, "I have it. Come see me, right now!"

Hurrying to the lab, Ryder strode in.

She shooed him back, demanding, "Close the door."

He complied, then returned back to her work table. She had dark circles under her eyes from lack of sleep, yet the irises were bright with excitement.

"I'm not going to put you through all the visuals. Rather, I'm going to explain what I've discovered." Her words were fast paced.

"Sure, go for it."

She shifted on her stool, waggling a finger at Ryder. "So, our problem was we didn't have the code to read the colour banded messages. We assumed that was because we didn't have the light message from the very first beacon."

"I do recall it that way."

"Well, I recovered a video of the first strobed message."

"How did you manage that?" Ryder could not hide the surprise in his voice.

"From what you told me, the explosion of the first beacon was massive. I got to thinking maybe that big an event might've been captured by someone else."

"Who?"

"I got my hacker friend on Haven to dig into it. He found out there were three Haven military ships shadowing the *Predator* while it was examining the first beacon. One of the vessels was equipped with a long-range scope. It caught the whole timeline, including the explosion, on video." She slapped her hands together. "From there, it was easy for my associate to hack into the Haven military archives and retrieve the data. That's what was on the hard drive."

"So far, you're doing really well, Kid."

She laughed. "Oh, there's more. As we suspected, when I reduced the frame rate, the coloured bands were a representation defining our alphabet." Before Ryder could let loose the words from his open mouth, she added, with finality, "From that, I was able to decode all three messages."

"Don't just sit there all smug. Out with the messages!"

"Sure, but they're not really messages. They're names."

Ryder paused, his brows furrowing with confusion.

"From the second beacon, the coloured bands revealed the name, Natalie Lowe."

"What? My grandmother?"

Her response was a nonchalant tilt of her head before she continued. "The second beacon sent out your name, Ryder Gunn. And this third beacon, presently outside the hull of this ship, is broadcasting the name, Marjorie Gunn."

"Who?"

"Mar-jor-ie Gunn." She emphasized the syllables.

Ryder had been briefed by the Mabuza see'ers about the concept of time travel. They also confided in him about Romy's burgeoning ability to do so.

With that knowledge, he knew it was possible Marjorie was someone from their future, but it was not something he was willing to share with anyone. Rather, he said, "I don't know a Marjorie Gunn. It must be an ancestor I'll have to research when I have some time."

Marty's lips twisted like something sour was in her mouth, and wrinkles appeared at the outer corners of her eyes. She thought, *well, la-de-da. That's a casual an answer as I've heard.*

Her brief bewilderment was interrupted by Ryder. "We can send a message to the beacon, now, one that makes sense."

"Sure, but I need Lieutenant Jenholin here to help me."

"Why?" Ryder retorted. "You're the smart one figuring all this out."

She threw her hand up in the air as her head tilted back. When her face fell and her eyes met Ryder's, she elaborated, "Yes, I'm the techy scientist type. I *discover* things and find codes. Engineers *make* things. Jenholin is an engineer, and she needs to *make* a signaling device."

Ryder strode to the door, depressing a button on the stainless-steel console beside it. He spoke into the comm unit. "Lieutenant Jenholin, come to the lab, immediately."

Almost immediately, the response came back, "On my way, Sir."

Two minutes later, the lieutenant strode into the room, her deep breaths an indication of her fast pace. "What can I help you with, Admiral?"

Marty was about to begin a lengthy restatement of the earlier explanation. With a snap of his fingers, Ryder stopped her. "The Kid will bring you up to speed after I leave. I'll give you the short version. Marty has broken the code and has all three messages revealed. We're at a point where we need to send a message to the beacon, but she thinks she needs your help to make a messaging machine."

"Why?"

Ryder was about to answer, when he heard Marty snap her fingers, followed by, "I got this, Admiral." She turned to face Jenholin. "We could make something rough and ready, and program your light bar to send that message." She glanced at Ryder, who had a look on his face with the obvious question, *why not?* Marty continued, "If the beacon understands it, and it will, they will likely send out a follow-up message."

"Great," Ryder offered.

"Maybe not so great, since, with the apparatus I have here, it'd take two hours to translate it, then another two hours to create another response."

"That would not be good for us," Jenholin said.

"I get it now," Ryder conceded. "Lieutenant, Marty needs you to make the communication device."

Exactly," Marty interrupted. "While you do that, I can write the code and create the interface."

"How long before this communicating device will be ready?" Ryder asked.

The two women, looked at each other and, oddly, both said, "two days," at the same time.

Ryder smirked. "Glad to see you two are in such good unison on this. He turned his gaze to Lieutenant Jenholin. "Don't leave this lab until this device is complete. Get all the help you need on my authority. Have them bring whatever tools and materials you need, to you. Understood?"

"Yes, Sir," came Jenholin's reply.

Marty lifted her hand.

"That goes for you too. And I know, lots of snack food." They were making progress, putting Ryder at ease. "If the two of you could give me an update every 12 hours, that would be much appreciated."

The two-day mark came and went. Ryder became uneasy. Two hours later, just as he was about to contact the two women, they contacted him over the ship's intercom. "Please come to Cargo Bay Two," Jenholin requested.

When Ryder entered the cargo bay, he saw Marty and the lieutenant beside a device—a cube, two metres long on each side. As he walked closer, he saw a mass of wires and circuit board covers, along with several small thrusters. Across the top of it was a light bar, a metre in length.

"Will it work?" Ryder questioned.

Marty began the explanation. "I created an interface and code so we can type words in my console, and after 30 seconds of processing, the strobe emitted from the light bar will send the message."

"You're sure?"

"There's also a light sensor here." Marty pointed at a large parabolic disc on the front of the machine. "This can read an alien light message, and within 30 seconds, working in reverse, it can translate it into words. We've done several tests back and forth. It works."

On the left side of the wide console in front of Marty, Jenholin pointed to two joy sticks. "These will control the thrusters on the device."

Giving a wide grin, Ryder said, "Excellent! When can we send our message."

For a minute the two women whispered amongst themselves, then Marty answered, "It'll take four hours to move the console to the lab and run a few more quick tests. Meet us in the lab then, and we'll be ready to go."

Ryder clapped his hands together as he turned to leave.

"Easy there, Spaceman," Marty blurted.

"What?"

Shaking her head, Marty elaborated. "What message do you want to send?"

Feeling foolish, Ryder blushed. "I guess that would be important, wouldn't it?"

They spent the next hour discussing different ideas. After all, a first contact with an alien species was important beyond belief. In the end, since the messages were names—so personalized—they agreed, rather than sending a general greeting from the Korians, or the Metronians, a message just as specific should be returned.

"Greetings. I am Ryder Gunn." Ryder voiced the selected message. "Sounds fine to me."

Ryder left the two women to their work before travelling to the command deck. There, he ordered the *Wayfinder* to move away from the beacon, changing the radius of the orbit from ten kilometres to 200.

Four hours later, he met the two women in the Kid's lab. Everything was ready, so Ryder gave them the go ahead to begin. An hour earlier, the messaging device was sent out from the cargo bay, and Jenholin was handling the joysticks as it was still forty kilometres from the beacon. The view from one of the cameras integrated into the light machine, still had the beacon as a small dot. Forty-five minutes later, it almost filled the screen mounted on the wall, as the light machine was only 30 metres away from it.

Ryder walked to the wall communication console and gave an order. "All crew members, secure yourself. If this doesn't go well, we might be in for a rough ride."

He moved to a position beside Marty's work table, rocking back and forth on his feet, fingers intertwined behind his back. "Proceed," he said in a quiet voice, not indicative of the fast pace of his heart.

Marty waited until the beacon just completed its strobe cycle. She waited 30 seconds, then she simply pressed one key. Perhaps one of the defining moments in their history, initiated by one simple movement of her finger.

A bright, white light exploded on the screen. The message was sent— then they waited.

After a minute with no response, Jenholin whispered, "The 125 second signal hasn't been sent."

"So, if it's going to explode, this is when it'll happen," Ryder added.

But it didn't explode. Another 30 seconds later, off cycle from it's 125 second pattern, a white burst left the beacon.

Marty leaned forward, pressing a few keys, starting the translation process. As she promised, 30 seconds later, words appeared at the bottom of the screen.

Greetings, Ryder Gunn. Will you come?

They huddled together for a few seconds before Marty typed in a response.

Where should I come?

The beacon flashed again.

It is far. We will help.

Another huddle, another response from Ryder.

We don't know how to travel so far.

Another flash from the beacon.

We will help.

Ryder was worried more questions might irritate the beacon, but he had to ask one more thing.

How will you help?

Another flash covered the screen.

Patience.

Then, the beacon began to move, slowly beginning a rotation. Ryder didn't have to tell Jenholin who was already manoeuvring the light machine away from the beacon. By the time the machine was ten kilometres distant from the beacon, the rotation was incredibly fast. Yet, at fifty kilometres distance, it was even quicker, the rotation so fast the beacon could no longer be distinguished. There was only a golden, blurred shape where the beacon once was.

As they watched in amazement, a golden trail began to form off the side of the shape, getting longer and longer, while the round shape elongated into an oblong. Then, as if it had been held back and finally set free, in an instant, the oblong shape blasted towards the tip of the golden trail, only to vanish when it arrived there. It was gone without a trace.

Marty pushed her fingers up through her bundles of red hair. "I can't believe what just happened."

The lieutenant was leaning back in her chair, all the blood drained from her face. She did not offer a response.

Ryder was as shocked, but gained his faculties quickly. "I guess it left the same way it came here."

"What now?" Marty replied.

"We do what it said," Ryder replied, trying his best to hide the child-like excitement he felt. "We have patience and wait."

Jenholin finally recovered from her temporary stupor. "Marty, take the controls and bring the light machine back. I'll wait for it by the cargo bay." Rising to her feet, she didn't wait for a reply. Someone did need to go to the cargo bay, but she hoped, on the way, she made it to the bathroom before she threw up.

Ryder was following her out, when he stopped at the door, turning back to Marty. "Hey, Kid. You want a job?"

She turned on the stool to face him. "Doing what?"

"I don't care. Make up a job description. Something tech or science." He shrugged.

"Working for the Explorer Corp.?" she asked.

"If you want. Might be better if you work directly for me. Special advisor of something or other. Just fill in the blanks."

"I'll think it over," she said, her face a conundrum, her eyes bright with pride, her lips set in a smart-assed grin.

"I'm counting on it. You're good, Kid," were his final words before he left the lab.

As he walked down the hall, something was bothering him. Something wasn't quite right. That's why he felt like there was more to come, and he would need better than good people to stay on this project. He knew what was causing the hair on the back of his neck to stand up. The first name the beacons had sent was, *Natalie Lowe*. Yet, her name ever since she arrived on the asteroid, Talus 3, was *Natalie Gunn*, her married name. *Natalie Lowe* had been her name on Earth. That meant, even though the aliens knew about the Korians, and from that, Jenholin had assumed the beacons were meant for them, the message was for Natalie Lowe, the woman from *Earth*.

And that was troubling.

Chapter 17: The Bracelets

The 38th day of the 5th month, Alpha Centauri year 0024.

Lucky Postree Ridge, The Harshlands.

Prodding the dead Mabuza's leg with his foot, Romy said, "What do we do with him?"

"We could bury him," Efi offered, "But it might be better if he was brought to Cliffside. The Mabuza officials there might be able to identify him." She glanced at Shayne. "Do you think you could do that?"

With the dead body laying at his feet, Shayne omitted the sarcasm he usually laced into his responses. "Sure. But obviously, it's not safe here. We should all go back to Cliffside."

Efi shook her head. "We've been making great progress since we came to the Harshlands. I also know how Mabuza think. They work well with an element of surprise, but now, since that is gone, they will be hesitant to repeat something that failed the first time."

Romy interjected, "When you see the Mabuza officials, ask them for a set of electric short spears, the kind more than a few of them favour." He winked at Efi. "I have my weapons with me, but from here on, if we are to remain, you need to be armed."

With that agreed, they went about loading the body into the back of Shayne's shuttle. Shayne told them he would be back in a few hours with the weapons and motion sensors.

Efi did not mention the circumstances whereby she was sure Romy's younger brother had used psychic powers to deflect the bullet from the assassin, thereby saving his brother's life. She assumed, if Shayne wanted Romy to know, he would have told him. She felt it was not her place to accelerate that discussion. But it was good knowledge for her to know, since it would likely be important one day.

When Shayne returned, he wore a pistol at his waist. He provided the electric spears to Efi along with the double scabbard. She immediately fitted the scabbard and tested the spears. Satisfied, she put them in place over her shoulders.

Shayne retrieved the sensors from the hold of the shuttle and said, "I brought ten sensors. Each is a combination motion sensor and vibration sensor. In the Harshlands, since there isn't wildlife over half a metre in height or 25 kilograms in weight, I've set the parameters to only sense activity over those levels."

Romy took half the sensors while directing Efi to go with Shayne. Heading in opposite directions, they equally spaced the sensors at a radius of 60 metres from the camp. Once this was complete, Shayne retrieved the small monitor from the shuttle and met Romy and Efi at their camp on top of the ridge. "This monitor is set to the frequency of the sensors. It's pretty easy to use," he stated as he flipped it to his older brother.

They shared a hot meal together next to a small fire. They were almost out of firewood, so it was fortunate Shayne had the foresight to fill the shuttle's hold with a large quantity before he left Cliffside. Shayne still didn't reveal information about his psychic powers, and again, Efi didn't question him on it. The notion was left unconfirmed when Shayne rose, slapped the dust from his thighs, announcing his departure.

Romy rose, giving his brother a great hug, while thanking him for all the help. Efi also gave him a hug, thanking him in turn. Once they pulled apart, with a sly grin, Shayne added, "No problem, Sis." The wink that followed confirmed he was back to his sarcastic self.

The next two weeks were spent continuing Romy's training, almost exclusively in transpositions and only short teleportations. When Romy hopped, sometimes Efi went with him, sometimes he went alone. It was good for Romy's confidence to do these independent trips. Each hop took about three hours since that was what Romy had been able to get his recovery time down to.

He also practiced local teleportations. He became quite proficient, not having hit any slabs of rock, or materialized suspended in the air. Having no new bruises to show from these efforts, Efi had him focus on longer teleportations. He was able to make several psychic trips back to their apartment at Cliffside. It was at this point, with Romy showing significant expertise in his abilities, when Efi made an announcement.

"It's time to start hopping in time," Efi stated, much too simply for such a monumental inference.

"Just like that," Romy said through a smirk. "Just do it?"

Efi showed him that beautiful smile, the one that always melted his heart but also caused his confidence to grow. "It's not like I can show you. It's something you just have to do."

"Where do I start?"

She was laying beside him on the blanket on the far side of the pond. "We'll start in the morning. Do you remember when I asked you to leave my silver bracelet in the apartment back on Shalkar?"

"How could I not? It was the first time we coupled. Then, you made a request, one I still don't understand, to leave your bracelet by the clock." He glanced down. "The one that matches the one—" His words stopped for a few moments as he saw, where there should have only been one silver bracelet, there were two "—I left back on Shalkar?"

Efi rolled on her side, facing him. "It was. While you were on one of your transpositions, I went and retrieved it from Shalkar."

Rubbing his temple, Romy mumbled, "I'm confused."

Ignoring the comment, Efi said, "I want you to go back in time and get the bracelet."

"But why? You have it on your wrist. I'm even more confused."

She repeated the request. "I want you to get it because, in that timeline, it is there, not here."

"You're really hurting my brain. What will happen if I am successful? Will you then have three bracelets instead of two?"

Through a giggle, Efi said, "I really don't know, but we're going to find out."

"Do you remember the time on the clock in the apartment?"

"It would be difficult to forget," Romy replied. "You only made me repeat it ten times. It was exactly 10:44."

The next morning, after their breakfast, Efi gave Romy some last instructions for the hop. She told him, after he arrived in the room and checked the time on the clock, he should see the owner on the first floor. Ask him the date. "After that, you need to wait about three hours before you attempt to hop back, hopefully with my silver bracelet."

Air escaped from Romy's lips, somewhere between a grunt and a laugh. "Right—bring back the bracelet you're wearing on your wrist right now."

She shrugged. "It's not an easy concept."

"Actually, it's kind of mind bending," he clarified.

She shifted closer to him, letting his arms wrap around her. He kissed her ear, then whispered, "I'm not too proud to say, I'm scared. There is a possibility, I might not make it back."

She returned the hug, her heart skipping a beat as she heard his words. With her cheek pressed against his chest she replied, "Remember, I am clairvoyant. I know this is not the end for you and I. That I am certain of."

The words buoyed his confidence. Romy released her, pressing his arms outward. She took several steps back. It was time for action and for Romy to fulfill his destiny.

Muttering, "Here we go," Romy closed his eyes, his lips tight together in a straight line. He began to shimmer, and soon, he could no longer be seen in the opaque ripples. Then, after they dissipated, he was gone.

Now, Efi noticed the silence, feeling more alone than she ever had in her past. She didn't move for a minute. From what she knew from the history of the previous time drifters, when they successfully travelled back in time, no matter how long they were there, they always came back to the same instant. So, if Romy had successfully travelled back in time, and returned, he should have come back immediately. Yet, he wasn't here.

There were now two possibilities. The first was he just transpositioned without any time shift, in which case he should be back in three hours. The other option, the one she didn't really want to consider, was that he did travel back in time, but was lost there.

It was at that point when she rose to her feet, deciding she needed to keep busy. She made a round to all the sensors, ensuring they were functioning properly. After that, she chopped some of the firewood into smaller pieces. Since the perspiration was flowing off her, she stripped and swam for a time in the large pond.

She dressed and made herself something to eat. Then, there was nothing to do but wait. She continued to look at the time on her tablet, but each time, frustration filled her since only a few minutes had passed. As the three-hour mark passed, her frustration turned to all out fear. When the opaque circle finally formed in the middle of their campsite, she jumped for joy. As soon as Romy materialized, she ran forward, throwing her arms around him, the force knocking him off his feet. She landed on top, giving him one kiss after the other spread across his face. Hearing him wheeze in a breath, she rolled off, but she kept her face buried into his chest.

"I didn't get your bracelet," he admitted. "I arrived there, but without a shift in time."

"I'm just happy you're back. We can try again tomorrow," she suggested.

Sliding out from under her, he sat up and stated, "No, I will try again in three hours." The lower tone in his voice told Efi it was not open for debate.

Romy wanted to be as ready as he could be, so he ate some food, then went for a short nap. He awoke just before the three-hour mark and mentally prepared himself.

Efi walked him through everything he needed to do: focus on the apartment, focus on the time on the clock and focus on the date—the 20th day of the fifth Alpha Centauri month. He took up the same position and began his focus. A moment later he was gone.

Unfortunately, the cycle repeated. He did not return. Efi worried to no end, until Romy materialized three hours later. Romy said he would try again in another three hours, but Efi put her foot down, insisting, that was enough for the day.

Romy finally agreed, and they both went for a swim. He thought they would go to their blanket, where they had often made love during their stay in the Harshlands. However, Efi pulled him to the near shore and their tent on the ridge.

"You need to get your rest," she insisted as they settled underneath their blankets.

Romy quickly fell asleep—as sound a sleep as he had in some time. But it was only to be interrupted a few hours later by a weight on his lower stomach. His eyes opened to see Efi, naked, straddling him. She leaned down, pressing her breasts against his chest. Just before she kissed him, she whispered, "I need you."

They made love. Romy was surprised at the level of Efi's passion. She was a sensual woman, but this night she was different, her every touch, kiss and movement a clear indication of her carnal desire.

It was midmorning when Romy finally stirred. He pushed Efi's leg off him before he sat up. He looked at her as she rolled to face the wall of the tent, hoping there would be time for more sleep. That was not the case as he gave her butt cheek a sharp slap. She yelled as her face snapped around, her golden eyes boring through Romy.

He lifted his hands in a defensive posture, his face the epitome of innocence. "Easy girl. I saw that dark look last night, but it wasn't anger."

She let out a low growl as her fingers snaked upwards along his thigh.

Slapping it away, he scolded her. "Enough of that. I feel great this morning. It's a good time to retrieve your bracelet."

They dressed, then had a meal, whereby they both ate double portions, as famished as they were from their exertions the night before. It was time to go back to the apartment on Shalkar. It was now after midday, and Romy felt invigorated—as if anything was possible.

He clapped his hands together, yelling out, "Let's go!"

This time he did not close his eyes, yet he was more focused than he had ever been. His form disappeared in the ripples. Efi moved to sit on the camp chair, but with herself half lowered, she noticed the shimmer reappear. A moment after that, Romy was back.

"I did it!" Romy exclaimed. The words that followed were fast paced. "The time on the clock read, 10:44. I checked with the man in the lobby and it was the 20th day of the fifth month. I did it!"

Tears flowed down Efi's cheeks; she was so happy. He had completed his first independent transposition in time. She was at a loss for words, and for a moment, they just stared at each other.

Romy broke the awkward moment. "Oh, I have your bracelet."

"What bracelet?"

Tilting his head, Romy added, "You sent me back to get your silver bracelet. I have it."

She let out a nervous laugh. "I have no idea what you're talking about. You went back to verify the time and date, then return. I know nothing about a silver bracelet."

Pressing his fingers into his pocket, he pulled out the silver bracelet, the one he now noticed was missing from her wrist. Only one from the pair was there.

She strode closer, her eyes examining the bracelet. Her eyes lit up. "That's my missing bracelet! I had no idea where I lost it, but it must have been in the apartment. Thanks!" she added, snatching it from him before placing it on her wrist beside its twin.

Grasping her shoulders, Romy asked, "You don't remember us leaving it there, or asking me to retrieve it?"
Efi's brows furrowed, "The time travel has affected you. You need to sit down and clear your head."

Romy did sit down, but again insisted on his version of the story. "You asked me to leave this silver bracelet on Shalkar. You asked me to leave one of your black bracelets in our apartment at Cliffside." He again glanced at her wrist. Both black bracelets were there. "I must be going crazy," he grumbled as his fingers swept back through his hair.

"You're not going crazy. I retrieved the black bracelet yesterday, while you were away on one of your hops. I was going to make you go back in time and get it."

"No!" he replied. "It was the silver bracelet."

She stepped closer to him and was about to sit, when he shooed her away. "Not now. I need some space and time to think this through."

Efi decided to go for another swim, leaving Romy alone with his thoughts. He was certain of the events in his mind. However, what he did not anticipate was that all memory of the bracelet from the time it disappeared from the apartment, would be lost. *That must be it,* he thought. *If the bracelet was not there from 10:44 on the 20th day of the 5th month, then all memory left with it!*

Having finished her swim, Romy called Efi over to sit beside him. He explained his theory and his conclusion. At first, she thought he had gone mad, but ultimately, with the realization he had no reason to lie, and that the theory from a time travel perspective was plausible, she accepted his version.

The following day, they decided to rest. The day before was a milestone, and they celebrated, drinking a little too much fruit wine. They had a good night's sleep in preparation for the following day.

The morning after, Efi explained the task. Just as he had gone back in time by hopping, now he would attempt time traveling utilizing teleportation; that meant he would travel back in time within the same plane.

"Remember, just as we were leaving Cliffside, I asked you to leave one of my black bracelets under the clock in the living area," Efi said.

"Sure. It was 11:22 in the morning. And before you ask me ten times, I am absolutely sure of the time!"

Chuckling, she said, "Okay, I get it."

Romy began the teleportation cycle, and the events played out just as they did the day before. When he returned with the black bracelet, Efi had lost all knowledge of that bracelet from the time it had been left in the apartment. He had to explain the logic behind her memory loss all over again, albeit, it was much easier since Romy had convinced her of the silver bracelet scenario.

Efi gave a concerned look towards Romy. "Your ability to time travel is powerful. It means, if you take something back in time, an object—or a person—they could be lost in time and eliminated forever.

Letting out a heavy sigh, he then added, "It also means, when I do go back in time and make a change, it can have profound effects. It could be beneficial, or it could be deadly to billions of people."

Efi laid a hand on top of his. "That's why you need the see'ers to guide you."

"*Guide* is a good word. I can work with that, but if the sentiment becomes words like 'direct' or 'insist,' we will have a problem."

She gave him that great smile, the one that always melted him. "I repeat, I will be on your side in this, no matter your decisions."

For the next four days, Romy practiced time travel, both hopping to different planes of reality and teleporting to different places within their plane of reality. He made two hops per day, and with each trip, he became more proficient. No one would say time travel had become second nature to him, but he was becoming comfortable with it.

Efi laughed uproariously when, on one of his teleportation trips, he had returned from the training area on the *Aramis* with his hideous, red and green vase. He joined in her laughter as he placed it on a high point in a swath of purple flowers, indeed a worthy place of honour.

As they ate their dinner, they summarized their accomplishments to date. After a slow start to his training, he had progressed rapidly. He offered that he would soon be ready to consider missions from the see'ers.

Holding up her hand, Efi offered, "As far as hopping goes, I agree. But considering teleportations, you have only gone back a short time span, a few weeks at the most. We need to work further back with much care, ensuring you are extremely comfortable before you attempt missions."

Begrudgingly, Romy agreed, but, that night, the thought bothered him. He was progressing well, and he felt strong—so strong he felt he could do anything. The restlessness kept him awake, until he could take no more. Hearing heavy breathing coming from Efi, he rose in the middle of the night, retrieving his clothes and boots before sneaking out of the tent.

Donning his clothes, a plan came to mind, and he set it in motion. Walking down the rough-hewn stairs, he moved down to the base of the ridge where their tools were kept. There, he retrieved a shovel, one with a sharp pick on the opposite end. Returning to the top of the ridge, in the dim visibility allowed by the tendrils of light shooting upwards from the pond's rocks, he inspected the base of the postree. He finally saw what he was looking for, picking up a small, round pod before slipping it into his pocket.

Romy didn't want to wait through weeks and weeks of additional training.

He was going to accelerate those plans drastically. Shayne, on one of his visits, had explained in detail the story of Lucky Postree Ridge. He had said, through testing, it was determined the tree was 850 years old.

That was what Romy needed to know. With the shovel in one hand, he closed his eyes, thinking back 850 years while, in his mind's eye, he pictured the massive tree as nothing more than a small sapling. He invoked the Athar in his mind. When he hopped or teleported in time, the Athar looked much different. Whereas the Athar usually had layers the mind's eye would accelerate through, when he invoked time travel, the entire layered view began to roll, end over end. He didn't understand how the process worked, or how his mind's eye knew when to stop the roll and acceleration through the layers, but it did.

When the view cleared, he was moving through the layers towards a bright yellow light. He focused on it, and a few moments later, he felt queasy along with the sense of falling forward. By now, he knew better than to step forward, since a moment later, the mind's eye view of the Athar was gone, replaced by the grey panorama of Metro.

The trip took much of his energy, and as a result, he fell to his knees under the morning sun. He stayed there for a time, taking several deep breaths. Eventually, he rose to his feet, inspecting the view around him. As expected, there were no signs of a campsite. The pond was there, but it was smaller, yet it sat higher against the ridge. As for the ridge, it looked lower, but in fact, it was the ground below the ridge that was higher. Romy assumed, over time, the winds had slowly eroded the softer rock at the base of the ridge, something that had not yet occurred in the time he just left.

It was only then he noticed there was no shade on the ridge. The massive postree was not there. His hopes grew as he circled in small steps, inspecting the rock face. Bent over, he picked at small irregularities until, finally, his eyebrows rose. "There it is!"

He took two quick strides, falling to his knees. There, in a crack within the surface of the sedimentary rock was the sapling, no more than ten centimetres high. He didn't know if fortunate winds had blown the seed here, or perhaps an Armatod had planted it. It really didn't matter.

Rising to his feet, Romy continued to inspect the top of the ridge. There were many other cracks, but none as large as the one the fortunate postree sapling had found. Finally, he decided on a crack that was about the same distance from the pond as the sapling was. Taking the pick end of the shovel, he attacked the crack. Sedimentary in nature, small chunks flew off in every direction. Once he thought the hole was large enough, he strode towards the pond. Finding a soil deposit, it took four trips to fill the hole he'd made. Satisfied, he pulled the seed pod from his pocket and buried it in the soil. He completed the planting by bringing four shovelfuls of water to soak into the soil.

He thought the work complete, but then had a second thought. He brought four shovelfuls of water to the sapling, thinking the two brothers deserved equal care. He knew the sapling would grow. Once the roots took hold, they would crack the rock, burying deep until they found the moisture laden surface below the ridge.

He waited longer than he should have, enjoying the view from the ridge. It didn't look that much different, although the Wilderlands were closer. He was enjoying it immensely, sitting by the edge of the pond, his feet dangling in the cool water, when he saw the dust cloud in the distance. He rose, pulled on his boots and, with a hand shielding his eyes, watched the dust cloud coming closer.

It was time to go, he thought, but at the same time, he was curious about the cause of the cloud, so he waited while moving to the highest point on the rock. He almost waited too long as the cloud was almost on him. Within it, he saw a mass of grey arms and legs—Armatods, and they were on the run! Naked, there had to be several hundred of them, some running upright, some on all fours, a few somewhere between.

Now, it really was time to go! He focused on the campsite. The Athar appeared. He was accelerating through the planes once again, but the rolling action was backwards. The bright yellow light in his mind's eye brought him back to his own time. When he opened his eyes, it was dark. Once his pupils adjusted, he could see the tent in the dim light of the pond. He was exhausted and all but fell into the bed before pulling the blanket over him.

In the morning, Romy awoke to the sound of a shuttle. He reached to his side, but Efi wasn't there. He must have slept late. Still tired, it took a few minutes for his vision to clear, and he took a few more minutes to enjoy just being lazy for a bit.

Finally, he did rise, immediately noticing he was still in his clothes. Poking his head through the flap of the tent, he spied Shayne and Efi. "Good morning."

As he climbed out, Efi handed him a yellow breakfast packet, identical to the one Shayne was already devouring. Between forkfuls of food, Romy asked, "You're back early. What's up?"

Efi thought the scene comical. The two brothers, sitting across from each other, resembled each other more than she had noticed in the past, made more evident by the similar bad habit of talking between huge mouthfuls of food.

After a massive swallow, Shayne answered, "A Mabuza official came to me yesterday. He told me one of the see'ers, Elki, asked for your presence at Hagaza, the Mabuza capital on Haven."

Pointing his fork at his brother, his eyes narrowed, Romy asked, "Was it a request, or did he insist?"

"It was a request, but it seemed urgent."

Romy glanced at Efi, and in return, she gave a barely perceptible nod of her chin.

"It seems like we will be leaving Lucky Postree Ridge. It was inevitable," Romy replied.

Both Efi and Shayne looked at each other, confusion filling both their faces. Shayne was the first to reply. "I'm not sure what you've been up to here, but whatever it is has given you memory lapses. I've never heard of Lucky Postree Ridge. This is Twin Postree Ridge; always has been."

Knowing what he would see, Romy tilted his gaze up, seeing two massive bundles of huge leaves, each bundle attached to a massive postree trunk. When he tilted his gaze back down, Efi and Shayne didn't understand the silly smile on his face, or the unnecessary, obvious words that followed.

"Of course, it is." Romy's smile turned from one of joy, to determination. He was ready.

Chapter 18: Return To Hagaza

The 8th day of the 6th month, Alpha Centauri year 0024.

Hagaza, capital city of the Mabuza people, Haven.

Hopping had become second nature to Romy, and he was now equally as proficient at the task as Efi was. Having just transpositioned to Hagaza, via an off-plane layover point, they successfully arrived at the transposition platform in the Mabuza government building. A guard, who had been expecting them, asked them to be seated and wait a few moments. He moved to an intercom on the wall, making what appeared to be a scheduled call.

A few minutes later, Grodin appeared, striding through the doors on the far side of the large room. He had a wide smile on his face as he approached. By now, they had been through quite a few experiences together, whereby Efi and Romy considered him as much a friend as an associate.

"Grodin! It's great to see you again." When he was within range, Efi gave him a tight hug.

When she released him, Romy slapped him on the shoulder. "Good to see you again, Friend."

Grodin maintained the wide smile. "My greetings to you both. The see'ers have a busy schedule, so they will be seeing you this evening, after dinner. I have been told to make you comfortable in room 510, just upstairs from where we are."

"Lead the way," Romy offered with a wave of his hand.

It was a short walk down a nondescript hallway to the main atrium. From there, one of the three elevators took them up to the fifth floor.

As they entered room 510, Romy said, "I think this is the same room…"

"We stayed in when we first met with the see'ers," Efi interrupted. Her gaze rose, scanning the room. "It certainly brings back memories."

"You have five hours before the meeting," Grodin informed them. "You can stay here, or you can travel the city, including the beach area."

"The other Korians and Sholites visiting the beach area might recognize Romy. They might have issues with that," Efi suggested.

Through a laugh, Grodin replied, "There are no Korians or Sholites in Hagaza Prime or the beach area. The recent reveal of our technology and psychic powers shook the people of both races. Things are not the same as they were; they probably never will be. They stay in the north now, and most of our Mabuza people have returned to the southern islands."

"That's sad," Efi said, her mind contemplating the future inferences. "In time, when they see we are not a threat, the tensions will ease."

"Nevertheless, if you leave the building, know that I will be shadowing you," Grodin said.

An orange fireball appeared at Romy's fingertips. "I have progressed, Grodin. No one will be harming Efi or I."

Grodin raised an eyebrow at the show of Romy's power. "I am sure of it, but I have my orders. You will need to indulge me as I carry them out."

Laughing, Romy slapped the warrior on the shoulder again. "I would have it no other way!"

Once Grodin left, finding two closets full of clothes, they changed from their travel attire. Romy donned a black, casual suit with a red open collar shirt, while Efi pulled on a yellow dress, the fabric falling to just above the knee.

When Romy saw the dress along with the sandals Efi slipped into, he let out a low whistle. "It's not the same dress, but it is very close to the one you wore during my first visit to the city."

She came close, pressing against him. "That's why I'm wearing it," she replied, barely above a purr.

Growling in response, Romy slid his hand up the back of her thigh, under the dress.

With a giggle, Efi spun out of his clutches, stepping back to lean against a dresser. Her nostrils flared and her cheeks were flushed. Yet, through it, she said, "Save that energy for later. I'm hungry."

People have different *sighs*. Romy was no different. Sometimes it was boredom or fatigue, sometimes it could be surprise. The one Romy let out now, was one Efi had seen before, although not so much in the last month during their time in the Harshlands. She knew from it, Romy was frustrated.

He let out a second, similar sigh, but since Efi did not show signs of sympathy, he opened the door, holding it for her. "Well, if we're not going to—you know—we might as well eat."

She walked by him, her hips swaying more than usual, her shoulders rolling to the same rhythm, and at the same time, her eyes fluttered.

Closing the door, Romy followed her. "I can't believe you just batted your eyes at me."

She turned her face, repeating the gesture suggesting innocence.

"Yeah, and that sultry walk. That's called a 'sashay.' Totally not fair."

They made their way to the tourist area, hand in hand, young lovers in love. As cliche as it was, that's exactly what it was. They spent the afternoon on the beach, visiting the rock outcropping at the north end. They let their feet dangle in the water, just as they had on their first visit. The difference this time, however, was they hugged and kissed without a care who was watching. The beach wasn't busy, but it certainly wasn't empty. But it could have been packed with Mabuza, Sholites or Korians; it would not have mattered. Even Grodin, off in the distance, wasn't noticed. They were lost in each other, and nothing would interrupt that.

They stopped and ate a wonderful fish stew before returning to their apartment. There, Efi pulled off the dress, and was flipping through the pant suits hanging in the closet.

"I was hoping you would keep that dress on for later," Romy said.

Without turning, Efi pulled out a bland, dark-brown suit. "The dress was for you, Handsome, not for the see'ers." She turned, holding the pant suit to the side, so it didn't cover her naked body. Now, there was no look of innocence. Rather, her golden eyes were dark, and her voice was deeper with a sultry tone. "You sure you want that dress on later, or maybe just like this might be better?"

Romy felt like his eyes were rattling. Before turning for the door, he managed, "I'll wait for you outside."

Grodin, waiting in the hallway, noticed the few beads of sweat on Romy's brow. "Everything okay, Sir?"

Romy was caught off guard. He opened his mouth but no words came out. Wiping his brow, he tried again, but all that came out was, "Doing great."

Grodin smiled a crooked, sly smile. "Very good, Sir. Say no more."

To get to the see'ers chamber, they needed to travel down to the ground level, then take a second elevator back up to the third floor. There were guards present when they boarded the elevator, two more when they left it and two more at the great wooden doors to the see'er's chamber. Malakay, the senior advisor, was waiting with them.

They all gave their warmest greetings. Malakay seemed genuinely happy Romy had survived to this point. Ruut Nkosi, a former advisor revealed now as a rebel leader, almost killed Romy during his first visit. However, Ruut was now in custody, with no end date to his incarceration.

After entering the large chamber room, Malakay, his fingers benevolently intertwined together in front of him, led them to a casual sitting area, not much different from the living area in their assigned apartment. Malakay, in a formal manner, announced Romy and Efi to the see'ers.

The five see'ers rose to greet their visitors. First, Jalli gave her greetings. She was the shortest of the see'ers, made to look even shorter by the extremely long ponytail she wore. As Romy reciprocated the greeting, he thought, *someone should tell her that.* Kory was next. The man gave a wide smile, but it didn't help. His shaved head still looked too big for his body.

Romy hoped his hesitation wasn't obvious when he greeted Arinol. The man, with slicked-back, black hair, held a close resemblance to Ruut, the man who tried to kill him on his last visit.

Finally, he turned to greet Mist and Elki, standing side by side. They were the two Romy had spent the most time with. Mist, usually more reserved, could not hold back her wide grin as she gave both Romy, then Efi, a hug. Elki, not to be outdone, also embraced each of them. Romy appreciated the smile on the older see'er's face, and he noticed her eyes were moist. He could see she was genuinely happy to see him.

Elki told everyone to sit, then pointed at a server on the far side of the room. "Bring drinks!"

Once everyone was served, the bottles were left on the table before the server was asked to leave. They were alone.

The large room, with excellent acoustics, left an ominous echo when they spoke.

Elki began. "Romy, tell me how you are?"

Romy gave an extended answer, detailing the events that had transpired in his life. He talked about his father, his father's beacons, his brother and his mother I'lish—everything except anything to do with psychic powers or time travel.

"That's wonderful," Elki replied. "How about your training?"

Shrugging, Romy gave the impression the topic bored him. "It has gone well. I am comfortable with both transpositions and teleportations. I have travelled back in time, up to 850 years, doing so within plane and passing through to other planes. Easy-peasy," he added before taking a drink from his glass. Then, he glanced at Mist, noticing the edges of her lips were quivering as she fought to contain her laughter.

"That's wonderful," Elki concluded. "It sounds like you are ready to proceed with some missions."

Leaning forward, Romy quipped, "Are they missions, or assignments?"

"What's the difference?" Elki asked.

"To me, a mission has military connotations. Assignments are more sinister and covert—like spying."

"Although I disagree with the sinister description, let's call them assignments, then. Are you ready?" Elki asked for a second time.

"He needs two more weeks of training," Efi interjected. She had decided to keep quiet so far, letting her man answer the questions. But here, she needed to give her unbiased evaluation.

"What do you think, Romy?" Elki asked for a third time.

"Efi said he needed two more weeks," Jalli said, her voice firm. "She has been with him all along, so she would know."

Elki scanned the other see'ers, but no one took sides. Her white afro shook as she clapped her hands together. "Very well. We will meet here again in exactly two weeks. We will provide you with your first assignment, then."

Elki made ready to rise, thinking the meeting concluded when Romy lifted a finger, indicating it was not.

"With all due respect to you, Elki—" he gazed in turn to each of the see'ers "—and the rest of the see'ers, I don't like the way that comes across."

"How so?" Arinol asked.

"When you have an assignment for me, I would like to receive a docket on the assignment a week in advance. In that docket will be details of the people I will be involved with, details of the location, the reason for my intervention and the expected result from it. I will expect all this information in detail," Romy stressed. "Then, I will decide if I will proceed, and how."

"Of course, *we* will advise you how to proceed," Elki clarified in a low voice.

"I would expect no less."

They rose and stretched their legs. The formal part of the meeting was over. While they finished their drinks, they mingled. Romy made a point to give Elki another great hug. He knew she was doing what she thought was best. Hopefully, the hug, and it was a truly sincere hug, told her within that purpose, he needed to find his way as well.

Just before he and Efi were ready to leave, Mist came over and hugged Romy. In his ear, she whispered, "Well done."

The next two weeks were filled with training. Romy did not find it taxing; in fact, the more he practiced traveling in time, the easier it came to him. Even his recovery time improved, now reduced from three hours to two. He was strong, and his strength was increasing. The change was obvious to Efi.

Throughout the training period, they shared their time between Hagaza and Cliffside. After all, their hops could initiate from any location. It was during one of the stays at Cliffside, in the middle of the second week, when Romy and Efi received an invitation to a party at the Metronian prime minister's government building. However, surprisingly, the invite was from Romy's stepmother, I'lish.

Apparently, during the peace negotiations between the Metronians and the representatives from Haven, she and the prime minister found each other to be excellent company. In fact, as rumour would have it, after the prime minister invited her back to Cliffside, the thought was they might be closer than just associates. When I'lish accepted the offer of a stay at a villa adjacent to the government building, typically reserved for visiting dignitaries, the rumours grew. Prime Minister Ren Jacoby was a widower, and I'lish was unmarried. It made for excellent gossip on Metro, and, eventually, on Haven as well.

Two days later, Romy and Efi arrived at the villa. Romy wore a dark-blue pair of slacks and a grey short-cut turtleneck—smart but casual. Efi, having brought the yellow dress from Hagaza, wore it once again. It never got old on Romy, and Efi knew it.

"Mother!" Romy shouted across the room as he waved his hand over his head.

I'lish waved back, the motion soon changing as she motioned for him to come over to her. Romy and Efi joined the group: I'lish, Ryder, Naala, Shayne and Prime Minister Jacoby. There were hugs all around, except for the prime minister, of course. This was the first time Romy and Efi had met him, so formal introductions were made.

The party itself was called a *Shanty*. There is no direct translation, but it is similar to a cocktail party, just with a little more class. Drinks were offered constantly, and exquisite finger foods were served every 30 minutes over a three-hour period.

It was during the second serving when Romy took Ryder aside. "Who are they?" he asked, pointing to a young couple conversing near the open doors to the balcony. The Mabuza woman was young and pretty. The young man with her was odd looking, having short clumps of ragged, red hair.

Ryder, pointing his drink at the woman, explained, "That—is Shayne's girlfriend."

Blurting out a laugh, Romy's drink swished, spilling out over his fingers. "Really!" After gazing at her for a minute, he mumbled, "I would say, 'not bad at all.'" After downing what was left in his glass, Romy asked, "Who's the guy?"

"That guy is a girl. That's Marty."

"And who is Marty?"

"Marty is the smartest person I've ever met," Ryder clarified. "That means, she's the smartest person you'll ever meet. She cracked the code for the messages from the beacons. And the thing is, even with how much she knows, she's like a sponge for more learning."

Obviously, Romy's next question was about the messages. He was flabbergast when his father told him of the three names: Natalie Lowe, Ryder Gunn and Marjorie Gunn. Romy had the same confused look on his face his father did when he heard the last name. Romy had no more idea than his father as to who Marjorie Gunn was.

I'lish wandered over to them, joining the conversation. "Why are you monopolizing our son?" she said through a smile.

Romy did a double take. His mother looked ravishing. She looked happy, but there was something else he could not put his finger on. Then, his eyes grew mischievous as he discovered what it was. He leaned over, whispering in her ear. "Why, Mother, you have makeup on."

Leaning back, she playfully slapped his shoulder. "You're the first one who's noticed."

Having placed his empty glass on a tray carried by a passing waiter, Ryder turned and said, "Noticed what?"

Both Romy and I'lish burst out laughing. It turned out to be a great night enjoyed by all, one they would remember for a long time.

The next day, Romy completed two more training missions. He found time travel was coming second nature to him now. The following day, they travelled back to Hagaza. Grodin met them, and led them up to room 510, which had been maintained for their return.

Three hours later, there was a knock on their door. Grodin, his lips set in a firm line, said, "Elki requests your presence in the transposition area. She would like to see a demonstration of Romy's time hopping abilities."

When they arrived, Elki was waiting with Mist. The senior see'er, with as much effort as she could to make it not sound like an order, requested Romy to time travel back. Mist showed him data on her tablet: the target plane, coordinates and the year.

"It's the coordinates of P Central, before the establishment of the pureblood colonies there," Elki clarified.

Romy tried to make his snicker not sound like a snicker. His words came in a low, suspicious tone. "I feel a bit like an animal in a circus show. Will you have treats for me when I get back?"

Sighing, Elki's eyes became rounder and her chin drooped. She turned, taking small steps to the exit.

After only three steps, Romy stated in a loud voice. "Okay! You want to see me time travel. I will do it." He raised his arms, creating a space. "Move back."

Mist, Elki, Grodin and Efi, hustled to the far wall. When they turned, Efi saw Romy was staring at her. She didn't understand the look until it was too late. She was about to yell out, but Romy's form began to shimmer, then he was gone.

An instant later, the shimmer returned. Romy materialized, but he was different. When he left, he had light-brown clothes. Now, he wore a black outfit. Efi gasped when she saw his face. He had left clean shaven, but now, he had a good three weeks growth of beard.

When Romy finished materializing, he fell to his knees. Efi rushed forward, and by the time she was beside him, he retched. The second spasm had bile vomiting up. Efi slipped under his arm and helped him to his feet.

By now, Elki and Mist were beside them. "What have you done?" Elki asked, the creases covering her forehead an indication of her concern.

Lifting his gaze, he let out a mocking laugh. "You wanted me to time travel. I did. I went to your location, but from there, I went to Talus 3."

Elki let out a loud hiss. "What did you do! You told me you wouldn't go there!"

Shrugging while rolling his eyes, Romy said, "You're wrong. I said, 'Romy Gunn would not travel to Talus 3.' I went as Soren Pym. You should remember that name. It was the name you gave me on my first visit to your illustrious city."

Mist closed her eyes and held her hands in front of her in a meditative position. After a few moments, she said, "I don't sense any changes in the Athar."

"Relax. I didn't do anything. I thought about killing the woman who caused the destruction of my people, but I couldn't do it."

"Thank our ancestors for that!" Elki said. Her eyes focused on Romy. Even though her words might seem harsh, they were said with the love she felt for the young man. "You can be a rogue, Mr. Gunn. You need to understand, on any given day, you can be a saviour or killer of millions of souls. I'm not saying that to scare you or convince you of anything. I am just objectively explaining your reality." That said, she turned and curtly walked from the room.

It was curious that Mist stayed, but it became clear she had an added question for Romy. "Why didn't you kill the woman and save Talus 3?"

Although the see'er had asked the question, he looked down into Efi's eyes with the answer. "I didn't change history because I didn't know if you'd be here when I returned."

Chapter 19: The Assassination

The 20ᵗʰ day of the 9ᵗʰ month, Alpha Centauri year 0024.

Hagaza, capital city of the Mabuza people, Haven

As Efi had foretold, the next two weeks were filled with more training missions. It was a week later when Romy's cycle of time travel assignments began. For each, he was given a docket with the details, just as he had requested. He realized quickly, over the next few months, these were simple missions. The see'ers were easing him into the workload to come.

The four missions he had completed were easily handled, most often simply being a matter of providing the authorities covert information of a mass murderer or diabolical psychopath's intentions.

In another trip, he was tasked with stopping an assassination of a prominent political figure. After his death, his world became corrupt with a hundred million people killed in the chain reaction of events. It was a bit more challenging, but shutting off the main power, thus the lights, at the convention centre where the assassination was to take place, eliminated the possibility of success for the sniper.

In another case, he avoided mass death from a terrorist bomb by simply pulling the fire alarm and evacuating the building. However, he was not as inconspicuous as he should have been. He was arrested by the local authorities. They were confused, since the bomb did go off, but his criminal act saved thousands of lives. Three hours later, they were on their way to his cell to release him, but they found his cell empty. The ability to transposition out of such situations was a definite advantage for a pureblood time drifter.

Over this time, Romy had only seen Elki occasionally, since she left the duties of providing Romy's assignments to Mist. As such, it was a surprise to Romy when he was summoned to the see'er's chamber for a meeting. Once he and Efi arrived, all five see'ers were in attendance.

Elki, seemingly on her best behaviour, handed a folder to Romy. "We feel it is important you accept this assignment."

The folder was thick, yet Romy began to flip through it.

"There's a lot there," Elki explained. "Let me summarise it for you, then you can review it in detail."

"Please," Romy replied as he closed the folder.

"The Athar has spoken to us of a planet in plane 6433. The planet is a scull world called *Franklin*. It is on the far edge of their sun's habitable zone. As such, it is perpetually cold, covered in snow and ice. But even though it might be a surprise to us, when that is all a people know, they find a way to thrive in it."

"That sounds like a good thing," Romy suggested.

"Most often, yes, but what also thrives on this world was and is organized crime. Up until 210 years ago, there were three primary crime families. They were kept in check by two things: the authority's superior organization and abilities, and, perhaps more importantly, the fact the three families were constantly battling each other. They were a bigger deterrent to themselves than the authorities were."

"I'm still not hearing why I would need to go there."

Elki continued, "As I said, that was up until 210 years ago. At that time, there was a meeting between the heads of the three crime families. They created a truce, one that has stood the test of time and is still in force today. They gained more and more power. The authorities were quickly overrun such that the crime syndicate rapidly took charge of the government of the planet, eliminating anyone who might stand in their way."

"Okay, you've painted a good picture," Romy admitted.

Leaning forward, Elki's voice became a tone lower, yet more direct. "Since the time of the truce there have been 85 million Franklinians killed by the organized crime syndicate. That is the extent of their oppressive power."

Romy couldn't help his eyes from opening wide. "Wow—85 million!"

"And the deaths continue each and every day." Elki took a moment, her next words measured. "We have concluded the only way to avoid these deaths is for one of the crime bosses to be assassinated before the meeting 210 years ago. One of them, a man named Carl Morgan, was the glue holding the syndicate together. Without him, the other two, who hated each other vehemently, would not have agreed to any type of collective agreement."

"You want me to kill someone?" Romy asked, his voice soft.

"Yes, one life to save 85 million," Elki clarified in case the proportion had not registered in the drifter's mind.

"No, I get it, Elki. But there must be other opportunities that would cause the meeting to be disrupted," Romy offered. "Can't we blow up a roadway leading to the meeting, or kidnap the man until the time of the meeting has passed? There must be something."

It was good that Mist had a great sense of timing. She answered Romy's question. "Our researchers have scoured the history books from Franklin. I have worked with them to ensure not one possibility was missed. This crime boss, Carl Morgan, was always secluded, and always at an unknown location. He had an army of highly trained guards with him at all times. We only found this one opportunity to assassinate him."

"Explain the opportunity," Romy requested.

Mist continued, "We know, three days before the meeting, Carl Morgan and his band of soldiers were staying at a massive house in the foothills of the Karson mountains, 30 kilometres from the small city of Van Selton. There is a tiny airport on the outskirts of Van Selton. Two days before the syndicate meeting, an affluent business man flies into the airport with his private jet. You see, he also has a large house in the foothills. Four hours before the meetings, the businessman is returning to his jet to fly to his next destination. Morgan and his associates hijack the plane and fly to a city, 500 kilometres away, for the meeting with the other two crime bosses."

Romy asked, "So, what do you expect me to do?"

Elki answered his question. "This is the only opportunity we can find when Carl Morgan is vulnerable. When the plane is moving down the runway, one of your fireballs would make short work of him and the jet."

Raising an eyebrow, Romy glared at Elki. "How many people were on the jet?"

"Eight," Elki said, a little too matter-of-fact for Romy. "The pilot, copilot, one attendant, Morgan and four of his thugs."

"It is then eight lives for 85 million," Romy corrected. "And three of them are innocent souls."

"Unfortunately—yes—there will be some collateral damage."

"Why can't I just damage the plane so that it never leaves for the meeting?"

"We thought of that," Mist answered. "However, there are two more private jets in another hanger at the far end of the airport, half a kilometre away. If you damaged the one jet, they could divert onto one of the others."

"Why couldn't I destroy the other two jets after damaging the first?"

Romy proposed.

Mist sighed. "We thought of that. You would have to run the half kilometre across open ground from the first aircraft to the other hanger. Morgan will have at least 50 armed guards with him. You would be mowed down by their weapons before you made it to the hanger." Mist felt Romy's pain. She tried to make her words as soothing as they could be in such a situation. "Romy, we really have researched every possibility. Destroying the plane is the only option."

Running his fingers back through his hair, Romy took a moment, staring at his feet, until he tilted his head, gazing at Efi. Her face did not reveal anything. This was a decision Romy had to make himself.

Straightening his shoulders, he took a prolonged moment to stare at each of the see'ers. "Understand, you are all party to this. It's not just me committing these murders. I will do as you ask. I will ensure Carl Morgan does not arrive at the syndicate meeting."

Elki was about to add some words, something Romy surely didn't want to hear right now. He stopped her by rising to his feet. Glancing at Efi, he said, "We better get going. I have a lot of reading to do," he said as he hefted the thick folder.

Not waiting for any type of formal dismissal, Romy led Efi towards the heavy doors. Malakay scurried along, catching up to them. It allowed him to hold the door open for them as they passed. Barely above a whisper, he said, "Best of luck, Sir."

Once they were well away from prying eyes in their apartment, Romy said to Efi, "You know I will do everything in my power to accomplish the task without killing those innocent people."

Efi held back the chuckle. It wasn't a humorous time. "I would expect no less from you."

Three days later, Romy was leaving from the transposition platform. He was dressed in a thick, white parka and matching insulated pants. After pulling the attached hood up over his head, Efi gave him a long kiss.

When she pulled back, she asked, "Do you have everything with you?"

Romy did a check. He pulled the map of the airport from his pocket. From another inside pocket, he pulled out the small binoculars. The last thing he checked for was a small wallet containing the pictures of Carl Morgan, the pilot and copilot. Of course, he, just as it was for any pureblood, could not take energy sources with him. He placed the items back in his pockets and prepared to hop to Van Selton Airport. At this time, it would be 7:00 in the evening there, so he would be arriving in darkness.

Efi gave him a quick, last kiss, before Romy moved to the middle of the transposition platform. He pulled the white hood tight before he shimmered and then disappeared.

He arrived on Franklin to a blast of frigid wind. It almost blew him over. In front of him, just a metre away, he saw the back of the small warehouse on the south side of the airport. As the Bantu intelligence had shown, there was a back door only a few metres from him. He ran to it, peering through the small panes of glass set in the top of the metal door. In the dim emergency lighting within the warehouse, he saw it was empty. He broke the lower pane of glass with his elbow, then reached through to unlock the door.

Once inside, he saw the west wall had a series of windows set in it, while another door was on the north wall, and beyond it would be the runway. He had timed his arrival to two hours before the hijacked plane's takeoff. That way, as soon as he destroyed the plane, he could hop back home.

He took the extra time he had to inspect the airport complex through the windows. The small terminal building was at the west end of the tiny complex, near the far end of the runway. On the other side of the runway across from the terminal, was a small hanger, and in it, he saw the jet in question. Moving to the door on the north wall, he opened it and checked his surroundings. He saw two more buildings, opposite from him, on the other side of the runway. He pulled the map from his pocket and verified one of them was a fuel storage facility, while the other was another small general storage facility. Looking to his east, in the far distance, he saw the other double hanger, and in it were two more jets. It was far away, and would be much farther if Morgan's gunmen happened to be shooting at him. Mist was right. Damaging the first plane and destroying the other two planes was a two-man job.

Back in the warehouse, Romy was interrupted by sounds coming from the main terminal. There was a large group of people walking from the terminal to the jet in the hanger. Needing a better look, Romy took off his gloves, retrieving the binoculars from his pocket. He placed the gloves on an empty barrel beside the window before lifting the binoculars to his eyes. He scanned the group, and after checking the pictures in his wallet, he found Carl Morgan, the pilot and copilot within the group. Both the pilot and copilot had their hands tied behind their back, while the other men surrounding the prisoners were heavily armed. It made a kill shot towards Morgan impossible without risking the innocent flight crew members.

He waited and watched. If Elki knew of his modified plans, she would be livid. He watched as the plane came out from the hanger, the guards now forming two lines, one on either side of the runway in front of the terminal. Flames blew out from the two engines, then the jet shot down the runway. He poked his head out the door, watching it speed by, just before it lifted into the air.

His modified plan was in motion. He never intended to destroy the plane—at least, not yet. This part of the plan was for him to obtain information: the configuration of the jet, the number of guards and their placement, and the exact weather conditions. With the information in hand, he was moving on to the next phase of his plan. If it failed, he could always hop back and destroy the plane in a repeated timeline.

On the back of the airport map was another map of Van Selton. He reviewed it and pressed his finger to a point in a wooded area beside the only hotel close to the airport. He knew, by how he felt, two hours had passed since he had hopped in, so he set his own plan in motion.

He shimmered, and a moment later he materialized in the woods beside the airport. He trudged through the thick snow until he found himself in a parking area adjacent to the three-story hotel. The building was small, but elegant, with a large lobby area. A doorman greeted him and seeing no vehicle, he asked Romy's intentions.

Romy, speaking with an air of importance, said, "I'm here from the airport with a message for Captain Blake Tilley." He didn't wait for a reply as he headed for the elevators. He glanced at the time display on the wall, seeing it was 10:00 pm, and the date indicated he had drifted back a day from his original arrival at the airport.

He knew, from the Bantu researchers, the captain was in room 211. Once he arrived on the second floor, he pulled the knife from his coat pocket, the knife not even Efi knew about. He knocked on the door, whereby a short, thin, bald man answered. Romy peered over the man's shoulder and saw there was no one else in the room.

He pulled the knife from behind his back, flashing it to the pilot's neck. "Back up!" he hissed.

The pilot shuffled backwards as Romy kicked the door closed behind him. After asking the man to sit in one of the room's chairs, Romy removed his coat, placing it on the bed. Lowering himself in the chair opposite from the pilot, he saw the fear in his eyes. The man was visibly shaking.

"Relax," Romy said. "I'm not going to hurt you."

"Why the knife?" the pilot replied, his voice quivering.

Romy put the knife on the table to his right, but still close enough so he could retrieve it, if need be. "I'm from a secret organization in the government. Our intelligence says, when you fly out tomorrow, your plane will be hijacked. We need both you and the copilot to keep away from the airport tomorrow. In fact, we need you to leave the city tonight."

"What agency?" the man asked. His voice still trembled, but at least his hands had stopped shaking.

"If you knew about it, then it wouldn't be a *secret* agency, would it?"

"Who is going to hijack the plane?"

"Carl Morgan and his associates."

The pilot blurted out a laugh. "What would Carl Morgan be doing in Van Selton? He hasn't been seen in years."

Romy's eyes darkened, his voice deepened as he stressed each word. "You don't have to believe me. But then, tomorrow evening, you will be dead."

Taking in a deep breath, the captain glanced at a cabinet a metre from him. "I need a drink. Do you mind?"

"Go for it."

"Would you like one?"

I'm good," Romy replied.

The man shuffled to the cabinet, pulling out a glass bottle, half filled with an amber liquor, and a glass. He filled the glass, and took a heavy drink. "That's better," he mumbled.

Over the next hour, the pilot relaxed. His hands no longer shook, as he drank most of the bottle. In fact, he and Romy had a polite conversation. The captain even thanked him for the warning. It seemed the captain had accepted he would not be flying the following evening.

"My life is more important than this damn contract," the pilot said. "I'll be on the train later tonight. The copilot is a good friend. I'll make sure he and the flight attendant come with me. Our next contract flight is in two days, so better safe than sorry."

"Make sure of it, Blake. You seem like a good fellow. I don't want you to get hurt."

That said, Romy was convinced the pilot would be on a train later that night. In any case, he would wait at the train station to make sure. He smiled at Blake, who returned it. Romy turned to retrieve his coat. His turn was only half complete when he felt the empty liquor bottle slam into the back of his head. "Damn," he cursed, before he lost consciousness.

The Van Selton Airport Police Station was in a small building adjacent to the terminal building. Since they only handled issues at the airport, and the airport was small, there was only one cell and only one officer on duty at any time.

That's where Romy woke up, immediately holding the back of his head. Once his vision cleared, he looked through the bars, seeing a burly officer glaring at him.

"Bout time you woke up," the officer sneered.

"How long was I out?"

"It's been about two hours. The weather outside is bad. Things aren't expected to clear up until tomorrow evening. That means we won't be able to transport you to the state jail until the following morning. They can do a mental evaluation there." He chuckled. "A hijacked plane, huh? And you're a secret agent," he added with a sarcastic snicker.

"I tried," Romy managed. "You'll probably be dead tomorrow night."

The guard, held his belly as he laughed. "Get some sleep," he said, before he walked into the station's front room.

Romy did just that. He had time, so he slept until midmorning the next day. He was thankful when they brought him a meal. The sarcastic guard had left, and now, a man, short on words, was left on shift. He seemed nice enough, being courteous to Romy, asking often if there was anything he needed. Romy felt bad for what he would have to do to him.

When the digital clock on the wall showed 5:00 in the afternoon, Romy teleported out of the cell. He didn't have to wait long before the guard came through the door to do his quarter hour check. Having picked out a hefty riot club from the storage closet, Romy smacked the guard on the back of the head. After putting him in the cell and locking the door, Romy moved into the front room of the station house.

He saw his white coat hanging on a hook on the wall, but when he retrieved it, he noticed the long tear in one arm. He had no idea how it came about, but it was fortunate there were three heavily-insulated grey, police coats hanging from similar hooks. The second one he tried fit well, but there wasn't a hood attached. So, he reached up and pulled the black, wool hat from the shelf. Pulling it tight, then dragging the flaps down over his ears, he was ready for the elements.

He took a moment to retrieve his map and binoculars from the ripped jacket before moving to the officer's desk. With a pen, he scribbled a short note, folded the paper and thrust it into the pocket of the coat. As he walked towards the front exit, he glanced at the mirror on the wall and thought, *this will work very well. He looked every bit a believable police officer.*

It was a short walk down a hallway to a side door, leading to the main, wide hallway of the terminal. The disguise did, in fact, work very well. Even though there were only a few people in the terminal, no one took a second glance at him.

Once outside in the light snowfall, he walked to the small storage warehouse on the south side of the single runway; the one he had been in before. He fingered the two items in his pocket, leaving them where they would be found before retracing his steps out from the building.

One of the black hat flaps lifted a bit, so he pulled it down before lowering into a crouch. Then, he ran across the runway to the fuel storage building on the other side of the runway. He jumped into the entryway alcove, shifting into a corner to wait. He looked at the timepiece that was attached to the sleeve of the police coat. "He'll be here soon," Romy mumbled as he pulled the binoculars out, pulling them to his eyes.

Even in the small storage warehouse, with the sound of the heaters working at their maximum, it was cold. Romy pulled the white rim of the hood tight around his face. About to survey the area through the window, he retrieved the binoculars. Removing his gloves, he put them on the barrel next to him. He froze, his blue eyes narrowing at the two objects on the barrel. He lifted the map, and his suspicion was verified. It was his map of Van Selton Airport. Instinctively, he thrust his hand into his coat pocket, expecting the map to not be there. But it was!

He pulled it out, placing it down beside the one on the barrel. They were identical! His mind felt like it would explode. *What was going on?*

He turned his focus to the folded paper. It might explain why there were two maps. Unfolding it, he read the words:

> *Romy*
>
> *I am here to help you. It will take two of us. Look outside the door.*
>
> *Romy*

To most people, their confusion would have grown. However, Romy had spent many hours thinking about time travel, the possibilities and the paradoxes. Yet still, a shiver went through him, causing him to pull his white hood even tighter around his face. He moved to the door, cracking it open. Seeing nothing odd, he slid out into the small, protected entryway. The storm had passed, but still there was a light fall of snow. Through it he saw nothing, but he heard a high-pitched whistle. He jumped back, pressing his back against the door. Pulling the binoculars from his pocket, he scanned across the far side of the runway towards the sound.

He saw a change in colour and a slight movement. In the doorway of the fuel storage facility, on the other side of the runway was a man. He was wearing a grey coat and a black hat pulled down tight over his eyes. Romy could not make out his face because of the binoculars covering it. The man was looking directly at him, so they were at a standoff.

When the man in the black hat pulled the binoculars away, Romy sucked in a deep breath. He was looking at himself! He pulled the binoculars from his eyes, wiping them. When he brought them back up, he was still looking at Romy Gunn.

The Romy Gunn in the black hat motioned to him. He lifted his hand, spreading his fingers. He then repeated the motion. From under the white hood, Romy understood the signal from his time with the PAT military forces. That meant, *ten minutes.*

Then, from under the black hat, Romy with two fingers, pointed to his eyes, then pointed at the single plane in the west hanger. Next, he pointed his two fingers at his double in the white hat, then the two planes in the hanger half a kilometre down the runway.

Romy's head, in the white hood, nodded up and down. He understood. In fact, he understood everything. His plan always was, if he could not complete the task himself, he would go back an extra day in time and convince the pilot to abort the mission. He must have done that, time shifting back a day, but failed to stop the pilot. Eventually, time catches up such that in this exact timeline, now there were two Romy Gunns, and that was fortunate since they needed two people to complete the mission.

Romy's face was flushed from the bitter wind, and his heart was racing. He lifted his hand, pressing his thumb up, indicating he understood the plan. He knew Romy was watching from under his black hat. From the fuel storage facility, he would disable the first jet. That left Romy in the white coat to disable the two jets in the double hanger. The countdown had begun. They had ten minutes.

By now, Romy was continually pulling the hood tight, and he did it again. It was more of a nervous reaction thinking about the task to come. He then stepped out from the alcove before moving around to the back of the building. A long berm of snow ran just in front of the perimeter fence line.

Romy climbed over the snow bank, then ran as fast as he could along the fence to the double hanger. Once there, he crept around the far side, peering into the massive hanger opening. It was dark, with not a soul in sight.

He only had a minute to spare. Focusing towards the far end of the runway, he saw the jet begin to accelerate. It was halfway down the runway, when he saw an orange lightning bolt of energy fly out from behind the fuel storage facility. It hit the front tire. It was a precision shot. The tire, along with the undercarriage assembly, was blown off. As a result, the underside of the nose, lowered with sparks showering in every direction. He realized his alter persona was, in all likelihood, already hopping back to Hagaza—and home. His part of the mission was done.

Now, it was his turn. From under the white hood, he focused. His arm pulled back and he let out an identical firebolt of energy. It exploded into the first jet. Before that explosion had settled, a second energy burst was on the way to the second jet.

He realized he had to teleport back a day to the hotel area. If he didn't, the second Romy Gunn would not be here in this timeline. His brain hurt as he tried to comprehend the obtuse reality he was in. It was the only thing that made sense. He had to teleport back a day. Focusing, he expected to feel the similar vertigo that came with any hop or teleportation, but nothing happened. He focused again. Still nothing, except he felt a burning sensation against his side. *Was he injured?* he thought.

In any case, he didn't have too long to contemplate it. Since the double warehouse was engulfed in flames, an emergency vehicle was speeding towards it. Heavily armed men were hanging off both sides. Romy knew he needed time to figure out what was wrong, so he ran towards the old, abandoned military barrack on the opposite side of the runway. He heard yells as the armed guards on the emergency vehicle saw him. They changed direction, speeding after him.

Fortunately, he arrived at the derelict building well before the vehicle. He burst open a door and fled up a flight of stairs, two at a time. Once on the third floor, he sped down a hallway, lined with offices and bedrooms on either side. He found one unlocked, jumping in before closing the door behind him.

Moving to the window, below him he saw the emergency vehicle had arrived. Four armed guards had jumped off and were surveying the side of the building. Romy heard them say, they would begin on the first floor, checking every room until they found the culprit. He shrank back from the window. It would not be long before they found him. He tried again to teleport back a day. Nothing happened. He tried, over and over, with the same result. The only change seemed to be the burning feeling in his side. He lifted his coat and shirt, inspecting the area of pain. There was a red mark, hot to the touch, but no wound.

He let the coat back down, and immediately, his side felt hot again. He pressed his hand into his pocket, then rapidly pulled it back out due to a hot, burning sensation. More carefully this time, he gingerly pressed two fingers in. With the tips, he gripped the edge of the paper and pulled it out. Releasing it immediately, it fell on the desk beside him.

If he was confused before, it was magnified now. It was the note the other Romy had written him, the one he had placed in his pocket after reading it.

He heard voices on the floor below him. The gunmen were on the second floor. Soon, they would be on the third floor. He said to himself, "Think! Think! What's happening." Then a thought came to him. In his training, Efi had told him of a time shift paradox. Even though he could travel in time, the Athar made sure logical sequences were not violated.

The other Romy had given him the note. It was a note he wrote after teleporting into the past. Now, if he teleported into the past with the note, then there would be no need for him to write the note. It was a circular cycle with no beginning or end. *That must be it!* He thought.

The note was now on the table. He focused again, even as he heard the footsteps in the hallway. As the doorknob turned, he began to shimmer. By the time it was opened, the gunmen found nothing except for a cryptic note, addressed to and signed by the same person.

Efi knew Romy should be right back, and he was. Right after he dematerialized, he rematerialized in the government transposition room. She thought it odd, a moment ago, he left with a white coat, and now, he returned wearing a grey coat and a silly black hat.

Once he smiled at her, indicating all was well, she said, "Nice look, Fella."

He pulled off the coat and hat, throwing them to the side. He wrapped his arm around his woman, leading her from the room. "That was a crazy assignment," Romy said.

"Did it go as planned?"

"Yeah. It's all good," he replied. But he was questioning that. It was a wild, mind-bending mission, one he was still having trouble contemplating. What was troubling him, perhaps more, was even though he didn't like being pushed into these missions, his adrenalin was flowing. He enjoyed the adventure, like an addict enjoying a bad drug, and it was a habit he might not get over.

Chapter 20: Not So Simple After All

The 15th day of the 10th month, Alpha Centauri year 0024.

Hagaza, capital city of the Mabuza people, Haven

A slight breeze came from the east, carrying the scent of the ocean. All bodies of water on Haven, with only a few exceptions, were fresh water. Yet still, this ocean carried the fresh scent of fish and birds and the flowering, long grasses growing along the rocky shorelines.

Romy took a deep breath of the scented air just before he took another drink of the ice-cold fruit wine in his glass. At the large table situated in the middle of the semicircular veranda, hanging off the back of the see'er's government building, were all five see'ers, Malakay, he and Efi. It seemed, Malakay, although not a see'er, was a trusted part of the group, never straying far from them.

The plates on the table were cannibalized, some empty, others with only a few scraps left on them. Lunch had indeed been excellent.

"How has your respite been, Romy?" Elki asked, a genuinely warm smile monopolizing her face.

After Romy's mission to Franklin, and the debrief, Elki realized the assignment was significantly more involved than she had forecast. As such, she insisted Romy take a month off.

"I can't complain," Romy responded. "Efi and I have been travelling to different worlds, both on this plane and others. I'm learning a lot."

"Very good," Mist added. "That way you practice navigating the Athar."

There was a blue folder on the table beside Romy. Elki pointed to it. "What do you think?"

The day prior, he had been given the folder. It contained his next assignment, and he had read it thoroughly. "It seems simple enough."

Chuckling, Elki said, "At least, this time, we're not asking you to take a life. Rather, we want you to save one."

"That's refreshing," Romy said. There were a few quiet moments, so Romy carefully worded a delicate question. "You haven't said much at all about my recent transgressions. I went to Talus 3. Then, I improvised a solution on Franklin where the three innocent people were not killed." He took another drink, after which he held it in front of his lips. Focusing on Elki above the rim of the glass, as if he was hiding behind it, he whispered, "I did not follow your advice."

Throwing back her head, Elki laughed. When her face came back down, her eyes were bright. "It wasn't advice. I gave you direction, and you disobeyed it."

"I made a decision in the field. With a military background, it comes naturally to me."

"That's a good thing," Elki quipped.

That surprised Romy. "Really?"

"Listen, Romy," Elki said as she leaned forward. "I have taken the advice of the other see'ers. We know you have a strong mind of your own, and as well as our objectives, you have your own. I accept that. The task of being a time drifter is not an easy one, so yes, you need to be able to think quickly on your feet. You were on Franklin. I was not, so it is difficult for me to be critical of your decisions." Her eyes narrowed, and her voice gained a noticeable edge. "As long as you continue to be successful, I am fine with this type of arrangement."

Romy tilted his head, giving her a curious look. He thought their relationship was much like a mother and a son coming of age. The son was testing boundaries, daring to stretch them, while the mother, knowing the change was inevitable, still tried to delay the power shift.

Tapping his finger on the folder, Romy asked, "This man, Tor Gent. Why is he so important that he needs to be saved?"

Mist had led the research into the assignment, so she answered. "Gent, 400 years ago, was a 35-year-old engineer. Thirty years after his death, there was a great civil war on his planet, *Teston*, where 200 thousand people were killed. However, our dreams show us, if he lived, he would have moved into Politics when he was 50. He would become a key leader and the force behind the reasons to avoid the civil war."

Glancing at each of the see'ers, Romy asked, "What is the confidence level this is the correct path?"

"Eighty per cent," Mist replied.

"That's low," Efi interjected. She had kept quiet, but now, when the low probability might be a risk to her partner, she had to speak up.

Elki, who was sitting beside Efi, patted her hand. "I know it is lower than the 90 to 95 per cent confidence levels we usually provide, but this is still acceptable. After all, we are not killing someone. We are saving a life. What could possibly go wrong?"

Showing he agreed, Romy slipped his plate aside, replacing it with the assignment folder. He opened it to the map of Colton, the city Tor Gent lived in. He pointed to a circle on the map. "As I understand it, Gent will be driving past this petroleum pumping station when he is on his way to work. There is a fault and one of the gas lines explodes. With their safety measures, the explosion is contained, but a piece of debris flies out, hitting Gent's vehicle, killing him. With no other casualties, it's really a freak accident."

"That's it," Mist agreed.

Shifting his finger on the map, he pointed at a bridge. "There are several bridges over the river, but Gent always takes this one when travelling to work."

Her voice soft, Elki asked, "So what's your plan?"

Romy closed the folder. "I'm not sure, but it shouldn't be hard to stop him from going to work that day, or just slowing him down."

Elki snapped her fingers over her head, then pointed at a servant on the far side of the veranda. He disappeared, then returned quickly with a small, wooden box. Elki took it, then handed it directly to Romy. Opening it, he saw the four small bars of platinum.

Money was different on every plane he went to. On some gold and silver were scarce, making them valuable, but on other worlds they were common. But the one thing Romy had found on every plane or world he travelled to, was platinum was *always* scarce. Whenever he went on an assignment, he took some of the rare metal with him to barter for the currency in use at his destination.

The transfer of platinum usually indicated the meeting was over, and, in this instance, it was no different. Romy and Efi left the see'ers to enjoy the rest of their afternoon on the veranda in the forever twilight.

Romy thought, *there's nothing like having the luxury of taking a nap after a filling lunch.* He and Efi took the opportunity, returning to room 510. They stripped down to their underwear, then crawled under the blankets. They didn't make love. Instead, they just curled into each other, arms and legs intertwined. Soft music played in the background, completing the perfect setting.

They kissed and touched, but not in a sultry way. They were soft and caring movements, showing each other their relationship was much more than just a sexual one.

"You know I'm going to be with you forever," Romy whispered.

"I'm counting on it."

Caressing her cheek, he added, "I like this—just the two of us."

She kissed the tip of his nose. "Well, two of us for now, until we have children."

Romy let out a "Ha! How many children?"

Closing one eye, feigning a calculation she had already completed long ago. "Three, I think. More if a daughter is not within the three."

"Three, or even more!" Romy blurted.

Giggling, Efi replied, "I am almost certain you don't have to worry about *more*."

"I really don't like that word, 'almost.'"

"Remember, I am clairvoyant," Efi reminded him, waggling her eyebrows.

He could not help but laugh at her as he rolled on his back. After a few moments, looking up at the ceiling, he asked, "Have you thought about coming with me on some of these assignments?"

"Not really. I know we accidentally travelled back in time in that first emergency with the bears. It might be dangerous to try again."

"Just as you are clairvoyant, I also know my abilities." He tilted his head, glancing at her. "I am strong, stronger than the see'ers or even you, know. I know I could take you, or really any pureblood, in my wake."

"Why would you want to take me?"

"For most assignments, I would not. For example, this next mission is simple. Now, the last one took two people. I had to do some crazy things to accomplish it. If you were there, it would have been simpler."

"Of course, I have no problem helping you," Efi stated. "But let's handle that when another such situation comes up."

"Thanks," Romy managed, just before his eyes closed, his breaths becoming heavy in his slumber.

The next day, at midmorning, Romy and Efi arrived at the transposition platform. Based on Mist's researchers, Romy was provided with clothing appropriate for the city of Colton: heavy, dark-blue cotton pants, a polyester shirt and an old, faded, light-brown leather jacket, one that looked like it came from a museum. He checked for the platinum bars in his pocket and the long knife in the sheath under the jacket.

Mist hustled into the room. She was happy she hadn't missed them. "What is your plan, Romy?"

"I've found, by now, things go better if I travel back a little further before the incident, maybe a few days. Then, I can get a good idea what the city is like, the people, and the situation. My plan will be based on that."

"Where do you plan to arrive?" Mist asked.

"I found an inconspicuous location on the east side of the city. There is a vacant building beside a pawn shop. There, I can obtain some local cash for one of the platinum bars. There are also a few hotels a couple of blocks away—inexpensive ones—the kind that doesn't draw attention to strangers."

Romy rolled his eyes when he saw Efi's eyes were moist. He placed a passionate kiss on her lips. "Silly girl," he whispered. "From your perspective, I disappear, then reappear immediately."

"You better," she muttered back to him.

Taking a few steps backwards, Romy gave her a wink just before the opaque, shimmering oval formed around him. Then, he was gone.

When he rematerialized on the planet Teston, plane 2844, it was the middle of the night. The darkness was broken by light from above. Looking up, he saw an odd sight. There were two moons, one lit to a one quarter crescent, the other slightly larger. *Two moons,* he thought. *That's crazy.*

He returned his focus to the three-story building in front of him. There was enough light to see it was made of concrete, coloured by a red pigment. A metal door, hung off the hinges, and there were two window openings on each level. Two of the openings were empty, while the rest were covered by some type of thick plastic sheet.

He was able to open the door far enough, such that he could squeeze through the tight opening. He walked carefully, sliding his feet. The plastic allowed some light to come through the windows, but not enough to see all the objects scattered on the floor. Trying to be quiet, he took his time. He hoped the building was empty, but there could be other people with more unfortunate circumstances than he had.

In fact, that was the case, as when he looked in the doorway of the front room, he heard a shuffling noise. Cowering, covered by a blanket was a young man and woman. The man's hand, holding a small knife, was shaking with fear.

Romy smiled at them, raised both hands and backed out of the room. He took the stairs up one flight and found the four rooms there empty. There was a mattress and a cushioned chair in one of the rooms, and thankfully, the door worked, allowing him to close it. He dared not use the mattress, so he chose the chair. He moved it into a corner, placing it on an angle so he faced the window and the door. He rested with the knife in his hand, trying not to fall into a deep sleep.

His plan failed. A noise bolted him upright. Light splashed through the window, revealing the young couple standing in his doorway. Seeing the knife in Romy's hand, they looked at each other, checking the wisdom of coming to the second floor.

Romy placed the knife in its sheath under the coat before smiling at them. "Good morning," he offered.

The young couple glanced at each other again. Seeing Romy smile, the girl smiled back while pulling her hand from behind her back. She held out the bread roll for Romy, whereby he took the bun. It was a little stale, but edible, and he was hungry. He pointed to the mattress, offering the young couple a place to sit, as he returned to the chair.

Their conversation was limited. Romy didn't want to explain why he was there. The young couple stated they were running away from their parents who refused to allow their courtship.

"It was hard, but at least they were together," the young man said.

Romy had to get moving. He wished them good luck, then strode to the door. The young woman's eyes followed him, pleading. It was obvious they had no plan and no idea what to do. Romy walked back to them, reaching his hand into his pocket, pulling out one of the platinum bars. He held it out to the young man. "Take it," he said.

The man's eyes were as big as saucers. He couldn't move.

"Take it before I change my mind," Romy scolded.

Hearing that, the young man snatched the platinum bar. It was enough to buy a nice house and a vehicle. He brought it to his eyes, his mouth gapped open.

Romy strode to the door. From behind him, he heard the girl's voice. "Thank you so much, Mister!"

As Romy skipped down the stairs, wondering why he gave the precious bar away, he muttered to himself, "A sucker born every minute."

As planned, he visited the pawn shop. The owner's eyes lit up when he saw one of the platinum bars. He was a good negotiator, but still, Romy thought he did well, obtaining half what the bar was really worth.

His next stop was the used vehicle sales depot he knew, from the map, was three blocks away. There, he undertook his second bout of negotiation, haggling over the price of a used, blue bubble car. That's the best description he could come up with. The vehicles on this world all appeared to be similar. Each looked like a big bubble on four wheels. Smaller ones were just that, while others had the bubble cut in half and an insert set in between. The longer the insert, the longer the vehicle.

A deal was struck. He showed the salesman his forged identification papers, and Romy Gunn was the proud owner of a blue bubble with a one metre insert.

He had chosen this location for a reason. He was on the very edge of the city, and he knew, in the distance, was nothing but country roads. It was a good place for him to learn how to drive a foreign bubble car. His slow and irregular exit from the car depot had the salesman scratching his head. But after that, he glanced at the money in his hand, and didn't give it a second thought.

Having decided to arrive at the city of Colton four days in advance, it allowed enough time for Romy to learn how to drive the bubble, obtain a room at one of the hotels, and test drive Tor Gent's travel route. Mist's intelligence information provided Romy with Gent's address. On the third day, he shadowed the engineer's white bubble car from his home, across the bridge, by the petroleum pumping station, to his office building in the city.

This would be simple, he thought. He just needed to create a small accident on the bridge. Even a five-minute delay would be enough. So, the next day, he repeated his actions. He shadowed Gent from his home, but this time, he was right on his tail. They travelled several roads to the four-lane highway. After five minutes, they were on the bridge over the wide river meandering around the city centre.

There was only light traffic, and that would make it more difficult. Romy kept an eye on his watch. There were seven minutes to the explosion. Once they were halfway across the bridge, Romy sped around Gent's white bubble. He could have side swiped him right there, but Romy had an escape plan.

In front of Gent, he paced himself beside a small, black bubble car, driven by a woman who looked too old to drive. They drove side by side. Romy saw his watch showed four minutes to the explosion. It was time. He pulled the steering wheel to the right, hitting into the front corner of the black bubble car. It forced the nose of her vehicle into the far guard rail. Romy knew they weren't going fast enough to cause major damage or harm to the woman, but the lane was blocked.

He backed his damaged car so it covered the other lane. With the task complete, he slid out of the bubble. Romy saw the old lady had managed to come out of her vehicle as well. She was angry and about to scold Romy, when he pressed a platinum bar into her hand.

"That should buy you twenty of those ugly vehicles!"

That said, Romy turned to the walkway along the edge of the bridge, where he knew the stairs were. By the time he took the two long flights of stairs down to ground level, he heard the explosion far in front of him by the main roadway. As he ran down the sidewalk running alongside the river, he thought, *assignment accomplished!* He ran to the fork he had previously reconnoitred, taking the left path into the woods. There he stopped, took a deep breath and began his transposition process. He was on his way back to Hagaza and Efi.

However, just as the shimmer began to form around him a jolt of pain seared through his head. His hold on the Athar within his mind's eye faded. The pain continued as he fought against it, trying to regain focus on the destination beacon. However, the view of the Athar that usually had him speeding towards the target while the planes rolled end over end, was mutating. The lines and beacon lights twisted and elongated. *Something was wrong!*

He fought against the pain, pushing back the fear he felt. Slowly, he made headway towards the target. He knew he was almost there since he felt the sensation of falling forward.

On the platform in Hagaza, Romy's transposition shimmer formed, then slowly cleared, leaving him in the middle of the room. The pain had left his head, leaving him feeling numb. Typically, after a planer hop, it took a few moments for his vision to clear. When it did, he saw there was no room to speak of. He stumbled back. There was a crumbled wall to his left. Above it, he could see the five-story government building was nothing but a mass of rubble.

Muttering, "What the…," he turned to his right, when he was surprised by a person directly in front of him. Seeing the black jump suit with a black balaclava over the person's head, a dazed Romy asked, "Who are you?"

The person pulled off the balaclava, revealing a pretty woman with light-brown skin, short, red hair and a long scar down the right side of her face. Her eyes were angry.

"Efi!" Romy screamed.

The woman pressed an electrical device to Romy's chest. The electrical charge caused his body to shake and his knees to buckle. Before he lost consciousness, he heard the woman snarl, "No one calls me Efi! I'm Efia!"

Chapter 21: A Changed World

Date: Unknown.

Hagaza, former capital city of the Mabuza people

The splash of cold water against Romy's face brought him instantly awake. He turned his gaze from side to side. He was sitting on the ground, his back against a broken column. His knees were drawn up with his arms wrapped around them. He tried to pull his hands free, but failed. However, he was able to lift them over his knees, and when he did so, he saw they were restrained by handcuffs.

Tilting his gaze up, he saw Efi against the forever twilight. He tried to speak, but the tape over his mouth stopped him. Lifting his bound hands, he was about to remove the tape. Moving quickly, Efi stepped forward, her fingers grasping his hand.

"I'll allow its removal, but I warn you, you must be quiet. There could be others close by who'd harm you and I," she warned.

Once her firm grip released his fist, he pulled the tape free. He took her advice, keeping his voice subdued, yet the words were sharp. "Efi, is all this really necessary? Bound and gagged—really? And the shock from the electrical device—was that necessary?"

She leaned down, her eyes narrowing. "This is the second and last time I'm going to tell you, "I'm *Efia* Kuma." Her finger flashed in front of his face. "Call me Efi again, and—well—I have more of that tape."

"Okay, *Efia*," he spat out the words. "Tell me what is going on, *Efia*. Tell me how I arrived to find Hagaza destroyed, *Efia*." Each time, he sarcastically emphasized her name.

A sideways grin came across her face, brightening it, notwithstanding the scar down the side of her jaw. Her finger relaxed as her hand slid under his arm. "Let me help you up," she offered.

Once on his feet, Romy lifted his hands. "Are these restraints really necessary? Don't you recognize me?"

"Yes, and no," she replied.

Romy shook his head. "What does that mean?"

"Yes, the restraints are necessary. No, I don't recognize you. This is the first time I've ever laid my eyes on you."

Taking a deep breath, Romy needed to think for a moment. It was Efi— now apparently, Efia—the woman he was in love with. Yet, she was different. Her short-cropped, red hair, the scar down her cheek and her more aggressive tone, were certainly not characteristics of his Efi. Even her short spears were missing. Rather, she had a sword in a scabbard at her waist, two knives in the continuation of the scabbard across her chest, and a pistol of some type hanging from the other side of the belt. Before Romy said more, or asked questions, he needed to think and gather his thoughts, even though the gut-wrenching feeling he had deep within him, signaled the initial horrific thoughts crossing his mind were a likely reality.

"Where are we going?" Romy asked.

Putting her hand behind his shoulder, she gave him a nudge, a clear indication she wanted him to move. "My orders are to take you to my see'er. She dreamt you'd be here on this day at this hour. She told me your name is Romy, and you have pureblood powers. That's why you have the bracelets on. They inhibit whatever psychic powers you have and also inhibit your ability to hop away from this plane."

Romy was guided down what once was the hallway from the transposition platform. One wall was still standing, and after walking a couple of metres, he had a good view of the city, or at least, what was left of it. He walked to the floor's edge, the wall now fallen into a mound of rubble. Growing through it were green plants and vines. As he looked around, he saw the jungle had overtaken the city of Hagaza, and by how large some of the trees were, the destruction of the city occurred long ago.

After he picked his way through the rubble to the courtyard beyond, he tilted his face back, asking Efia, "You said, 'see'er.' Shouldn't that be 'see'ers.' There are five of them."

"Our *see'er*—" she emphasized the singular "—told me you'd say things that wouldn't make sense. She also told me not to give you too much information, warning me it could drive you from acting foolish to stupid."

"Now, that's the Efi I know," he mumbled.

Ignoring his words, she gave him another push on his shoulder. "Towards the ocean. Let's be quick. I was serious when I said there might be enemies lurking about."

The shove pushed Romy towards the broken iron fence that used to separate Hagaza Prime from the beach area. He was forced to follow a serpentine path, avoiding rubble, bushes and trees that, over time, pushed the once beautiful courtyard stones askew. Finding an opening in the fence, he slid through followed by his captor. The steps he remembered leading down to the lower city were gone. He jumped down the two-metre distance, tucking and rolling. Efia, being nimbler, jumped down and landed on her feet, her bent legs easily absorbing the impact.

"That way," she ordered, pointing to the rock outcropping at the far end of the beach.

Romy continued the trek through the beach area. The buildings that would have made up the entertainment area, were in shambles. Any wood had been burned long ago, leaving only parts of the brick-and-mortar buildings left standing.

Hitting him on the shoulder, she pointed to the rocks in the distance on their left. "That way," she ordered.

He adjusted his direction, stepping out onto the sand. It brought back wonderful memories of his time with his Efi. The thought was only momentarily replaced by another thought, one that was slowly turning into a realization. *His Efi was gone, replaced by Efia.*

He stopped at the rocks only to be prodded forward by another shove into his shoulder. Using his hands for balance, he climbed up and over the jagged rocks with Efia following closely behind. From the top of the rock outcropping, on the other side, Romy saw a large swath of reeds in the shallow water. Hidden within was a small pontoon boat.

"We're going on a cruise," he scoffed.

"Help me push it out," she said.

They skittered down the leeward side of the outcropping, Romy jumping into the knee-deep water. They pushed the small boat clear, after which Romy jumped into the front. Efia, climbed into the rear and sat on the built-in bench, just in front of a motor seeming much too big for such a small craft.

With the press of a button, the engine roared to life. She turned to face forward behind the narrow control console. Romy almost fell back into the boat when she pushed the throttle heavily forward. He clutched a grab handle just in time, the sharp turn on the steering mechanism almost throwing him into the ocean. Once he regained his composure, he saw they were bouncing across the waves, heading straight out into the open ocean.

"Shouldn't we be traveling along the shoreline?" he yelled back to her.

"Relax!" she yelled back.

It had been an hour since they left the transposition platform. It was an hour of time for Romy to consider his situation. It was obvious to him the world he came back to was not the same as the one he left, just as the woman he was now with was not the same woman who kissed him goodbye. He had completed his mission flawlessly. The see'ers talked about their communication with the Athar, the collective consciousness of all living things. What he was asked to do was for the greater good so, what could possibly go wrong? *That's what the see'ers told him!*

Well, something did go fucking wrong! Damn their 80 per cent probability! That still left 20 per cent, and that 20 per cent had come into play. The pain he had felt in his head and his distorted view of the Athar during his transposition were because of his close psychic connection to the Athar. These symptoms were the Athar's way of telling him a significant disturbance had occurred in the cosmic consciousness. His actions had changed something else that set the Athar and everything he knew askew— severely fucking askew. He had made the right choice to not share much with Efia. He would wait to see the see'er. Surely, that person would have more answers.

They had been travelling out into the open ocean for 20 minutes. There were less waves, and the ones they encountered were rolling, smooth waves, but still, Romy was getting sprayed much too often for his liking. He was cold and wet.

He turned his face back to Efia. "This is crazy! If I don't fall in the water and drown, surely, I will die of some bacterial infection!"

Pulling one hand from the steering mechanism, she turned her wrist up to her gaze. "We're almost there! Only a few more minutes!"

Efia's idea of a few minutes turned into ten, before she idled the engine. The boat was just rocking on the waves in the middle of nowhere. Romy was about to voice another complaint when he saw bubbles on their starboard side—lots of them. The water churned and spewed until a black tower pressed from the middle of the chaos. Romy held on as the water's motion pushed the pontoon boat backwards. Once he was secure, he looked back across the water to see a long, narrow submersible had risen out of the ocean. It was black with a blue stripe down the side.

Efia fired up the engine, then coasted the boat towards the side of the submarine. By the time they pressed against the side of it, hatches had been opened and several Mabuza seamen were scurrying across the deck, throwing ropes down to the smaller boat.

Wrapping one of the ropes around her fist, the other hand gripping just below, she looked at Romy, then pointed with her chin to the pitching deck four metres above them. "Climb!" she ordered, as her feet pressed against the rungs hanging off the side of the vessel.

Not to be left behind, Romy followed suit, gripping the second rope as best he could with the restraints on his wrists, allowing him to fumble his way onto the deck.

They were no sooner on the deck, when a deep voice bellowed down from the top of the submarine's tower, "Clear the deck!"

Romy glanced up, but the captain had already gone. A Mabuza sailor grabbed his arm, "This way, Sir. The ocean waits for no one."

Sure enough, the vessel lurched forward, and already the bow was angled down. He, Efia and the men hurried into the hatches that were clicked shut behind them. The captain came and greeted them, a greeting Romy found to be no more than an obligatory, duty-bound effort. He led them to a cabin Romy thought quite large for an undersea vessel. Giving his apologies and blaming his duties, he left them alone.

Just before the door closed, Romy noticed the two guards in the hallway. "I could be mistaken, but I feel like a prisoner," he quipped.

Sitting back on a cot, Efia replied, "You're not mistaken. The handcuffs you're wearing and the guards outside are good clues." She smiled at him, not sarcastically this time. It was genuine and playful.

As she removed her weapons, placing them beside her on the cot, Romy lowered himself on the cot opposite her. For a moment, in that smile, he saw some of the Efi he knew and loved. It was difficult for him to not blurt out his feelings and pull her into his arms. "Surely, there are some things you can tell me," Romy probed.

"I can tell you we're travelling to *Citrean,* our Mabuza capital. There, you'll visit the see'er, and she'll answer your questions."

"She? Is her name, Elki?"

"No questions," she reprimanded him. After a few moments, she offered, "I don't know an Elki."

Against her warning, he was about to ask the name of the see'er, when the sound of the door opening, distracted him. A porter brought in dry, folded clothes for each of them. She left them on the bed, then left the two of them alone again.

With a coy smile, he gazed at her. "I can't get out of these wet clothes with these on." He lifted the handcuffs.

She rose to her feet, lifting her pistol as she did so. She took aim at the centre of his chest as she said, "I won't hesitate to shoot you if I see you try any sudden moves, or if I see even a semblance of a transposition circle. Understood?"

Rising to his feet, he hoisted his cuffed hands in front of him. She reached into her pocket, pulling out a tiny electrical device. She pressed the button, and one of the handcuffs opened, leaving the other tight on his wrist.

"Absolutely no trust at all," Romy muttered. He slid the jacket off his back and was about to undo the pants, when he asked, "You just going to watch?"

"Yes, and yes," she replied.

"That's confusing."

"Yes, I don't trust you, and yes, I'm not going to take my eyes off you for a second."

"Enjoy," he said as he kicked off his boots, just before he let the soggy pants fall down around his ankles.

"You're not the first man I've seen naked," she stated, her tone a little too bored for Romy's liking. "You're not even the first *white man* I've seen naked. What are you anyway: a Toltec or a Celtae, I imagine?"

"You can imagine all you want. I don't answer questions until I visit with your see'er."

"You're funny," she said, not being able to hold back the smile. But her smile faded quickly when Romy turned to face the cot. She saw the long scar on his leg and several other wounds on his back. Once his pants were pulled up, he turned, revealing three more scars on his chest, one quite large. She didn't know who Romy was, but from the scars she knew he was a warrior and a survivor.

Romy was true to his word. He didn't answer any of Efia's questions, and he refrained from asking any of his own. They greedily ate the food that was brought. He managed even though the handcuffs had been replaced on both wrists. With his stomach full, he leaned back on the cot, his back against the wall of the cabin. Then, sleep overtook him.

"Wake up!"

Romy's heavy eyelids opened barely a crack.

"Wake up!" Efia repeated. "We're here!"

Romy wasn't sure how long he had slept, other than it must have been for a long time. Beside him, pressed and cleaned were his clothes. Efia had changed as he had slept, and now she allowed him to change back into his original attire. Once he was ready, she opened a door where a guard was waiting. The young Mabuza man led them to the command deck, then up a steep rise of stairs to the tower deck where the crisp ocean air hit them. The captain welcomed them, seeming happier since they were almost at their home port.

Leaning out over the front railing, Romy saw the vessel was headed towards an island, and the majority of the island in his view was monopolized by a massive, high concrete wall coming out of the water just offshore. Buildings filled the sloping landscape behind it to a high pinnacle where a massive flag hung from a tall pole. As the submarine plowed towards the wall, he expected to see the Mabuza flag he knew; a light blue iris within a white eye, set on a dark-blue background. Instead, fluttering in the breeze was a light-blue background, adorned with six yellow stars, equally spaced across the flag's surface. It was just additional affirmation this was not his reality. It was a reality changed by his actions on Teston.

The submarine slowed, yet still, Romy thought the vessel was about to ram into the wall, when a massive groan came from the concrete structure. A wide section of the wall opened, allowing them to slide through. In front of them, now, was a long bay, one side filled with fishing vessels, while the other side had three military vessels docked there. Two were identical submarines to their own, while the third was a smaller surface vessel.

It was not lost on Romy that everything he had seen since his arrival was evidence there was a war of some type, and it might still be ongoing. Hagaza destroyed, military submarines and massive fortifications told him this reality wasn't as peaceful as the one he left.

Once Romy and Efia left the submarine, they found a vehicle waiting for them. The driver nodded to Efia as they boarded, then the vehicle shot forward, a little too fast for the winding road they were following. The road snaked back and forth as they climbed the hillside. Romy took in the city, finding it drab, with most buildings simple concrete structures with very few of them painted or decorated. At least, there were quite a few trees adding some colour to the bleakness of the houses.

After ten minutes, they stopped in front of a large, three-story building, this one painted light-blue. While Romy had seen only a few military guards at the bay, here, there were many. A few were posted guards, but it seemed even more were busy, on their way to meetings or tasks of some sort.

They all gave Romy a suspicious look since he was still handcuffed, but even more of a curiosity was the fact he was white-skinned. On the submarine, and now in the town, he only saw dark-skinned Mabuza.

As they walked through the tall, arched doorway, Romy asked, "Are we going to the see'er now?"

"Thankfully, yes," she replied. "Then, my mission will be complete, and I'll be done with you."

They went up one flight of stairs, then down a long hallway. Romy realized, with how far they were walking, this building and maybe many others, burrowed deep into the hillside. The bland facade of the building was only a tiny piece of the complex. As such, they left the natural light coming through the front windows behind, now replaced by bright ceiling lights attached every ten metres.

Even if Romy wanted to escape back to the bay, perhaps with a thought to steal a fishing vessel, he would not have remembered the way out of the complex. They turned down one hallway after the other, a maze of corridors and doorways that had his sense of direction baffled. Now, if these bracelets came off, then he could leave whenever he wished.

Turning another corner, they came face to face with four burly guards in front of a massive, wooden door. Efia approached the guard near the communication console, and stated, "She's expecting us. Efia Kuma and—" she turned and pointed at Romy "—him. What's your second name?"

Intentionally ignoring Efia, he turned to the guard. "And, Romy Gunn."

The armed guard took a few minutes at the console, then turned to Efia. "She's on the Heights. Take the pinnacle elevator at the…"

"I know the way," Efia interrupted. "I've been here many times."

Once beyond the doors, a hallway to the left brought them to a series of elevators where Efia led them to the far one. Having entered, Efia gave a voice command, and the elevator shot upwards. It was a long ride, but when it ended and the door opened, they stepped out into a small enclosure built of natural stone. The twilight hit Romy from the opening opposite the elevator. Once they were out in the fresh air, Romy saw they were indeed on the highest point on the island with a panoramic view of the surrounding ocean. However, now, with the improved view, he saw the city fortifications only covered the tip of the island. The remaining rugged landscape spread 15 kilometres in the opposite direction.

They were on a large circular patio, 40 metres across. There were several small groups of people, and amongst them, were many uniformed guards. Romy noticed one woman standing alone. Her back was to them as Efia led Romy towards her. Her shoulder length, jet-black hair, brushed against the straps of the ankle-length, dark-blue dress. The dress was covered with a matching, waist length cape. The woman was looking out over the stone railing at the natural beauty of the island, fixated on something in the distance. As such, she did not notice Efia and Romy approaching.

"My apologies for interrupting," Efia offered in a loud voice. "I've returned with the cargo."

Romy blurted out a laugh upon hearing the reference to him. However, his laugh was cut short when the woman turned. Her hair was shorter, and she had wrinkles showing years of stress, but her stunning beauty was still very much evident. "Mist! Thank the stars in the sky!" Romy blurted.

Efia thought she would be done with the man soon, but she raised an eyebrow in interest when he said the see'er's name. *It might be worthwhile to stay and listen for a time,* she thought.

Mist stepped closer to Romy, smiling the beautiful smile he remembered. The movement worried Efia, causing her to place her hand on the trigger of her pistol.

Lifting her hand to stay the younger woman, Mist said, "Take these handcuffs off our guest."

A moment later, Romy was rubbing his wrists. It was only now, after a gust of wind shifted Mist's cape, that he saw her arm. He could not hold back the gasp that left his lips. Her left arm was gone below the elbow. Composing himself, he said, "Things are very different from when I left."

Mist wrapped her good arm around Romy's shoulder, coaxing him towards chairs situated around a small table. She gave a nod to a man by the stone building housing the elevator, whereby he rushed inside. "Unfortunately, I know only a little about your predicament, but let's talk over dinner, and we can see if we can figure things out." She tilted her face back to Efia. "Come along, woman. You're a part of this, and you look like you need to eat."

They each sat in a chair, then Romy began the discussion. "You know, without the shackles, I could leave here whenever I want to."

"Of course you could," Mist replied. "But you won't, at least not yet. After all, where would you go?"

Romy grinned. The Mist in front of him was another sign this reality was different. But at least, her demeanour was similar to what he knew of her, not like Efia whose personality was very different. "You're the first friendly face I've seen," Romy confided. However, he was sorry as soon as he said it, seeing the dark sadness come over Efia's face. It was the truth, but in his heart, he loved her, even this altered semblance. He turned back to the see'er. "You were expecting me."

"I'll be blunt, Romy," Mist stated. "I speak with the Athar. We are as one. I dream with the collective consciousness often. It guides me, yet, two nights ago, I woke in the middle of one such dream. It was pleasant until there was a mighty flash of pain in my head. There was an obvious change in the Athar, a great, instantaneous change that troubled the collective. The following night, the Athar told me you would be on the platform at the ruins of Hagaza. I was told your name, and I was told of your importance." She whispered the next few words. "It appears you are critical to our destiny."

A cart rumbled towards them, clicking across the stone platform. Food and drinks were served before the servant scurried away.

Romy was hungry. He took several mouthfuls of fruit before replying to the see'er. "So, you don't know much about me?"

"No. But I—" then, Mist looked at Efia "—*we* are prepared to help you in whatever tasks you have."

Taking a deep breath, Romy explained, "My name is Romy Gunn. I am a Korian, born in space, but raised on this planet, Haven." Efia was going to interrupt, but Romy stayed her with a raised finger. "I left this world earlier today, but when I returned, the reality here is horrifically different. It is not the same place, yet it is."

Solemnly, Mist whispered, "You said you are a Korian?"

"Yes, the son of Ryder Gunn, famous outlaw of Haven." He wasn't sure he should reveal who he really was, but there seemed to be no sense in delaying the inevitable. He leaned closer to Mist. "I am a time drifter."

The see'er almost choked on the drink at her lips. "You are a msafiri? We have not known of a time drifter for five thousand years."

"Yes. I was on an assignment to fix a catastrophe about to occur in the Athar. I was successful, at least, the assignment was completed. When I returned, everything was different. Hagaza, a thriving Mabuza city is gone. You are different." Then he gazed at Efia, and he could not withhold the momentary crackle in his voice. "She is different."

Even if Mist wasn't a powerful see'er with the power to peek into the future, some things were quite obvious. "You love her," Mist whispered.

Taking in a deep breath, Romy said, "In my reality, we were in love. We were mates, devoted to each other."

Efia had a blank look on her face. She decided not to reply. The last thing she wanted was to get more involved in something she wanted no part of.

Thankfully, Mist let Efia off the hook, interrupting the awkward moment.

"I am sorry your world is gone, even more sorry because this one does not sound as favourable as the one you left."

"What do you mean?" Romy asked.

Placing her fork down, Mist leaned back in her chair, a clear indication a long explanation was coming. "In our reality, there are two factions of Mabuza: those that use our powers to work with the Athar to improve the existence of all people within it, and those who would use the powers we have to selfishly enrich our own people and our prosperity, no matter the consequences to others."

Romy interjected, "It is the same in my reality. The helpful Mabuza are prevalent, with only a scattering of selfish Mabuza rebels."

"On hearing that, I am even more sorry, Romy. You see, in this reality, 120 years ago, there was a great civil war between our two factions of Mabuza. Ultimately, the greedy Mabuza, with more resources, prevailed. Those we call the Northern Mabuza inhabit the two main continents on this planet. We are known as the Southern Mabuza, having been pushed into the smaller, southern islands. It is a fragile peace, with many outbreaks of violence and the never-ending threat that, one day, they will come and finish us off."

"I can't see how the Korians and Sholites would have allowed this to happen," Romy offered. "I am sure, even in this reality, they aren't as powerful as the Mabuza factions, but surely, they would have influence."

For the second time, Mist leaned close to Romy. "Twenty-four years ago, your fleet of Korian and Sholite ships approached this planet. The Northern Mabuza thought them a threat, and they have a vast space armada." Mist placed her hand on Romy's wrist. "I'm sorry. The Northern Mabuza annihilated your joint fleet. It was a slaughter."

Romy's eyes were moist as he looked at Mist, a pleading look seeking for her to recant the story. But even though her lower lip trembled, she remained silent. Romy squeaked out a few words. "Every last one of them, dead?"

"About thirty ships managed to escape, but the Northern Mabuza did not pursue them. Why bother, when there was nothing for them but a cold death in deep space?"

Running his fingers back through his hair, he muttered, "So, I am the last Korian."

Mist squeezed his wrist. "Yes. All the other Korians and Sholites are dead."

Chapter 22: Decisions

Date: Mabuza year 2417

Citrean, capital city of the Southern Mabuza people

His hands under his head, Romy lay on the bed in the room Mist had assigned to him. One second, the pillow was too hard, so he would lift himself and punch it several times. Then, it was too soft, resulting in his efforts to bunch it into a tighter ball. But there was nothing wrong with the pillow. Rather, everything else was wrong; that was the thought monopolizing Romy's mind. Even though he was exhausted, it was that thought keeping him awake.

As a sign of his submission to his insomnia, he fell back on the pillow, hands now over his head, his eyes focused on a spot on the ceiling. This was the first night in as long as he could remember that his Efi was not beside him, except, of course, for the durations of his time travelling missions. Otherwise—and as he thought the words, he looked over at the vacant spot beside him—she was always beside him. This felt wrong.

Everything here was wrong. The Korians and Sholites were long dead, except for perhaps a few that escaped, and again, that was only because the Mabuza didn't think them of any consequence. Even these Southern Mabuza were different. Their priority was the defence of their islands, resulting in a military priority, yet, from what he saw, these people were scared. They lived in the shadow of the more aggressive Northern Mabuza.

Finally giving up, Romy rose to his feet. He replaced his night clothes with a fresh set of clothes that had been provided him. He pulled on the same boots and the weathered light-brown coat just before he slid open the glass door leading to the patio. He realized, and it was an ironic realization, even though he was raised on this planet, he was surprised by the forever twilight in the early morning hours. It seemed Metro was his new home with the contrasting warm days and cold, pitch-black nights. That was his new normal.

Placing his hands on the half wall, he easily side slipped his body over it. As his gaze panned from side to side, he saw there were small verandas identical to his every 20 metres at several levels.

Romy was restless; he needed to think, and for him, often, the best results were during a walk. His apartment was half way down from the pinnacle to the valley below; the distance between was over a gradual slope, so his descent was started at a relaxing pace. Once he arrived at the valley, he entered a forest of small-leafed trees, the trees being from two different, but similar species. The leaves of one were light-green, while the leaves of the other were a darker variety.

His footsteps crackled against the brown, fallen leaves covering the short grass visible only in a few areas where the tree's spacing was wider apart. He took a deep breath, enjoying the scent of the vegetation mixed with the ocean breeze that reached even here, on the other side of the tall hillside hiding the ocean on the opposite side.

After walking a kilometre into the wooded area, Romy squatted, leaning back on his haunches. Picking up two handfuls of leaves, he crunched them between his fingers, enjoying the closeness to nature. Yet, the calm didn't last long. His mind returned to his dire situation. He, singlehandedly, had wiped out his reality, replacing it with this horrible world of death and destruction; there really wasn't a better description.

His consciousness must have zoned out for quite some time because when his mind refocused on the present, it was to see a massive mound of crushed leaves pooled at his feet. Rising to his full height, he brushed his hands together, removing the few remnants of loose debris, before continuing his walk further into the forest.

As the distance from the pinnacle increased, the signs of wildlife grew. What he noticed first was the chirps and songs of different birds. Then, he noticed the insects the birds fed on, as well as a few different lizards who competed for the same food. He came upon a shallow stream, which he crossed, expertly stepping across a few conveniently placed rocks.

He assumed, by now, someone in Citrean would have noticed him missing. He really didn't care. He made a mistake submitting to the see'ers in his former reality—for what—for the destruction of everything he loved? *Besides,* he thought, *they're supposed to be clairvoyant. That means they shouldn't be surprised too easily.*

He turned, looking behind him, but he didn't see the pinnacle. His path must have curved to the south such that another larger, steeper hill blocked his view. By now, he had travelled six kilometres, when the sounds of nature were replaced by the tell tale sounds of machinery: the hum of electrical generators and the click-clack of moving gears. He slowed his pace until the forest ended. He waited at the edge, looking into the clearing in front of him.

It was a military base, with a wide runway on the side closest to him.

There were many cargo planes and even more small jets. Most of these were fighter jets with missiles hanging from the wings. Romy thought it odd. *It was one thing to be on high alert, but it was a whole next level of readiness to have so many planes with armaments loaded.*

He lowered himself with his back propped against the trunk of a stout tree. He watched for some time, seeing a few planes take off, then a large contingent of perfectly aligned soldiers on a fast-paced running drill on the far side of the airfield. *Everything I see here stinks of war,* he thought. As he rose to his feet, he spat on the ground, as if it would rid him of the memories of the civil war he had fought in within his own reality. He had lost many friends in that horrible war, including, Jax, his childhood best friend. He knew, with little consolation now, that was one of the reasons he accepted the assignments from the see'ers in his reality. It was because, usually, completion of his assignment would result in massive wars and the associated death of many millions, being averted.

He had been walking back to the pinnacle, still in a day dream, when he heard a snort. It was right after a particularly loud crackle from his foot crushing a mound of leaves. Looking up, the instant view of 20 sets of wide eyes looking towards him was comical. It only lasted a second as the herd of half-metre tall, furry beasts sprinted off, following the edge of the stream. Yet one remained, its eyes above the two curled tusks not so wide open as those fleeing. The gaze was proud and challenging as it lifted its snout, letting out a boisterous snort of indifference.

Romy chuckled, a light chuckle as to not offend the beast. He lowered down into a squat, bringing his eye contact level with the intelligent eyes of the creature. He raised a hand in greeting that set the beast to waggling its large head back and forth. Grinning, Romy had the impression the beast was amused by him.

Picking up a small stick, Romy threw it towards the creature. It sidestepped, and the stick fell beside it. Lifting its head, the front legs of the beast danced. Another stick was thrown, and the beast sidestepped, once again—and again the quick, triumphant dance. There were two more sticks, so Romy threw them. He didn't know who was enjoying the game more, he, or the beast.

There were no more sticks. The beast gave one last snort and began his trek, following in the direction of its herd. Now, Romy saw why only the front feet danced. This creature had a damaged rear foot, providing a noticeable limp. And his brown fur was riddled with grey streaks. This creature had lived a long life, and even through the limp, somehow, the gait was a proud one.

As the beast moved along the shoreline, Romy rose, dusting off his hands on his thighs. He heard the sharp twang, then the loud squeal. When his gaze snapped up, he saw the beast on its belly, an arrow stuck in its side, its eyes open and lifeless. Whoever shot the arrow had perfect aim.

A moment later, he heard the crunch of leaves to his right, followed by a figure appearing into the short clearing. It was Efia. She was replacing the bow over her shoulder as Romy strode towards her.

His eyes were smoldering as he yelled, "Why did you do that?"

"It'll provide a good meal for many Mabuza," Efia retorted. "It's good you distracted it."

"You...you saw us playing?" Romy sputtered. "And you still killed it?"

They had walked over to where the dead beast lay. Efia gave it a casual glance. "It was old. It didn't have long left in this world."

Romy felt the distaste in his mouth created by Efia's casual attitude towards taking a life. He understood hunting. After all, he ate meat on a regular basis, but knowing he was distracting it into a playful, unguarded mood, and then taking advantage of it—he deplored the callous message it provided. But, even more so, he despised it because it came from the woman resembling his Efi. The feelings of love were becoming lost as his subconscious locked them in a remote part of his memory.

"Why are you here?" Romy asked.

With a smirk plastered on her face, she replied, "I was following you. You set off the motion sensors outside your veranda, and since Mist has charged me with your safety, I was required to follow you."

"So, I'm a prisoner?"

"No, but for some reason Mist considers you to be of great importance. For me, I think you're a bit irritating, at best."

Romy's shoulders sagged as he let out a slow exhale. He found it difficult, even though the woman was not his Efi, to hear such words uttered from the lips of the double standing in front of him.

Noticing the impact her harsh words had on him, her eyes opened wide giving her a softer appearance. "I'm sorry," she offered. "I tend to think the worse of people and throw out insults easily." She placed her hand on Romy's arm. "You're not irritating at all. In fact, I find you quite interesting. I realize I'm not the same as the Efi from your reality, but who knows. One day you might come to have feelings for someone as crude as I."

His eyebrows lowering, creases formed across Romy's forehead. *Now that's confusing,* he thought. *Just when he had determined Efia was a cold, selfish woman, his conclusion was shattered by a moment of remorse and empathy.*

Removing her knife from her sheath, Efia lowered to one knee beside the beast, ready to begin the cleaning process.

Gripping her shoulder, Romy urged her back to her feet. "I'm not going to stay here and watch you gut it. We're going back to Citrean."

"We can't just leave it here!"

Romy was already walking towards the stepping stones in the stream. "Stay if you want to, but I am leaving. Call someone else on your radio to come and retrieve the carcass." He knew, since he was in her charge, she would have to follow his recommendation.

As such, she was half way across the stones when Romy's feet landed on the far shore. A few fast strides, and she was beside him. They walked at a slow pace, both enjoying the isolation from other people. They both had reasons to think.

Finally, she broke the silence. "Tell me about your Efi."

Tilting his head towards her, he raised an eyebrow, surprised by the request.

"Please," she added.

They still had five kilometres yet to travel back to the pinnacle. Romy carefully chose his words as he described his Efi. Although it was difficult, he tried his best not to place her above the Efia walking beside him. He didn't want to demean this woman, even though she was very different. Romy, several times, maybe in error, put the difference in the two of them onto the Mabuza wars this Efia had been through, and his Efi had not. He even tried to reason with Efia's sensibilities, explaining the debate on what has the most influence on a person's character: nature or nurture? He didn't go so far as to tell her the difference he saw between his Efi and Efia, convinced him nurture was the driving factor.

When they were almost at the pinnacle, Efia placed her hand on his arm again, stopping him. Looking up into his face, she asked, "Is your Efi beautiful? I bet she doesn't have such a scar as I have." She brought her finger up, dragging across the long disfigurement down her cheek and under her jaw.

He asked a question in reply, "Did you get the scar in the civil war?"

She gave an impish grin. "Nope. Bar fight."

Even though he gave a momentary smile, she could not help but notice the pathetic look on his face. His eyes were relaxed, fully open, his jaw having a slight sag. It was a look of pity.

For a moment, Romy was at a loss for words. He watched as Efia's eyes became moist, but when he saw her reset her lips in a tight line, he knew she would not let the tears flow. He did feel sorry for her, but even more so, he felt sorry for himself. This woman was not the one he loved. It didn't matter what he told her, she would know he was lying. When it came to his Efi, he was like an open book.

He put his hand on the back of her shoulder, coaxing her towards the rise up to the pinnacle. "We better get back," he whispered.

Their walk together and their discussion had finalized his decision. He felt a pang of selfishness, but thrust it aside immediately. He thought, *no matter the cost to this reality or this Efia, I'm going to go back to Teston and undo what I have done. I'm getting my Efi back.*

Chapter 23: Hiding Out

Date: Mabuza year 2417

Citrean, capital city of the Southern Mabuza people

Rostman Cheenan had an odd gait. He was able to provide a quick pace, even though his steps were short. It was more of a shuffle with his feet sliding across the floor. It was even more awkward when he was irritated, as the shuffle was quicker, and that was the case now.

As a senior assistant to Mist, she had charged him with finding Romy Gunn. Yet, 30 minutes later, after checking his apartment and Efia's, and also the building cafeteria, he found no sign of them. He was a loyal servant of the see'er, and he was not privy to what the white man was doing here. White people from the other races never came to Citrean, yet he was here, treated with extra special attention and privileges. He had faithfully served Mist for 30 years, and from that, he understood the see'er would tell him what he needed to know, and no more. Yet, it did not mean he could not be irritated.

He was on his way back to Romy's apartment when he heard an outside door open, the sound coming from a side hallway he just passed. When he turned, it was to see Romy and Efia turning the corner, walking towards him.

Clapping his hands together, he said, "There you are! I have been looking for you all morning."

Efia had known Rostman since her parents died when she was a child. He was as close to a father to her as could be. Once she was near, she gave the older man a hug. "Well, here we are. What's so important?"

He slid his fingers across her cheek, but the moment was fleeting and quickly lost as he turned his attention towards Romy. "Mist requests your presence in her state room. If you could follow me, I can take you there now."

"It'd be better if we clean up first," Efia volunteered. "No need for you to wait. I know the way."

The old man's fingers slid inside his jacket, pulling an envelope from a hidden pocket. He handed it to Efia. "Mist has given you an assignment, one she says needs to be completed immediately." Assuming that closed that portion of his assignment, he turned to Romy, glancing up and down from the top of his head to his boots. "We can stop along the way where you can wash your hands. Other than that, you look respectable."

Ten minutes later, Rostman held the large wooden door open for Romy so he could enter a small, elegant waiting area. Rostman whispered a "wait here" just before he passed through the second, inner door. It was only a few moments later when he returned to usher Romy into the see'er's state room.

The room was two stories high with full, floor to ceiling windows filling one wall. The walls were painted red and trimmed out with natural wood. Even though it was not stained or lacquered, the unfinished wood seemed the correct choice for the room Mist used for official state business.

Romy didn't see her until her voice gained his attention.

"Good morning, Romy. I hope you slept well," she offered.

Walking towards her, he replied, "I appreciate the sentiment, but as you can imagine, my night was restless. Maybe it was for the best as I went for a long walk, and that helped clear my mind."

Peeking around Romy, she gave direction to her assistant. "Rostman, thank you for your help. Please leave us now."

After he left, Mist pointed to a well-cushioned armchair. Once Romy was seated, Mist turned to a side table, pouring two large cups of water. She returned to the chair opposite Romy, placing the drinks on the table between them before sitting down.

After taking a short drink, Mist asked, "So, what thoughts keep sleep from you?"

Running his fingers back through his hair, Romy let out a sarcastic chuckle. "Where do I even begin?"

"Maybe start with what your plans are?"

Romy lifted his face up, raising an eyebrow. "That's odd. In my reality there were five see'ers, and they tried to control me at every turn. Not once did they ask me what my plans were."

A warm smile came across Mist's face. "Well, in this reality, I am asking."

"Why isn't Efia here?"

"From what little you told me, you have strong feelings for the Efi in your reality. I didn't want that to spill over here and affect your words or decisions," Mist stated.

Taking a moment to drink from the glass, Romy gathered his thoughts before the words formulated. "When I walk amongst your people, I see the looks on their faces. I see anger, frustration and despair. Very few people smile, and I can see they are unhappy. Everywhere I look, I see war, or the readiness for war. This morning, I went for a walk in the beautiful forest behind the pinnacle, yet, even there, the calm beauty is destroyed by a massive airbase with armed planes ready to take off at a moment's notice."

Shrugging, Mist quietly replied, "I can't argue with your observations."

"In my reality, of course we had crime, and we just came out of a civil war of our own, but the Mabuza were not involved. The Mabuza there are a happy people with a purpose in life that did not involve war and power."

After a long sigh, Mist said, "It sounds wonderful. I am envious of your reality."

Leaning forward, Romy's gaze connected with Mist. "Then, you know why I need to go back in time and try to fix what I have done. This reality is wrong."

After a few moments to consider his words, she shifted the conversation. "Was there a Mist in your reality?"

Leaning back, Romy could not help but smile, even if this Mist took it as an insult. "I knew you as soon as I saw you." He shrugged. "The Mist in my reality had both her arms, there were very few stress wrinkles on her face, her hair was much longer, and she smiled quite often."

Mist's face flushed. Romy noticed it just before she brought up the glass to take a drink, but really to cover the sign of her embarrassment.

"I'm sorry, Mist. My goal was to answer your question honestly, not to insult you."

She quickly recovered, lowering the glass. "Don't worry yourself." She laughed. "I've had much worse said to me over the years." Crossing one leg over the other, she continued, "How does reality work? Are there many realities and you're just hopping from one to the other, or is there only one reality that changes based on your actions?"

"You might think it unfortunate, but from what I have experienced, there is only one reality. So, when I did my see'er's bidding, I replaced the reality I know with this one. My goal now is to go back again and undo what I have done. Then, this reality would be replaced by the one I destroyed."

"If that is true, then your Mist—beautiful and happy in her life, would replace me?"

"Yes, not only you, but everyone you know and everything you see around you."

"I just want to make sure, by helping you, I'm not committing suicide."

Raising his eyebrows, Romy asked, "Then, you will help me?"

Mist slapped her thigh at the same time she let out another laugh. "Young man, I knew I was going to help you before you came here today. I knew when the Athar told me you would arrive in Hagaza yesterday." She leaned forward, and her face changed. Beauty came into her appearance, a regal beauty of a confident leader. "I know this is a horrible world, full of hate and the quest for power. If I could snap my fingers now and change my reality to yours, I would not hesitate for a second."

"You're brave. It must be difficult being a leader here."

"Romy, I am a see'er, more powerful than any of the six in the north—it's not even close. However, all six of them together, if they put their mind to it, could destroy me. As a see'er, I know our existence as Southern Mabuza's is limited. It isn't a matter of *if* they will attack. It is only *when*. So, let's get started. What do you need from me?"

"My original mission that changed everything was on the planet, Teston, within plane 2844. There was an engineer, soon to be politician, Tor Gent, who I saved. He was to die in an explosion that day, 400 years ago, but I saved him. Somehow, that started the change. Can you have your historians bring me every piece of information about that planet, and any connection to the Mabuza and this world?"

Mist pressed a button in the arm of her chair.

A voice replied, "Yes, Madam."

"Find Allard. I would speak with him immediately."

"Right away," came the instant reply.

"I will also need an office to work from, perhaps near my quarters," Romy requested.

"Of course, but it won't be here. You must leave Citrean."

"Why?"

"The Northern see'ers know you're here. They don't know why, but they have the sense you're important. Yet, they don't know how important. A team of Northern elite soldiers is already scouring your landing site at Hagaza, looking for clues."

Romy was puzzled. "I have only been here for a day. How could they possibly know so quickly?"

"Well, the North have see'ers, although they are weak ones. However, it is more likely that their spies here have informed them." She saw the look of puzzlement on Romy's face grow. "Yes, they have spies here, just as we have spies in their cities."

"Where am I going?"

"I dare not say it out loud. You never know who is listening. It is written on the paper within the envelope Efia was given. She is provisioning an ocean shuttle. By now, she must have it ready to go."

"Wouldn't it be easier for us to hop to an off-plane way station, then hop back to this secret destination?"

She rose to her feet, a cue for Romy to do the same. Her hand came up and touched his face. "I wish I had the innocence you have in your mind. In this reality, we minimize the time we hop into this plane since the three-hour lull after transposition is our most vulnerable time. You see, if we are attacked at that point, we cannot hop out to safety. Consequently, it is safer to scull travel to your destination."

A knock on the door interrupted them. There was a squeak as the door opened, and a middle-aged Mabuza slid his face around the door's edge. "You called for me, Mist?"

Mist gestured Allard in. Without giving too much detail, after a very basic introduction to Romy, she repeated the pertinent facts about Teston that Romy had relayed to her. It appeared to Romy that Allard was a highly trusted person within Mist's circle. She told him the importance of the work, directing him to stop all other activities and to focus only on this assignment.

Once he left, Mist had a last few disconcerting words for Romy. "Time is of the essence. The Northern Mabuza will eventually find you. My estimate is that will happen in two weeks. You will get updates sent to you every day, but no matter what, you need to leave this reality in one week, no longer. From there, you will need to go with whatever information you have and my best wishes." By the time she finished her words, her eyes were moist.

Romy wrapped her in a hug, kissing her cheek. He thought it might be the last time he would see this version of Mist. Thus, the hug lingered. Finally, without looking at her again, he turned, striding towards the door. As tears came to his own eyes, he tried to convince himself he was saving this world, not destroying it.

Chapter 24: Escape

Date: Mabuza year 2417

Citrean, capital city of the Southern Mabuza people

Sitting in the left seat of the sea shuttle, Romy was relieved the ride was smoother than he had expected. They had left Citrean an hour earlier, and not by the public harbour. After his meeting with Mist, he had been led to the buildings lower level, then through a damp, dark tunnel leading deeper into the island's core. After fifteen minutes, he and Rostman walked out onto a short plateau within a dark cavern. On the other edge of the flat area, a large vessel bobbed up and down on shallow waves coming in through a narrow opening leading to the sea.

Efia was loading supplies through the cargo door. When she stepped out, she saw them and waved. The smile on her face surprised Romy. He assumed she would have been disappointed at having to babysit him.

Rather, when he was close enough, Efia gave him a hug. There was a sparkle in her eye. "It seems we're going on an adventure."

Romy replied, "If that's what you want to call it."

She poked him in the chest. "I do."

She took a moment to give Rostman a warm embrace, then said her farewell.

The sea shuttle was entirely enclosed in a sleek housing, sharply angled at the front to reduce their drag. *This vessel was made for speed,* Romy thought. Once he entered, he saw the passenger compartment was tight, but could comfortably hold four people. Seeing Efia jump into the front left seat, behind the controls, he lowered into the right seat, beside her.

As Efia went through the startup process, pressing four buttons, he heard each of the engines roar to life. All four were idling at low revolutions, the deep sound echoing throughout the cave. The sound was intimidating, telling him they would likely be travelling at a high rate of speed. When Efia turned towards him, asking him to fasten his shoulder belts, it was to see them already locked in place.

The sea shuttle barely fit through the crooked sea entrance. Once they were clear of the rock outcropping and out on the open sea, Efia flicked several switches. A radar screen in front of her came to life. There was a keypad beside the monitor, where she keyed in coordinates. As a result, a target location lit up on the map. With nothing in front of them but open water, she pressed the four engine levers 20 per cent forward. The bow lifted as they shot forward, but quickly, as she adjusted the trim, the vessel leveled out.

Romy was worried as the choppy water bounced him around. Three hours of this wouldn't work. The bumps became worse when Efia pressed the levers to 50 per cent. He was about to raise a complaint when he saw the levers pushed to a 70 per cent position. The rough conditions in the passenger compartment immediately stopped. Now, rather than complaining, he mumbled, "That's better."

Efia gave him a wink. "This is a hydrofoil. At this speed and trim, we're riding on two sets of water wings with the bow clear of the water."

"Well, thank the stars for that."

The view out the angled front glass changed. Initially, it had been open ocean, but now there were spots of colour in front of them. As they travelled further, they became tree-covered islands, some quite large, others tiny. Efia maintained the sea shuttle's impressive speed as she manoeuvred the vessel through the channels between the islands.

On one larger island, Romy saw another expansive, modern city with overhead monorails between the tall buildings. The smaller islands had smaller communities, but from what he saw, they were no less modern.

Thirty minutes later, the scattering of islands was once again replaced by the open ocean. They hadn't said much to each other, and the silence was bothering Romy. He finally said, "I'm thinking I said some things earlier this morning you might have taken the wrong way."

Keeping her eyes focused on the front glass and her hands on the controls, she replied, "I don't think I took anything the wrong way. Your reality was a more peaceful place than this one is, and you love the Efi you left behind. I'm not her. I get it."

"It's not that simple…"

Efia interrupted, "It's not complicated." She finally turned her gaze towards Romy. "I've had my share of disasters and disappointments. Me not being at the same standard as your Efi, it's just another bump in the road, so, don't sweat it."

"All that said, I appreciate your help. Not everyone in these circumstances would be so willing."

After letting out a laugh, she looked at him, a sultry look. "You never know. If you don't change this reality and get your Efi back, you might find me more attractive. After all, you're not hard to look at."

Romy's mouth was stuck halfway open. He could tell he was blushing.

Another laugh from Efia broke his embarrassment. She leaned to the side, punching him in the shoulder. "Relax, Romy. The focus is on the mission, but we can be friends. I'd like that."

Averting his gaze to the front window, Romy was confused. He was seeing bits of his Efi in the woman sitting beside him. Although, she was rough around the edges, there was a personable kindness inside her. "I would like that as well—friends. After all, I can then count two people on this world as friends—you and Mist."

"It doesn't put you at much of a loss. This world is shit. I know your mission is to bring your reality back and replace this one."

"Wait a minute," Romy said. "You weren't at the meeting with Mist and I. How could you know my plan? In fact, she asked me what my plan was."

"Are all Korians so gullible? You met with a see'er," she emphasized. "When you meet with a see'er and they ask you questions, understand, they already know the answers. When she first set eyes on you on the Heights, she knew the change you would propose. Shortly thereafter, she gave me a summary of the events to come."

For the next hour, there were no words between them. Efia had put the vessel on auto pilot, leaving one hand resting on the controls. She began to hum a song. The humming changed to soft lyrics. *She had a wonderful singing voice,* Romy thought. He was enjoying it as she sang one song after another in the Mabuza tongue. It calmed him.

He was startled as he was pressed hard against the shoulder belts. He had fallen asleep and was now struggling to pry his eyes open. He realized they had slowed down, and they were bouncing across metre high waves. In the distance he heard the sound of waves breaking on rocks before his vision came fully into focus.

He saw a great spire of rock spiralling into the air, 100 metres in front of the shuttle. Something seemed odd, and then he saw it. Carved into portions of the almost vertical face were more than a few window openings and several balconies.

"That's Ventura," Efia stated. "About 100 years ago, this was a settlement of Mabuza, a group not agreeing with the policies of the North or the South. One day, a supply ship came into the lagoon and found all of them dead. The cause appeared to be some type of virus. In any case, between the colder climate of the Eastern Ocean and the fear of the mystery death, no one ever came back here after the bodies were discarded into the sea."

"Is it safe for us?"

"Our medical experts say it is, but according to Mist, it's safer than you staying in Citrean. The Northern Mabuza won't think of looking for us here."

Efia had set the engines to no more than a low rumble, enough to keep the vessel pointed at the shoreline as it rode the waves towards it. After one wave, she pressed the levers forward and the steering mechanism sharply to the left. The sea shuttle reacted, skipping across the wake before the next wave hit them. They sped around a high grouping of jagged, black rocks, surprising Romy when they turned into a calm lagoon on the other side of the natural break wall. Ahead of them, there was a dock Efia expertly guided them to.

Once the vessel was secured, they popped out onto the wood planks, where Romy held a hand over his eyes. "That's a lot of stairs," he mumbled.

He turned, hearing Efia crack open the cargo door. "It'll seem like a lot more than that on our third trip," Efia offered as she pointed to the mountain of supplies in the hold.

Panting, Romy dropped the last fuel can beside the generator on the fifth floor of the interior structure carved from the rock. They were in one large room—a safe house of sorts—outfitted and maintained for just such a situation as Romy was in. There were four bunks along the far wall, three desks and two tables, with two of the desks having computers on them. He was thankful there were heaters mounted to the walls, and with the wooden shutters covering the windows, they should stay warm. If that wasn't enough, there was a cabinet full of blankets beside the warm coats hanging from hooks on the wall.

"I've lived through worse," Romy said.

Efia, having just filled the fridge with food, turned and placed her hands on her hips. "Well, thank you for that. There are many men who'd beg to be here alone with me for a few days."

"You know what I meant!" He looked at her, noticing the silly grin on her face. "You're not going to be like this the whole time we're here, are you?"

She interlocked her fingers behind her, swaying her hips as she approached him. "Not the whole time. But it might get cold. We could always pull two of the bunks together—just for body warmth, of course."

Romy couldn't help but smile. He was starting to really like Efia. For a moment, he thought the shared body warmth might be an excellent idea. Then, the image of his Efi came into his mind's eye, with her light-brown hair, tipped with gold. He was confused, and these thoughts wouldn't help him.

To clear the confusion before it became a distraction, Romy set about organizing a workstation. Then, he made sure the fuel reservoir for the generator was full, and he verified it was running efficiently. In a drawer, under one of the tables, he found a tablet. Once he turned it on, he was satisfied, finding it communicated with the computer on the top of the desk. After some fumbling through programs and files, he found the encrypted messaging centre. He checked for updates from Allard, but there was nothing. He was an optimistic man, or so he thought, but having news this early stretched that notion.

Having some idle time, Romy convinced Efia that a tour of the facility was in order. They walked through the accommodations that ran a 50-metre length on the level they were on. Stairs at the far end gave them access to each of the four other floors which were identical to the one they were occupying. Romy found the complex drab and simple. He assumed the people who lived here didn't have much. There were remnants of furnishings and broken plates in several locations. It looked like looters had likely taken anything of value long ago.

The next morning, Romy checked the messaging centre, and again, there was nothing. This waiting had him anxious and with the feeling he needed to blow off some steam. As such, even though the air was brisk, he removed his shirt and set about exercising. He had a routine for just such a time, and he went through it, working up a good sweat.

Finding it entertaining, Efia sat in an armchair, one leg thrown over the side. She held a large fruit she was devouring. "Just watching you makes me hungry," she said between chews.

He gave her a sinister look, creases forming on his forehead as he lowered his brows. "So, why exactly are you here?" he quipped.

A large chunk of fruit was pushed to one side inside her mouth, filling her cheek. "I'm here to protect you in case things get tough. I was also told to make sure you don't hurt yourself—so make sure you don't strain something."

Ignoring the last comment, Romy left the quarters to continue his workout. He spent the next 20 minutes doing stair climbs—down to the bay, then back up—over and over and over. Finally, making his last trek down, Romy removed his clothing before diving into the cool lagoon water. He was doing his second length across the water when he noticed Efia was beside him. Romy was an excellent swimmer, but she had no trouble keeping up. Two more lengths and Romy was ready to climb out. He hesitated, realizing Efia would see him naked. She saw his predicament, rolling her eyes as she walked up the steps carved in the rock.

Apparently, she was not embarrassed to show him her naked body. Picking up one of the towels she had brought down with her, she turned to face him, giving him a more enticing view.

Grumbling, "So, that's the way it's going to be," he strode up the stairs, lifting the second towel to his chest.

Glancing down, she grinned, "I'm not sure why you hesitated. You've nothing to be embarrassed about."

Turning to face away from her, he finished the drying process, then wrapped the towel around his waist. He pointed a finger close to her face. "Separate bunks—remember that."

Romy heard her snickering and chortling all the way up the stairs to the room they had moved into. By the time they finished dinner, it was getting late. Against the rule he had set out, they did, in fact, push together two of the bunks. However, it was only with Efia's promise to keep her distance. But it would allow conversation without shouting across the room.

And talk they did. Efia told the story of her early life being raised on an island 300 kilometres north of their present location. She gave him a more detailed history of the scar on her cheek and a few of her failed relationships. They took turns with Romy telling her the history of the Korian people, their arrival on this planet, the civil war and the new life he was beginning on Metro.

Romy wasn't sure when they fell asleep, but it must have been late because when they woke it was midmorning. Even before they prepared breakfast, they both hurried to check if there was a message from Mist or Allard.

Romy almost jumped out of the seat he just sat in when he saw one was there. With Efia looking over his shoulder, he opened the file. It was from Allard, and it read:

Romy and Efia

This is the information so far. Keep in mind, our original thought was to investigate the connection between Teston and the general Bantu race. We also know there was a general shift in the Bantu philosophy from a more pious existence to one where wealth and power became the priority. We know this happened 130 years ago. Our search, therefore, was from 130 to 400 years ago, and the target was an association between Teston and the period of change in philosophy.

Romy slid his fingers back through his hair, muttering, "It certainly is the long-winded version expected from a historian." He continued reading the text...

When you visited Teston, 400 years ago, there was a Bantu population there. At that time, there were 120 thousand Bantu on a continent one thousand kilometres away from the city, Colton. There was only a sprinkling of these people living with the Testonians in the populated, urban areas.

Today, there are 900 million Bantu living with four billion Testonians, fully integrated in a multicultural society.

We know the change in Bantu culture to a more aggressive approach to life began about 200 years ago.

That's all I have for now. I will send you an update every morning at the top of the ninth hour.

Allard

Efia said what Romy was thinking. "It's not much, but it's better than nothing."

Knowing the next report was a day away, the time seemed to drag at a painfully slow rate. They decided to follow the same routine: exercising, then stair climbs followed by a brisk swim. They both began to enjoy each other's company, talking about the very different worlds they came from. Sleep did not come to them as easily as the prior night. His fixation on Allard's messages had Romy continually looking at the computer.

Efia noticed this and placed her hand on his arm. "Go to sleep. Watching the computer won't make the message come any faster."

It was early when Romy woke. There was still two hours before the messaging time. He moved a chair by the window, watching the waves break offshore. The ocean had a cruel beauty, crashing against the rocks below, sending up geysers of spray.

He needed to keep busy, so he moved to the kitchen area and set about preparing a nice Sholite-style breakfast, the kind his mother used to make on holiday occasions. When he brought the two hot plates of food into the main room, Efia was awake, sitting on the edge of her bunk.

After Romy placed the plates on the table near the bunks, Efia rose and inhaled the scent of eggs and fried meat. Walking closer, the sight of the food matched the aroma. "You can cook! Not just a pretty face, after all."

They ate and shared some idle banter until 30 minutes before the messaging time. Romy rose, stating, "The message might come early." He checked the computer, but there was nothing. Efia just shook her head as he hit the *load* key every ten seconds, hoping the message would be coerced into appearing. It finally did, one minute before the ninth hour.

As they did the day before, they read the contents:

Romy and Efia

I took the liberty of sending three Mabuza agents to Teston to scour through their history records. Here is what they have found, so far.

As I wrote yesterday, 200 years ago, the Bantu on Teston took a more aggressive approach to life. A group called the Bantu Global Association, BGA for short, formed and represented the Bantu interests. Their goal was to be less pious, and to target wealth. We don't know much about the BGA other than they were an amalgamation of four smaller Bantu groups.

At the same time, when it came to warfare, the Bantu were not as powerful as most other pureblood races. They were often attacked, often resulting in mass casualties. With this backdrop, the BGA joined with a growing number of Bantu worlds. This governing group, known as the Bantu Universal Council, or BUC, has, today, grown to over four thousand worlds. This world you knew as Haven, and we call Aeo, is one of them.

The agents are now digging into the details of the four smaller groups to see if there is a critical link to your bridge traffic jam, 400 years ago.

Next message is tomorrow at the top of the ninth hour.

Allard

"I think they're getting somewhere," Romy said.

The rest of their day followed the same routine. Earlier than usual, they both rolled onto their cots, pulling the blankets over them. They typically spent some time talking about their histories, but Efia chose a different direction, focusing on the future.

"You really are going to go back in time and try and change things back to your reality?" she asked.

"You know the answer," Romy whispered back. "You have lived your entire life on this world. You know better than I, it's not a good place. In fact, it's horrible."

"What happens if it doesn't work?"

Romy frowned. He hadn't really thought of that eventuality. A realization startled him. If he really could not have his Efi, what would he do? "Then, I would come back for you. We could leave this place and go somewhere else in the Athar."

Her voice was soft as she stammered, "You...you would learn to love me as you loved your Efi?"

Reaching over, he intertwined his fingers into hers. "We're getting ahead of ourselves. Get some sleep."

They fell asleep hand in hand. Somewhere in the night, they had shifted and they were facing in opposite directions when they woke. Maybe it was for the best. It would have been awkward waking, looking into each other's eyes while still holding hands. They had slept later than anticipated. It was only ten minutes before the ninth hour. As he had done the morning before, Romy continually clicked the *load* key. He did so through the next ten minutes, then ten more.

Finally, when 30 minutes had passed, Efia said, "Something's wrong."

"Agreed."

Moving quickly to the sleeping area, Efia said, "Get dressed, now. Pack what you need. We might have to leave at a moment's notice."

They dressed quickly, Romy into the original clothes he wore on his arrival to Aeo, including the weathered leather jacket. Just as they finished, a shimmer appeared close to the window. Someone was hopping in. Pulling her pistol from its holster, she pointed it at the rippling waves forming in the circle.

When the fuzzy image cleared, to their relief, they saw it was Mist.

Efia had a second thought that it wasn't good at all. Mist was alone, without guards, and she hopped here, leaving her vulnerable without a simple escape route. "You shouldn't be here!" Efia exclaimed.

"Hush, Girl," she said as she approached the two of them. "There is a problem. We found Allard early this morning—murdered. The Northern Mabuza are closer than we thought."

"But why would you put yourself in danger by coming here alone?" Efia asked.

"Right now, I can't trust anyone but myself. Allard had given me an update last night. It was urgent you receive it, so here I am."

The feeling of panic Efia felt was heightened by a rolling thunder coming from outside the window. All three of them moved to it and peered out, but there was no storm. However, in the distance there were five black dots, and they were becoming larger as they closed on Ventura Island.

Efia's voice was shrill. "It's too late. They're here!"

The black spots had grown into five massive gold and black airships, rumbling towards them.

Mist casually looked at Efia. "It's time for the two of you to leave. You have a greater purpose than to die here."

"As long as you're here unprotected, I'll not leave you," Efia said.

A moment later, ten opaque circles formed within the room. Then, ten members of the see'er's elite guard were with them. However, Romy noticed, with no ability to hop with energy sources, they were armed with simple swords and knives. Motion from the rocks below caught Romy's eye. More transposition circles were appearing there. When he finished counting, there were 30 soldiers, dressed in the gold and black regalia of the Northern Mabuza. Mist's guards wasted no time when they saw the enemy. They ran for the stairs, ready to defend their see'er at all costs.

Beyond the rocks, the five airships were idling a half kilometre off shore. Their decks were bristling with guns, all pointed at the tall spire, now seeming fragile. Ten more of Mist's guards hopped into the room, quickly following the first ten down the stairs. Unfortunately, Romy saw wave after wave of Northern Mabuza soldiers hopping in on the small beach head below.

There was a clash of steel as multiple swords met near the lagoon. The southern group was heavily outnumbered, and Romy meant to even the odds. From the window, he could see the mass of northern soldiers. Tentacles of orange energy formed on his fingers, quickly growing to a massive ball of energy. He heaved back, then snapped his hand forward, releasing the energy from his fingertips. The energy stretched into a line as it accelerated to the enemy group. They didn't know what hit them, but it did hit hard with ten soldiers blown into the air, bits and pieces of flesh and bone splashing into the tranquil lagoon. He threw another burst, but more and more soldiers clad in gold and black were appearing and overwhelming the fewer Southern soldiers.

Efia was frantic. "You never should've come here. You can't hop to safety!"

"Child, I am a see'er, more powerful than any in the north!" Her eyes were bright, fueled by her energy. "There is nothing that has happened here, and will happen today, I have not foreseen in my dreams. It is called, *destiny!*" She flashed her finger towards a developing scene in the west. "We have come prepared."

In the direction Mist indicated, the ocean was alive. Five large submarines were riding the surface, shooting up a tumultuous spray. Above them, were five massive airships. From the airships, fighter jets were launching, five at a time. All the ships in the armada were coloured with the black and light-blue of the Southern Mabuza.

Having heard a whistle from above, Efia cried, "Look!"

High in the sky, but dropping quickly, were three more gold and black airships. There was a point, when the Southern Mabuza fleet was within range, that complete pandemonium erupted. Missiles crossed the space between the two fleets, some with powerful warheads, others defensive armaments to destroy them before they hit.

Below, more soldiers from both sides were hopping into the land battle. "It's a horrible sight, Mabuza killing Mabuza" Mist declared. "But this day of reckoning had to come. We have been preparing for it."

From the north, Efia saw another five Northern airships speeding to their location. "We're outnumbered!" she exclaimed.

"Perhaps not," Mist replied. Before her words were complete, a massive bubble of water appeared in front of the five Mabuza airships parked in front of the spire. An instant later, the nose of a massive vessel thrust through the churning water. It cleared the surface in an almost vertical ascent. It was adorned with the black and light-blue of the southern forces. When it was in line with the enemy ships, from its belly, cannons fired into the northern ships from a close range. With no time for defensive measures, the charges slammed into two of the enemy ships. One cracked completely in half, the two sections dropping into the sea. The other remained in flight, but was heavily damaged.

"That's something the Northern military doesn't know we have," Mist clarified as she pointed at the massive southern vessel continuing to accelerate skyward.

Now, wave after wave of missiles fired from it's bow towards the three northern airships still in their descent towards the battle. Missiles were fired in return. One of the northern ships was crippled, flying on its side, slowly spiralling towards the water. Three Northern ships, seeing this new technology vessel as their major risk, focused their fire on it. Eventually, one missile made it through to a critical area, resulting in a massive explosion. Bits and pieces of the vessel showered down over the other ships below them. That might have been the decisive moment for the North, but two more similar amphibious flying ships, painted black and light-blue, rose from the water.

In the air, at least fifty fighters from each side were dogfighting around the spire. A few of the Northern Mabuza pilots took a run at the spire, firing missiles towards it. They were intercepted by defensive ordinance from the Southern fighters. However, it was enough for Romy to pull the two women away from the window.

The timing was fortunate because a minute later, Romy heard a high-pitched whistle. Simultaneously, in his mind's eye, Romy had a vision of the window destroyed and the floor of the apartment covered in rubble. Instinctively, he willed his energy shield to life, throwing it around the three of them.

When the missile hit, the front wall of the building blew apart. Romy felt himself lifted off his feet and thrown against the back wall. Fortunately, his shield absorbed most of the energy. He spat dust from his mouth as he opened his eyes. Dust filled the air, making it difficult to see, but beside him he saw an arm. Crawling over, he saw it was Efia. She was unconscious with a cut on her head, but a quick inspection of her limbs and her pulse indicated she wasn't critically injured.

With the dust settling, further away, he saw Mist—at least the upper half of her. Her lower half was covered by a mass of heavy rock. She was awake, and with her good arm, she feebly waved Romy to her. Rising to his feet, Romy stumbled over, kneeling beside her. What he saw was heart-wrenching. She was barely breathing. Covered with an unbearable weight of rock, he glanced down to see her foot, but it wasn't where it should be. He knew she would not survive this.

"I'll go for help," he stated.

Somehow, she managed a smile. "Don't be silly. This is my end."

"It doesn't have to be."

Blood was coming from her mouth as she coughed. "I told you, I am a see'er. Everything that has happened today I have seen in my dreams, including my end."

"What…what should I do?" he stammered.

"You have your assignment to complete." Mist opened her hand to Romy, revealing a folded paper. "This is the information from Allard. You need to go now."

"I can't leave you alone."

"Soon, I will be dead. Change things back to your reality. Bring me back to life. I love to think of myself whole, with long hair and beautiful."

Romy glanced at Efia, still unconscious.

"Take her with you."

"I'm not sure I can." He replied.

Even though there were only a few breaths left, she managed to roll her eyes. "Silly Korian. I am a see'er. Take her with you."

Romy was about to answer, but Mist's head lolled to the side, her eyes open. She was dead.

Rising to his feet, he glanced out the massive opening where the window had been. The battle was raging, and he could not tell who was winning. He assumed Mist knew, but that knowledge died with her.

Running the few steps to Efia, Romy lifted her, a rag doll held up by his hand at her waist. He pulled his mind's eye of the Athar into view. He focused on Efia, into her subconscious, forcing his view of the Athar into her. He moved them through plane after plane, shifting and rolling. Around them a shimmering circle formed. A moment later, they were gone.

Romy was going back to Teston, 400 years in the past, to fix the damage he had done, and Efia was going with him.

Chapter 25: Return To Teston

The 233rd day of the 2388th Teston solar year.

Colton, largest city on the southern continent, planet Teston

Romy almost lost his balance with his first step to the abandoned house, the same house he came to on his first hop to the city of Colton. He steadied himself as best he could with his arm tight against Efia's waist, her limp weight pulling on his shoulder muscles. A grunt escaped his lips as he realized his mind was groggy, likely because it was only the second time he had hopped with another person while shifting in time.

Efia's toes dragged along the ground as he covered the few metres to the back door, half open and hanging off its hinges. Although it was the more difficult path, he stumbled up the stairs to the second floor. Fortunately, he did not hear any sounds that would indicate others were in the building, but it was only early evening; if other squatters came, more than likely, it would be later in the darkness of night.

Once his steps were on the creaky floorboards of the second floor, he turned towards the larger room at the front of the house. From his first visit, he remembered it having a fireplace and two well worn but sturdy arm chairs. He lowered Efia into one of them before examining the cut on her head. The bleeding had stopped, and as it is with most head cuts, the superficial wound initially provided a grotesque amount of blood, making it appear much worse than it was.

Yet, Efia was still unconscious from the jarring impact, but likely now even more so from the hop 400 years back in time. Romy had targeted their hop so they were exactly two weeks after his original hop to Colton. That meant an earlier time version of himself had already arrived, blocked the bridge and prevented the future politician, Tor Gent, from being killed in the roadside explosion.

Now, in hindsight, he knew that part of his mission was not the issue. The see'ers would have foreseen this and not recommended he go. Something else, unforeseen by Elki, Mist and the other see'ers, must have been changed, something that created a cascade of events, throwing the Athar into chaotic turmoil. He let out a deep sigh, knowing that trying to find that single event would be an almost impossible task. He chuckled sarcastically as he pondered the word, 'almost.' Yet, he had to try. He needed his Efi back, and he would make every effort to reverse the detrimental changes in reality, knowing some would suffer from such a reversal. He could not help but to glance at Efia, her slumbering appearance much more innocent than the personality she provided when she was awake. It was likely she would be one of those suffering if and when he reversed this reality back to the one he knew.

He needed to move, hopeful the activity would put those thoughts of human collateral damage from his mind. He checked Efia's pulse and her breathing, all appearing normal, so, he set about searching the rest of the house. He started on the third floor, then to the first, finishing back on the second floor and the room he left Efia in. He checked her again, and when he put his hand on her forehead, she tilted her head, and a barely audible groan slipped through her lips. This time, when he bent over to check her, he felt something in his pocket. Slipping his fingers in, he retrieved the note from Allard that Mist had given him.

The two windows in the room were covered with hard, thick plastic boards. They let through some light, but more came through two large, irregular holes near the top of one of the boards. Taking advantage of the added light, he unfolded the note and began to read. It was long, and when his gaze was running along the hand written lines, two thirds of the way down, his eyes opened wide. His one free hand came up to join the one holding the paper. Yet, between both of them, the paper was vibrating. When he finished reading, sweat broke out on his brow. He lifted his arm and dragged the sleeve of his leather jacket against his forehead. He closed his eyes tight and clenched his teeth. When he opened his eyes, he looked down and realized he had squashed the note into a tight, round ball.

He now looked at the ball of paper with disdain. It was something he needed to be rid of and as quickly as possible. He moved over to the block fireplace where, on the stone mantle, a box of matches lay. The box was covered in dust, but when he slid it open, he saw it was half full of dry matches. He struck one against the block surface of the fireplace. It exploded in a spark, followed by a strong flame. Without hesitation, he held the ball of paper over the flame, allowing the yellow and blue fire to spread over the entire surface before dropping it deep into the recess, as far back on the hearth as it would go.

"What's that smell?"

Romy shot around to face Efia, now sitting a little more upright in the chair, her fist rolling on one eye socket as she tried to clear her vision. Feeling much like an adolescent who just got caught in an infantile act, Romy's face turned a deep shade of red.

Her eyes wide, Efia blinked repeatedly as she tried to improve her vision. "Are you burning something?"

"I was trying to start a fire, but I realized there isn't any wood."

Efia laughed, but it was stopped by the pain across the right side of her head. As she brought her fingers up to touch the tender wound, she said, "Tell me where we are, although where ever here is, you're just as stupid as you were on Aeo?"

It was then, as Efia's mind began to clear, that the memories of the last couple of hours came back to her. "The battle!" She snapped her head from side to side. "Did we win? Where's Mist?"

Moving to a squat beside her, Romy pulled her hand away from the wound. "The wound isn't bad, but you've been unconscious for about 20 minutes."

"I don't care! Where is Mist!" she yelled as she tried to pull her hand away.

Romy's grip on her hand tightened, not allowing it to be released. In a soft voice, he whispered, "Mist died."

"No!"

Their eyes were both filled with despair; hers for hearing the horrible news, his for providing it.

Romy explained, "We were watching the battle. A missile was coming towards the room we were in. Instinctively, at the last moment, I threw my psychic shield around us, but even with that the force threw the three of us against the back wall. You were knocked unconscious, but Mist landed in an area where the back wall fell on her. I went to her, but she passed away a few minutes later. After that, I hopped out, taking you with me."

Efia's eyes narrowed. "You should have left me there to fight. We might have won!"

"I couldn't leave you there."

"You coward! Why did you run?"

Romy's eyes became darker as the emotions inside him changed. "I left because Mist told me to. On her dying breath, she told me to take you with me. I had no choice!"

Turning away, hiding the tears, Efia replied, "There is always a choice."

Releasing her hand, Romy rose to his feet. "Mist didn't know who would win the battle. But she did know if the Southern Mabuza won, then there would be another battle, then another, until the Northern Mabuza eventually became victorious. That she knew, as did you."

"Then, where are we?"

Romy moved over to the covered window and lifted up on his tip toes, peering out one of the broken holes. "We are in the city of Colton on the planet Teston, 400 years in our past."

"So, it begins. You plan on changing my reality to yours?"

Turning, Romy gazed at her. "Yes. I'm going to reverse your shit reality back to mine." Without waiting for a reply, Romy returned his gaze outside into the twilight while Efia managed to rise to her feet.

After a few minutes, he heard her voice. "Well, if I'm going to help you, you'd better get me some clothes more befitting of this world—and some food."

Now realizing Efia was still wearing her military attire, he agreed with her. "There's a pawn shop across the road. Wait here, and I'll get you some clothes and some medical supplies. Then we'll get some food."

"Do you have money?" she questioned.

Romy winked at her before walking towards the fireplace. There, his fingers slid around a broken piece of block, coaxing it out far enough so he could slide his fingers in behind it. When his fingers came back out, held within two digits was a small bar of metal.

"That looks like a bar of platinum."

Grinning, Romy agreed. "Yup, and it could keep us going for years."

"But how did you know it was there?"

"Because I put it there when I was here two weeks ago," Romy replied, matter-of-factly. "In my reality, the see'ers would give me platinum bars to take with me on my assignments, most often much more than I needed for my expenses. One of my rules was to never take any platinum back with me. So, when I was here two weeks ago, I left an extra bar here. And if I hadn't, I could have retrieved any of the many little stashes of platinum I have at various locations around the Athar."

Two hours later, Romy and Efia were sitting at a booth in a restaurant, two short blocks down from their abandoned house. The restaurant wasn't great, and the food was adequate at best, but their hunger was such that they both felt it was one of the best meals they had ever eaten.

Efia was now dressed in dark-blue pants and a thigh length matching jacket with a grey shirt under it. Her head wound had been dressed and now it could barely be seen under her short, red hair.

"What do we do next?" she asked as they waited for dessert.

"It's getting late, and there's a hotel near here I used on my last visit. We need to get a good night's sleep, and then we begin trying to solve this mystery of what changed in the timeline."

"How do we go about that?"

He knew this time would come, and here it was. He said, "We need to find a man here by the name of Mick Dulan." He saw the questioning look on her face, and her lips began to mouth a response. He lifted his finger before she could. "Mist gave me a note from Allard just before she died."

She nodded.

"I read it once we arrived here. It fed the burning you smelled when you woke in the abandoned house. It was short and simple. When Allard looked back in Teston's history to this time period, he found a private investigator by the name of Mick Dulan had investigated the pumping station explosion and the many factors surrounding it. In fact, Allard was confused by the fact Mick Dulan was obsessed with the entire event, investigating it for years on end."

"I take it tomorrow we'll try and find Mick Dulan."

"That would be a good start," Romy agreed. "You still sure you want to help me?"

Efia clasped her fingers in front of her. Her head was tilted slightly down, but her eyes were angled up. "If you are successful in changing the time line back to your reality, you don't really know what will happen. If you take me back with you, I might fade away and your Efi will be waiting. On the other hand, you might be stuck with me and your Efi might be the one gone in any case of reality. Then again, you could leave me in this timeline. But perhaps your Efi will not be there in that case." Her head tilted to the side, her eyes softening. "Are you sure you want to do this?"

"I have to try. You know I love Efi. I…"

Efia lifted her hand, stopping the uncomfortable moment. She gave him the smile he needed. "I get it. No need to rehash old ground. But I'll ask you one thing in exchange for my cooperation."

"What?"

"Promise me you won't leave me here. I'll take my chances hopping back, new reality or old, but I want to live out my days there."

An odd thought hit Romy. "You just got here. What if later you decide you want to stay?"

She could not hold back the laughter. "I won't, but I'll give it to you that if I *beg* you to leave me here, then you have an out from your promise." She shook her head as the laughter continued.

Through it, Romy made the promise to her. He was thankful the two pieces of pie came at that opportune moment. They both ate in silence. Romy was thankful for it, knowing there was much more to the Allard note than what he told Efia. He knew he just lied to her, but he had no other options. He was beginning to understand there was reality, but destiny could destroy the best of plans and intentions.

Chapter 26: Mick Dulan

The 234th day of the 2388th Teston solar year.

Colton, largest city on the southern continent, planet Teston

"A couple more minutes, and we'll be there," the cab driver announced.

After a restful night at the hotel and a light breakfast, Romy and Efia asked the hotel manager for assistance using the computerized directory in the complimentary business suite. Initially, the manager rolled his eyes and began to make excuses until he saw the paper bill in Romy's hand. The manager tilted his gaze downwards, surprised at the large denomination for what appeared to be a simple task.

He snapped the bill from Romy's fingers, then said, "Follow me."

The hotel was middle class at best, so not the type frequented by business people, yet it was good for their advertising to indicate they had a business suite. Unfortunately, the dank room, emitting a musty smell from lack of ventilation, was proof the advertisements were not effective.

The manager sat in a chair in front of one of three computers before placing his fingers on the keyboard. "What are you looking for?"

"A person by the name of Mick Dulan. He's a private investigator."

The manager's fingers flashed across the keyboard, causing various windows to appear. With each one, a barely audible "ah—huh" was whispered by the manager. After another flurry of keystrokes, his index finger lifted higher before pressing hard on the *enter* key. The printer came to life, and a moment later the manager held the paper in his hand as he read from it:

"Dulan Investigations

322 Rislow Laneway

West Morton."

He snapped the paper over his shoulder where Romy retrieved it. Romy thanked the manager, but he paid Romy and Efia no more attention as he was occupied with closing down the many screens he had opened.

Outside the front door, several cabs were waiting for prospective passengers. Romy and Efia hopped into one and gave the driver the destination.

After a few minutes, the driver, an older man with a ring of grey hair around a bald head, glanced at the passengers through a mirror in front of him. "You're a Bantu," he said.

Efia grinned, glanced at Romy, then replied. "I think he's talking about me."

The driver let out a quick staccato of laughter. "Of course I'm talking about you."

"It's that obvious?" Efia continued the patronizing responses.

His smile turning upside down, the driver said, "Oh, now. You're playing with me. Of course you are the Bantu, and West Morton has a high population of Bantu. It's also not a very nice place."

"Is there a lot of crime there?" Romy asked.

"No, not at all. It's just their culture is different."

"You mean different from yours," Efia added.

The driver glanced in the mirror again, his eyebrows lifted. "Yes, different from mine." The driver's eyebrows quickly lowered. "I mean, that's what I mean, but I don't mean it in the way you think I mean it. I'm not like that." He waggled his finger at Efia's reflection in his little mirror.

"I meant nothing by it," she replied through a grin. "But it's best you now keep your attention in front of you. The roadway is getting busy."

Twenty minutes later, after travelling on a wide multilane highway, then two smaller but still hectic thoroughfares, they arrived on a quiet side street. The cab stopped in front of a brown brick, three story building. A metal sign was tacked to the wall with the address:

322 Rislow Laneway.

When they departed the cab, it was just before lunchtime. The sky was overcast and the temperature was on the cool side. They entered the drab office building, and after checking the directory, they took an elevator to the second floor where they quickly found a wooden door with a frosted glass window in it. Stenciled on the glass was:

Dulan Investigations.

After entering, they found themselves in a small outer office where a woman was seated behind an old desk that looked like it was made from the same tree as the door. The woman was a middle-aged Bantu, slim with salt and pepper hair down to her shoulders.

She smiled. "Well, good—" She glanced at the clock on her desk "—almost afternoon. How can I help the two of you?"

Seeing the Bantu woman looking at the two of them, but spending more time focusing on the unusual white guy, Efia answered, "We'd like to see Mister Dulan about a contract we'd like to pursue."

"I can make you an appointment," the woman offered as she turned to her computer.

"We're from out of town, and we came a long way," Efia interjected. "So, is it possible to see him now?"

"You seem like a sweet girl," the secretary said. "So, let me see if he can fit you in." She rose and scurried through the door behind her.

Romy lifted his hands, palm up, as he glanced around the room and the few empty chairs aligned along the far wall. "Fit us in between who?" he asked. "There's no one here."

"Stop it!" Efia said, followed by a slap on his chest. But she couldn't hold back the grin. However, it stopped abruptly when Efia heard the doorknob turning.

"Mister Dulan says he can fit you in for a few minutes now." The secretary held the door open as Romy and Efia walked through the doorway into an office that didn't look much different from the outer office, just a bit bigger. The desk near the far window was similar to that in the outer office, and there was similar wood paneling on one wall. Romy thought, *it must have been one really big tree.*

A man rose from the other side of the desk when they entered. The first thought Romy had was, he doesn't match this office or this neighbourhood. Mick Dulan was a good 30 centimetres taller than Romy. He was lean with black hair, parted at the side. His facial features were sharp and striking. He glanced at Efia who had a smile on her face, a variation of which Romy hadn't seen before. It was obvious she agreed with his positive evaluation.

Mick wore maroon, pin-striped pants and a thin, black sweater with a white shirt collar protruding at the neck line. He wore two silver rings on his fingers, and he had a fashionable watch on his wrist, the first Romy had seen during his short time on Teston.

Romy's first impression was this private investigator wasn't a working man, but when he looked closer at his hands, he saw there were a couple of callouses and a small cut. That was a positive, but what really changed Romy's initial negativity was Mick's eyes. They were brown, nothing unusual, but they exuded honesty. At least, that's the impression Romy received.

On Teston, people do not shake hands or have any type of physical greeting. Mick just pulled back one of the two seats in front of his desk and looked at Efia. "Have a seat, and tell me how I can help you?"

Efia took the offered seat, her smile towards the suave man widening, and Romy sat beside her. Mick returned to his own chair opposite them, intertwined his fingers on the desk and said, "I'm all yours. How can I help you?"

Tilting his gaze towards Efia and seeing her smile turn more sinister, Romy placed his hand on top of hers. "Let me start," he said to her, causing the smile to fade away.

"My name is Romy Gunn and this is Efia Kuma. Are you familiar with pureblood castes?" Romy asked.

"Of course. Efia is a Bantu. I suspect you are a Celtae," Mick replied.

Romy's brow furrowed. "She is obvious, but how would you know about me?"

Mick laughed. It was a deep elegant laugh that matched his appearance. "I'm an investigator. To do that effectively one needs to be an excellent observer." After a short pause, he asked, "Am I right?"

Leaning forward, Romy willed the green energy shield across his chest.

In response, Mick lifted one hand, palm up. "I got it," he said. "No sense burning the place down. Lots of wood as I'm sure you have noticed."

The energy sputtered out as Romy returned his focus on Mick. "We have an interest in the explosion that happened in the city two weeks ago," he explained.

"You mean the pumping station," Mick surmised. "It was a big explosion. At least there was some good luck in the disaster since the main highway leading to the station was blocked by an accident. If that had not happened, some people would have died. The driver who caused the accident fled, even though, in reality, he would have been seen as a hero." He glanced at the large video screen on the far paneled wall before continuing. "What's your interest in the explosion?"

Efia couldn't help but notice the distracted glance at the video screen. "Is there something you're waiting for?"

"There's a hajiball game starting in an hour. It's our global final."

"That means we have a little time before it starts," Efia interjected. "By then we'll know if you're willing to work for us."

Mick's eyes lit up. "Usually, my cases are men or women wanting their unfaithful mates watched. This sounds like espionage, and, to say the least, so much more intriguing." He leaned forward, focusing on Romy to the chagrin of Efia. "Why are you interested in the pumping station?"

"You will have to bear with me as I explain. It will take a few minutes," Romy advised.

"My interest is certainly piqued," Mick said.

After a deep breath, Romy began. "You seem familiar with purebloods, so I take it you know the specific powers of the seven races?"

"Indeed, I do. The shield you showed me, the Toltec who can conjure up energy balls, the Kush with the power of illusion…"

"Point taken," Romy interrupted. In fact, he was impressed with Mick's knowledge. "However, there have been a few, and only a very few purebloods with mutations. One, was a man who led the Ionians and the other races such that the ongoing race wars across the Athar were minimized."

Mick replied, "You are speaking of Nolan Harrison."

Romy and Efia's jaws both dropped. "How could you know that?"

"We do get purebloods who visit our planet from time to time. The southwest coast has wonderful resorts. I met a few Ionians who came through a few years ago." He shrugged. "With all those psychic powers, you would have thought some gossip control would be in order."

Romy's brow lowered. "Here's something you don't know. Nolan Harrison was an ancestor of mine."

"Do you also have multiple powers?" Mick asked.

In response, Romy lifted his fingers and for the second time enabled his psychic powers. This time, a small orange energy ball formed on his fingertips."

"Okay. Okay," Mick said. "Remember the wood."

"I don't have all seven psychic powers. I have a few, but I do have a very unique one that even Nolan Harrison did not have."

Mick turned to Efia with a wide smile, making his appearance even more handsome. "I hope you're enjoying this as much as I am. The intrigue is building."

"I have the ability to travel in time."

Mick's eyes widened, and he let out something between a gasp and a cough. "Say that again."

"Did you not hear me, or did you not understand?" Romy answered.

"Just say it again."

"I can travel in time. I can do it within plane, or I can do it plane to plane."

Mick leaned back onto the padded back cushion of his chair and let out a sigh. "You started with so much promise, but this is when I am going to ask you to leave."

Efia began to rise, but Romy stopped her as he lifted his hand. "Wait." He turned his gaze back to Mick. "If I do something to prove I can travel in time, then can we continue?"

"Sure. Humour me, but as you do so, we are going to watch the game." He pressed a button on a console in front of him, and the video screen came to life.

Rising to his feet, Romy moved to a clear space behind the chair he had occupied. "Have you seen purebloods transposition before?"

"Not often, but a few times."

Romy nodded, and a shimmer began around his form. It spread across and in front of him until the oval shape was opaque. When it cleared, he was gone.

Efia said, "With time travel, if he is successful, he will be back immediately. It's not like…"

Her words were interrupted as the shimmer reappeared, but worked in reverse. When it faded, Romy was once again in the room.

"That doesn't prove anything," Mick offered.

Once again, Romy took his place in the chair. "You said there was a hajiball game that will begin shortly."

Mick glanced at his watch. "In 15 minutes. It's between the North Coast Jets and the Colton Flames."

"Do you bet on the games, Mick?" Romy asked.

"From time to time. I have money on the Colton Flames right now," Mick confessed.

Pulling out the heavy wallet from the inside pocket of his jacket, Romy opened the zipper and pulled out a 200 val bill. He laid it on the desk in front of Mick. "I want you to place a bet with this. The Jets are going to win 23 to 18. A forward named Milic will score the 23rd goal for the Jets with 11 seconds left. I want you to call your bookie and bet the 200 on the game. What are the odds for predicting the correct score?"

"This morning it was 15 to 1."

"Here's the deal," Romy explained. "The 200 is a small fortune unto itself. But if the bet wins, you keep the 200 plus all the winnings as your fee for working for us for the next month."

"I have two other jobs on the go," Mick stated.

Romy waved his hand. "Cancel them or subcontract them." He pointed at the 200 val bill. If you win, that's more money than you would make in many months."

Romy could see in the way he was rubbing his chin, Mick was considering the offer. He put his finger on the bill, pressing it closer to Mick.

Finally, Mick reached forward, snapping the bill out from under Romy's finger. "Done." He then pressed a button on the communicator on his desk. "Racine, order lunch for the four of us. We're going to be watching the game together."

During the first 30 minutes of the game, Mick explained the rules and the reasons things were happening as the action played out. He was sitting next to Efia—quite close, in fact, and Mick was spending most of his time explaining things to her. It didn't bother Romy so much. After all, he had already watched the end of the game when he teleported away from this office.

But as he watched it for longer, he got a basic understanding of the game. There were ten players on each team, and they all had specific tasks and positions. Each had a hooked, hard sleeve, half a metre long, attached to their hand. There was a small ball they could carry in the sleeve, or when need be, sling it to another player. The game was physical with significant body contact allowed. The ultimate goal was to put the ball in one of three small quarter metre holes in the other team's end of the indoor stadium.

The game only had a minute left to play when Romy turned to Efia and Mick. He wished he hadn't.

Mick was leaned over close to Efia. "I used to play hajiball, semi pro, but then I broke my ankle."

Looking upwards at Mick, Efia placed her hand on his chest. "That's why you're so athletic looking."

Romy pushed Efia in the shoulder, and the force caused her to bump into Mick. "Pay attention. The score is 22 to 18. There's thirty seconds left."

So, they did watch. With twenty seconds left, Milic was running down the left wing with the ball in his sling. A defender lunged for him, but Milic stopped on the spot, evading the effort. Two steps later, he flung his arm forward. The ball was released at an incredible velocity, finding its way into the centre of the left target. Game time was shown on the left top corner of the screen. There were 11 seconds left.

After the restart, the game finished with no further goals. All three of them rose to their feet. Mick's legs were a little shaky as he moved in front of Romy. He pushed his fingers back through his hair and stated, "It seems you are indeed a time traveler."

Romy grinned. "And it seems, you are indeed somewhat rich."

Chapter 27: The Happy Couple

The 259th day of the 2388th Teston solar year.

Colton, largest city on the southern continent, planet Teston

Pulling back the dark curtain, Romy peered out the window at an angle, watching Mick and Efia approach along the sidewalk from the distance. They were close together, walking in unison with Mick's arm wrapped around her shoulder. As they came closer, Romy saw they weren't talking, but they did have wide, satisfied smiles on their faces.

Romy didn't mind the situation at all. He was foretold Efia and Mick would hit it off. The three of them had spent most of their time together on their investigation, but they needed breaks, and in those, Mick and Efia always seemed to wander off by themselves. They even took two days off at one point to recalibrate. Romy had difficulty when he heard that. He had never heard the activity he knew was happening behind closed doors as— recalibration.

It had been 25 days, or five Korian weeks, since they met Mick Dulan. For the majority of their time, they had been working almost exclusively on their project to find people who could be related to the blockage on the bridge and the pumping station explosion. They were making headway through many possibilities, thanks primarily to Mick's information network that even now still amazed Romy. Mick had his fingers in politicians, newspeople, celebrities and even the city's criminals. Yet still, with this network resulting in many leads, they were no closer to finding a solution.

Turning, Romy glared at the far wall of the main room of the apartment, one Mick had allowed them to use. Upon learning more about Mick, they discovered he owned the entire three-story building his office was in. He insisted Romy and Efia use the furnished, two-bedroom apartment on the third floor during their stay. With the travellers using the apartment and Mick spending his evenings in the overnight room adjacent to his office, they were able to focus more time on the case.

There were 75 faces pinned up on the far wall. Walking towards them, Romy scanned them again, just as he had done 100 times before.

He heard laughing from the outer hallway, and a moment later, Mick and Efia spilled into the room. They both gave a brief hello to Romy who faced them with his fists against his hips.

"It must be nice to have free time," Romy quipped.

Rolling her eyes, Efia replied, "Oh, come on. We were only gone for 45 minutes. You should try getting some fresh air for yourself. You wouldn't be in such a perpetually bad mood."

"The only thing that will get me out of my bad mood is solving the puzzle of what needs to be done to fix the timeline." As Mick and Efia lowered onto the couch facing the collage of faces, Romy shrugged. "But you might be right. Let's go through this one more time to see if we missed anything, then I'm going to go for a walk to clear my head; that's if we don't come up with something." With a wink he added, "Then when I come back, hopefully, I won't be such a bitch."

"Sounds like a plan," Efia said through a smirk.

Romy made a wide circle with his hand towards the collage. "We have a total of 75 people we have or have had, at some point, on our hit list. It is appropriate to consider the change in the timeline was caused by the death of someone. So, we found eight Coltonians who died the day of the explosion and another 17 who died in the four days after. And since we know the shift in the timeline happens some time well in the future, the person who died would have to have children. Of the 25 people who died, ten did not have children, so we shifted them to the left side of our board. These are the unlikely ones and low priority. The remainder we shifted to the right as high priority.

Then we added a filter, thinking, if the timeline was going to be severely shifted, the death would likely be in a political or military family. That shifted another dozen names to the left."

Romy was lost in the sea of faces. Mick and Efia were listening, but Romy didn't even notice them. "And then the idea came that maybe the time shift wasn't triggered by a death; rather, maybe it was just a family member of someone who got killed who was despondent enough to make a career or life change."

Romy kept talking, but soon his words were moving in circles. Mick and Efia added input from time to time, but, once again, Romy was getting frustrated. He finally slapped his hand on the wall and growled, "We're getting nowhere. We do our research every day. Through that, we discount a few people, but we come up with even more people who potentially could be the source of our time shift."

Efia rose to her feet and placed a hand on Romy's shoulder. "I think that's enough for tonight. Let's get some dinner, then a good night's sleep."

Turning, he pulled her hand off his shoulder, but did not release it. "You know, there are times you do remind me of my Efi." Before the awkward moment became even more so, he released her hand and glanced at Mick over her shoulder. "I think I am going to go for that walk. I'll get something to eat while I'm out." Romy's eyes darkened as he continued. "Just make sure you take care of her."

Without waiting for a response, he strode towards the door and removed his leather coat off the hook next to it. He knew he had to take more drastic action, and knowing that, he didn't dare look back as he closed the door behind him.

A few minutes later, he was out on the sidewalk. It was early evening, but darkness had settled in. He walked a few hundred metres, giving himself a last opportunity to change his mind. A colourful food truck passed him, moving in the opposite direction. His thoughts were troubling him, so much so, he didn't notice the odd circus music emitting from the truck. He was just delaying what must happen, so, after whispering a curse, the shimmer appeared around his form. A moment later, he was gone.

He had targeted the old abandoned house on Teston that he had arrived at twice before, but when he rematerialized, the house was not there. Instead, he was between a line of trees and the roadway on the other side of a grass-covered field. Now, far in the future, things had changed, and the abandoned house had finally been demolished. Walking to the roadway, he turned right since he saw lights in that direction. He wasn't surprised to see the hotel was still there, but it had been renovated and enlarged. Once he entered through the revolving doors, he saw the establishment was now upscale and elegant.

Off to the side of the main foyer, he saw a uniformed attendant rocking on his feet behind a high desk. There was a pad of paper and a pen on top of it Romy used to write down a name. After pulling out a large denomination bill, he handed it to the attendant with the paper.

"Do you think we could go to your business suite? I need an address for that name."

Romy already knew how the attendant would respond by the way his eyes lit up.

"Of course. Right this way."

Ten minutes later, Romy was walking out the revolving doors with the same piece of note paper, now also bearing the address he was looking for. He handed it to the cab driver after entering into the bubble car.

The driver put the vehicle in gear, and after he made a U turn, he said, "Wow! North Suburbs. That's a nice area."

Romy just nodded, without giving a reply, nor did they talk for the remaining 30 minutes it took them to get to the street they were looking for.

Once they made their final turn, the driver stated, "It's just at the end of this road."

"Let me out here," Romy responded. "I'm going to walk the rest of the way."

"Anything you say," the driver offered.

Romy paid the man along with a large tip before he began walking along the sidewalk bordering the street, counting down the house numbers. When he was two houses away, he stopped and slid under the wide branches of a tall tree. Even though it was dark, the tree provided shade from the street lights. He stayed there for a time, building up the courage to knock on the door. But just when he was about to leave his hiding spot, the front door of the house opened, and an older couple walked out.

The man was tall, although a little stooped, and he walked with a slight limp. The woman was pretty with long white hair, tied in four thick bundles, falling down her back to her waist. They moved onto the sidewalk, turning in the opposite direction away from Romy. They held hands as they headed towards the intersection about 400 metres away.

Romy followed, keeping in the shadows. He tried to keep his footsteps quiet, although he suspected the older couple would have no idea he was there. *Why would they?*

After 200 metres, Romy continued on the grass beside the sidewalk, when his ears perked up. He thought, *were those footsteps behind me?* He turned, but after a lengthy inspection, he saw nothing out of order.

When his gaze turned forward, he saw the couple turning the corner at the intersection. He hurried after them while still trying to remain silent. When he turned the corner, he heard the footsteps behind him once again. Ahead, he saw the older couple entering a well-lit building. A sign hung from a post in front of it. It read:

Siros Street Sports Tavern

Realizing he had time, he snuck into a group of three trees beside the sidewalk and waited. From behind the thick trunk of one of the trees, he didn't have to wait long. An older man was walking by, his eyes shifting from side to side. He had white hair tied back in a short ponytail and a short white beard and moustache. Romy could not tell much else because of the knee-length, black coat the man wore.

Once he was ten metres past his position, Romy stepped out onto the sidewalk. "What do you want?"

The man spun instantly into a crouch, and the green energy shield of a Celtae formed around him. Instinctively, Romy conjured up an orange ball of energy, and flung it at the man. Romy was surprised since this fireball was his more powerful variation, and the man's shield easily deflected it. He was just in the process of creating a second energy ball, when he was surprised for a second time.

The man dissipated his shield and held up his hand. "Romy Gunn—wait!"

With one eyebrow raised, Romy walked carefully towards the man. "You know who I am?"

The older man rose to his full height and relaxed. "My name is Gracin. I'm here to help you."

Walking closer, Romy replied, "What makes you think I need help?"

"Since I am not so different from you, I know things you know, and even some things I know you wished you knew."

"You're talking in riddles," Romy quipped.

"This will help with your confusion, then." Gracin reached into his inside coat pocket and pulled forth a small, black book. He threw it to Romy. "This is what you are looking for. And with that my assignment is complete."

Romy opened the book and saw the first two pages listed many names in a lineage format. Further in the book were details of the names—at least as far as he could see with such a quick inspection. He turned back to the first page and recognized one of the names. It matched one of the names on his collage of faces in the apartment!

The man had already turned when Romy called after him. "I don't understand! How could you know this?"

The man turned his face and chuckled as he continued to walk away. "Many things are revealed in the future, especially to someone far in the future." He saw the confusion had not left Romy's face. "What—you don't think you're the only time drifter wandering the Athar with assignments from see'ers, do you!"

Romy could do nothing but stand there, mouth agape as a shimmer appeared around Gracin's form. The oval became opaque, and then a moment later he was gone. "Well. I'll be damned," he muttered as he put the small book into the inside pocket of his jacket. Even though the solution to his dilemma was now at hand, he still had to finish what he came here to do.

He walked up the stairs, into the tavern, and stopped just inside the doorway. It was large, and right away, he could see it was dedicated to fans of hajiball. There were jerseys and pictures hung on every portion of the wall. Two different screens were playing different games the patrons were watching while letting out constant cheers.

He saw the older couple in a booth, facing away from him, watching a large screen behind the bar. Taking a deep breath, he strode towards the booth and slipped onto the bench opposite the couple. The man looked shocked—the woman, not so much.

The woman said, "That was a long walk. It's been 50 years."

"I know Efia. I apologize." He looked at the man. "Same to you Mick. I'm sorry."

Efia, although now in her 80s', was still pretty under the long, white bundles of hair, and in spite of the long scar she still carried on her jaw. She smiled widely. "It's good to see you again. We knew you'd come one day, and here you are. But don't get me wrong, I'm irritated, but we're not angry. We've had a wonderful life, one I wouldn't change for anything."

"I know," Romy whispered.

One corner of Efia's lips curled up. "How could you possibly have known?" She saw Romy's face darken as he blushed. "Why do I get the feeling I'm going to become more irritated?" she added.

Romy explained, "Do you remember when I first brought you to the abandoned house in Colton, and there was a note from Allard?"

"Yes. It was the note with Mick's name on it."

"There was more on the note I did not tell you about. Allard's research found a married couple, Mick Dulan and Efia Kuma, with 3 children and eight grandchildren and a number of great grandchildren."

Efia elbowed Mick and through a grin, said, "Hear that! We're going to have great grandchildren!"

Romy continued. "The note also said the two of you continued your investigation into the explosion into your senior years. That's why I came to you now, hoping for a solution."

Reaching out and placing a hand on top of Romy's, she said, "We don't have a final solution. We came up with a short list of five names that had the highest probability." She then listed them off.

Pulling the small book he received from Gracin from his pocket, he opened it to the first page. "Nope. The name of the person we need to find is Manda Fisk."

Mick, who had been silent so far, said, "Now I'm confused. I thought you said you came here looking for the solution."

"I did," Romy replied. Then, he explained his encounter with the time drifter, Gracin, who was the source of the book.

"That's unbelievable," Efia said.

Romy tilted his head and shrugged. "Yeah, who would have thought someone we don't know at all, from far in our future, would bring us the solution."

Letting out a low giggle, Efia clarified, "It's not that. It's incredible that there is another one like *you* floating around the Athar."

Both eyebrows lowered, Romy quipped back, "You're over 80 now, but still, you're the sarcastic smart ass."

"It's like we left the apartment only yesterday, still fighting and bickering," Mick interjected. "And as I told you many times there, you two need to give it a rest." He lifted his hand in the air, catching the eye of the bartender. He then lifted three fingers, and the bartender, knowing Mick very well, knew exactly which three drinks to bring.

With their joking set aside and the three fruit wines in front of them, it was time to understand how Manda Fisk fit into the time shift.

Efia began. "Manda Fisk was one of the people we removed off our list early on. She had no children, and she was a construction worker, so no political or military ties. How could she be the cause of this?"

Romy opened the book to the detail pages and began to read out important facts. "We never would have figured this out—not in a million years. It's more convoluted than we ever imagined." He flipped the pages and continued to read. "The paradox also involves Jay Son."

"How so?" Mick asked. "He was a ten-year-old boy who broke his leg the day of the explosion. He was on his way to the Brash Street Hospital in an ambulance, but the bridge blockage forced the ambulance to go to the West Colton Hospital."

"It reads here, as we know, the Brash Street Hospital is five kilometres northeast of the bridge. The West Colton Hospital is 15 kilometres west of the bridge."

"Was the distance an issue?" Efia asked.

Romy answered, "No, but remember, the ambulance carrying the boy to West Colton was in an accident. It was only a fender bender, so another ambulance came for the boy, but the initial ambulance in the accident was out of commission for some time. That might not seem like a problem on its own, but it was a factor. There are six ambulances assigned to each of the two hospitals."

After a long drink of wine, Mick stated, "The damaged ambulance was assigned to Brash Street Hospital, so they were down to five. Not a big deal."

Lifting a finger, Romy read out more facts. "Two days later, in the morning, a Brash Street ambulance was dispatched to West Colton to transfer the boy. That left only four ambulances for the Brash Street region. There was a flurry of calls, and one of them was for an industrial accident at a demolition site."

Elki cringed. "It was a horrible accident. Manda Fisk fell off a short platform when the railing gave way. The concrete wall they had been tearing down had iron rebar in it. It was a fluke, but she fell on a piece of rebar held by a broken block of concrete. It pierced her leg, hitting a main artery. She bled out on the way to the hospital."

Romy continued to fill in details. "However, with one broken ambulance, and a second transferring the boy, the ambulance dispatched from Brash Street Hospital was delayed. Normally, the ambulance would have arrived in ten minutes, but instead, it took 22 minutes. That was the difference."

"I'm still confused," Mick admitted. "Manda Fisk had no children. How could her death affect the future?"

Flipping through a few pages to a point near the end of the book, Romy said, "Here it is. Manda was married to Rory Mason with no children. When she died, two years later, he remarried a Bantu woman. They had two children." He lifted his face with a satisfied grin. "Five generations later, a descendant—part Bantu, part Testonian—started a cult-like group that proposed the Bantu use their powers for wealth and power. Over the following generations, the movement grew throughout the Athar, including Aeo."

"You need to go back and make sure Manda Fisk doesn't die. That would be the easiest way," Efia proposed.

Romy leaned back and took a deep drink of wine. He considered Efia was probably right. But he would finalize the plan with the younger versions of Mick and Efia when he got back to them.

Efia nudged Mick. "Can you give us a few minutes alone, Love. Maybe get us another round before Romy leaves."

Mick paused for a moment, unsure what Efia was up to, but her loving gaze told him all was well, so he shifted out of the booth and strode to the bar.

Romy asked, "What's up?"

It took a moment for Efia to find the right words. "We still don't know under what conditions your Efi will be waiting for you when you fix the shift in reality. If you take me back to our original time, or you leave me behind, just as you did 50 years ago, we really don't know the result."

"True, but I have my hopes."

"As do I," Efia replied, her eyes becoming moist as she fought back the flow of tears. "Mick and I have had a wonderful life here. We do have three children and eight grandchildren who I'd not trade for anything. I knew shortly after you left, and it has been reinforced every day since, that this is where I have always belonged."

"I understand," Romy whispered.

"Do you? I need to make sure you really do. Romy, long ago, I made you promise to take me back to my home world with you. Jokingly, there was a condition that would veto that demand."

"I remember."

"Good, my friend. To be clear, I'm not only asking you to leave me on Teston with Mick, I'm begging you."

Chapter 28: Manda Fisk

The 259th day of the 2388th Teston solar year.

Colton, largest city on the southern continent, planet Teston

Romy reappeared in the timeline he had just left. The teleportation 50 years into the future and the return would appear almost instantaneous to anyone watching, even though for Romy, he had been gone for over four hours of his time.

When the shimmer around him dissipated, he heard the circus music from the food truck far behind him. The wide yawn was a sign of his weariness, but more than that, he was hungry. Thankfully, ahead, in a parking lot the food truck had just left, three more were parked, their awnings up and the aroma of wonderful, spiced food spreading from their narrow smoke stacks.

It didn't take long to cross the street and arrive at the lot. He looked at the menus of each truck and chose the second one. There, he ordered a hot meat and vegetable sandwich. Once the steaming sandwich was in hand, he retraced his footsteps back to the third-floor apartment above Mick Dulan's office. By the time he was walking up the stairs, he had devoured the sandwich. He opened the door and was startled by the sight of Efia and Mick, entangled on the couch.

Pulling herself free, Efia scoffed, "Don't you ever knock?"

Frowning, Romy replied, "I live here. Why would I knock?"

Mick straightened up and interjected, "Technically, you're both guests."

Romy closed the door behind him, then clapped his hands together. "The two of you need to pull yourself together and listen. I have great news!"

Efia's interest was immediately piqued. She hadn't seen Romy's smile so wide, or his eyes so bright, since they arrived on Teston. "Don't stop. Tell us what's going on," she urged.

Pulling out the small book, he explained the details of his run in with Gracin. The time drifter from far in the future gave him the book that held the exact information they were looking for.

Both Mick and Efia were silent, the looks on both their faces showed they were more than a little dumbfounded.

Slapping the back of his hand against the book, Romy said, "The solution to our problem is here. We know what we have to do!"

If Efia ever had a skeptical look on her face, it was now, her lips scrunched to the side, one eyebrow lowered. "Where did you run into this man, Gracin?"

Romy opened his mouth, but paused for a moment before saying, "I was walking towards the food truck lot to get a sandwich when we ran into each other." He pointed in the general direction and added, "Three blocks from here."

In an instant, Romy had decided it would serve no purpose to tell them he had gone into their future and visited them in their senior years. In reality, it was an invasion of their privacy. And such knowledge of their future could affect decisions they would make now. The last thing any of them needed was another forced alteration to the timeline.

Pushing her hand out, palm up, Efia said, "Give me the book."

Romy tossed it to her, and even before she leaned back, she had the book open. Mick shifted closer to her, so he could also read the critical information within. They read to the back of the book in 20 minutes, then turned the pages back to the beginning and read it all for a second time.

When the second reading was complete, Efia snapped the book closed. "So, it's Manda Fisk."

"If we make sure she doesn't die, generations later, her husband's ancestor will not create the extremist Bantu cult," Romy concluded.

Rising to his feet, Mick was already walking to the office when he directed, "We need to have another look at her file."

Romy and Efia followed Mick, until he sat at the chair in front of the computer. As he started tapping keys, he explained, "Manda Fisk died in an industrial accident. That resulted in a mandated investigation by the Construction Safety Board. I know someone there, and they sent me the file a while ago. Fortunately, I didn't discard it after we initially deemed her a low priority."

Mick was advancing through a series of pictures within the file when he found the one he wanted. It showed a thick concrete platform set on pillars, a metre above ground level. On one side of the platform, a wooden post and railing system was attached. A section of the railing was broken, with the two sides hanging. Below, were broken concrete sections, some larger some smaller, and two of the larger blocks had iron rebar protruding from them. One in particular, was gruesome looking with the iron bar and the block covered in blood.

Efia said, "That's where she fell through. Her leg hit the bar and it pierced her main artery. The ambulance was late, and she bled out." She brought her hand up, rubbing her chin. "We need to find a way to help her." She shrugged, then glanced at Romy. "It shouldn't be difficult for you to go back in time and figure out a way to save her."

Placing his hand on Mick's shoulder, he said, "I need to talk to Efia alone for a few minutes."

Rising to his feet, Mick looked down on Romy and replied, "I thought we were in this together?"

Efia crossed her arms, showing she agreed with the sentiment.

"Bear with me, Mick. You've been an integral part of what we need to do here, but I just need a minute alone with Efia," Romy repeated.

Shrugging, Mick let out a frustrated sigh as he left the room. A moment later, they heard the front door of the apartment close behind him.

Efia's face had a distinctively darker hue. "That wasn't nice!"

"I think, once you hear me out, you'll understand." Romy took a deep breath before continuing. "When I go back to save Manda, you need to come with me."

"Why? It doesn't seem like it would be difficult."

"That's not it at all," Romy elaborated. "When we fix the timeline and the reality reverts back, I'm not sure, but I think it is important where you are in the timeline when that happens."

"But you're not 100 per cent sure?"

Romy slid his fingers back through his hair. "No, not 100 per cent. But it is a much higher probability that if I leave you here, you will disappear with the alternate, corrupted reality."

"Can you bring me back here after the reality is fixed?"

"If you want me to bring you back here, I will do that."

Efia gave a curt nod. "Okay. Then, we'll leave in the morning." She turned and headed out the door.

Romy yelled after her, "Where are you going?"

Her hand caught the door jamb, and she turned her face to him. Her eyes were wide and sad, as sad as Romy had ever seen them. "I'm going to spend the night with Mick."

He didn't need to know anything else. Romy understood, his own eyes now as sad as hers while he watched her leave the apartment.

The next morning, the three friends ate breakfast together. Efia explained to Mick she was going with Romy. Mick wasn't altogether surprised, but still, he did ask her if she was coming back. He smiled wide, placing his hand on top of hers when she told him she would see him again.

From their apartment, with Mick watching, Romy and Efia left in a shimmer of hazy light. When they reappeared, Efia didn't recognize where they were.

"I thought we'd be near the construction site," she said.

Romy had transported them to a back alley on the far east side of Colton. "There's a nice hotel on the main road ahead. We need to stay there for a couple of nights." On his last word, Romy began to walk up the alley.

In a half run, Efia caught up. "Why are we wasting two days here?"

Without breaking stride, he explained, "It's important I bring you back to a time before the pumping station explosion and the blockage on the bridge. I told you, I'm not sure, but I believe everything associated with the alternate reality will go away if we change it back to the version of reality I came from. By bringing you back to a point before the change, you're at a point before the alternate reality was created. Here, I think you'll be immune to the affects of the change."

She punched him in the shoulder. "You think?"

Rubbing his shoulder, he responded, "Yes, I think, but with a high probability. But what I do know with a much higher probability, is if you were left with Mick in a time after the event in question, you would disappear."

"This gives me my best chance?"

"Absolutely."

Two nights later, Romy and Efia were lying prone on a shallow rise of land across the road from the structure being demolished. Through the tall grass, both of them were looking through binoculars they had purchased.

Romy whispered, "I don't see any security guards."

Efia let out a snort. "Why would there be guards? It's a building being demolished."

Romy rose to a squat. "Let's go, then."

It was the early hours in the morning, and the darkest time of night. They were both dressed in black for their planned covert activities.

Efia rose, shuffling down the hillside, Romy beside her. There were a few lights hanging from high posts around the work site, providing lit areas, but also shadows. They ran across the narrow roadway until their backs were flat against the metal, mesh fence in one of those shadowed areas.

The fencing was poor at best, with only two ties at each fence section joining to each post. Retrieving the cutters, Romy cut the lower tie beside him. He lifted the section of fence, allowing Efia to crawl under. Then, Efia held the fence and Romy followed her. Bent over, they ran towards the concrete platform they had spied from across the road. Rubble was scattered at the base of the platform under the wooden railing. It was easy to find the two blocks with the protruding rods, and they immediately set in place the simple plan they had previously decided on.

"Start with this one," Romy directed. He placed his fingers under the edge of the block while Efia firmly gripped the iron bar. "Pull!" Romy urged.

The block was heavy, but between the two of them, they were able to shift it.

"How far do we need to go?" Efia said through panting breaths.

"Three metres should be enough," Romy replied.

Once it was moved to the set distance, they proceeded to move the second block to a spot beside it.

Looking back at the area Manda would fall to, Efia saw it was still covered with a lot of awkwardly shaped rubble. "It's still more than likely she'll be injured."

"That might be a good thing. We need for her to live, but outside of that, the change to the timeline should be minimal. We don't need another alternate shift."

"You sure the rods are far enough?"

Turning towards Efia, he gave her a sarcastic snicker. "Unless she takes a running leap, sure it's far enough!"

"Then we're done. Let's get out of here."

Romy woke with a start. He felt the warmth of the sun on his back. Turning his face to the side, he saw Efia beside him, the binoculars held to her eyes.

"It's about time you woke up. Workers in bubble vehicles have been arriving for 30 minutes now."

Propping himself up on his elbows, he looked through his own binoculars. He scanned across the worksite. "Has Manda arrived?"

"Not yet—wait—the red bubble car that just arrived. There's a woman just exiting it."

Romy adjusted the magnification knob. "Yup. That's her." He glanced down at the watch he had purchased the day before. "We have four hours to wait."

"Wake me when it's almost time," Efia said. She placed the binoculars down beside her, then laid her head on the ground, closing her eyes.

Romy lay his head on his arm, watching Efia sleep. He missed his own Efi, and this woman was her double except for the hairstyle and the long scar along her jawline. In that moment, he missed his girl terribly, but if all went well today, she would be back in his arms soon. He was more concerned for Efia. In this altered reality, he knew Efia and Mick had a full and happy life. But if they were successful in changing the reality back to what he knew, there was a strong likelihood, but no certainty, that this outcome would be the same. He put his faith in the fact their personalities were the same, no matter the reality, and as such, he was hopeful they would be just as happy.

He glanced at his watch often, until the time was 15 minutes before the pending accident. He nudged Efia awake and whispered, "Fifteen minutes."

She yawned, propped herself up and brought the binoculars to her eyes. They both did, watching the work being undertaken across the road. Manda was on the platform with a massive drill, making holes in the far side of the platform. It concerned Romy because she was no where near the suspect railing. Another worker came up to her and, at first, they seemed to be having a playful discussion. At one point, the man put his arm around her shoulder. That made her angry, and she pushed him away. As he threw his hands up, she stomped to the opposite side of the platform, leaning back against the wooden railing. The railing snapped, and, with her arms flailing, she fell backwards.

"And there it is," Romy mumbled.

A loud, high-pitched scream echoed across the work site, loud enough for it to reach them across the roadway. A man ran over to Manda, kneeling beside her. She was holding her thigh while the man looked lower, seeing her ankle bent at an awkward angle. Cupping his hand to his mouth, he yelled across to a man with a red vest, "Her ankle is broken! Call an ambulance!"

Pulling the binoculars from his eyes, Romy turned on his side, and whispered, "We have 22 minutes."

Efia also turned to face him.

He reached over and put his hand on her shoulder. "You okay?"

She nodded. After a few moments she muttered, "If I disappear, tell Mick—well tell Mick I'll miss him." A tear was sliding down her cheek. Once she realized it was there, she angrily brushed it away.

Romy slid closer, wrapping his arms about her. She returned the embrace as they waited. They heard the ambulance siren in the distance. It grew louder until they knew it was at the site just opposite from their location. It didn't take long until they heard the screech of tires, then the siren began to fade as the ambulance raced away.

"I'm still here," Efia whispered.

"The critical time will be somewhere in the next 20 minutes. That's when, in this alternate reality, she died."

Efia's fingers gripped tighter into Romy's back. There were no words as they waited.

Romy groaned, followed by a louder wail as a jolt of pain shot through his head. A second jolt was even more intense. Romy only felt this type of pain once before; the time right after he blocked the bridge and he heard the pumping station explode. That was his last thought before he lost consciousness.

When he finally woke, it was to Efia's fingers gripped into his shirt, shaking him violently. "Romy—wake up—wake up!"

His eyes fluttered open, and he saw her smiling wide. She slapped him on the chest. "You've been out for 20 minutes, and I'm still here! Woohoo!"

Romy grimaced, one hand on his chest where Efia slugged him, the other holding the side of his head. He grumbled, "Yeah, I'm fine. Thanks for asking."

"What happened to you?" Efia finally asked.

Romy explained how it seems a massive shift in the timeline and the associated reality shift, causes a significant disturbance in the Athar. "As a time drifter, my mind must be more sensitive to this type of colossal event."

Efia could not keep the wide smile from her face. "So, the correction was successful, and I'm still here!" Now sitting on the ground, her knees drawn up, her feet did a happy tap dance against the ground. "What now?"

Romy rose to sit beside her. "You tell me? Do you want to go to my version of your reality, or do you want to go back to Mick?"

Her eyes brightened at the mention of Mick. "He's the only person I know here. My Bantu people are in your reality. My parents might be there."

Romy's voice was soft. "They will look like your folks, but they are Efi's parents."

Through a sigh, she replied. "True, but if I meet them, they'd surely accept me. Would Efi allow it?"

Shrugging, he responded, "I think so, but I can't speak for Efi. However, if you go back with me, you will recognize people including Mist. But they will not know you. You would require a great amount of strength to overcome the adversities of life on a world you know, but it does not know you."

"I will think on it," she stated. "But my initial sense is I belong with my Bantu people."

"Okay, I'll need to know tomorrow. Right now, I'm exhausted and need some food, then some sleep."

"Tell me again, why are we here?" Efia asked.

Before explaining, Romy took a moment to consider his words. The sharp pain he had felt in his head was a good sign reality had changed for the better. However, he needed verification. The simplest way was to see if something that occurred in the altered corrupt reality was still going to happen. That meant they needed to travel into the future to a point where such an event would be obvious. Consequently, they were now two weeks in the future from the time of Manda Fisk's injury, standing in a store front entryway across from Mick Dulan's building.

"As I told you earlier, we need to verify the reality has shifted to the one I know," Romy replied.

"How are we going to do that?"

"Remember, after the battle at Ventura, I pulled you out and brought you, unconscious, to Teston. The next day, you and I came here to find Mick Dulan."

"Of course, I remember."

Continuing the explanation, Romy said, "That day is today. That's why I brought us here. In about 15 minutes, we will know if we really were successful in fixing the timeline."

Efia shook her head. "I'm not following."

"In the altered reality, you and I hopped from Ventura Island to Teston, and today we would arrive here at Mick's office. However, if the reality has been changed, then the battle on your world did not happen, nor would there be a reason for you and I to hop to Teston or meet Mick Dulan."

"Your mind has been twisted by the possibilities of time travel, but even more frightful is the fact, I understand you."

A cab arrived at the building, the same colour as the one they used in their first arrival. Romy began to sweat, but he sighed with relief when the vehicle continued further down the block. They waited 30 minutes after the expected arrival time, and there was no sign of Romy and Efia on their original arrival. It was another sign the reality shift had been corrected.

"I think we're done here," Romy concluded.

Grabbing his arm, she said, "Not so fast. We need to go see Mick."

Turning and softly grasping Efia by her shoulders, he said, "At this point in the timeline, Mick has not yet met you or I. We could see him, but he would not know us."

She smiled. "I know, but Mick helped us. Without him, the correction would not have been possible. I think he should be rewarded before we leave."

"How?"

She held her hand out. "Give me that 200 val bill for the bet on the hajiball game."

He reached into his wallet and pulled out the bill as he grinned. "I get it. You want to play out the exact same scenario as the first time we met him."

"Yes, just let me give him the money and the score for the game this afternoon."

That's exactly what they did. They entered the outer office and met Mick's secretary. She led them into Mick's office where he was wearing the same pin-striped pants and sweater. Romy began with the pureblood story, and Mick believed him until he told Mick he was a time drifter. However, this time, rather than Romy hopping forward in time to obtain the score in the game, Efia pushed the bill across the table and told him the score and attached game details.

The same arrangement was made whereby Mick could keep all the winnings, but he would need to believe the time traveller story. Of course, the money was compelling so Mick agreed. Once they were in front of the video screen, Romy saw it as a good sign when Mick arranged to sit beside Efia. It was even more positive when half way through the game, the two had shifted closer together, seemingly obsessed with each other and barely paying attention to the game.

Romy rose, and told them he needed the bathroom.

Without looking away from Efia, Mick pointed to the office door and said, "Just down the hall."

Efia and Mick were so focused on each other, they were oblivious to Romy, his lips quivering as he stared at them for a few moments. But he saw they were smiling and happy, and that brought a satisfied smile to his own face. With that, he left, walking into the outer office.

There, for a second time, he said hello to Mick's Bantu secretary. He spied a pad on her desk. "Can I borrow your pad and that pen for a moment."

"Of course." She handed the two items to him.

Walking to a high side table against the far wall, he placed the items on it. He pulled out his wallet, still filled with many large denomination bills, and still, there was a platinum bar half the size of the original one.

When he had visited the elderly versions of Efia and Mick in the tavern near their home, as the three of them were leaving, Romy asked Mick about a large, wooden plaque hanging off the wall near the front entrance. Mick explained, hajiball was big all over Teston, and there were many sports bars. Within them, it was a custom to have a hajiball plaque with brass placards, each one showing the score in each year's final championship game. The board they had been looking at had 68 plaques secured to it.

Romy was impressed and took a moment to admire the plaques, with increased interest on one in particular. *It might come in handy*, he thought, at the time.

Now, with his lips pulled wide in a grim frown, Romy began to write.

Mick:

Once the game is over, you will have confidence in my abilities. You made a lot of money today, but I am giving you the opportunity to be both happy and even more wealthy.

The final score in next years final game is Harty City Raiders 18, West Coast Rams 16. Bet everything in this wallet on the game. The two of you will have a great life together.

Take care of her.

Romy

He placed the note in the wallet and zipped it closed. Returning to the secretary, he returned the pad and pen, then handed her the wallet. "Make sure you give this to Mick, but only after the game is over."

"I should tell him you're leaving."

"No, he knows. He told me to tell you not to disturb him until the game is over," Romy clarified.

Angling her head back, she laughed. "He tells me that for every game he watches here."

"It was nice meeting you," Romy said. "All of you."

He turned and walked out, then down the hallway. He had a few moments to change his mind. He thought Efia wanted to leave with him, but he could tell she was unsure. The older version of Efia was very sure, and she appeared genuinely happy in her old age. Even though Mick, today, did not know Efia at all, people do not change. Of course, they would fall in love, just as they had in the previous, altered reality.

He was satisfied. He brought forth the vision of the Athar in his mind's eye. He found the lit beacon he yearned for. It drew him in as the shimmer grew around him. He had a satisfied smile, knowing his Efi would be waiting. He was going home.

Chapter 29: Unfinished Business

The 16ᵗʰ day of the 10ᵗʰ month, Alpha Centauri year 0024.

Hagaza, capital city of the Mabuza people, Haven

As she had done so many times before, Efi waited for the shimmer to reappear. For each transposition, she was worried. If Romy did not return right away, it meant something went wrong, and there was a good chance he would never come back. So, she held her breath and only exhaled when she saw signs of his return.

However, when Romy appeared, she knew the assignment had not gone as planned. He appeared exhausted, but more than that, he looked older, as if this hop back in time had drained him of some of his life's energy. When his tired eyes caught hers, she heard him gasp. By the time he rushed to her and wrapped her in his embrace, he was doing his best to hold back his sobs.

"What happened?" she asked as her arms wrapped around him.

They were frozen there for a time, his face buried in her neck, until Romy took control of himself and pulled back. He cupped her face with his hands and kissed her passionately. "Things did not go exactly as planned, but all is well now." He smiled, even as the back of his hand came up and wiped away the moisture from his cheeks.

"How long were you gone?" Efi questioned.

"Almost three months," he replied. "I will explain it all to you when we are alone."

Elki was standing a few steps behind Efi, Mist beside her. He saw both their faces were solemn, their cheeks hollow. By that look, Romy saw they sensed the relationship he had with the see'ers would never be the same. All their clairvoyant visions of their future entanglement with the Athar had been shattered in that moment when they saw the look on Romy's face.

Nevertheless, Romy slid past Efi and gave Elki a hug, and even a greater one to Mist. When he pulled away, he reached down and grasped Mist's fingers. Raising them up, he chuckled and said, "I wasn't sure I would ever see you again—and with both arms intact."

Elki interrupted, "Romy, what are you talking about? Are you sure you're okay?"

Efi stepped forward beside Romy. He put his arm around her shoulder and answered, "I'm better than I have been in quite some time," he said through a feeble grin.

"I know you're tired," Elki added, "But it's obvious things did not go as planned. The two of you will meet us in the see'er's chambers in one hour for a report, then you can rest." She turned, heading for the exit from the transposition room.

"No."

Elki froze before turning to face Romy.

"That's right. I said no," Romy repeated. "Efi and I will give you an update after the dinner hour, this evening." His arm slid down, his fingers grasping Efi's hand, and without waiting for a response, he brushed past the two see'ers.

On the way to room 510, Romy inspected everything that came into view; he peered down every corridor and out every window. He was checking for anything that looked out of place. Thankfully, everything appeared the same as when he left.

Once they were in the apartment, Romy wasted no time, making his way to the bedroom, peeling off pieces of clothing along the way. His timing was perfect as he was only in his undergarment when he flopped onto the bed. Kicking off her boots, Efi joined him. Her mouth opened, about to ask a question when Romy lifted a finger to his lips.

"Later," he muttered before he lay on his side, dragging her against him.

She was about to make another attempt to ask what happened, but she heard his heavy breaths. He was fast asleep.

Efi had closed her eyes and had also fallen into a light slumber. She woke with a start when Romy jolted upright, and a scream escaped from his lips. He was shaking, and his body was covered by a sheen of sweat.

She sat up, placing a hand on his shoulder. Pushing backwards, she coaxed him back to a prone position. When his head hit the pillow her arm swept across his chest, settling on the far side. "Tell me what happened while you were gone."

For the next hour, Romy explained everything that had transpired. He told all, not sparing any detail. He told her about the initial successful mission that caused the horrendous changes to reality and the horrible place

Haven had become. Hagaza was nothing but rubble, and that's where he met Efia. He described her very well and explained the circumstances whereby he left her behind with Mick Dulan.

Her gaze lowered, her voice quiet, she asked, "Was she much different from me? Were you close?"

"She looked like you, but her personality was her own, and in many ways not like you. After a rocky start, we became good friends, and we trusted each other."

That satisfied Efi, now embarrassed because doubt crossed her mind. And if any negative thoughts remained, they vanished when he continued his words.

"I love you, Efi. While I was gone, and even when I was with Efia, all I could think of was returning to you."

She leaned over and kissed his cheek. "I told you before, you own me, and I will love you forever."

He pulled her close while leaning his face to the side, glancing at the clock. "We still have a few hours before we meet the see'ers."

Letting out a snicker, she replied, "I don't think Elki appreciated it when you denied her request for the report. I'm surprised she accepted it without a further argument."

"I could tell by the look on their faces they sensed changes were coming," he stated. "Elki has no idea."

Romy inhaled and scrunched his nose. "I need a shower. Care to join me?"

"Mmm, it's tempting, but we still need to eat before we meet the see'ers council. Besides, for me, it's only been a few hours since we had a shower together earlier this morning."

Sliding free, Romy shifted his feet off the side of the bed. "Can you do something for me, please?"

"Sure."

"I am guessing there is a man in your research department here—a historian by the name of Allard."

"Well, yes, but how would you know?"

He waved his hand. "It would take too long to explain. Can you have him located, and have him meet us in the research library after we have met with the see'ers."

"For what possible reason?" Efi asked, her brow scrunched, showing her confusion.

Rising to his feet, he said, "I'll explain it as we eat dinner. Can you have something sent up from the cafeteria?"

Romy was already turned away by the time she nodded. She picked up the communication receiver and made both calls, first for the food, then to Grodin, giving him the task of finding Allard.

After their dinner, Romy felt much better. He was clean, outfitted in clean clothes and well fed. Efi saw the difference, telling him he looked almost back to his normal self.

Not much later, Romy rose to his feet. "We better not keep the see'ers waiting."

Once in the hallway, Grodin, who had been waiting, fell in just behind them. "Good to see you again, Sir," he said.

Turning his head, Romy stated, "You've met my father. You can call him, Sir, if you like, but not me."

They passed several Mabuza guards along the way, and when they arrived at the heavy wooden doors to the see'er's chambers, Malakay was waiting for them. After he opened the door, he followed Romy and Efi in. Romy knew the way, having met with the see'ers here several times in the past.

He found the five see'ers where he expected, sitting in the comfortable seating at the far end of the massive room. The three junior see'ers sat on the wide couch, while Elki and Mist each sat in matching armchairs flanking them. Romy grinned, thinking of bookends.

There were two empty chairs facing the couch, and Efi was about to sit in one when Romy slipped his fingers between hers, stopping her from lowering. He turned to the see'ers. "We won't be staying long."

That said, Romy gave a clinical report about the assignment. It was detailed but brief, lasting all but 20 minutes. He emphasized the fact the reality they were in was almost lost. An effort for good had almost turned to complete disaster.

Surprisingly, Elki did not interrupt or ask questions. She sensed Romy had changed. Things were different, but she needed to ensure what she suspected. She clapped her hands together and said, "We all thank you for your efforts. I am sure those words are not enough to compensate what you have been through." For a moment she looked at Mist, looking for a sign, but Mist was stone faced, leaving Elki alone with her intentions. She turned her gaze back to Romy and continued, "You and Efi need to take a long vacation. No work, just relaxation. When you return, we can discuss further assignments."

"There will be no more assignments." Romy stated in a firm voice.

"What do you mean? What of all the good you can continue to do in the Athar?" Elki replied.

Romy smiled at Elki much as he would to his grandmother if she was still alive, a mix of comfort and sadness. His words came in a softer tone. "I know you have to try, for what would the see'ers do without me? Your race waited for me for hundreds of years. You prepared earnestly and in good faith. You prepared Efi, and for that, I will be forever thankful. The five of you are not stupid. You understood what I just described. You understand how close we came for this reality we know to be snuffed out, replaced by an evil, chaotic similarity. I will no longer play with the fate of the Athar. Destiny shall be what it has to be. To be very clear, I am retiring as your time drifter."

Elki and Mist, as powerful see'ers, both knew all of this when they saw Romy's face after he hopped back to this reality. Consequently, now neither showed any emotion on their faces. Elki stayed silent, but Mist chanced a few words.

"Are you saying you will never travel in time again?" Mist asked.

"Not at all. I am sure I will. It is addicting, to say the least. There is a need that draws me even now, but I will never travel in time with a goal of changing the past or the future. Fate will have to be what is ordained by someone much higher than any of you or I."

Elki interjected, "What if it is something critical and Athar changing?"

"I consider you all close friends. Any of you can always talk to me about such affairs, but in all likelihood, the answer will always be no."

Elki, as the leader of the see'ers, replied for the group, "We understand."

Taking a moment to look at each of the see'ers, finishing with his gaze back on Elki, his voice was again firm as he stated, "So far, I have worked for you. If, and I don't see why—unless I should lose my mind—if a collaboration would ever occur, you will all work for me. You are my advisors now. Is that understood?"

Romy saw Elki's throat move as she swallowed heavily. "Of course. We understand."

As Malakay led them back to the large wooden doors, Romy leaned in, whispering to Efi, "Was I too hard on them?"

She whispered back, "Oh, yes, but it was wonderful."

Once outside the doors, Grodin came to them. "Allard has been waiting in the research library for some time."

They hurried to the building next door, housing the research library. On the way, Efi asked again why Allard was needed?

Romy told Grodin, "Go ahead. We will be there in a few minutes." Once he left, he grasped Efi by the shoulders. "In the altered, corrupt reality, as I told you, I knew Efia and Mick lived a full and happy life. However, since I woke up, it's been bothering me to no end that I cannot say I am sure of that result in this reality, now that it is changed back."

She saw the sadness and despair in his eyes. He was not at peace, and he would not be until he knew. She slipped her fingers between his and said, "Then, we had better find out."

They caught up with Grodin, now waiting on the second floor with Allard. The middle-aged historian was confused, since he had never met Romy Gunn, yet the younger man acted as if they were familiar associates.

"I need your help, Allard, "Romy explained. "I would like you to pull up some information on a planet named, Teston."

Snapping his fingers, Allard said, "Come along then," as he led them to one of the many computers facing the far wall.

The older man sat with Romy and Efi looking over his shoulder. Grodin had the sense to move in the opposite direction, and he took up a position at the main entrance.

"Plane and coordinates," Allard asked.

Romy gave him the information, and Allard's fingers flashed across the keys. A graphic of the planet popped up on the left side of the screen while statistical data flowed down the right side.

"If you could do a search for a man named Mick Dulan. He lived there between 300 and 400 years ago in a city named Colton."

Allard complied, and it didn't take long for a data sheet to pop up on the screen. "Here he is," Allard said. He was reading the screen, repeating information he thought was pertinent. "He was actually born 440 years ago, and he died at the age of 105, apparently what would have been a long life for a Testonian." The older man suddenly pressed his finger against the computer screen, and leaned his face close to it. He mumbled, "This is the oddest thing I've ever seen..."

"What?" Romy interjected.

Keeping his finger on the screen, he spun around facing Efi. "It says here he married a woman named Efia Kuma. That's your name."

"Actually, I go by Efi," she clarified.

Allard just shook his head. "This is also odd. She died a year before Mick Dulan, but she does not have a birth date. It's like she just appeared from nothing. No recorded parents or history."

"What else?" Romy asked as he pointed to the screen.

"Of course," the older man said as he turned back to the computer. "They were married for 74 years with three children and eight grandchildren. It looks like they ran into a vast amount of money when Mick was 40. They became popular philanthropists, working with and donating to many worthy causes on Teston, and also on other nearby planets."

Placing his hand on Allard's shoulder, he whispered, "That's enough. Thank you."

Allard rose to his feet, more than confused, and the confusion grew when he saw Romy and Efi wrapped in a tight embrace. He shrugged and scurried away.

Hearing him depart, Efi whispered, "Are you okay?"

His cheek was pressed against hers. He was crying, but they were tears of happiness. "Efia and Mick lived a long and happy life. It was important for me to know I didn't abandon her to a life of despair. I would not have been at peace, otherwise." He pulled his face back, placing one hand on her cheek. "If it wasn't for her, and I shouldn't forget Mick, I wouldn't be back here with you. They lived a happy life, and now we will start our life together. My hope is we will be as happy as they were.

Chapter 30: The Monolith

The 10ᵗʰ day of the 8ᵗʰ month, Alpha Centauri year 0030.

High orbit around Metro.

The monolith appeared exactly six months after the last beacon. Several navy ships were in orbit around Metro when alarms sounded on each ship. Sensors had picked up a massive electrical disturbance resulting in each vessel's captain thinking they were under attack. They armed their weapons and engaged their cloaking devices.

They didn't have to wait long as an area of space near the planet began to ripple until a small tear appeared at its centre. The tear expanded into a massive rift with tendrils of electrical energy flickering around its perimeter.

A rock formation appeared in the void, becoming larger as it made its way into Metro space. The observers were wide-eyed as they expected the length of the asteroid to end, but it just kept coming. It wasn't until the asteroid revealed itself at its full two-kilometre length, that the void behind it closed.

The first cloaked vessel approached tentatively, making a circle around the asteroid, much the shape of a flattened cylinder two kilometres long, 500 metres wide and 100 metres tall. It became readily apparent this was no ordinary asteroid. First, its arrival had placed it in perfect orbit around Metro. Second, there were golden metal protrusions at regular intervals along its length, the most notable being a massive golden sphere, easily five times as large as the golden beacons the Metronians had previously intercepted in deep space. This massive sphere embedded into the top of the asteroid, near the front, had a similar ring of white light, strobing every 125 seconds, the same frequency used by each of the previous beacons. It was easy to understand why the massive asteroid was dubbed—*the monolith*.

Although military vessels remained in the vicinity, several Explorer Corp. vessels were assigned to lead an investigation. This initial investigation was led by Ryder Gunn with Marty Mortenson close by his side. However, after the monolith was secured and deemed not to be a threat, Ryder assigned Marty as Project Manager with the task to investigate the large chunk of rock.

Marty deciphered the messaging from the strobe which was a basic welcome and directions to open an exterior doorway, allowing entry within the structure. Once inside, the Metronians discovered the monolith was hollowed out, not unlike Talus 3, but on a smaller and more efficient scale. On their initial venture, led by Marty, they discovered emergency lighting throughout the many corridors. The monolith was not just an asteroid; it was a spaceship the unknown aliens had sent them.

The vessel was void of simulated gravity, and there was no atmosphere. It took Marty six months to decipher the alien's light circuits and make those two functions operational. They found a powerplant room with a mysterious, unknown power source, and a large control room, but there were literally hundreds of thousands of circuit boards with light energy powering them. They were not electrical in nature, at least that's what the Metronians had determined.

Since Marty preferred to keep far away from political elements, she gave regular reports to Ryder, who relayed them to Metro government and military officials. At the same time, those officials were becoming increasingly frustrated. Progress was slow, but Ryder explained the nature of the advanced unknown technology, far beyond their comprehension. The engineers were making their way through the masses of light circuits and manuals, all utilizing light as the medium of communication. Estimates from Marty indicated it would take 20 to 30 years for them to understand the vessel and be able to control it for space flight.

Now, six years after the monolith's arrival, Ryder and Romy were in a shuttle, speeding upwards towards it. As they came close, they saw the familiar sight of the three massive Explorer Corp. ships now permanently grappled to the side of the monolith, equally spaced along its length. Enclosed gangways from each ship connected to each of three portals in the side of the asteroid ship.

Ryder visited more regularly, Romy not as often since he did not have the same level of fixation with the monolith as his father did. Ryder led them off the shuttle, now docked at the Explorer Corp. ship, then across to the gangway. Crossing that had them in a corridor aboard the monolith.

Little by little, Marty had been able to fire up systems aboard the monolith. One of them was a transportation train that ran down the central length of it. They boarded it, and Ryder spoke into the makeshift translator mounted near the alien light receiver. The translation only took a few seconds before the doors closed and the train sped towards the front of the vessel.

A minute later, they offloaded and continued to what they had discovered was the vessel's command deck. Ryder had been there many times, but for

Romy, this was only his second visit. He turned, looking up, whistling. "Wow!"

The room was half a sphere with a flat floor, 30 metres across and 20 metres high. For the most part, it was empty with a round, five-metre-wide, raised platform at its centre. There were 20 large, smooth orbs on raised pedestals around the perimeter of the round platform. Long ago, Marty had discovered these were primary controls, working in conjunction with a ring of lights that ran around the wall of the larger room.

"Good, you're here," Marty said to Ryder. She then glanced at Romy who appeared wide eyed and star struck. "I'm glad you could make it for the show."

"When can we start?" Ryder asked.

There were two dozen technicians with light translators in hand, milling about the room, some of whom were at control panels on the outer wall, communicating with the light panels located there. "There's just a few final checks, then we'll see if we can fire my baby up!" Marty exclaimed.

"You're going to fire up the entire ship?" Romy asked.

Waving a hand, Marty replied, "No. We're years away from that. We know where the powerplant is, but short of figuring out how to open the doors to it, we have no idea how it works. Today, we're ready to fire up the exterior sensors and the interface to this room."

A senior technician came to Marty and told her they were ready to begin.

Marty nodded and yelled out, "Everyone to their places!"

The technicians looked like they were scattering randomly, but in fact, while most left the room, those remaining rushed to predetermined locations. Once Marty was satisfied, he moved in front of a control console the Metronian team had jury rigged to the alien technology on the platform. The console had both a microphone and a large keyboard. Marty chose the keyboard as her fingers pressed against the keys. When she hit the enter command, a strobe connected to the console flashed.

Alien sensors in the room, as expected, deciphered the message and immediately the appearance of the room changed. Romy almost toppled as he was hit by the immediate sense of vertigo. It was as if the command deck was gone, and the small platform they were on was now hovering in open space.

Marty clapped her hands in joy as Ryder yelled out a "Wow!"

For a few minutes, the three of them made a slow circle on the platform.

They could see the connected Explorer Corp. ships, and below them, the planet Metro. Beyond it, making up the backdrop, was their sun.

Marty noticed one of the raised orbs lit up when the holographic view was enabled. She mumbled, "If our research is correct, this should work."

She placed her hand on the orb and shifted it across the smooth surface. As she did so, the entire room's view rotated. She continued to move her hand until they were looking out into deep space, away from the planet. She waved to Ryder. "Come try this. It's awesome."

Ryder's hand replaced Marty's. He shifted it from side to side and up and down. The holographic view tilted and turned until Romy could not hold back his request.

"Enough already!" Romy exclaimed. "You're making me feel sick!"

Ryder released the orb, and the view became stationary. Marty moved back to the keyboard on the console, and another strobe burst was sent to the room's sensors. Immediately, the hologram disappeared, leaving the large room as it was before the test.

Ryder slapped Marty on the back. "Excellent progress Kid! Keep up the good work." He glanced at his wrist interlink, then at Romy. "We better get back. If we're late, Shayne will never forgive us."

Ryder and Romy made the return trek in their shuttle. Once they were almost at the space port near Cliffside, Romy asked, "How much time do we have?"

"Ninety minutes," Ryder replied. "It's enough time to get to the hospital." He glanced at his wrist interlink again. "Naala and Efi are already there."

Once out of the shuttle, they took the local air shuttle to level 2, pod 18, located just outside the hospital. They made it to a large double door with the stenciled words, *Obstetrics and Delivery*. On the other side, they found Naala and Efi in the waiting room.

Naala said, "It's good you're here. Shayne just went in with Moira."

Moira was a Metronian woman Shayne, now 22, married a year earlier. She was being induced to have their first child.

Naala's update was interrupted by a flurry of high-pitched words. "Daddy! Daddy! You're here!" Romy's daughter, now five years old, left Efi's side and ran towards her father. She jumped at the last second, landing in his waiting arms.

Moira's birthing process had begun, and the time to delivery could vary.

They all waited, until three hours later when a nurse came out and extended her congratulations on the delivery of a healthy baby girl. The nurse knew the question before it was asked, telling them only two at a time to visit, with parents first.

After giving Romy a playful nudge, Ryder started towards the recovery area with Naala close behind. Romy and Efi waited with their daughter. Romy put his hand on the bump on Efi's stomach. "How's my son doing?"

"You don't know it's a son," she scoffed.

Grinning, Romy said, "You could use your psychic powers and find out."

"I choose not to use them just to appease you. I prefer a surprise."

Thirty minutes later, Ryder and Naala returned. Romy picked up his daughter, her arms instinctively wrapping around her father's neck while his arm moved to support her weight. A few moments later, Romy, Efi and their daughter were in the recovery room. Moira was already sitting up on the couch, leaning back against a pillow. Shayne was sitting beside her, a tiny bundle of baby flesh wrapped in a blanket held in his arms.

Romy and Efi gave their congratulations, while Romy's daughter yelled out, "I want to see the baby!"

Shayne rose to his feet, a proud smile on his face. He brought the baby close and pulled back the blanket to uncover a beautiful, pudgy face. He tilted the baby up so that the two children's faces were close together.

Shayne winked at Romy, then, in a low voice, announced to Romy's daughter, "Meet your new baby cousin, Marjorie Gunn."

Epilogue

September 25ᵗʰ in the year 2084.

Zurich, New European Union

"Don't stop now!" I exclaimed.

Romy had turned off the tablet and placed it on the table in front of him. "I've been reading to you for a long day and a half with only five hours sleep last night. We missed lunch, and I'm hungry."

"But I must know what happened to Marjorie Gunn! How did the aliens send her name with the fourth beacon when she was not even born yet? What happened with the monolith? Did Marty ever…"

Romy rose, waving his hand as he interrupted," I don't know."

"What do you mean, you don't know?" my eyes wide, showing my insatiable addiction to the story.

He walked to the large picture window, gazing out over the trees towards the river snaking through Zurich. "We are now at the same point in the timeline as my niece, Marjorie Gunn. She is now eight years old. Marty continues to make progress on the monolith, but it is slow work."

I watched as Romy intertwined his fingers behind his back. He continued to gaze out the window, appearing to be lost in his thoughts.

I stood up and moved beside him. "Something is bothering you?"

"Several things, Yevgeni. You are correct in that the aliens, who we now refer to as light beings, knew about my niece before she was born. Time does not appear to be an obstacle for them."

I shrugged. "As it is not an obstacle for you."

He tilted his head towards me. "Point taken. But there are other disturbing aspects."

"Like?"

"The light beings are obviously far advanced compared to us. If they wanted to meet us, why wouldn't they just come? Why wouldn't some of them have been on the monolith? Why send us an advanced ship they knew we would struggle with?"

"Good points," I replied. "Your people will need to be careful."

He nodded as he returned his gaze to the scene out the window.

It was my turn to bring up a curious point. "Romy, something has been bothering me while my mind has been spinning these past few days with the tale you have told. At first, I couldn't put my finger on it, but now I have."

"I will try and help you with that, if I can."

"My question goes back to the point where the story all began, on Earth, several generations ago. Your great grandfather, a man we knew on Earth as Logan Russell, and my grandfather, a man Logan knew as Nick Anderson, made a pact whereby Logan, or his descendant, would bring the story of the Korian people back to Nick, or his descendant."

"You know I know all of this. I am here, fulfilling this family pledge for Logan Russell."

"Of course, Romy, but you traveled back to my time to deliver the story to me. It would have been just as easy for you to go back further in time and deliver the story directly to Nick Anderson. Why didn't you?"

Romy put his hand on my shoulder. "I probably will tell the story to Nick when we are done here. But there is a reason I came to you and not your grandfather."

"So, there is more to the story, after all."

"Only in that I left one part out until now, and it explains why I am here with you," Romy clarified. "You see, I did not tell you there was a fifth beacon that came two months after the fourth."

"Was there another coded name?"

"Predictably, yes, but it was a name we did not know. My father, knowing I have see'ers at my disposal and the ability to travel in time, gave me the assignment to discover who this person was. My father and I only came up with one clue, and that was a minor aspect of the names only my father had noticed. Natalie Lowe was the first name, not Natalie Gunn. Since Lowe originated on Earth, I began my search for the person in this part of the Athar."

"Did you find the person?"

"I did indeed, but I have not discovered a reason as to why this name would be important to the light beings." Romy took a deep breath and turned his gaze to me, his eyes piercing as if he was searching for something. "The name transmitted from the fifth beacon was you. The coded name was Yevgeni Ivanov."

Dear Reader:

Reviews are important to every author. We are thankful that many readers take a few moments to return to the purchasing website, in this case, Amazon, and leave a rating and a review.

If you could do so for this story, it would be much appreciated. Keep in mind, a Hollywood style review is not needed. Even a few simple words would be great.

Thanks again, and I hope you enjoyed the story.

Peter Sandor

www.ingramcontent.com/pod-product-compliance
Lightning Source LLC
Chambersburg PA
CBHW051310250626
47155CB00012B/845